The B

Beyond Time

The Book

Beyond Time

A Novel by

A.M.CARTER

"There are far, far better things ahead than any we leave behind."
—C. S. Lewis

"If you don't know where you're going, you might end up some place else."
—Yogi Berra

eLectio Publishing

Little Elm, Texas

www.eLectioPublishing.com

ISBN: 0615931162

ISBN-13: 978-0615931166

eLectio Publishing, Little Elm, Texas

www.eLectioPublishing.com

KRINTON

N

Mt Zorbin

Kalpos
(Guard Post)

Penryth
(shop)

Treacherous Mtn

Brundel City

Shakel

Horcum Hill

Camp

3

Grentham
(Tavern)

Trynn Goth

For my sons,

Daniel

Joel

and Marcus—

with whom it all began, when I began telling a bedtime tale one night back

in 2010

In memory of my Dad,

Anthony Edward Corner – 1937-2012

Thanks for being an inspiration to me

Contents

Acknowledgments.. 1

Prologue 3

Chapter 1 15

Chapter 2 25

Chapter 3 37

Chapter 4 51

Chapter 5 61

Chapter 6 75

Chapter 7 89

Chapter 8 103

Chapter 9 117

Chapter 10 129

Chapter 11 139

Chapter 12 157

Chapter 13 173

Chapter 14 189

Chapter 15 201

Chapter 16 213

Chapter 17 227

Chapter 18 239

Chapter 19 251

Chapter 20 265

Chapter 21 279

Chapter 22 295

Acknowledgments

My heartfelt thanks to everyone who has helped make this book a reality.

Faye: thanks for spurring me on, believing in this project from the outset and for providing the otter artwork; Claire M.: for your honest critique and encouragement; young James: for your enthusiastic feedback; Mike: for running with my ideas and bringing them to life through amazing graphics; Rachel Starr Thomson: for taking on the vision for this novel and providing guidance, structure and superior editing skills; Gio, Sue: for listening and praying; Dee: for general enthusiasm and promising to buy the first copy; Ivona from Cambridge: for convincing me to pursue publication; Sarah C.: for proofreading, Everyone at eLectio Publishing: thank you for taking on this book. And Tim: thanks for all your reading and faith in the story, despite my endless doubts. You've stood with me throughout everything. I love you.

To my British readers, please note: The use of American English throughout.

Prologue

Trumpet blasts resounded across the bustling city square. A towering knight, almost eight feet tall and clad in full platinum armor, marched back and forth on a creaky wooden stage. The platform had been specially erected for this momentous occasion. Throngs of people flocked toward the ancient, crumbling walls of the historic city of Erundel. The day had come for the chance to see the legendary Treanthor, their admired Emperor. His yearly visit had been long anticipated.

Ree-Mya, a young mother with long, dark hair, wove her way through the masses, clutching a small baby close to her in a sling across her slender body. Heart racing furiously, she breathed heavy sighs of relief upon realizing that she was among the last few to be let into the square. Looking back over her shoulder, she glared at the mammoth oak gates being pulled closed and bolted by hefty guards.

Wiping her brow with a checkered handkerchief, Ree-Mya winced as the cries of disappointed travelers rose up eerily before dissipating. Guards threatened to hurl boiling water at them if they didn't stop their banging. Ree-Mya turned away. She had walked the entire way from her village in the south, Trynn Goth, stopping en route for just one night at her grandparents' home. Her hazy blue eyes now reflected hope but also weariness after the long journey. While crowds pressed forward to catch a better view of the fearsome knight, she drank in the sights and smells around her.

Wafts of smoke from stallholders cooking chickens on spits mingled with the scent of tangy ale and chopped wood. Ree-Mya's nostrils tingled with the fragrance of strong potions that traders were hawking at the entrance to the gates. Hordes of bodies, all dressed in thick woven cotton and leather, jostled against her and warmed the air. High above the crowds swayed flagpoles and colorful banners. Ree-Mya sensed a unique atmosphere in the air, and she found it both enchanting and overwhelming at the same time.

Young children dashed past her, waving flags enthusiastically and joined as everyone began to chant Tre-an-thor! Tre-an-thor! Tre-an-thor! Several boys climbed the willow trees that lined the furthest side of the quad, waving to those below, while some older ones pointed their prized ska-swords into the air, showing off the gleaming light and sound feature on their xanth-powered gadgets.

Rumors had circulated that one day, xanth would be able to power electricity once again in people's homes – perhaps a return to the way of life before the Great Catastrophe of 2025. Treanthor always declared that he was working toward it – but insisted that it would take time and, for now, the people should be content with all that he had already achieved for them. But Ree-Mya was not content; she longed for the return of technology which could change everyone's way of life, particularly the poor, the sick and the uneducated.

Today would mark the beginning of a new era. That was the message that had been sent out into all the towns and villages. Those who came to Erundel would be the first to witness Treanthor's latest, marvelous invention; something far greater than ska-swords or xanth games or magic tricks.

An unkempt man with silver hair and chipped teeth approached Ree-Mya and touched her arm. "I have something very special for the lovely lady today," he croaked. She shook him away, alarmed, but he persisted. His eyes darted around, and he shifted from one foot to the other, not pausing to be still even for a moment. From a hidden pocket in his jacket, he pulled out a little black velvet pouch. Pulling open the string, he showed her a powdery gray substance. Its strong aroma stung her nose, and she could see that it almost glowed, as though strands of silver were contained in the grains.

"Sniff these wonderful grains, and you'll think you're in heaven," the man whispered, his eyes still shifting. "It's the strongest blend ever made!"

Sekrin. Ree-Mya closed her eyes, assailed by the smell, by the sight, by the memories it conjured up. Her husband was back at home even now, drug-delirious and no good to her, no good to her son. He probably didn't even know they were gone. She thought of the last time she'd tried to win his heart back—to make the father see his own baby and care. Marcus, cast aside by his own father in favor of this—this powder. This poison. She clenched her jaw, certain that her husband was indeed already familiar with this stronger strain of sekrin.

"No, thank you. I need to think of my son." He started to wheedle again, but she promptly turned away. "Please leave me alone."

All who managed to get into the city square became delirious with delight at their good fortune. Screams and shouts pierced the air, such was the excitement. Some joined in a chorus of clapping, while others began punching the air vigorously. One young man repeatedly banged a drum hung around his neck, his rhythm noticeably out of time with the claps of those around him.

Treanthor had not only promised to unveil his new, amazing structure in the city, but also announced small rewards for everyone who came on this special day. The people – both young and old, rich and poor – could hardly contain their euphoria over this event. One girl fainted and had to be carried away from the commotion, her parents anxiously sprinkling water over her face.

The crowds began to surge forward around Ree-Mya, pushing her sideways and causing her to stub her sandaled feet. Starting to feel uneasy about her visit, a slight fear grew in her stomach when yet another person elbowed her in the back. Looking across at the imposing structure behind the stage, concealed mostly by a thick, purple curtain, she wondered, *What could it possibly be?*

Perhaps I shouldn't have come today, she thought. *Perhaps Grandfather was right about me wasting my time.*

But she had to see for herself. She wanted to know if Treanthor really cared about the people and whether she might get the chance to speak with him for even a moment. Might he be favorable toward her idea for new xanth inventions? Did he really have the best intentions for the future of Krinton?

Officials in her village had claimed that if she could only get near the front, she would be able to persuade a guard to let her speak personally with the Emperor after the crowds had dispersed. "All the guards would go soft for a lady with a pretty face like yours!" they said. "He usually stays at the end to talk to a few lucky ones." Deep down, Ree-Mya was aware of the unlikelihood of being able to approach Treanthor but she refused to quash her hopes.

As her young son began to wriggle and squirm, Ree-Mya looked down at him and began to stroke his wavy, brown hair. Marcus was six months old; he would never remember this historic occasion – only hear about it from his mother and other relatives.

As the last trumpet sounded, the knight stepped forward and held up his shield toward the people. "Silence!" he bellowed. A series of hushes whispered across the tree lined courtyard, until the only sound to be heard was the wind in the leaves and a lone cry from an upset child.

Everyone fixed their eyes on the knight, captivated by the shiny, rotating rings in the center of his shield. The largest ring glowed red and white and spun furiously, almost mesmerizing those at the front. The burly man raised the shield and twisted the large ring several times. Gasps echoed through the square as a massive beam of red light flooded out from the circle on the shield, casting a dazzling spotlight wherever it was directed. The knight held the shield up to shine across the stage and cried, "Ladies and gentlemen, wait for it—I now bring to you our one and only, great, most awesome—quiet now . . ." The knight swept an outstretched hand from left to right as a call to silence.

The hush almost buzzed with excitement before building in intensity.

"Treanthor!"

The Emperor swept through the rear gate at the hill of the Old City and onto a specially prepared walkway which led to the raised platform.

"You may now show your appreciation for the Emperor!" bellowed the knight.

An almost deafening uproar of shouts and hurrays arose. Ree-Mya joined the chorus at first but felt twinges of uncertainty. Looking around, she became convinced that she was the only one not impressed by Treanthor's presence. Everyone else was cheering and clapping with all their might, while she regarded him with suspicion and disdain. But she'd had to see for herself. That was why she had come. She had desperately hoped her grandfather was wrong about him and that she might get a chance to approach the Emperor with her idea.

But her instincts told her that he would never listen, that he was not as benevolent as he seemed.

Treanthor's beaming face revealed how much he enjoyed the adoration and applause. His two greyhounds strutted around the black-and-gold hem of his robes, wagging their tails and equally enjoying the limelight. He reached down to pat and stroke them, momentarily expressing that the dogs were more important than the crowds, than his people.

Treanthor's flowing robes were black, with red paneling stitched into four wide, vertical stripes. At the hem, impressive gold tassels communicated his position as a statesman. Light from the knight's beam followed him wherever he stepped and bounced onto the tassels, causing them to glimmer red, silver, and gold interchangeably. Entwined among the tassels, little bells jangled gently, producing a hypnotic sound as he moved back and forth across the platform.

Row after row of knights formed a barrier, preventing anyone from touching Treanthor or climbing onto the wooden platform. The people frantically tried to get closer to his presence, and they pushed and shoved to catch a better view. Scores of officials, dressed in smart jackets and shiny shoes, tried to maintain order. They were instantly recognizable by the large gold embroidered "T" on their felt hats, which they wore with pride. Ree-Mya curved her shoulders inwards and tried to distance herself from the seething pockets of people around her.

Clouds had begun to descend over the square that morning, but now the wind picked up and the clouds started to disperse, allowing some rays of sun to shine through.

"The shadow!" one man exclaimed, pushing aside an elderly lady and her grandson to find a way to step inside Treanthor's shadow. Others began to stream forward, but the imposing, threatening guardsmen prevented them from climbing over their human barrier.

Ree-Mya could feel her own disdain choking her. It was rumored that anyone who stepped into the shadow of the Emperor would magically receive a measure of his superior knowledge and power. One man from her village claimed that his strength had more than doubled after he stepped into the shadow of Treanthor. It had been observed that this man could indeed lift boulders at the coal mine which would usually require two men to shift. But Ree-Mya had her doubts about this story.

Once again, people were hushed, this time to allow Treanthor to speak.

"Good people!" he declared, his eyes wide and captivating, his hands stretched out in a gesture of openness. He smiled, his thin lips curling upward to reveal shining white teeth, and waited for silence. "The time you have waited for has come!"

Whispers greeted his announcement. This was why they had come—to see the unveiling of Treanthor's latest gift. He had delighted them before—with roads, with rebuilding, with new technologies. Their excitement was palpable.

Treanthor moved to the far right of the platform, toward the eastern wall of the Old City. He pointed toward the curtain covered structure which was built into the wall.

"I shall now reveal my gift to you," Treanthor announced, reaching up to pull a long white cord. The purple cloth was drawn back to reveal a massive, metal building decorated with glowing glass panels.

The people let out gasps in wonderment at this strange new thing. Steps led up to an enormous angular door, which was opened by the push of a huge, sparkly blue button, and Treanthor positioned himself at the entrance.

Something about it unsettled Ree-Mya. She wondered what ulterior motive the Emperor might have for this glitzy new construction, and she eyed it with suspicion.

Treanthor raised his voice. "This, my dear people, is a grench port. It is what you have always wished for" — he paused —"though you did not know it. The powers of this spectacular gift are beyond your wildest dreams!"

The people began to cheer, but Treanthor held up his hands to quiet them, smiling.

"I have traveled far and wide and visited many a wizard and superior craftsman to create this port with my team of NewTech inventors. It shall rescue you, not from raiders or wild beasts, which no longer trouble our civilized cities, but from the far greater enemies of boredom and monotony. Inside, there are many delights for you."

Ree-Mya glared at the grench port and its distinctive silver door. The etchings in its angular surface reminded her of the strains of silver that ran through sekrin.

"It shall be open to you daily at the east gate of the Old City. One hundred and fifty people may enter grench at any one time, and you may stay at least one hour — longer if there are no crowds. This port will amaze your senses and thrill your souls, for it is a structure filled with the power of xanth, which I have brought back from the volcanic Mount

Zorbin. Until now only small amounts of these crystals have been discovered to build gadgets and toys for your children. Within the mountain which no man dare approach, I—your beloved Emperor— risked all to source large quantities of xanth to create for you this marvel."

Once again cheers erupted, and once again Treanthor raised his hands to quiet them. This time, he held up a red disc in one hand. "Xanth crystals have been used to build you an experience that will fascinate and enchant you for as long as you will. Today, however, everyone will get a chance to visit, so your time will be limited to five minutes each. The person to catch this red disc will be the first to go in!"

"Here, here, me, over here, Treanthor, give it to me!" the people shouted frantically, jumping up and down.

Treanthor closed his eyes, smiled, and threw the red, glassy disc into the crowds.

A skinny, older boy wearing a blue flat cap leapt to catch it mid-air. "Yes, I got it!" he exclaimed, waving it to catch the Emperor's gaze.

"Come here!" said Treanthor. "What is your name?"

"Wesley," the boy replied.

Treanthor moved away from the entrance and ushered the boy in with a gracious bow. He pushed the blue button again to close the unusual door.

"Now, before any more go in, let us choose the color of this grench port. The panels are purple and yellow, but xanth has the power to change color. So what would the people of Erundel like to see at the entrance to the east gate, to light up the whole city from its ancient core? Red, green, purple, blue? Let the people decide!"

The roar of approval nearly drowned out the answers shouted by the crowds. "Let the people decide" was a common phrase from Treanthor, passed down by officials into the towns and villages. He wished them to know that they had a say in the way Krinton was governed, that their voices mattered—that their beloved Emperor did nothing without their best interests at heart.

If only Ree-Mya wasn't so sure it was a lie.

Even back when she was a young girl, Ree-Mya's grandfather had warned her about Treanthor's "schemes," as he called them. "He steers their intentions toward his own will," he had said, his voice quiet but full of bitter certainty. Anyone who disagreed publicly with the intentions of Treanthor, as voiced by the mayors and magistrates, was shouted down in the local streets and bars. Anyone who continued to disagree . . .

Well, no one talked about that.

Thousands of voices shouted out their preferences, while Ree-Mya's throat grew tighter and the bitterness of her certainty made her eyes ache. Amidst the noise, it was clear that most were shouting for green and blue.

"So shall it be!" declared Treanthor as he climbed to the top of the imposing grench structure and pulled a lever down. Immediately, the glass panels decorating the port changed from purple and yellow to bottle-green and ocean-blue.

"Hurray! Amazing!" cried everyone in the square, many jumping up and down wildly in their excitement.

Moments later, Wesley appeared at the door to the port, breathless, eyes wide. "You are not going to believe this!" he yelled. "I've never seen anything like it, it's amazing . . . there are lights and rooms and buttons to touch and levels and platforms to jump across and . . . and . . . I'm going back in!"

Wesley darted back inside before any guardsman could stop him, and Treanthor laughed along with the crowd. Then he stepped aside again and announced, "Let another one hundred and forty-nine enter in!"

As the crowds pushed forward, Ree-Mya turned away. She had seen enough.

"Far beyond your wildest dreams," he claims! As if this grench port will even benefit the lives of the people! It's just a gimmick to distract everyone from questioning his power and authority. Sounds like a fancy playground to me, just with some lights.

She had almost hoped it would be different this time, though she should have known better. Most people did not bother themselves over the governance of Erundel, or indeed, the entire land of Krinton. The majority were descended from the Wryxl folk, renowned for their simplicity and easygoing natures. It was common among the Wryxl to just accept things the way they were, and not to bother to ask any questions or worry about their current or future way of life. "Whatever may happen shall happen. So be it," they would say.

Ree-Mya was different. Her grandfather was half Treegle, a minority group infamous for their fierce and strong-willed natures. Most had been destroyed by Treanthor's knights when they began a revolt over a hundred years before. But their blood still flowed in Ree-Mya's veins, and she hungered to learn, to find things out for herself — to doubt. And to believe.

She pushed against the tide of the crowd, back toward the Old City gates, glad that no one cared to pay attention to her. "All knowledge has been attained, and I possess the utmost knowledge. There is nothing new to learn!" Treanthor had long ago declared. Why should they seek any other ruler, any other way? They should be happy he was so learned and cared for them so well, that he had provided jobs for everyone and that food was plentiful.

More cheers and laughter erupted behind her as the shift changed in the grench port and scores of waiting people rushed in. Ree-Mya felt her mouth twisting with unhappiness. Today, Treanthor had become even more popular in the eyes of the people, who were enthralled by this fantastic new attraction. The Emperor had succeeded in securing their allegiance—but not hers.

A small part of her had genuinely believed that Treanthor might use xanth and NewTech to help people's health. Or to invent some kind of computer system, like the ones told of in tales handed down for several generations that allowed people to access knowledge and create on their own. But having set eyes on him and this new grench port, she knew that her grandfather was right:

"Don't get your hopes up, Ree-Mya," Grandfather had said when she was about to leave his home that morning. "Treanthor controls NewTech and uses it only for his purposes. Why would he ever agree to a return to the former way of life? He knows that if people inform themselves, they might turn against him and try to rule Krinton themselves." He had squeezed her hand tight and taken several slow, labored breaths before continuing.

"He certainly doesn't want them to be able to communicate with each other easily, as they used to with those things called phones and other devices. He realizes that they might use NewTech to oppose him in future. That's why only he has access to xanth crystals—until another source is found elsewhere."

Ree-Mya looked down, her face despondent. She no longer wished to try to approach the Emperor; it was obvious that Treanthor cared only about his image and appeasing the people with entertainment.

I should have listened to Grandfather, she thought. *Why was I so foolish as to think that maybe he was too old to know anything about NewTech and the Emperor?*

As she pressed closer to the gate, a uniformed man stepped directly into her path and held up a silver trinket, shaped like one of the Emperor's greyhounds, on a long chain. A woman nearby all but snatched it out of his hand.

"That's right!" he said, pulling more trinkets and a bowl full of kroens, shiny silver coins, out of a cart decorated in the Emperor's colors.

"Gifts from Treanthor to commemorate this special day—the beginning of a new era!"

From the platform, Ree-Mya could hear those same words being echoed. *A new era.* She shook her head as the man thrust more trinkets toward her, but children and adults on either side received them ecstatically. A thin teenager handled his shiny coin and examined it over and over, staring at both sides, incredulous at his luck.

Somehow Ree-Mya ended up with a kroen in her hand. She turned it slowly. One side showed a bird of prey—something like a vulture. The image made her shudder, but she did not understand what it signified. On the other side were the letters "EoP"—Era of Pleasure.

Ree-Mya stood still, not moving for several minutes, as she watched everyone clambering to get a coin. She turned slowly and watched as the crowds intensified around the platform and Treanthor began throwing the coins out into the square, laughing as he did, as the people fought to get their hands on one.

Ree-Mya simply observed others as they gloated over their treasures. Her head hurt. Her eyes hurt.

Marcus began to stir and fidget, and soon he let out piercing shrieks and cries.

As the crowds surged around the platform and the vendors moved with the tide, the area around the gates cleared a little. Ree-Mya turned to leave the square and make her way home. On the road beyond the river, an elderly man offered her a ride. She blinked back tears as the wagon bumped and jolted over the road. Why, oh why, did she feel so dismayed at the day's events, when everyone else was so overjoyed?

Looking down at Marcus in her arms, settled comfortably in the quieter country air, she covered her aching eyes against the assault of the sun and said, "One day, Marcus, you will get the chance to leave the land of Krinton and escape Treanthor's influence. You will flee this shallow world and find the ancient Kingdom of the North."

Chapter 1

Marcus MacMillan opened his eyes, looked up at the battered red kite that had hung over his bed since the day he and his father had crashed it six years earlier, and felt a mixture of excitement and worry. Stretching out his body and wriggling his toes, he turned on his side and ran his fingers through his hair. Something had stirred a change inside, like he was no longer the brown-eyed, tousle-headed boy he'd been only twenty-four hours earlier. The sun was only just rising, streaming light through the window across the room and onto his face. As he kicked his covers to the end of his bed, they disturbed a thin layer of dust on the bedside table by his head. Marcus screwed up his face and sneezed loudly three times before rubbing his eyes and wiping his nose with the back of his hand.

So this was it—April 17th, 2325; he was thirteen. The day his father used to talk about, the day he would become a man, had arrived. Moving his hands across his chin, Marcus felt the new hair growth, although sparser and finer than many of his peers, on his maturing face. His eyebrows and the hair on his arms and legs had grown thicker and darker since last year, and his voice had already deepened. *You'll be way taller than me and your mother by the time you're thirteen,* his father had told him many times. *Crops are so much better than they were when I was a boy. Treanthor's technologies have changed everything. Your generation'll be a race of giants compared to mine!*

Marcus sat up quickly, ducking his head to avoid bumping into the kite. He didn't quite duck far enough, and the battered patchwork of sticks and worn red fabric swayed gently overhead as he stomped his feet on the cold floor and shook his shaggy hair back.

He'd grown up learning about the way life was *before*—before Treanthor came to rule with his promises of peace and happiness forever. His great-grandfather had never let him forget that in his day, boys had gone hungry as often as they'd eaten. In his day, they didn't have knarl-

15

knives to help them catch game or good milk from cows to make their bones strong. They had lived subject to famines and storms and terrible want, just the way everyone in Krinton had lived in the three hundred years since the Great Catastrophe.

Today, Marcus almost envied them. At least they didn't have to make terrible choices on their thirteenth birthdays—on the days when they should have been celebrating their newfound manhood with all their energy. Most boys his age would follow their fathers into some profession, but his father was gone, and his choice was between moving away and apprenticing with his mean uncle Nomit or joining an orphan work gang overseen by Treanthor.

He swallowed and looked down at his hands. They were clenched. He released them slowly and tried to get his mind off his impending doom—*Choice*, he reminded himself. *It's a choice, not a death sentence.*

Marcus walked across the room to find his pile of clothes draped messily over a rickety old chair. He pulled his leather-edged tunic over his head and tied it around his waist with a corded belt. After pushing his black linen trousers into his brown ankle boots, he put on a navy blue waistcoat which had belonged to his father and tied a cotton scarf around his neck, tucking the ends into his shirt.

Just as he was tying his boots, he heard a gentle knock at his door.

"Are you up yet, Marcus? It's your big day, son!"

"Yes, Mum! Can you believe I'm thirteen already! I'll be down in a moment."

"Eggs for breakfast," she said, "just to begin the celebration."

When Marcus walked out of his room into the wood-paneled hallway, Ree-Mya gasped and turned away.

"Are you all right?" Marcus asked, his forehead creasing.

To his surprise, she wiped away a tear. "You just—you're just so grown up," she said. She looked up and smiled at her towering son, grown into full physical maturity already, just like most of the boys of

16

his generation. The film over her eyes kept her from seeing him clearly, and she did not tell him the real reason for her tears. *In that cloak, I thought for a minute he was his father.*

Ree-Mya stood on her tiptoes to kiss Marcus's cheek. "Go on downstairs and see to the eggs," she said. "I want to finish wrapping your present."

Marcus grinned, happy to think about something other than his newly adult worries, as the smell of fried eggs wafted up to the top corridor. Lunging down the hall, he hopped along the last few steps and then decided to do something he often did when he was in a happy mood: jump down four or five steps at a time, only slightly holding on to the rail.

This time, his clumsiness got the better of him. He misjudged the final section of the stairway, falling down the last few steps and hitting his head on the kitchen door, which was halfway open.

"What *are* you doing, Birthday Boy?" his mother called from upstairs.

"Nothing!" he called back. Ree-Mya had often found Marcus in a heap at the bottom of the stairs as a young child. Once he had tried to leap all the way from the top to the bottom in one swoop and had nearly landed in the arms of a deliveryman who was waiting in the hallway with sacks of wheat and corn. Marcus had landed on one of the parcels, and flour went everywhere. It took him all morning to sweep it up, and his bottom had ached for a whole week.

As the sound of eggs sizzling grew louder, Marcus scrambled to his feet, rubbed his sore head, and burst through the kitchen door. He managed to flip the eggs just before they would have burned, and he smiled at the open spice jars all along the top of the woodstove. His mother had spiced breakfast just the way he liked it. In a larger pan on the back of the stove, fried chicken was spitting and crackling.

He could hear her moving around upstairs, and he let his thoughts go to the mysterious present she'd been hinting at for weeks. He did not yet own a ska-sword, and he had often looked longingly at those owned by the men and a few lucky boys at the weekly village market. Ska-swords were impressive, broad-handled instruments with retracting blades which could be adjusted according to one's size and age. Each was constructed according to a unique design, decorated with bright stones, and incredibly light—which meant that it was easier to learn swordplay with a ska-sword. Unlike the blades of the old days, ska-swords offered all the fun and impressiveness of being a swordsman, but required very little work. Designed by NewTech, each one could light up when in motion or be used as a torch. The glow was powered by something called xanth, but Marcus didn't know much about this.

One thing he did know was that ska-swords were often given to boys on their thirteenth birthdays, and Marcus had always imagined his father presenting him with a silver and black model and taking him out for the day to practice using it in the woods. But he knew the swords were costly and that his mother could not afford the same things as other families—families with responsible, hardworking fathers. Still, he couldn't help but dream.

Marcus turned from the heat of the stove and noticed that one of the dishes set for breakfast was cracked. He pulled it off the table and replaced it. The reminder of his mother's failing eyesight joined his bittersweet feelings as he was reminded again that his father would not be here to celebrate with him. A little part of him secretly hoped that his father would return just for this one day, just to wish him well and shake his hand, to give him a manly hug. His mother had somehow sensed his secret hopes and warned him that this was most unlikely.

Marcus could still remember the day he'd discovered hakrin in the cabinet by his father's bed. The drug, a more potent and mind-altering version of sekrin, was banned in Krinton. Sekrin had had a powerful grip on Marcus's father for years, causing him to distance himself from his loved ones and stop communicating with others. Hakrin was even worse. Somehow, mountain folk smuggled it into the towns and villages, selling it cheaply at first. After the first try, consumers always wanted more—at inflated prices, of course. Marcus's best friend, Rindel, had a mother who was ensnared by the poisonous stuff. Once lovely and friendly, she became sickly thin, convinced that clawing creatures were trying to force entry to her house every night. "Away, away, keep them away," she would repeat endlessly, her eyes vacant and inhuman. In the end, Rindel's father sent her to a special home to receive treatment from herb doctors and guru healers, but she had not improved.

By Marcus's tenth birthday, his dad too had become increasingly strange and scary in his behavior. He often lurked around the house and ranted weird complaints all evening. His mother called him "delusional," though Marcus hadn't quite understood what that meant. All he knew was that the father he'd once known was not the same person anymore, and it saddened him deep inside. Many nights he would lie restless in bed and hear his mother crying over what was happening to her husband. One time she shared with Marcus that he had promised to never touch any such substances again when Marcus was still a young infant, but a few years later had returned to his addictive habit.

Eventually, his father left. He said he needed more hakrin. Ree-Mya had been forced to sell a number of family treasures to afford food and repairs around the house, including the one original, damaged painting of the old world they owned, which depicted an impressive city with huge towers and water all around.

Marcus often wondered whether the Wryxl builders would ever develop the ability to construct such huge towers again. All Treanthor's improvements had not yet returned them to the splendors of the world before the Great Catastrophe, even though Treanthor's promises of a brighter future seemed truer with each passing year. Their days of hardship, toil, and hunger were nearly forgotten, and as long as they were provided with food, housing, and entertainment, no one complained about Treanthor's rule, even though he had once been viewed as an outsider. He had charmed everyone with his talk of making Krinton great once again and even more majestic than it had ever been. Even better, he did it all for the people, requiring little of them beyond their cooperation.

Mother had also been forced to sell some of her books. Most families didn't think reading and writing was important, though they would allow people to learn to read if they desperately wanted to. Ree-Mya was one of those people—and so was Marcus's father, before the sekrin got hold of him again. Books were scarce, nearly all destroyed along with most of the former way of life. The only things people would read were simple road signs or town placards. Perhaps also their own names, which were often inscribed rustically on their possessions.

Ree-Mya, however, had three or four treasured volumes that her grandfather had salvaged, and she had insisted that Marcus too learn to read. As a younger boy he had tired of reading the same old stories again and again. This was when Ree-Mya decided she would write some stories down from memory that she had heard in her childhood, but it was hard to get hold of paper or ink. Still, she saved as much as she could to purchase more sheets to pen her precious tales, and she wondered aloud when iron, ink, and other materials would one day become easily available to make those amazing printing presses which her granny said had once been in abundance. There were even tales told of every family possessing their own miniature printing machine, along with magical machines called "personal computers"—but the books had outlived these machines, which ceased to function once their electric power sources and cables were destroyed in the Great Catastrophe. A generation or so later, nearly everything else was also completely destroyed. Resources had been low ever since.

Ree-Mya often said that she could not even imagine what life must have been like before the dreadful date which ushered in another dark age, a time devoid of hope or enterprise, when creativity had been destroyed and people struggled to see another day. In his more sympathetic days, her husband had imagined with her and read and cared about those things too. Later, he only grew irritated with her "obsession." He would not have been sorry to see her sell the books.

But despite his harsh demeanor and the tense atmosphere at home, Marcus still hoped that his father would return. He missed the way his father used to tousle his hair and call him "Little Fighter"—especially when they would wage play battles after dinner. It wasn't the same without him around. Marcus had to chop wood and take care of other things around the home himself, and he missed the company of doing things with his father.

Plus, if his father had stayed home, he wouldn't have the choice to make today.

The sound of cautious footfalls on the creaking stairs announced Ree-Mya's return, and she entered the kitchen looking breathless but happy. She had been plotting things for weeks, and Marcus was sure that she had something special in store for him. She'd hinted that she had amazing news, and as he pulled out her chair and served her eggs, the excitement on her face was uncontainable.

"Thank you, young man," she said. "I should be serving you, not you me."

"That's all right," Marcus said. He grinned. "Just so long as you come through with that surprise."

"Oh, I will," she said. Her tone altered. "It's a rather unusual surprise, son, but one that's just right now that you're thirteen."

Marcus plunked himself into the wooden chair across from her and attacked his breakfast as though it were all that stood between him and Ree-Mya's secret. Perhaps she had organized a party—maybe lots of village boys would come, and even some of his cousins from the town of Arron. Rindel at least would be there. Maybe they'd have an archery competition or play ball in the nearby forest. Maybe she had managed to get hold of the newest ska-sword model after all, even though Marcus was sure they couldn't afford that.

Or maybe she was going to announce that his father was better and was coming home for good.

When Marcus had polished off a heaping plateful of the wonderful eggs and fried chicken, along with a small freshly baked loaf of granary bread, Ree-Mya smiled and gave his arm a little push. "Wait for me out on the deck, in the sun," she said. "I'll go find your present."

Marcus went out as she requested, but he soon moved his chair into a shady position to look across their neighbor's fields to watch the horses grazing. When Ree-Mya came out carrying a package wrapped in blue cloth and twine, she nearly tripped over his feet. Thankfully she managed to steady herself, but Marcus swallowed hard at yet another realization that his mother was nearly blind. She had tried to keep it from him, memorizing every inch of her way across the house and yard as well as keeping strict mental notes of the whereabouts of everything in the home, but he had noticed.

Ree-Mya sat down at the table beside her son, laying the package on the table but not handing it over. Marcus eyed it eagerly but said nothing as his mother went into her usual ritual of keeping the gift from him as long as possible. It wasn't in the shape of a ska-sword, but Marcus put aside his disappointment and tried to guess what else it could be as they chatted about Marcus's recent growth spurt and memories of when he was a little boy who loved to climb trees and play tricks on people. After a while they sat and listened to birdsong in the yard; in the distance they could hear Mr MacKinney chopping wood. Ree-Mya sat still, enjoying the sunshine on her face, while Marcus began to get restless and fidgety.

Marcus could only contain himself so long. Finally he blurted, "Well, what have you been conjuring up for my birthday, Mum?"

She smiled and swatted his head playfully. "So impatient," she said.

"I want to know," he pushed.

"Well, breakfast was only the beginning, let me tell you," she said. "We'll have a small feast by the river's edge later today."

"With guests?" Marcus said.

"Rindel's family," she answered. Her voice grew a little quieter as she finally pushed the package across the table toward her eager son. "I hope you'll realize how important this gift is, even though it may not seem like much."

Marcus wasn't really listening as he pulled open the string and unwrapped the blue cloth packaging. And there it was—a book. A book! His heart sank as he looked at it, with the title on the front in what seemed like gold-embossed lettering: *The Book Beyond Time.* Well, his mother might well be excited by books, but she should know by now that they didn't really get him very excited—particularly not on his birthday. When would he even have time to read it? He wasn't a child anymore!

Suddenly all his attempts to ignore the realities of turning thirteen without a father came crashing down. Marcus dropped the book on the table, muttered, "Thanks, Mum," and got up to walk away. He went down the steps into the yard and headed for the gate at the right end, planning to wander into the village to let off steam and hide his anger from Ree-Mya.

"Wait," she called, picking up the book and following him, taking her steps carefully. "I need to tell you about the book . . . and what I saw the other night. Marcus, this is the most important thing I could ever share with you!"

Marcus slowed his steps but kept his back to her as he approached the gate. His body was rigid and tense. Ree-Mya reached her hand out and touched his arm. "Please, listen just a moment. This is all about your future."

Chapter 2

"Marcus, you were gone, kayaking with Rindel on the river. I was busy getting ready to go apple picking in Farmer Jeshrun's orchard. I picked up my wicker baskets and remember noticing the blue sky and bright red robins from the kitchen window. It was a glorious, sunny day. My dreams are always crystal clear and vivid, as you know.

"But as I opened the door to go out, all my surroundings shifted violently, as though crumbling away, and brilliant colors and shades merged to form the strangest spectacle of moving light. Everything was transformed. Trees blended together, their branches extending out to each other and joining into one; plants emerged as if from the sky—and yet there was no sky, just a fusion of blue and gray which seemed eerily haphazard and unwelcome. There was no sun. The grass no longer shot up from the earth, but faded to one side, a heap of green and brown."

Ree-Mya's words came rapidly, and Marcus shifted uncomfortably at her intensity. "I looked down at my feet, only to find that I was not actually standing on anything—no doorstep, no ground, no foundation; yet somehow I was still upright and fully in control of my own movements. Stepping into what had been the garden, I began to search desperately for the gate. Seeing part of the fence, I reached out to touch it, but it melted away in my hand, transformed into dust particles which fell away into a little heap. I wanted to step on the pile of dust, but it too disappeared."

Marcus tried to interrupt her, but Ree-Mya continued to speak, faster still, her voice increasingly urgent.

"Suddenly afraid, I turned to go back inside the house, but though I neared the door, I could never quite reach it. I ran, my heart quickening and my body hot with the effort, but the door was always just beyond my reach. That's when I stopped, exhausted and full of fear, and dropped my head into my hands. Then I started to sob uncontrollably until I could cry no longer. I thought I would wake up. But when I finally opened my eyes again, I screamed when I saw only a few floating pieces of wood and random parts of furniture. The house was no more.

"Desperately, I tried to grasp whatever I could. When I finally managed to touch the lid of a wooden chest, it faded away, crumbling like sand before disappearing altogether." Ree-Mya gestured with her hands as she spoke, trying to demonstrate the urgency and reality of what she had seen. She seemed unable to stand still.

"I spun around to get hold of a cherry tree nearby, and it waved around like a rag doll being shaken. Then all the brightness around me started to fade until everything was gray and black, and the tree no longer appeared to be a tree, but rather a strange structure like a wall of knotted ropes. This too eventually faded. The house was gone; Trynn Goth could not be seen; all of Krinton had faded away."

Marcus leaned against the fence and folded his arms as his mother finally slowed down and her voice grew quiet. "But Mum —" He paused. "It was just a dream. What does it matter?"

Ree-Mya hardly seemed to hear him. "I woke sobbing and hugging the bed frame as if it were a long-lost friend. It was *more* than a dream, Marcus. It was meant to tell us something, and to remind me — to remind me of something my grandfather shared with me many years ago, when I was still a child."

As the breeze stirred her long hair, Ree-Mya smiled fondly. "His croaky voice and squinting eyes come to life again in my mind as I remember it. He looked at me intently and said, 'Ree-mya, I'm giving you a book which must be treasured above all others. I have not followed its quest, and I'm counting on you to take the risk and do it. Our world is gripped in a lie, my child. We must have someone who will stand against the coming tyranny and deception. This book will be your only hope, the only escape from a kingdom that won't last. I'm counting on you because your father wouldn't listen to me; he was always too busy building his business or drowning his sorrows in sekrin. It's up to you to find the truth — to find the Kingdom of the North."

Marcus cleared his throat. "I don't get it," he said. His mother was scaring him. She never got worked up about anything—she was always calm, always gentle. He didn't like how disturbed she sounded, and he wondered if she too had started to sniff sekrin secretly. He looked searchingly at her eyes, face, and skin, but he saw no signs of the drug, and her breath was untainted.

She didn't seem to notice his examination. "A kingdom that won't last. A world gripped by a lie. Grandfather was talking about my dream—about the fading away. When I remembered his words, I knew immediately what my dream was all about. Grandfather had handed me *The Book Beyond Time,* and I had promised that I would find the truth. But I was only nine years old. I didn't have a clue what he meant, and I hadn't even learned to read yet. By the time Grandma taught me two or three years later, the book had been mislaid, and we couldn't find it. After that, Grandma insisted that he stop talking about it, and soon after they moved away from the village. She thought it was just a crazy story. But he wouldn't stop telling me about his mistrust of Treanthor whenever I visited him, even on the day I ventured into Erundel when you were a baby."

Ree-Mya's voice grew almost frantic as she took Marcus by the shoulders and looked into his eyes with her clouded ones.

"Last year, I found the book in the attic and tried to read some pages, but my eyes were already—well, I could not make out the words. I tried to tell you about it once, Marcus, but you wanted nothing more to do with books after your father left, and you refused to go looking for it. But this is not just any book, Marcus. Since having my dream, I'm certain of that. I now know why my grandfather spoke with such urgency: he knew that we have to get out of Krinton."

Marcus pulled away, suddenly alarmed by his mother and everything she was telling him. The green trees and Farmer Jeshrun's fields called to him, and all he wanted to do was run. "Get out? Mother, what are you talking about? There *is* nowhere else but Krinton, unless you're talking about rumors of other planets! This isn't like you!"

Once again, she all but ignored him. "It's up to you now, Marcus," she said. "I dusted the book down and wrapped it up for you, for this most important day of your life, because I'm convinced that it holds your destiny. I cannot follow the quest. I can't even read anymore. I need you to see what the book says and go where it leads you."

"Now?" Marcus squeaked. It was a bad answer, but it was all he could think of. She set her jaw with a determination he had never seen on her face before.

"Now is your chance!" she exclaimed. "You are thirteen now, a man. You must leave home one way or another. Do you really want to join the other orphan workers or go to Uncle Nomit's farm?"

Marcus remained silent and stared at his mother. For the first time it began to occur to him that his mother might be crazy.

Ree-Mya broke the silence by holding the book up and flipping it over, turning back the pages feverishly. "Here, let's see what it says in the first page. I'm sure Grandfather read it to me, but I don't remember." She stretched out her hands, holding the book out to him.

Marcus reluctantly took it from Ree-Mya and scanned the ancient pages. He licked his lips and began to read in a monotone voice. "Let all who search for truth and hope to escape destruction read here. The journey on PathOne that leads to the Kingdom of the North is long and hard, but the rewards are beyond your dreams. Listen for a voice calling you and be sure to—"

Marcus stopped midsentence. He shut the book firmly. "Who knows what 'truth' means, anyway? There is no such thing! Treanthor and all the Wryxl say that truth is whatever you want to believe in. And Krinton is on its way up—everyone knows that. 'Let all who hope to escape destruction'—there won't be another destruction for thousands or millions of years. We don't need to worry about that! And as for voices—what kind of nonsense is that? Sounds like that suspicious, hocus-pocus stuff you're always telling me to ignore!"

Pushing the book back into Ree-Mya's arms, he said, "I need to go for a walk, to think. I'll be back for that feast down by the river later."

Ree-Mya released her hold on his arm and listened to him walk out the gate and across the pathway leading to the village. When she could hear his footsteps no more, she went slowly back inside and took the book up to Marcus's room, where she placed it carefully on his pillow.

* * *

Marcus wandered into the village, where he encountered some local people who were keen to chat with him and share idle gossip about other townsfolk. None seemed to realize it was his birthday, although one of the old women commented on how big he was getting. He was in no mood to talk, so he left Trynn Goth, heading toward Frenham Forest. A winding, stony path took him away from the village houses, the market, the tavern, and the farmers' fields. As he walked, he contemplated everything his mother had shared with him.

Why was she so concerned about that book? Was her dream really so vivid that she would stake her son's life on it? Why should he trust some nonsense passed down from a disappointed old man who hadn't bothered to take up the quest himself . . . whatever that meant? And why should her dream affect him? Surely he should have a say in his own destiny and make decisions for himself now.

He growled and kicked a rock away from the path, watching it bounce over a rough patch of ground and knock chips off the bark of a tree. *What decisions? I can't do anything but go to Uncle Nomit or the workforce.* To his annoyance, he found tears stinging his eyes. He just wanted to be normal like everyone else his age!

Starting with a normal birthday, he thought. This was meant to be his special day; he had wanted a different kind of surprise. *The Book Beyond Time* was just . . . well, weird. It didn't seem exciting at all, simply weird.

Why would anyone want to put their future into the hands of some ancient book?

Marcus reached the center of the forest where he came to his favorite tree, a vast, imposing oak that stretched across a huge clearing. If he climbed up high enough, he could see the whole forest from here.

Twenty minutes later, sitting across a broad, sturdy branch about halfway up, Marcus listened to the sounds of birds and squirrels moving around the forest and thought about his mother again. She hadn't meant to upset him, he knew. She was probably sitting at home crying over his angry response. Guilt and pity assaulted him together. His poor mother, her eyesight all but gone, had struggled to give him all she could. Selling apple pies at the market, sewing curtains for local women who were never quite satisfied with the work—lately she had even spoken of taking in lodgers. And she didn't just do it for herself. Mostly, she did it for him.

No, she didn't deserve to have her only son turn his back on her and take away her hope for the future. He couldn't just abandon her like his father had.

Marcus straightened his shoulders and made up his mind. He would return to the house after the birthday meal and promise to read the book. That would satisfy his mother and make her happy, even though he had no intention of listening for voices or following the "PathOne" it talked about. Instead, he would make her see that the book was just another fantasy story that should not be taken seriously. He would show her that it did not contain his destiny or any such ridiculous notions, and thus they should simply enjoy the fun of the book and then ignore it. Let someone else waste his life chasing silly dreams.

As for his future, Marcus would go to the workforce in Erundel. His uncle Nomit had never been a nice man, and he couldn't bear the thought of being bossed around by his older cousins, who always played tricks on him and looked down on him. Instead, he would help in the rebuilding of Krinton and still be close enough to come home on his days off and bring his mother the little money he earned. Treanthor's men wouldn't work him too hard—and Erundel had a grench port and markets selling ska-swords and all the newest gadgets, as well as plenty of other amusements. When he had served the obligatory four years, he would return home to take care of Ree-Mya properly.

Marcus shinnied down the tree and started the trek home, whistling as he went. The decision made, he felt like a weight had lifted off him. He picked up firewood as he went, filling his arms until he spotted something shiny across the path, near some hedges just outside of the forest. Curious, he went to take a closer look and found that it was a knarl-knife someone had dropped. And it wasn't broken, but working fully, including the switch that snapped the knife closed. Marcus grinned—now *that* was something worth finding on his birthday! He practiced carving on a piece of wood and then tried using it to chop some bramble branches away. The best thing of all was the clip that attached to his belt and the smooth, effortless flick mechanism. He'd have to find some village boys tomorrow and ask them how else the knife could be used. He'd heard a rumor that this kind of knife could cut through anything. Maybe Rindel would know more about it; he was always up-to-date about the advances of NewTech products.

Rindel! The realization broke on him all of a sudden, and laughing, he began to run toward home. Rindel was still coming, to feast with him and his mother by the river. For his birthday.

It wasn't going to be such a bad day after all.

As promised, Ree-Mya had prepared a feast by the river, with fresh bread, grilled chicken legs with her special smoky barbecue sauce, and a cake filled with strawberries and cream. Marcus showed off his knife and played tag and tackle with Rindel and his brothers, all four of them laughing and shouting until they couldn't breathe. The game ended when they threw Rindel into the river.

Marcus felt like a young child again, and he thought he would never grow too old to play games.

Rindel was a few months older than Marcus, yet he was not much bigger, and he was always guaranteed to make Marcus laugh. He had mischievous eyes and hair that was a bit straggly and unkempt. He loved to pounce on people unawares and scare them witless, and he always had a hole somewhere in his clothing from his crazy antics. Although he had begun working with his father in the foundry when he turned thirteen, he was still reckless and silly, and he often teased Marcus for his clumsiness, but Marcus enjoyed his company and was thankful for a friend who understood what it was like to have a parent who had left.

As the sun started to go down, everyone sang "Happy Birthday" at the top of their lungs. Then they all packed up their things and said their goodbyes. Marcus explained quietly to Rindel that his mother had gone all strange that morning, promising to tell him more about it another time. As they waved off Rindel's family, Marcus took Ree-Mya's hand and said that he had something to tell her.

"I've changed my mind, Mum. I'm going to read the book, as you want me to." He forced a smile and tried to sound excited. "I'll read it all tonight if I can. We'll see about this PathOne business."

Ree-Mya's face lit up. "Oh, Marcus, I knew you'd see sense! Thank you. I can't wait to hear more of what it's all about. Grandfather pleaded with me to search for PathOne, to follow it to the Kingdom of the North and to never give up. He also had some Treegle friends who would talk in hushed tones about feeling trapped in Krinton and about the sense of absolute freedom on PathOne. I used to think it was a fantasy—some sort of game they all played—but since having my dream, I just know there has to be more to life than Krinton. Grandfather often said that PathOne wasn't for weak-willed people, only for the determined. For people who would continue on the way, no matter what."

She bit her lip for a minute, but Marcus couldn't tell if it was with sadness or excitement. "I will miss you when you go on your quest. But it is best, Marcus."

As they wound their way home in the twilight, Marcus was glad that Ree-Mya couldn't see the true feelings on his face. Reading that thick book was going to be such a waste of time — and there would be no quest, only his departure for Treanthor's workforce and his new life in Erundel. But he didn't want to disappoint his mother for the time being. At least once he started reading, he'd be able to tell her that her grandfather had been wrong, and she'd forget all about her dream.

When they had reached home, Ree-Mya went to unpack the picnic while Marcus disappeared to his bedroom. Finding the book on his pillow, he sighed heavily, kicked off his boots, and lay down on his back.

Opening the first page, he read the lines he had seen previously again, and then he continued reading. There was nothing particularly special about the text. *It's just words on pages,* he thought. It wasn't even much of a story, mainly a bunch of old teachings and some odd-looking maps with the occasional short story or anecdote thrown in. He didn't really take much of it in, concentrating more on getting through the huge number of pages and wondering whether it would take several days to read it all.

And then it hit him from nowhere. Marcus held his breath as a strange presence gripped him and everything around him started to disintegrate. His chest of drawers melted like wax and slithered downward, as if it were merely a fresh painting being washed away with a bucket of water. Beneath him, his bed was turning to sand.

He leapt to his feet. He was definitely awake; he could hear his mother pottering around in the kitchen!

Marcus slammed the book shut, and instantly everything was restored to its usual solid state. His breathing slowed down but was still heavy like gasps, and he realized that he was sweating profusely. *This is ridiculous. Maybe I've got sunstroke or something from being outside most of the day.*

He blinked a few times, looked around, and then opened the book once more. This time, everything in the room started to go jellylike

33

immediately. Marcus watched incredulously as his bed shrank away from him like an old rag and the window faded like a thinning cloud blown by the wind. He felt as if he were choking and life was being sucked out of him, though there was no one else around, no one strangling him. Fear wrapped round him like a blanket as he observed Trynn Goth disappearing like water through a funnel, and he seemed to be propelled toward a dark corner. All the while, there was a droning, near-deafening sound, which increased in intensity with every passing second. It was so horribly loud, Marcus wanted to shout "STOP!" but had no voice.

As he felt himself being pulled down to the funnel of darkness, in the distance he observed a small gushing waterfall cascading over a jagged black rock. Just beyond that, he could see a small door with a brass handle. The door was wedged open a crack, and brilliant light spilled out into the scene of chaos he found himself in. Willing himself toward the door, he drew right up to it and peeked through, managing to take one step inside.

A glimmering city of lights lay before him, surrounded by spectacular greenery, and he was immediately captivated by the awesome sight. A sparkling river ran through the center of the city, and sights and smells overwhelmed his senses in a rush of delight, though it seemed he could only catch glimpses—dances, fountains, fantastic creatures, and everywhere laughter and singing and music. The place was buzzing with all kinds of other amazing activities, too, such as he had never seen before.

The scene was welcoming and calm, yet also perfectly thrilling and majestic. The droning sound ceased, and Marcus felt a sense of freedom and elation and excitement.

Seconds later he was wrenched back toward the fading world. But what he had seen had impacted him deeply. As he turned around, he heard a voice saying, "First, find the BlackStone Waterfall. It is there your journey will begin."

Immersed again in the fading world with its harrowing droning, Marcus was desperate to get away. He at once became aware of the book in his hands, and he shut it forcefully despite his trembling hands.

Once more, everything returned to normal. He stared down at the ancient leather cover. The room around him *looked* solid—so why did he feel like it wasn't real, like the vision of a fading, melting world was more real than anything he'd known? And what kind of power was connected to this book? And what was the city he had seen—the glorious city of lights that was even now calling to his heart, making him want to cry and laugh at the same time? As he sat on the bed, his body was still shaking from the shock of it all.

He didn't understand anything. But he knew he had to tell someone.

Chapter 3

Clutching the book tightly in his arms, Marcus hurried to find his mother in her rocking chair, stitching curtains by instinct and touch rather than by sight.

He cleared his throat. "Mum, I —" He knelt down beside the rocking chair. "I understand what you mean now. It just happened to me! I was reading, and everything started fading around me, and I was wide awake — it was so strange. I thought I'd been transported to another world or something, and then . . . and then it just stopped when I shut the book."

Ree-Mya laid her hand on her heart.

"But what does it say, Marcus? What are you supposed to do next? Your grandfather talked about a quest — what have you learned of that?"

He cleared his throat again. "Well, I, er, I don't know yet. I was reading, but not exactly — not really paying attention. But then I heard — I think I heard — a voice. I was hoping you'd be able to explain it all properly to me. Did you ever hear anything of the 'BlackStone Waterfall?'"

She frowned. "No, Marcus, that doesn't sound familiar. I think I've told you everything I know." Then she sat bolt upright.

"No, wait! I do remember some other things he told me!" She clasped Marcus's arm and drew a long breath. "Grandfather said that PathOne is a way that can never be wiped out — it's a route that leads to an everlasting kingdom of infinite treasures and eternal friendships, a place where no one dies any more. Oh! And something about a city — a city of lights. The city must be part of the Kingdom of the North."

Marcus flinched a little. He hadn't told her anything of that part of his vision.

Ree-Mya loosened her grip on Marcus and leaned back in her chair. "There are some other things that my visiting Treegle relatives used to whisper about—but I'm not sure I understand what they meant. Something about PathOne changing their hearts and minds. It was as if finding it had made a difference to their lives in Krinton. They spoke as if they were following the path, even though they were here with us. And even though they were still searching for the northern kingdom, they appeared to be, uh, satisfied, content. Even their eyes seemed to sparkle, as if they had found . . . found something worth finding. They used to talk about PathOne being the 'only way.'"

She paused and placed a hand on Marcus's arm. "Won't you find out if there is truth in what they said, and search for a path to lead you out of Krinton?"

Marcus contemplated his mother's request. She was calmer this time, more poised and encouraging, and in his heart he knew that he could not just walk away and ignore the book.

"Let me try again. I'll try to concentrate this time. I think I'll just read here a while and let you know what I find out."

Cross-legged on the wood floor beside Ree-Mya, Marcus set about earnestly reading the first pages again. This time he was relieved that nothing was disturbed when he opened the book and that he wasn't transported back to the fading world. Still, he was unable to fully relax — his body was still on edge from the earlier experience. The first thing to catch his attention was a quote about "Believing, even when all others disbelieve," and again the mention of a voice. A voice he would hear that would start him on his journey, but which he must not ignore or it may stop speaking to him.

Marcus turned back the corner of one page, about twenty pages from the beginning, which contained a warning that filled him with anxiety: "Always be aware of your surroundings, stay alert and don't let yourself get distracted. Be always watchful for hidden foes along the way."

Marcus had not even considered the possibility of opposition. *But who are my foes? Why should anyone want to stop people from traveling this path, and how could anyone even know the direction I'm headed?*

For every captivating line that he read, Marcus also had a question, for not everything was clearly explained—and that frustrated him.

About a hundred pages in he read a description of the northern kingdom, something about a place "drenched in light," "shrouded in mystery," and the "ultimate destination of the free." The descriptions matched his momentary experience of the other side of the door in his very real vision, including all kinds of precious stones and a flowing river through the center. Once half his body had crossed over to that incredible place, all panic and dread about the fading world had dissipated, and his soul had felt flooded with vibrant feelings of happiness. He had experienced something so amazing, it wasn't possible to describe it properly. He knew in his heart that he wanted to find that place—if it really did exist.

Ree-Mya finished sewing the hem on a pair of blue velvet curtains, folded them, and closed her eyes as she leaned back in her rocking chair. Her thoughts were only interrupted occasionally by the turning of pages and the intermittent snuffle from Marcus.

He skimmed through each page quickly, hoping to read something about the BlackStone Waterfall, but he found nothing. Instead he read some words which caught his attention. "Everyone is beckoned toward PathOne, but many ignore the calling. Who will follow the calling toward the Kingdom of the North and listen to my voice?"

A slight chill went up Marcus's spine as he recalled the voice instructing him to find the waterfall. He had definitely heard someone speaking to him in the vision, but who it was remained a mystery.

He continued reading as much as he could and came across several maps which he examined briefly, but he couldn't really make sense of them. He'd never seen a map before, only simple town plans etched into wooden boards at the main entrance to most towns or villages. Most people didn't venture far beyond their town or nearest city.

And finally he came to a description of Krinton, and it chilled his blood as he read it.

Hours had passed. Marcus shut the book and looked up at Ree-Mya, who had fallen asleep. It was late now, probably around midnight, and Marcus was tired, but he knew she'd want him to wake her up.

"Mum, wake up. Mum."

He reached up and shook her arm gently, and she stirred.

Marcus spoke softly. "I've found out what I need to know. I don't understand it all. The book says Krinton is only temporary—that it's not exactly real, and a deceiver rules it, and time is running out. There are some mentions about increasing progress and inventions and a popular ruler. These things don't signify a better world, but the beginning of the end—something about 'everything getting better' before it will all get terribly worse."

Ree-Mya nodded, keen to hear more of what Marcus had discovered. He went on. "It sounds like people are being deceived about the prosperity of Krinton—because whatever we can gain here will fade away. It says that everyone who wants to escape destruction must follow PathOne to search for the Kingdom of the North, just as your grandpa said."

He grew quiet for a moment, thinking about Krinton and what the book said about its future. "My vision—it was so real, so alarming. The panic I felt was real—just like you experienced in your dream. I think it was a warning that I must go as you said. The book says that anyone who truly wants to find this kingdom *will* find it. And it's such an amazing kingdom, I caught a glimpse of it—the city of lights, exactly as the book describes. I've made a decision, Mum; I want to find that place. I want to leave tomorrow!"

* * *

40

Marcus had a restless sleep that night, wondering if he'd really be able to go ahead with this journey or find the BlackStone Waterfall. He began worrying about his ability to understand the book and follow its guidance correctly. And the voice — what if he didn't hear it again? What if he couldn't tell where to go next? He couldn't even read the maps in the book properly. How would he look after himself — and what about Treanthor's edict that no one must go beyond his home county without a valid permit of travel? If he stated "Kingdom of the North" as his destination, Treanthor's knights would launch an investigation and follow him. What if Treanthor really was the deceiver the book talked about? And what about dangers along the way? Wild animals, risky bridges, gangs of thugs?

Eventually he fell into a deep sleep, but he woke with a start at dawn, fully alert. *I have to tell Rindel,* Marcus thought immediately. Getting dressed hurriedly and grabbing an apple on his way out the door, he stumbled down the slope to the large, dark, timber house at the end of the lane. Climbing up the ivy on the right side, Marcus knocked on the window. Rindel's younger brother Lorik opened the window, bleary-eyed and bemused.

"What are you doing here? What time is it anyway?"

"I need to see Rindel. Where is he?"

"He's not here. He had to stay at the foundry too late, so he just slept there."

Marcus groaned. "Can you give him a message when he comes back? Promise? Tell him to come round to my house immediately — it's urgent!"

Lorik nodded and yawned before closing the window and heading back to bed. Marcus hurried back home to find Ree-Mya awake and pouring tea in the kitchen. Steam rose from the familiar blue cups.

"I'm getting ready to go, Mum. If this book is true, then I need to leave as soon as possible. Treanthor's men will be round in a few weeks to check on thirteen-year-olds and make sure they have work

41

placements. If I get on my way now, it will be harder for them to track me down later. I'm hoping that Rindel will come too."

Ree-Mya sat down at the table and picked up her cup of tea before responding. Her delay made Marcus nervous. "Is that a wise choice, Marcus? You know that Rindel can be a bit—unreliable sometimes. Silly."

"I know, Mum, but he's my friend. He hates working at the foundry, and I—I just don't know if I can do this on my own."

He threw himself into a kitchen chair, and his mother pushed a plate of sliced bread across to him. "I think you can, son. I've seen how independent you've become over the last couple of years, and I know that you always think things through properly. You can make this journey as well as anyone."

Marcus frowned and wolfed down a piece of bread with honey, wishing it would calm his growing nerves. "But I guess I'm still not really sure about all this, if I'm honest. What happened with the book last night—what if it's all just a trick which some wizard has put together, and the strange power will only lead me into trouble?"

"Grandfather would never have lied to me, Marcus. And what the book says about Krinton is true. It's strange, but the more I lose my eyesight, the more I realize that there is another side to life that is more *real* than all of this. The first moment I ever set eyes on Treanthor, when you were just a baby, I knew that I could never put my hope or future in his hands. He seemed so . . . so insincere; so . . . evil, yes, that's more like it. I'm sure the book tells the truth. Our only hope is to follow it."

Ree-Mya paused a few moments. "And Marcus, when you find it— come back for me."

Marcus swallowed a lump in his throat. "I will go, Mother, for you—and I will come back for you. Will you be safe here alone?"

"I'll be fine; Farmer Jeshrun says he'll have a whole crowd of laborers coming in soon in preparation for harvest, and he can send a couple of decent ones to me for lodging. They can also help me around here, with lighting the evening fire and so on. I'll be just fine."

Marcus nodded and then remembered that she most likely couldn't see the simple movement, despite his standing so close to her. So he took her in his arms, holding her close. "All right, then, as long as you're sure. I'll miss you."

Ree-Mya wriggled free. "Oh no you don't, young man! You're not going to make me cry before you've even departed!"

* * *

Marcus decided to take only two bags—one large cloth sack for clothing, a couple of blankets, and his tent; and his leather satchel containing other essential items—including matches and *The Book Beyond Time*. His newfound knarl-knife was clipped to his belt. Not everything he wanted to take would fit into the bags, and it started to frustrate him. He couldn't quite take it in that he was going to leave home and fend for himself; even more worrisome was the fear that he might not make it home to his mother and friends again.

"Eggs are ready, Marcus," called Ree-Mya from the kitchen.

"Coming," replied Marcus.

Leaving everything in a heap on the floor, he swung out of the room, already drooling in anticipation of a hearty breakfast. This time, Marcus and Ree-Mya didn't talk much at all. They simply ate and listened to the morning chorus of birds just beyond the back door. Marcus was distracted from his breakfast by a growing lump in his throat and very nearly had second thoughts about going, but he chose to say nothing about his doubts to his mother.

"Ooooo, wooo," came a low moaning sound from outside.

Ree-Mya jumped up.

Marcus's eyes widened. "What was that?"

"Ooooo, woooo . . ." There it was again! It sounded like a ghost in pain, or a—

Then there was a banging on the outside wall. *Thud, thud, thud.* "Oooo, wooo"

"I knew it!" shrieked Marcus.

Rindel's face appeared, grinning at the window. "I got you!"

Marcus dashed to the washbasin, soaked a sponge in water, and darted out the door.

"You rascal!" Marcus threw the cloth at Rindel and felt justified when it hit him squarely between the eyes.

"Don't do that again, Rindel," scolded Ree-Mya from the kitchen door. "You know I can barely see; you nearly scared the wits out of me."

Rindel apologized sheepishly more than once before he and Marcus headed into the yard, where they sat on a couple of huge logs.

After sharing his story, as well as Ree-Mya's, Marcus told Rindel of his plan to start his journey later that day.

Rindel was fascinated by everything his friend said. "You know, I heard a similar story from an old carpenter once—strange chap, he was. But he kept going on and on about such a kingdom and a path that led to it. Said his father had dug up some weird book in his backyard and told him all about it. I thought he was crazy or something, but maybe he was right."

Marcus cleared his throat. "Rindel, I want you to come with me."

"With you?" Rindel squawked. "But—work at the foundry, and—"

"You hate working at the foundry," Marcus said. "And your brothers can help your dad with the work."

Rindel snorted. "You're right about that. He's always complaining that I'm not careful enough with a hammer. When are you leaving?"

"Midafternoon—when it's cooler for traveling," replied Marcus. "Will you come?"

"It's crazy," Rindel said.

Marcus grinned. "I know. So will you do it?"

Rindel grinned back. "Yup."

"If you're not back here with your things on time, I'll leave without you. And bring any valuables with you; we might need to trade for food along the way."

"Sounds exciting!" quipped Rindel. He slapped Marcus on the back as he headed toward the gate. "I'll meet you in a while then," he said. "And sorry for scaring you earlier. Tell your mother I won't do that to her again."

"I will. Now don't tell anyone of our plans, or they might change your mind or speak to the village officials about it. They must just think we're going on some childish adventure, or going to Erundel to join the workforce. Nothing serious."

"You can trust me, Marcus," Rindel sang, and off he went back home.

Marcus finished sorting out his things upstairs, then stopped to rest a while on his bed. The old kite swayed gently in a breeze from the open window.

Moments later, it seemed, a door banged.

Rindel was back already! Marcus had fallen asleep. He quickly grabbed his things and went out to hug his mother goodbye. She was watering plants in the garden.

"Have you got the book?"

"Yes, it's in my satchel. I won't let go of it, ever. First we're heading to the Hill of Horcum—that's the obvious way north—then down into the next valley. We'll ask around and keep our ears open to find out anything we can about the waterfall. Until then, we'll just keeping heading north. If I can, I'll send a message back to you in a couple of days."

Ree-Mya laid her hands on her son's shoulders and looked up into his face. "Be strong, Marcus. Don't give up. I love you, dear son."

Marcus fought back tears. "I love you too, Mum."

Before they left, she handed them two parcels of bread and cheese. "This should keep you going a few days. I've just baked the bread."

Marcus and Rindel thanked her, hugged her again, and left without looking back.

They walked down the lane, past the village market, past the two farms and their old orchards. Neither of them said anything much as each one realized the huge journey he was embarking on — an adventure, but one where nothing could really be certain.

It surprised them both that they tired quite easily before they had even covered any great distance. Yet neither wanted to stop too soon to rest for fear that the other would urge him to turn back. The tension in the air was noticeable.

Eventually they reached the base of Horcum Hill, the most challenging landmark in their part of Krinton. The hill was practically a mountain, with grassy sides that rose up at an almost sheer angle. No one they knew had ever ventured up it. "It doesn't lead anywhere," old Wryxl men said when asked about it. The road went around it, but they would save hours if they went over the hill instead. They decided to rest and eat a little before ascending the grassy hillside, where sure-footed sheep were grazing. A rocky stream cut through the hillside all the way to the bottom, where it met with a narrow river.

Just before they started their climb, Marcus went to refill his water containers at the fast-flowing part of the stream at the foot of the hill. He talked to himself as he went. "That's where the freshest water is, my dad always used to say."

He had to duck under low-lying branches and push aside some bushes to get to the source of the river. He knelt down to fill the skins, and when he pulled himself up, he caught sight of the jagged black rock he had seen in his vision. Marcus gasped and nearly tripped back into the river. The rock was obscured by thick tree branches, but it was instantly recognizable — shiny like polished stone, with distinct jagged edges and streams of water flowing down it. The water was more of a

46

trickle than the flowing waters he remembered from his vision, but there was no mistaking the stone.

He had found the BlackStone Waterfall.

Marcus stared at it for quite some time, wishing something would happen to indicate what he was supposed to do next. Nothing—there was no voice, no further instructions. Still, this was the right place, and the voice had said his journey would begin here. He returned to Rindel full of confidence. It was a sign, he was sure of it. They were meant to ascend the hill. From there, they would press on toward the north and hope to find PathOne clearly marked out.

"We're definitely heading the right way! Come on, let's climb up."

Rindel didn't share Marcus's enthusiasm, but he thought it could be fun to go climbing. There were no hills in Trynn Goth, and tree climbing had long ago lost its thrill.

When they reached the top, sweaty and worn out, they felt a strong sense of achievement. It was exhilarating to have reached the summit, and they shook hands and congratulated one another. It was hard to believe they had never tried that before—it was so much fun! Now they could see for miles around. Trynn Goth looked like a miniature dolls' village. Across several valleys and plains to the north, they could just about make out the city skyline of Erundel and see the glistening tower of the popular grench port. Neither of them had been there since they were very small; both were keen to experience the thrill of city life without a parent alongside them. They had heard so many vivid tales about Erundel, and neither boy wanted to turn back once they had come this far. Marcus didn't know where else PathOne would take them, but at least this part of the journey would be exciting.

Rindel lay down in the grass, staring up at the cloudy sky. It looked as though rain could be on its way, but the air was still pleasantly warm. Marcus sprawled out nearby and listened to Rindel tell amusing tales about sheep and mindless shepherds. The stories weren't especially original—everyone joked about shepherds.

He thought they'd better be on their way, but the laughter felt good, and then Rindel started a play fight, grabbing Marcus by the elbow and tickling his armpits. Marcus responded by pinching his arms and poking his belly.

Rindel tried to escape by running around a clump of fir trees. "You can't catch me!" Marcus took the challenge and wrong-footed Rindel before grabbing him by the shoulders.

"All right, you win!" Rindel declared. "I tell you what, though — I bet you wouldn't dare to tumble down the hillside."

He headed across to the far side of the hill's peak and looked down. The sides weren't so sheer on this side, though they still sloped down for a perilous distance. Still, this side of the hill was lush, with very few rocks or other obstacles. "Quite a way to the bottom, but I reckon I could roll all the way. Watch!"

Rindel collected his bundle of belongings, clutched them to his tummy, and started rolling down like a bale of hay before Marcus could do anything to stop him.

"Hey!" Marcus shouted. "Don't leave me behind!" He tucked his bag of clothing and blankets to him and threw himself down after Rindel.

He didn't for one moment consider why there were no sheep grazing on this side of the hill.

As they tumbled full speed to the bottom, Marcus squeezed his eyes shut and held on to his bundles with all his might. As he heard Rindel yelp with elation, he opened one eye slightly to catch the rolling view. And that was when he spotted a bleak, moving shadow out of the corner of his eye. Turning his head to see up the hillside, he became fully aware of a hovering, fur-covered creature with red eyes and long claws. It wasn't a bear or anything he'd seen before. He'd heard stories of such beasts.

It was a gratsch.

"Rindel!" Marcus yelled at the top of his lungs. But before he could shout out a warning, his momentum carried him over a dip in the hillside and slammed him against the ground again, knocking the breath from his lungs.

Rindel had already landed at the bottom and was lying stretched out on his front. He didn't move. The gratsch spotted its opportunity to attack a still target, and as Marcus caught horrified glimpses, it made huge, bounding strides toward Rindel.

"Rindel!" Marcus yelled again.

It was too late. Just as Rindel turned to get up, the gratsch lunged for him, swooping him up into its apelike arms by the scruff of his neck.

"Auughhh!" screamed Rindel.

Marcus was still hurtling down, but he twisted his body so he rolled in another direction away from them both. He reached the base of the hill and grabbed at grass and rocks to make himself stop rolling, crawling to hide behind a gorse bush as soon as he could gain control of his limbs. He watched as the gratsch manhandled Rindel and roared in his face before thrusting him over its shoulder and walking off with its prized catch. Rindel wasn't even resisting, and Marcus couldn't tell if he was hurt or just in shock.

Marcus's head was spinning both with the situation and with his tumble down the hill. This had not been in his plan for the day. He cupped his head in his hands as he recalled the warning about "hidden foes" he had read in *The Book Beyond Time* the night before.

He had ignored the book's first major instruction! Why hadn't he stopped to think about it before following Rindel down the hill? Some quester he was. Now what could he possibly do to help Rindel? *There's no way I can overpower that gratsch, even with my knarl-knife. I need to find help, but we're miles from anywhere.*

Looking up, he saw Rindel being carried westward around the curve of the hill. Marcus felt despair in the pit of his stomach and wondered how on earth he would deliver the awful news to Rindel's family.

The sound of hoofbeats pounded his fears from his head as a mysterious man on a gray horse appeared, charging toward the gratsch with a long silver sword and a quiver strapped to his back. He retrieved an arrow and shot it toward the beast, wounding it in the mouth. As the gratsch stumbled and wailed with the pain, it released its hold on Rindel. Rindel collapsed in a heap and crawled behind a small rock, too scared to run further away. The man dived toward the monster, his horse neighing and kicking while the rider swiped his sword at the huge creature and finally thrust it into its furry chest. The gratsch stumbled to the left, then to the right, before losing balance and falling backward onto the ground with a massive thud. It lay still.

Marcus ran toward the scene.

"Rindel, Rindel, are you hurt?"

"He'll be just fine," the man replied.

Chapter 4

The stranger was an old man, but clearly strong, clothed in a dark cloak. His wavy, silver-and-gray hair reached down to his shoulders; his neat beard was trimmed short in a distinctive style, with an additional short, plaited section of beard hanging from the tip.

"Who *are* you?" Marcus implored.

"I am Brayman, and you, Marcus, should pay more attention to *The Book Beyond Time* before acting recklessly."

Marcus froze. He had told nobody else of the book—and how did this stranger know his name?

"I, er, I know. We didn't think . . ."

"No, that's it. You didn't think. Your friend here nearly led you both into a deadly trap. You would do well to consider your surroundings before plunging down a hillside. I watched you both before this lad made his move. The gratsch was lurking over there, waiting for you to move into its territory, but neither of you noticed. You did not even stop to ask why most travelers go *around* the hill. You must always be aware of your surroundings!"

"Thank you for saving us," Marcus said humbly. "You seem to know a lot about us. Do you know—that is, I'm not sure how to . . . do this. I thought—well, I found the BlackStone Waterfall, and I thought it meant we should come up here. I was wrong, then—but . . . I don't know where to go. What should we do now?"

Brayman's face was stern, but Marcus thought he saw a smile playing in his eyes. "You must be on your way at once, before sundown. You must take this quest seriously, for there are many who would oppose you—and not only mindless beasts. Go where you already knew you were to go. You *were* right to come this way, up the hill—avoiding other people along the usual route, but you must be aware of your surroundings and watch for hidden dangers. Go north, unless Merloy tells you otherwise."

"Merloy?"

"You've heard a voice, haven't you?"

Before Marcus could answer, Brayman untied a sword from his saddle and handed it to Marcus.

"Here—this is for you. You will need to use it in future."

Marcus took the sword and unsheathed it, awed. It was a sword, but old—much older than anything the boys in the village liked to daydream about. Its double-edged blade was a dark metal, almost black, and its handle was worn and inlaid with a dull green stone. Yet, it fit Marcus's hand perfectly and seemed balanced just for him. Brayman watched as Marcus inspected the sword and then proceeded to dismount before handing his horse over too.

"But—but I can't take your horse, sir! Then you will be without one," Marcus said.

Brayman really did smile this time. "She is not my horse, dear boy. I brought her especially for you today. I have another, nearby in the town of Woytl. Take good care of her; her name is Tress. She needs some gentle guidance and will need to get to know you."

Marcus climbed up and settled into the leather saddle. He was comfortable on horseback, having ridden with Farmer Jeshrun's son just for fun on occasion. But he had never ridden a horse any significant distance.

"Here, Rindel, climb on up behind me."

Brayman frowned as Rindel came staggering forward. "Will the lad here travel too? I thought you were to be traveling alone."

"Well, yes. Rindel's my friend, and he has agreed to go with me to the north."

Brayman stared at Rindel a moment, and the boy squirmed. Finally, the old man said, "Oh, if you insist. But do be on your way now. The night will soon be upon us, and you must get out of this territory. It has other dangers."

Marcus pulled Rindel up behind him, and Tress shifted uncomfortably, nearly throwing them both off. Marcus dug his heels in and pulled the reins tightly. "Will you tell us more about yourself, sir? Who sent you our way, and how did you learn to battle a beast like the gratsch?"

"There is no time to discuss such things at length right now, Marcus. But I can tell you that I have been sent here to guide you onward along PathOne, and that there are those who would seek to prevent your journey. Treanthor has tried to silence any talk of the path and is determined to wipe out any of its followers. He will no doubt soon send men after you and your friend here. You are not the only one sent on this quest, Marcus. Others are destined to travel this way beside you — though some paths you will have to travel alone. Everyone has to discover his own way along PathOne."

"That doesn't make sense," Rindel grumbled. Brayman ignored him. Marcus listened without interruption, subdued by the thought that people could be sent to track them down, wondering about the consequences of traveling forbidden routes.

Brayman focused his gaze on Marcus. "This narrow path, hard as it seems, is your destiny and will lead to a new life. Take care to befriend those who will encourage you along the way and who are also seeking what you want. I am overseeing a secret network of knights to watch over PathOne and help its followers find their way. Watch out for these brave ones, though they may not be immediately obvious to you.

"Look out also for Merloy, the one who can appear to you and help you. He holds all the answers to all of your questions, and he will ultimately show you where your way lies. Remember, many others seek only to deter you from your quest. Now be on your way! You must pass through Erundel before continuing north. Make sure you are not distracted by the city!"

Marcus nodded, and Rindel thanked Brayman for saving his life before Marcus turned east, away from the hill, on toward the city of Erundel.

They rode together in silence, Marcus exulting in the feel of the horse beneath him and the sword at his side. He started to wonder about this person called *Merloy* and began to think that this journey might be a real adventure after all.

* * *

A small fire crackled and spat while Marcus flipped pages in *The Book Beyond Time*. He growled in frustration.

"What's the matter with you?" Rindel asked.

"I don't understand this book," Marcus grumbled.

Rindel flipped onto his stomach. He was lying on the ground close to the fire, and his brown eyes sparkled as he watched Marcus. "Of course you don't. It's just a book. Books don't matter to us anymore, remember? They're so old-world."

"You should talk. You're following a book."

"No, my friend, *you* are following a book." Rindel grinned. "I'm just following you. To see what happens. 'Cause it's better than working another day at the foundry. What don't you understand, anyway?"

Marcus thumbed a few pages back. "Well, stuff like this. 'Do not set your heart upon the treasures of this world, for all are temporary and fading away. They are mere illusions. Rather, set your heart upon the treasures of the north.'"

"What's so hard about that?"

Marcus shut the book with a satisfying thud of heavy paper and leather. "How am I supposed to care about 'treasures' when I can't see them? And then a few pages later it says that the treasures of the north aren't things we can see at all, but 'freedom, happiness, and peace, even in the center of the storm.' Huh?"

54

Rindel shrugged. "Don't stress about it. Remember what the villagers say: 'Relax; don't worry your little mind about such things. There is no truth, it's all in your mind; whatever you wish for will be your future."

Marcus snorted. "You're such a Wryxl."

"And you're such a Treegle! Wryxl ways suit me just fine. They're better than worrying all the time, like you're doing. 'Whatever may happen shall happen. So be it.'"

Marcus made a face and flipped the book open again, thumbing pages until he came across words that already looked familiar. "The fool says in his heart, 'There is no truth, all things will be what they are. Nothing can be changed.' They do not know that the difficult path of right-doing leads to life, and that the path to destruction is full of ignorance and mindless wrong-doing."

"The difficult path?" Rindel asked.

"Don't ask me. Sounds like something Brayman talked about." Marcus breathed out heavily, scanning the horizon. The lights of Erundel could be seen, burning orangey in the darkness. The city was still some miles off, and they had decided to camp once darkness fell. Gratsch territory, thankfully, was far behind them. Tress, the horse, had patiently carried them until both boys were so sore they couldn't wait to get down. Their fire was a bit pitiful, but at least it was burning.

"I can't wait till we get to the city," Rindel said. "I want to see a grench port. And there will be merchants! Erundel is bound to have all the latest NewTech gadgetry! D'you think we can get a new ska-sword? Maybe we can trade that old thing the old man gave you."

"I don't think we should do that," Marcus said, laying a protective hand over the weapon.

"Why not? It's just a hunk of old metal."

"It was a gift. I just don't think we should get rid of it. Anyway, Brayman told me not to part with it, and he sounded pretty serious."

Rindel rolled his eyes at Marcus, then flipped onto his back and propped himself up on his elbows so he could see the glow of the city. "I've always wanted to go to Erundel. My dad would never let me. Said a fool like me would get sucked into the grench ports and never come out."

"He was probably right," Marcus said, tossing a small stone at Rindel's head.

"Ow! What was that for?"

"Revenge," Marcus said, grinning. "Payback for the bruises I got rolling down that stupid hill!"

Rindel scrambled up and fired a clod of dirt in Marcus's direction. Marcus ducked, shielding *The Book Beyond Time*. "*I'm* the one who almost got eaten," Rindel said. "No thanks to you."

"Well, we're even, then," Marcus said.

They laughed. After a few minutes, Rindel wrapped himself in a blanket and tried to sleep.

Marcus stoked the fire and stared down at the book in his hands. "All I can say," he muttered, "is that when I get to the Kingdom of the North, I'd better find some tangible treasures worth finding—not just some notional ideas of freedom. That's not going to fix Mum's eyes. Or help me start a new life."

Sighing, he flipped the pages open and scanned another passage. "Beware of trusting all those in fine clothing. The measure of a man is not to be found in his outward appearance but in his inner strength of character. What is inside you is of far greater worth than what you put on to impress others." There it was again—all this business about outward things being untrustworthy, not as real somehow as inward things.

He lay down and closed his eyes. Everything he had read in the book hung in the air like some kind of challenge he didn't really understand.

Is this world really fading away, like the book says? Marcus wondered. *Is it really going to be destroyed?* He flicked past large chunks of the book and began reading about unusual, glowing creatures called *cronjls*. The book described these winged beings as "guardsmen of the path" and "unseen warriors for good." Marcus thought they sounded awesome — but also like they belonged in some sort of fantasy story told by his cousins. *Could these even be real in Krinton?*

No answers came to his questions. Cold and uncomfortable, barraged now by Rindel's snoring along with his own doubts, he finally fell asleep.

* * *

Traffic was pouring into Erundel as they approached, crowding the wide roads and narrowing down a packed, noisy, shoulder-to-shoulder stream of people and animals attempting to cross the slender bridge over the River Quinn all at once. The city's gleaming stone walls were hung with black and red banners, matching the flags that flew from the high towers. Marcus knew that here, fronting the river, was the only place where the walls still stood. Beyond this place, work crews had dismantled the stone barricades, giving the city room to sprawl. Since Treanthor had installed the first grench port here, years ago when Marcus was still a baby, Erundel had become a center of commerce and progress, one of Treanthor's proudest achievements. He had concentrated task forces here, bringing the city into the new golden age of peace, prosperity, and pleasure for all. The Era of Pleasure, he had named it.

Words from the book tugged at Marcus's mind. "The treasures of the north are not food and drink, nor things present to the eye and gratifying to the body. The treasures of the north are the knowledge and strength to know and to do what is right, peace of mind when all around is confusion, and the deep happiness that remains no matter what desperate situation you find yourself in."

He frowned. *But I thought PathOne led to a destination, a new kingdom! Now it seems to be talking about a way of life—so confusing!*

Tress began to resist entering the city center, unsure of all the bustling activity around her, and Marcus struggled to control her properly. As an oncoming farmer's wagon approached them on the city street, Marcus tried to steer her to one side. But Tress resisted and crashed headlong into the cart, causing the load of vegetables to scatter everywhere. Marcus and Rindel spent a long while helping to pick them up, red with embarrassment as the farmer berated them for the mistake.

"You two should never be allowed out on that horse again! You're far too young to be journeying without a proper chaperone. What did you think you were doing? And where were you going in such a hurry? It can't have been that urgent!"

When she nearly collided with another street vendor's cart, Marcus grew frustrated with Tress's inability to judge narrow spaces and decided it would be easier to dismount and walk through the city streets.

Standing here, in the crowd, already smelling the heady aromas of Erundel, hearing music and laughter, and seeing the gleaming stones and banners, Marcus thought to himself that he wasn't so sure the treasures of the north could compete. A brief memory of the city of lights came to him, but that had been a vision—this was real.

A fat man, shining rings on all his fingers, elbowed Marcus and beamed down at him. "First time in the city, boy?" he boomed.

How does he know? "No," Marcus answered. "I've been here before."

"When you were a baby!" Rindel crowed. "You haven't been here anytime that *counts!*"

"Indeed," the big man said, nodding in a jovial way. "The city of Erundel has become a wonder! Treanthor has transformed this place." He leaned down and whispered, "Go to the grench port first. It will be busier later today, when the merchants close shop. If you go now, you needn't wait so long in line."

"Yes, sir!" Rindel answered, ignoring Marcus, who was quiet. Too quiet. He knew his mother hated the grench ports—always had. She associated them with sekrin and other drugs, things that people used to invent their own worlds and stay out of the real one. *If this* is *the real one,* Marcus thought to himself. *According to the book, this is all a bunch of lies.*

Of course, his mother's reaction to grench ports came partly because his father had loved them. Marcus's aunt had once confided in him that Ree-Mya's opinions were most certainly an overreaction—the grench ports were mostly just fun and games, after all. But over the years, his aunt had developed her own opinions about the ports. She associated them with layabout types who wasted all their time and energy doing nothing worthwhile or productive. They parted with their money, had a great time, but had nothing to show for it.

"Grench ports are a mindless distraction for young men and women," she would say. "The more they visit, the more they want to return, and then they come out looking spaced out and lacking creativity. It drains them of enthusiasm for life—have you seen the look on their faces?"

She did have a point. Even in his little town, Marcus had seen the effects on those who came back from visits to the city. Many of the young people had little energy to be creative or patience to develop new skills once they started visiting grench ports frequently. They seemed to lose their spark for life and became unhappy about everything—that is, until they could go back to play again.

Marcus looked around, drinking in the masses of people and color and animals—fine horses, oxen pulling wagons, even a few pigs and dogs running around. Ska-swords on display and gadgetry sparkling everywhere. It all looked real and solid enough. Nothing illusory or deceptive about it.

"Come on," Rindel urged. "I see a way to get through the crowd."

Hardly waiting for a response, Rindel took off, weaving through a nearly interlocked puzzle of wagons and carts. Marcus ran after him, breaking into a grin at the exhilaration of dodging, jumping, and pushing. He nearly collided with Rindel at the edge of the river.

"Whoa!" Rindel said, flailing his arms to keep from falling in. "Careful!" He grinned at his friend. "After you."

Marcus grinned back, and with a whoop, leapt into the water. Rindel jumped on him a minute later, and they wrestled each other, ducking one another's heads, pulling hair, laughing and splashing. Tress trudged along after them, a little reluctant to immerse half of herself in the cool waters. When they were done, they climbed out on the opposite bank, dripping, their sides hurting from laughter, and entered the hub of Erundel.

Chapter 5

The grench port stood within the crumbling walls of the Old City square—a cobblestoned square that had once been a small city in itself, long ago, in the days before the Great Catastrophe that changed the world. Whatever its history, it was mostly forgotten. All that mattered to people now was the present: the present of pleasure and happiness, represented by the strange machine at the center of the square. Once, the square had been graced by ancient willow trees, but they had been cut down to make room for more people to line up. All that was left of them was their wide stumps, upon which grench players sat or stood.

Rindel was sprawled out on one now, soaking up the sun and dreaming of the game that was just five people ahead of him. "It's going to be wonderful," he said.

"You don't know what you're talking about," Marcus said, frowning.

"You'd think you didn't even want to play."

Marcus just grunted. The book was heavy in his bag. More and more, its words seemed like nonsense. True, he didn't really like the idea of going into the grench port—maybe he just didn't want to join Rindel's enthusiasm, or maybe he wanted to stay out for his mother's sake. But the sunlight—the cobblestones—the willow tree—all of this was so *real*. The people looked so truly happy. Everything was dreamy, intriguing, exciting. He could smell food cooking from a hundred merchant stands and see the brand new ska-swords swinging from the belts of city men dressed in fine tunics. A gang of boys, wearing the uniform of Treanthor's orphan workforce, were racing up and down the crumbling walls, obviously happy to be here.

Illusion? Destruction? It couldn't be.

A thought came very suddenly into Marcus's mind, reinforced by the shouts of delirious happiness when someone came staggering out of the grench port and the line moved up one. *The Kingdom of the North is just a myth. This—what Treanthor is building—is real.*

He shook his head.

Even with the short line, it was another forty minutes before Rindel disappeared into the grench port. Marcus stepped out of line, ignoring the incredulous stares and remarks of those behind him, and waited. He needed to think some things over by himself.

* * *

Inside the port, the xanth-crystal lights were low, and Rindel weaved his way through a narrow entrance tunnel before finding himself on a square platform. Neon arrows indicated where he should go next. A girl with a long ponytail and a silver bag across her shoulders pushed past him and jumped across to the triangular platform opposite.

"C'mon," she said, looking back at Rindel. "Haven't you been here before?"

Rindel shook his head and followed her across.

"See, try this," she exclaimed, pressing a green button just above the rail. The platform dropped at an incredible speed, and Rindel nearly lost his balance and fell into the girl's arms.

She laughed at him.

"Awesome!" said Rindel, pulling himself up straight. He grinned and then pressed a blue, diamond-shaped button.

This time, he held on tightly to the rails at the edge as the platform spun round about five times. When it stopped, the platform tilted forward, propelling them both onto another walkway. Following the girl's lead, Rindel grabbed wires above his head, which swung him down to a lower level. Here, the multicolored xanth lights were flashing at random intervals, and loud, thudding music boomed into the air. Rindel had no idea where it was coming from—he could see no musicians.

Another neon arrow led him to a seat facing what appeared to be a blank white wall. Rindel pressed a green button on the top of his chair. *Vroom!* was all he heard as a glass cage dropped over his head. He was about to panic when he heard instructions. A clear voice said, "Use your feet to press the foot pedals on the floor, and find the buttons on either side of your seat. They will direct you."

Rindel did as he was told, and the blank wall before him disappeared, swallowed up by blue sky and rushing canyon walls. He was flying! Eyes wide and heart pounding, he flew over canyons and chased monsters, the buttons allowing him to progress to each new level. He felt a huge sense of power and pride in his ability to conquer beasts and travel at unimaginable speeds. A button on his helmet allowed him to change direction and visit different places, while the pedal on the floor controlled speed. Within minutes he'd been across mountains, skimmed over the surface of seas, fought in city taverns, and dueled strange knights.

"Proceed now to the next platform," the voice said.

Vroom. The helmet whisked up and away over his head.

Rindel followed the next arrow, crawling through a tunnel which was bumpy beneath his knees. With each movement the ground beneath him wobbled and made him feel strange, but in a nice kind of way. It was a bit like being tickled—annoying, but somehow enjoyable.

At the other end he was instructed to stand still on a red circle. Rindel was aware of a couple of boys watching him and grinning. Suddenly the circle was swept from beneath him, and he fell at an alarming speed for what seemed like an age, though it was probably only four or five seconds.

"Aaarrrggggh!" yelled Rindel as his stomach leapt and his hair stood on end.

He landed in a massive pile of soft hay and started to laugh. Following the arrows, Rindel continued to leap and swing across platforms, through tunnels, and across walkways. Xanth crystals, music, special effects, and dizzying adventures—all of it combined until Rindel had lost track of time.

When an alarm sounded, instructing everyone to leave after their hour's visit, Rindel's heart sank with disappointment. He hadn't gone up to the top floor yet, and he'd heard others talking about how incredible it was up there. He turned on his heels and looked for a place to hide, but before he could secrete himself away somewhere inside the port, a guard appeared and ushered him out.

* * *

When Rindel appeared in the grench port exit, he made a mad dash for the entrance, shouting that he'd waited long enough and he was from the country and they ought to let him in again. While Marcus blushed ferociously with embarrassment, Rindel was roughly escorted away from the port by two burly guards and tossed on his rear into the street outside the Old City square.

Before they shut the door, one of the guards called, "There's a time limit, you know, because of the crowds! Come back tomorrow!"

"Well, you've made an utter fool of yourself," Marcus said. "One goal completed. Now what?"

Rindel was quivering, his hair shaggier than ever after all the spinning around. He looked at Marcus, but he seemed to be seeing past him. "Get back in line, man! I wanna do it again!"

"They won't let you back in until tomorrow. You made an idiot of yourself, remember?"

"*You* do it then."

Marcus shook his head. "No . . . not today." He cast about for a good excuse, unable to shake from his mind Brayman's warning about not getting distracted in the city. "I'd rather not go without you."

The shouts of vendors hawking their wares carried to them from around the corner of the stone wall. Rindel's eyes were beginning to focus more sharply. He looked disappointed.

"We'll go to the market," Marcus said. "Okay? Let's tie Tress here with the other horses while we look around."

He looped a rope several times around a large post and patted the horse before heading into the square.

The Erundel market was at the center of the new-city sprawl. It covered several acres of smooth, stone-paved courts. Wagons and fantastically decorated caravans stood almost touching each other on every side, while wealthier merchants had laid out their goods under brightly colored tents, some of which stretched for blocks. Food, drink, jugglers, fire-swallowers, swordsmen, acrobats, performing monkeys and dogs, and vendors everywhere—hawking, pushing, inviting, calling, singing, summoning. Marcus had never seen anything so splendid, nor so overwhelming, in all his life.

Rindel was drawn into the tent of a thin woman who hovered around his head like a bat, her arms full of bangles, and opened little jars and waved them under his nose. "Love potions for the young gentleman?" she said.

Marcus grabbed Rindel's arm. "Not today, thanks!" he said, whisking his friend out of the tent.

"I could have used that," Rindel complained. Marcus ignored him. His gaze was drawn to a tall stilt-walker, juggling flaming torches as he advanced above the crowd. "Amazing," he breathed.

"This way," Rindel said and disappeared into the crowd.

"Oh, now where's he going?" Marcus rushed after Rindel, trying hard to keep his friend's shaggy head in sight. It was no easy task in the sea of people that surrounded them, and they were soon separated. The sun beat down on Marcus's head as he pressed through the sweaty, clamoring crowd—and suddenly burst through the wall of people into a quieter, calmer place.

It was one of the tents that stretched over blocks of ground, he realized. The awning overhead, drawn tight, was green, and the sun filtered through it with a pleasant, inviting air. The tent poles, placed strategically throughout a maze of tables laden with weapons, jewelry, clothing, and curiosities of all kinds, were covered with ivy and flowers.

Directly in front of Marcus, reflecting his own face and form back at him, was a tall, gold-framed mirror. It was easily the height of a fully grown man.

Marcus stared at himself. It seemed, suddenly, as though no one else was around. He forgot about Rindel, forgot about the crowds. It was just him and the mirror.

And he was not especially happy with what he saw.

The boy who was staring back at him was dirty, shaggy, and wearing clothes that were frighteningly old-fashioned and country style. He had none of the magic, none of the mystique of the people in this city. Marcus felt his ears burning as he studied his battered shoes, with one big toe beginning to peek through, and the rips in his cloak from rolling down the hill. The sack over his shoulder was even worse, and weighed down as it was with necessary items for travel—and the *book*, blast it—it made him look like some sort of packhorse. Even his sword, which had made him feel like a warrior, was nothing but dark, aged iron.

His mother, he thought, should be ashamed of him. He'd thought he was a man, starting out on this journey. But he was nothing but a confused, frightened, lost child.

"Like what you see?" a voice asked.

Marcus spun around. Facing him was a sharply dressed man with a green cape over his tailored clothing and a decorated ska-sword hanging at his side. The man's hair was cut short, and a goatee covered his chin. He wore a rakish hat with a feather in its brim, and on his cheeks was tattooed a spiral pattern in blue.

The man bowed. "Prelanor, at your service," he said. "A merchant, not of these parts, but glad to be here in your fine city. Or . . . it isn't *your* fine city, is it?"

Marcus's ears were burning again. "No, sir, I . . . I come from the country."

"Indeed," Prelanor said, looking a little amused. "And you have come to the city to seek your fortune, now you've come of age?"

"Actually," Marcus said, "I'm just passing through. I'm on a journey, you see."

Prelanor's eyes showed that he did see indeed. "Is that so? But you *are* legally of working age."

"I turned thirteen," Marcus said, "a few days ago."

"Would I be right to assume that you do not have the approved travel pass for this journey?"

The question was so unexpected, and spoken in so low a tone, that it took Marcus a minute to realize it had even been asked. Prelanor's body language hadn't changed; he still looked like he was just trying to help Marcus with a purchase.

"And you no doubt know about all the patrollers stationed in every town and city, sent by the Emperor to check that people are working, not just wandering off the main routes?

"I . . . er . . ."

Prelanor interrupted. "You don't have to answer that question. I too thought little of the choices I was given when I became a man. My travels are not officially . . . well, let us say, I pay my way." He swept his hand out so that Marcus looked again at the tables laden with merchandise — all of it fine clothing and weaponry to make a modern man of anyone, even a country boy. "My trade opens doors."

Smiling, Prelanor picked at Marcus's sleeve. "Of course, if you want to survive as a maverick in this world, you have to dress the part. The city, much less the world, will never take you seriously unless you look as though you are one step ahead of them all, in fashion and in weaponry." The merchant's eyes dropped to the sword. "That, for example, you might want to get rid of."

Marcus pushed the sword to his side as though he would hide it. "I'm a little attached to it."

"Ah," said Prelanor. "But not to the rest of it, surely?"

Marcus looked down at his dust-covered boots and homespun clothing. "Not at all."

"I'll outfit you, then," Prelanor said. "See to it that you're dressed so that no one will look down on you, no matter where you go. Although — well, where *are* you going?"

Marcus liked the merchant. He wanted, very badly, to be rid of his clothes and his lowbrow appearance. And suddenly, all of his doubts came boiling to the surface, and he wanted to be rid of those too. Where *was* he going? To some far-off bizarre kingdom that couldn't even promise him anything of value now? It occurred to him right then that he could have a fourth option: to go, not to Uncle Nomit's or the city task force or even to the Kingdom of the North, but to wander the world and make anything of it that he wanted. Perhaps the old Wryxl proverb was right after all.

"Whatever you wish for will be your future," Marcus whispered.

"What was that?" Prelanor asked.

Marcus met the merchant's eyes. "Have you really traveled all over Krinton?" he asked.

"I have that, lad," Prelanor said.

"Then perhaps you can tell me if — if a place I've heard of is real."

Prelanor quirked a finely shaped eyebrow and waited.

"The Kingdom of the North?" Marcus asked.

The merchant chuckled. Marcus felt his heart sinking. "The Kingdom of the North," Prelanor said, and this time Marcus wished he would lower his voice even more. "It is . . . not real. No. A myth. It has drawn many travelers over the years, but eventually they learn it is an idea, not a place."

Prelanor narrowed his eyes and smiled, his expression strangely frightening. "You might say," he said in a low, conspiratorial tone, "that the Kingdom of the North is the drug of choice for some people—something like sekrin, hmmm? And all that talk of an imaginary friend—Morlow, is it?—how ridiculous! Most of us grow out of such silly stories. They're just a way to deny reality and pretend. But nothing wrong with that, is there, boy?"

Marcus backed away, and suddenly he bumped into the mirror. He shook his head. "No . . ." he stammered. "No, nothing wrong with that." He thought of his mother and was suddenly angry.

"So you won't be going *there*," Prelanor said, and Marcus found himself nodding in agreement. It was a myth. He knew it. The book—that crazy book. He would throw it away. Into the River Quinn. Or perhaps sell it, in his first sale as a world-traveling merchant . . .

He looked around, blinking as though he'd just awakened. Prelanor was gathering up items—a cloak, tailored clothing, shoes with curled points on the toe ends, a small dagger. All of it cutting-edge, the very latest of fashions. "For you, young master," Prelanor said. He winked. "We'll work out a price."

Marcus dropped his sack on the ground and shoved it under one of Prelanor's tables, picking up a tunic with the same kind of blue swirls as were tattooed on Prelanor's face. In the other hand, he picked up the little dagger and twirled it in between his fingers, liking the way it made him feel dangerous and cool.

A sudden blast of trumpets almost made him drop the dagger.

"Treanthor," Prelanor said. "Go on, boy . . . go hear what the Emperor has to say. I'll keep these things aside for you."

Marcus turned on his heel and headed for the street, but Prelanor whistled and tossed him something—a cloak, black on the outside and lightning-yellow within. "It'll hide the rest of your clothes until you've got something better to wear," Prelanor said. "Might as well start being the new you now."

Marcus grinned. "Thanks!" he said. "I will pay you!"

"I'm sure you will," Prelanor said. "Get going—you don't want to miss this."

* * *

The already massive crowds seemed to have doubled in size, and Marcus fought his way to a good view. People had cleared a wide lane through the market, and a massive black carriage, studded with glowing red lanterns, was passing by, drawn by huge black horses. Marcus's eyes widened. He searched for Treanthor.

"Where is the Emperor?" he asked someone next to him.

The man didn't try to hide his scorn. "Not 'ere—he'll be in the sixth carriage. Just you watch."

Only then did Marcus realize that an entire procession was passing down the street. Each carriage carried greyhounds, men, and women wearing long gowns and elaborate hats. "Who are they?" he whispered.

"The court and councilors," the man said. "Today is important for all of them. One of Treanthor's advisers will be selected as the new governor of Erundel. It's the highest paid role in the city—and it's a position that comes with special powers, a measure of Treanthor's power. But first they're going to usher out an old adviser, who is nearly dying—and give him a special place at Treanthor's table."

"What do you mean by 'powers'?" Marcus asked.

"Hush, boy," the man said. "I'm trying to listen."

Another blast of trumpets quieted much of the crowd. In the sixth carriage, a tall man robed in black and red stood. Behind him was a massive globe, golden and glowing, which cast the man's shadow in many directions. People were scrambling and fighting to step inside scraps of the shadow.

"The shadow! The shadow!" they cried.

Treanthor raised his hands, and the people quieted. The Emperor was going to speak.

70

"My good people!" he said, his voice carrying impossibly well. There were cheers, but they died down quickly. Treanthor reached a gloved hand down and pulled a man up to stand beside him. The man was dressed like a king, with a crown upon his head. He was not old, but neither did he seem young—if anything, he looked like an old man who had managed to hide his age tremendously well.

"Behold, the one who is to be renewed!" Treanthor said. "I promised you, did I not, that those who serve me best will never die? This, my friend and adviser, has been one of my most faithful servants. As you know, he has been stricken with a wasting disease and has battled it for some time."

Marcus eyed the sick man from head to toe and felt sorry for him. He was a pitiful-looking gentleman, despite being dressed in fine clothing. He was hunched down and obviously in pain. Upon further examination, it became clear why the man looked so strange—he was wearing makeup and clothes that were supposed to make him look healthier than he really was.

"Today, by the power of my favor and my shadow, his body will be rejuvenated and restored to youth, and he will spend the rest of his days in bliss at my citadel. He will prove to you all that Treanthor's faithful followers are given pleasure and victory in all things. Those who serve me well are rewarded well."

At that, Treanthor opened his flowing cape and brushed it like a wave cascading over the official's body. Miniscule silver specks of dust wafted around the man, whose face appeared to immediately brighten, and he stood taller, somehow stronger. But only those very nearby could see the dusty substance float to the ground.

Marcus could hear the cheers, the crowd crying out its approval, some who were sick calling for mercy and a similar miracle of their own. But he heard it all as a distant buzzing—for he was seeing something he was quite sure no one else could see. Before his eyes, Treanthor's adviser was fraying, fading, disintegrating, bit by bit—just like the world had done when he first read *The Book Beyond Time.*

It was another vision. And somehow, he realized, no one else could see it.

A voice, a strong, manly voice, spoke in his ears. *"What you see is true, Marcus. Treanthor has no power to stop this man from dying. All he can do is deceive the people into believing that he has somehow given his adviser a renewed body and a healthy life. His words are lies meant to cloak the truth, just as he has cloaked the fate of this world in distractions and cheap thrills."*

Marcus swallowed hard. As he watched, the fraying grew worse—and then, even as the people continued to cheer Treanthor, the vision passed.

"This man will now live in luxury with me at my palace, spending the rest of his days in relaxation!" boasted the Emperor. The adviser appeared overjoyed and amazed as he was guided back into a seat beside Treanthor in the sixth wagon. He waved furiously at onlookers and shouted, "It's true! I feel like a brand new man, no more pain!"

Out of another carriage stepped another finely dressed, very tall figure, the man put forward to become the new governor. Treanthor had already preselected him, but he had stirred the people up to favor him on previous visits. After the man's new position was announced by trumpet blowers, the people cheered hysterically and waved flags. They chanted his name—"Vazurr! Vazurr!"—until he motioned for them to quiet down.

As the new governor, a slick man with beady eyes, began his speech, Treanthor and the rest of his entourage departed the square. Most people stayed to hear the speech, but a small crowd ran alongside the Emperor's carriage, desperate to get a closer look at Treanthor.

Marcus remembered the cloak he had been given, but he did not go back to Prelanor. Instead, he slipped into the crowd behind the procession and followed it as it resumed its journey out of the city—toward the famous citadel of Treanthor himself.

Treanthor had said one thing. The voice in his head—Merloy—had said another.

It was time he found out for himself which voice was telling the truth.

Chapter 6

The crowds cheered vigorously as Marcus darted after the black carriages carrying Treanthor and his minions. "Farewell, Treanthor, O Mighty One!" "Hurray, Treanthor, the Great!" Their eyes were glazed with excitement—they almost looked hypnotized.

As the last wagon was about to pass through the city gates, Marcus propelled himself forward, into the dust kicked up by the wheels, and shouted up to one of the drivers, "I'm Treanthor's shoe shiner, let me up!"

The man looked down on him like a horse might look on a flea. Marcus reached out to grab the side of the carriage, coughing and choking on the dust.

"Oh, hurry up then, man; let him up, Galwin!"

Galwin, one of the burly knights at the rear, grunted and reluctantly grabbed Marcus by the wrist, hauling him up into the carriage. "You shouldn't have stepped down into the crowds, young man. Treanthor says to always be ready for a swift departure—no daydreaming next time!"

Marcus nodded and bowed his head low, pretending to tie his laces in case anyone in the carriage actually knew Treanthor's real shoe shiner. A portly man who appeared to be a treasurer was busying himself nearby with coins and a little decorated chest. A young woman was preening herself in front of a handheld mirror, and she totally ignored Marcus. He began to breathe a little easier. It looked like no one was going to call his bluff.

Trying to contain his anxiety and breathlessness, Marcus retrieved a white handkerchief from his waistcoat pocket and covered his mouth. After a while he used it to wipe beads of sweat from his forehead.

"Oy, you lowlife!" bellowed an angry voice.

Marcus raised his head slightly and caught sight of the treasurer staring at him.

"Come here, boy, and shine my shoes."

"Yes, sir," Marcus replied humbly, and moved across to kneel before the haughty man. The treasurer glared at him with cruel eyes and waited to be served.

Marcus bent over the treasurer's black leather shoes, and panic struck him. *You don't have any shoe polish, idiot!* Any substitute he might have possessed had been left with Prelanor in the city. Forcing his heartbeat to slow, Marcus simply spit quietly into his hankie and began shining the black, square-toed shoes as best he could. Keeping his head down, he rubbed and cleaned for what seemed like an hour.

When he had finished, he wobbled back to a seat across the carriage. The motion nearly threw him, and he reached out to steady himself on the decorated chest—but the treasurer knocked his hand away.

"Don't even think of touching that chest, boy. Treanthor's dogs will tear you apart if I find you've been anywhere near it! They're a special new breed, those greyhounds you know. Vicious!"

"Uh, no, of course not, sir," Marcus mumbled, shielding his face with the now nearly blackened hanky and making it the rest of the way to his seat.

* * *

The citadel of Treanthor was a black, rocky spire that rose from the earth like the battered head of a spear. As they approached it in the darkness of the night, they could see lights—red and gold—glimmering all up and down its height. The citadel was a natural phenomenon, a strange mountain that had been mined, hollowed, and crafted into a home and fortress for the Emperor. It had been one of the first projects completed in Treanthor's rebuilding.

A dozen or more hefty, heavily armed guards stood watch all around the entrance and sides of the imposing structure. Just above the trees to the right of the entrance, several huge, strange-looking birds swooped across and around. They were too far away for Marcus to see clearly from the carriage, but he wondered about their screeching cries, unlike any birdsong he had heard before.

Not even a mile from the citadel lay the ancient volcanic Mount Zorbin—an intimidating monolith which spewed forth smoke and ash almost continuously. Anyone who happened to come across the citadel by chance would run away in fear once they caught sight of Mount Zorbin. The guards were almost an unnecessary feature. Sometimes the guards would make bets over how many steps an outsider would take before turning on his heels and running off in fear.

As he caught sight of the formidable mountain, Marcus gasped. For years he had believed the rumors that the volcano would begin to erupt if anyone came close. *And yet Treanthor lives almost at the foot of it? He must have started the rumors—he's just trying to keep people away. But why?*

Black wrought-iron gates opened at the base of the citadel, and one by one the carriages passed through, swallowed up by the darkness inside. Marcus shuddered. Part of him wanted to jump out of the carriage and bolt.

But part of him had to see what was going to happen to Treanthor's adviser. The book warned that Krinton was full of destruction and death—that so much of this world's happiness was temporary and that darkness was just on the other side. Treanthor told his people that he was immune to death and also had power to reward a few of his closest servants with immortality. He told them that Krinton would last forever, and that they could have all the happiness, satisfaction, and pleasure they wanted in his kingdom.

The book and Treanthor said exactly the opposite things about the world; they could not both be right. Marcus needed to know which was the liar.

Their carriage passed beneath the rocky entrance into inky darkness. For a minute they rode forward in total darkness and total silence. Then, suddenly, the passage gave way to a great cavern, lit with glowing golden globes and red lanterns. The smooth rock walls stretched up hundreds of feet, disappearing into the darkness of the spire. The carriages sat on a pavement, waiting for passengers to disembark. Across from it, steps led up to a polished dais the size of a banqueting hall and decorated as lavishly as any royal court.

"Everyone step down now," growled Galwin, opening the other side of the carriage before moving on to other carriages ahead and commanding everyone else out.

The woman across from Marcus swept up her flowing silk skirts and stepped down. Marcus followed her, shielding himself from view behind her elaborate headwear—a wide-brimmed hat with several long, floating red and green feathers which swept dramatically past her neck.

Up the steps, beneath the pulsing glow of an enormous golden globe, Treanthor's entourage gathered in a circle around him and the now-shriveling man beneath his cloak. The man appeared whole, yet weak and powerless: he had begun to hunch low again and clasp his head in pain. Treanthor had promised to give him new life, to rejuvenate him. But he didn't look like a man on the verge of renewal to Marcus. He started to cough and splutter, and Marcus noticed tiny droplets of blood settling on his gown.

Treanthor raised his hand and motioned for others to follow him. The adviser did, along with a few other regally dressed men and one woman. The other passengers from various carriages began to disperse as though they all knew where they were supposed to go. Marcus looked around wildly. Where should he go? Where *could* he go so that no one would notice him, but he could still see what was happening to the adviser? At any moment someone would see him standing there and figure out that he was an intruder . . .

But no one did. The great hall emptied, and Marcus stood alone beneath the glowing lights.

He could hear the voices of Treanthor and his lackeys drifting back from the long corridor they had taken. Gathering up all his courage, he followed them. They were moving slowly because of the sick man, and it didn't take long for Marcus to get them in his sights. Their voices covered the sound of his footfalls, and he crept after them, careful to stay in the shadows.

Why are there no guards? he wondered. *Why isn't anyone trying to stop me?*

And then he remembered the highly trained guards outside and the fearsome volcano with its terrifying protection. There was no real need to post guards inside the citadel. No intruder would be brave enough or skilled enough to get this far.

Except me, Marcus thought. *And I'm barely a grown-up. What do I think I'm doing, anyway?*

Really, it would be much easier to turn around and go back to Erundel. He could buy clothing and supplies from Prelanor and set himself up as a merchant, traveling all over Krinton. He would sell the book first thing and forget all about its advice and the voice and Brayman, and all about his visions of the world fading and disintegrating into nothing.

It would be much easier. But Marcus kept going forward anyway.

The corridor was narrow, but its ceiling was high. Dim red lights, powered by xanth crystals, flickered all along it. Narrow doors, eight feet high, opened on to other passages and corridors. Some gave way to steep steps, descending down into the earth. Marcus shivered as a cold wind blew up from one passage. He thought he could hear the sounds of moaning carried on that wind. Did the steps lead to a dungeon?

He hurried past it, careful to keep his steps quiet so the men ahead of him wouldn't hear. But it was another door, only about six feet further down the corridor, that made him halt, eyes widening and heart standing still.

The wind that came up from this passage was hot and smoky, like something was being cooked or forged below. And Marcus knew the smell it carried as well as he knew his own name.

Hakrin.

The drug that had destroyed his father's life, and Rindel's mother's, and so many other people. Officially, Treanthor had released statements saying that hakrin was dangerous and to be avoided. But this smell . . .

He was making it here.

Treanthor's own citadel was where hakrin came from! And after a short while, Marcus was sure he could also smell milder forms of sekrin. Surely it was no surprise that Treanthor loved sekrin—after all, it subdued the people and caused them to be laid back about everything. No one taking sekrin would bother to oppose Treanthor or his vast monopoly of power.

Marcus chuckled to himself as he imagined his mother's look of outrage when he told her what Treanthor was up to. But even as he laughed, thoughts of his father brought tears to his eyes. By producing these drugs, Treanthor had destroyed his father's life and stolen him away from Marcus.

Ahead, the passage was widening out and ending at two massive doors. They were made of some kind of metal, and they glowed blood red in the xanth light. Treanthor took hold of the rings on the doors and pulled them open, and his followers passed through.

Marcus stopped. What now? The doors were closing, and if he rushed through them, he would be caught. He scanned the sight before him, looking up the walls. There! Two openings were cut in the rock over top of the doors—ventilation shafts, maybe.

When the doors had closed completely, Marcus searched the rock wall beside them. Sure enough, it was rough and irregular—easily climbable for a boy who had spent much of his life shinnying up trees and climbing fences and house walls with his village friends. He grabbed

80

a handhold, braced his feet against the wall, and climbed as quickly as he could.

The doors were eight feet high, and the ventilation shafts were another foot higher. Xanth crystals embedded in the wall flickered, lighting up his way. By the time he reached the top, his muscles ached and sweat was pouring down his forehead. But he hauled himself into the shaft and was gratified to see a light not three feet away. He crawled forward and found himself looking into a circular cavern.

Stalactites spiraled down from the high ceiling, met by stalagmites that rose from the floor. Torches planted amidst them burned, making smoky smudges on the walls. A massive xanth crystal in the center of the room lit up the whole thing. Tapestries hung from the walls, the largest one featuring a vulture in flight, and a long dining table stretched through the middle of the room at the base of the xanth crystal. Greyhounds stirred on their beds. One of them raised its head and looked straight at Marcus, but its only response to his presence was to thump its tail.

This was Treanthor's personal meeting room.

At the table, Treanthor sat down in the light of the xanth crystal and motioned for the others to join him. They took their positions. The only one who did not sit down was the adviser who had supposedly been restored to health. He stood before the table like a man on trial, and all of their eyes fixed on him.

A voice lifted up to the ventilation shaft where Marcus waited. It was cracked, weak, and pleading—the voice of the adviser.

"Please," he said. "You must help me, I'm losing my strength again. I am dying, Treanthor!"

"You are not dying," Treanthor said. He sounded incredibly calm. "Just believe, my friend. I am setting you free."

The adviser shook as he pointed his finger at Treanthor. "You have nothing to do with this! You promised me you could stop my death, but you have done nothing. You lie!"

Treanthor didn't even bother to stand up. "Be calm," he said. "Take it like a man."

The adviser didn't seem inclined to be calm. He was shaking so hard that Marcus could see the motion from his perch. "I believed you and gave everything to serve you. You promised I would be repaid with power and deathless life. But I have been dreaming—seeing the truth about this world you have created. It is nothing but a lie and an illusion. The truth haunts me in my dreams!"

Marcus's heart began beating wildly as he witnessed the man bending down to his knees. Any effects of the sparkly drug he had inhaled earlier had clearly worn off now. He was coughing violently and begging to be returned to his family. A dark cloud formed in the air and swirled around his head like a cyclone. He pointed his finger one more time as he tried to accuse Treanthor of double-crossing him. The air filled with the smell of fire and smoke as an official approached the man with a glass canister filled with something like a murky chemical. It emitted a cloudy vapor.

"You are a liar," the adviser said. "And as I die, so will Krinton if it continues to believe you!"

Treanthor ignored his pleas and snapped, "Give it to him—make him drink it all!"

The Emperor's servant pulled up the man's head and forced the dark liquid down his throat.

The vain woman from the carriage snorted, "That should shut him up! They don't usually make such a protest until they taste the liquid. This one seemed to sense something was coming for him, ha ha ha!"

All the others in the room laughed in response as the man slithered to the floor, his body convulsing as it reacted to the strange, dark substance.

In a moment he was still, his voice silenced. The dark cloud dispersed, but the smell still lingered. The air felt thick with the sense of something evil. An evil which everyone back home, and all over Krinton, had always dismissed as a silly idea. "There is no evil in the world," they assured themselves—"just a bit of bad luck now and again."

But the book had said different. The book had said that evil was real and that it led to death and destruction. The book claimed that an enemy, a liar, threatened to drag all of Krinton down into this destruction. And as Marcus looked at Treanthor, leaning back at his table and sipping from a wine goblet without any sign of real concern, with the smell of hakrin merged with other chemicals in the air and the man's demise still filling his eyes, Marcus was certain that it was all true.

"What will we tell the people?" one of the other advisers asked.

Treanthor waved his hand in the air. "What we always tell them. That he has been rejuvenated to youth once more and that he will now live like a king in my palace. His suffering here has ended, as we promised."

The ruler looked each of his advisers in the eye, drilling them with the importance of his words. "We keep up this ruse for the good of the people. Soon our research will teach us how to fully overcome death. Until then, we can make good use of his half-functioning body. Otherwise, they will go looking for life and power somewhere else."

In the Kingdom of the North, Marcus told himself. He understood Treanthor's words perfectly. Real life was not found in Krinton, but in the north—and Treanthor would lie, cheat, and drug the people to keep them from going there.

Treanthor began to lead the circle in a chant, something about the power of darkness. Moonlight was streaming through the window behind him, and the Emperor positioned himself to cast a shadow over the helpless figure. And then the man on the floor began twitching. Marcus's eyes widened as he watched the man who had been coughing and convulsing now shake his head and stand to his feet. His eyes opened, except he no longer had normal eyes. His eyeballs were like dark stones, devoid of any signs of life. He didn't look human anymore.

When he opened his mouth to speak, no sounds came out—he was unable to speak.

Is this what is meant by the power of Treanthor's shadow? wondered Marcus. It seemed like an ominous power. *Treanthor does indeed have power over people, but it is only a power to destroy—not to heal.*

"Take him away!" Treanthor ordered.

Immediately, two officials led him out of the room and back along the corridor. Marcus barely breathed, fearful of being seen. Something started to irritate his nostrils, and he twitched his nose furiously, panicked that he might not be able to stop himself from sneezing. Clasping his hands over his face, he stayed unmoving until the door was slammed shut, then backed out of the ventilation shaft on his hands and knees and shinnied down the wall—scraping his legs and arms in the process. He continued to follow at a reasonable distance to see where the drugged man would be taken. Marcus stopped dead in his tracks when he saw them take him down the steps toward the place of hakrin production. He heard one of his captors say loudly, "We should get a couple of years' work out of this one—be able to produce enough hakrin for two large cities!"

They're using the sick and the dying like slaves to produce hakrin in an underground factory! And they think they're coming here for a wonderful new life of pleasure! Treanthor's double-crossing everyone!

Marcus was nearly sick with fear. He knew what his fate would be if he were discovered roaming the building. With a pounding heart he ran full tilt through the dark corridor, past the stench of hakrin and other chemicals. In the background he was sure he could hear the frightful moaning sound of prisoners. He ran until he had left the citadel behind, hauling himself deftly over the bars of the wrought-iron gates, not pausing to retrieve the torn shirtsleeve which caught on a spike. He hurled himself into the woods, glad to be away from Treanthor's presence and pleased that he had managed to keep Prealnor's fine cape from damage. Two guards noticed the dark figure running through the trees, but they were half-drunk and assumed he was Treanthor's fire boy, sent to find kindling wood in a hurry.

The night was deep and dark, and Marcus was aware that he was defenseless. How stupid that he should leave his sword, along with the knarl-knife, back in the city with a man he had only just met!

He had come so close to buying into Treanthor's lies and trying to make a life for himself in Krinton. He had come so close to giving up his journey north. But never again.

Without stopping, Marcus continued running, the adrenaline from the earlier events driving him toward the glowing city lights. When he was all out of energy, he collapsed on the side of a path, resting his head in his hands. Erundel was still about a mile away, night had fallen hours ago, and he was concerned that he might not find Prelanor.

More worrisome than that, however, was the thought that he might not find the book. What he once had dismissed as nonsense, he was now convinced held the answers to the future state of Krinton and the urgency of escaping its downfall.

The book had repeatedly mentioned "the enemy in your midst." Now Marcus was certain that this referred to Treanthor. *It must be true,* he thought. *Mum was right after all.*

But who was the "Spirit of Merloy" needed to resist him? Since their rescuer, Brayman, had mentioned this name, he had noticed that the book referred to this character in many places; he appeared to be someone of great knowledge and power. Marcus was aware that he was pretty powerless in himself to stand up against the Emperor and his legions of knights. Marcus was sure it was Merloy he had heard speaking—twice now—but didn't know how to contact him.

He was desperate for someone else to believe him and to be earnest in the quest. Rindel continually jested about it all; his mother was far from the city and knew no more than he did. Oh, how he wished his father could come alongside him and help guide him in what to do next! But he had fallen prey to Treanthor's trap of hakrin and sekrin. The book said that Marcus must stay on the narrow path toward the north, just as Brayman had told him, but he only knew of the main, wide path out of Erundel. No one had told him where to go from the city. Where exactly was this narrow path, and how would he know it was the right one? Hadn't Brayman said something about needing to find his own narrow path? He didn't have a compass—they cost a week's wages. And as for Tress, well, she was sometimes an unwilling companion, still getting used to her new rider.

"What am I supposed to do?" Marcus said aloud to himself. Screwing up his face and rubbing his neck, he felt incredibly frustrated.

"Call out, and I will answer."

He heard the words in his head—or maybe just in his memory. Hadn't he read that just this morning in the book?

Looking over his shoulder to ensure nobody was around, Marcus whispered earnestly, "Help me." He closed his eyes.

Nothing happened, and he felt like a fool.

As he moved to stand up and be on his way, a breeze blew his hair back, and a figure draped in silver and black garments stood before him. Marcus stepped back sharply, alarmed.

"Do not worry. I have heard you, and I will guide you." The voice was strong, yet reassuring and warm.

"Who are you?" Marcus inquired.

"I am Merloy," the figure replied. "Now that you truly believe in *The Book Beyond Time,* I have come to help you in your next step."

Marcus was silent, his eyes wide as a vein in his forehead pulsated furiously. He could hardly believe that a man had appeared from nowhere and was offering to help him. He reached out to touch Merloy on the shoulder, but his hands found nothing to touch.

"I am not of this world," said Merloy, whose face appeared like none other Marcus had ever seen. His blue-gray eyes seemed to gaze directly through to Marcus's soul. And he seemed familiar somehow—like an old friend, or a father. Marcus knew that he could trust this man. There was a calmness about him that was reassuring and endearing.

"You must take care to follow the instructions in the book, for many would try to stop you from reaching your destination."

"Will you come with me?" asked Marcus, intrigued.

"I am always near," was Merloy's simple reply. When he said this, Marcus recognized his voice. The same voice he had heard in his vision that night, instructing him to find the BlackStone Waterfall. The same voice that had spoken to him in Erundel, challenging Treanthor's lies.

Marcus sat down again, and Merloy sat across from him. The trees all around cast deep shadows, and yet Marcus could see the man clearly.

Marcus began to tell Merloy all about his travels so far, about his escapades with Rindel, and about his mother and her earnest plea. When he reached the story of Treanthor's citadel and the adviser's evil transformation, he choked up. "It was awful," he said. "But I believe now. I know that the Emperor is a deceiver."

Merloy listened intently, smiling and nodding occasionally. For the first time in a while, Marcus felt safe. Merloy made him feel comfortable and protected.

When Marcus finally stopped talking, Merloy instructed him to find his horse and other belongings and leave the city first thing in the morning across the bridge.

"When you have crossed the River Quinn, turn sharply left and make your way across the uneven, rocky path that is no longer used. After some distance you will find a stone archway, surrounding an iron gate. Go through the gate and head straight ahead for several miles. Do not turn to the left or right, no matter how attractive the other paths appear."

"I don't have a pass to travel there," Marcus said.

"No one does," Merloy said. "It is the road to the north, and Treanthor will allow none to travel it. You must be brave and faithful to remain on the road. Finally, stay strong. Don't rely on your feelings, Marcus. Trust what you know to be true. And remember that I am with you. I will always be near if you want me. If you reject PathOne, you reject me. You will find me when you look for me with a sincere heart."

Marcus listened carefully and was about to reply when Merloy disappeared. He leaned forward, clasping his head in his hands, pensive. One thing he knew for certain: he had not felt so safe or secure or content since his father had carried him firmly on his shoulders as a young boy.

Chapter 7

The morning stillness was interrupted abruptly by the sound of a blacksmith's tools on the workbench.

"Are you not up yet, lads? I'll be needing some more space in here shortly."

Marcus sat bolt upright, jerking Rindel from his deep slumber.

"C'mon, we need to leave!" Marcus pulled the still-sleepy Rindel out the back door of the workshop and nodded gratefully to the smith. "Thank you, sir, we're very grateful for your hospitality."

Marcus had arrived back in the city in the early morning hours the day before. He had managed to find Prelanor and return the fine clothes in exchange for his own bundle of belongings. Prelanor was unable to convince him to purchase even the shoes. He didn't seem too happy about it.

"Er, no, sir, I don't mean to have misled you. I, er, I was interested in doing business with you, but I've changed my mind. I don't need your fine clothing where I'm heading; you see, I'm leaving the city tomorrow. But it has been wonderful to meet you and hear of your travels."

Marcus had felt stupid as he excused himself from Prelanor's store, and he made a hasty exit as he waved goodbye. Prelanor had just raised his eyebrows and sighed.

After leaving the merchant, Marcus had gone in search of Rindel, who had been wandering aimlessly around the city, trying out games and food booths and flirting with the girls who sold flowers in the city square. After a couple of hours, Marcus eventually found him sitting outside a rowdy tavern drinking kelsch—the local Erundel ale—and chatting to a group of enthusiastic tradesmen. He was telling them the tale of his encounter with the fearsome gratsch; the men were captivated and burst into raucous laughter as he explained how he had rolled down the hill straight into the beast's territory.

Without a word of explanation, Marcus had grabbed Rindel by the scruff of his neck, pulling him out of his seat and literally dragging him away from the tavern.

"Hey, I was enjoying that ale!" complained Rindel.

"Well, I hope you didn't tell them your name," Marcus countered, "otherwise Treanthor's men will soon be on our heels. Your father will have reported you missing by now, and you know that the Emperor will issue a search for you."

"I can't remember what I told them."

"That's the trouble with ale," Marcus replied with a groan.

Once they had returned to the spot where they had tied up Tress, they piled their bags onto the horse and went in search of somewhere to spend the night. Marcus protested about Rindel wasting money on drinks and a new, fashionable cloth cap; Rindel protested that Marcus was being too serious, and besides, hadn't they come to experience some fun?

Marcus kept quiet about what he had experienced in the citadel and in the woods with Merloy; he wasn't quite sure how Rindel would react. Instead, he focused their attention on finding overnight shelter. They stopped several passersby to ask about a good place to stay.

One plump woman, carrying two baskets of fresh-baked bread, smiled at the two young men and said that she and her husband had room in their workshop—but they'd have to make do with blankets on the floor. And it would cost them, did they have ten kroens?

Marcus and Rindel only had six of the distinctive Era of Pleasure coins left, but Marcus persuaded her to accept a small gold signet ring instead of the money. It had belonged to his grandmother but was already too small for his fingers, and his mother disliked jewelry now that she easily lost small items around the house. The woman was delighted with this offer and promptly snatched the ring, pushing it onto her little finger. It wouldn't go past her knuckle, but she didn't complain.

The boys followed the woman across the city square and down a steep, cobblestone lane, passing several inns along the way. She led them across a small patch of grass where several goats were grazing and up another street lined with small, terraced houses. Tress was just small enough to fit through the alleyway which led to the blacksmith's yard. But she expressed her dismay at having to squeeze between a rough wall and a fence, scraping her feet on the ground and pulling backward. After resisting and snorting repeatedly, shaking her mane to demonstrate her displeasure, she finally allowed Rindel to coax her through.

The woman told Marcus to tie his horse to the fence, then fetched a bowl of water for her. Inside the house, she offered them some bread and chicken broth, which they happily accepted. Her husband was upstairs sleeping, having retired early—they could hear his snoring. Two little girls huddled by the fire were playing with a wooden toy and stopped occasionally to stare at Marcus or Rindel.

After they had eaten, the woman led them to the workshop beside the house. She threw some blankets on the floor and warned them not to open the door lest any rats come in overnight. Marcus wanted to tell Rindel what had happened, but his friend talked almost non-stop about stories and funny happenings at the tavern, and Marcus found that he lost his desire to talk about the citadel.

"Ooh, you wouldn't believe the things they told me, Marcus. It's a shame you weren't with me," Rindel muttered as his stories began to wind down. "A funny-looking chap, think his name was Tom, told the tale of a young Wryxl girl named Pryann. Think she lived around a hundred years ago. Anyway, this girl once started to question their way of life and why Treanthor should have all the power and stuff. Anyway, she was told to stop it but would not back down. In the end she was cast out of her town with her hands bound to her feet. Her shrieks could be heard for hours, and she was never seen again until her cousin searched high and low for her, as a promise he had made to her mother. All he found was her hair tied in a ribbon, lying in a cave to the east of Krinton." Her body was never recovered."

After a few more stories, Rindel had fallen asleep midsentence, while Marcus tossed and turned most of the remainder of the night.

As the blacksmith waved them off in the morning, they were on their way once more—Rindel somewhat worse for wear after one too many ales the night before. Marcus had not had much opportunity to read the book, as the lamp they'd been given had little oil remaining and it became dark soon after they settled in. Still, he clutched the leather volume inside his waistcoat and became excited at the thought of reading it once more. His journey lay ahead of him, and for the first time, he couldn't wait to see what would come next.

Marcus smiled to himself as they maneuvered through little streets and across the marketplace toward the main city entrance. He was glad to be heading out of the city—its alluring sights and sounds had become irritating. The noise never seemed to cease, and there were just so many people—he was always bumping into someone or being pestered to buy something. And after what he had witnessed and heard in Treanthor's citadel, it all seemed like a giant trap. Behind the glimmer and glamor lurked a sinister ruler who didn't care one bit about the people of the city.

Rindel, on the other hand, grumbled about having to leave so soon and questioned why they had to be in such a rush. Marcus wondered for a moment whether he should leave his friend behind, but then he remembered Rindel's family. He couldn't bear the thought of coming back someday and having to tell them that he had left Rindel all alone in Erundel. Besides, wouldn't he be leaving his best friend to destruction if he didn't take him north? Rindel needed to learn the truth too, even if he wasn't quite ready to hear it yet.

"I think you'll find it just as exciting where we're going," Marcus tried to cheer Rindel on, but he didn't sound very convincing. "Here, let's buy some fresh fruit and a pie for the journey. Do we have any money left?"

Rindel's eyes lit up; any mention of food always spurred him on. He smiled as he fished out some coins from his pockets. "Found more of these lurking in the bottom of my bag this morning!"

Marcus gave him a thumbs-up and brought Tress to a halt near a vendor.

They chose some cherries and a bunch of red grapes, as well as a tasty-looking meat pie. The lady selling offered them a special price if they also purchased a fruit cake, to which they readily agreed. She even threw in a red apple for Tress for free — so everyone was happy.

As they left the city and crossed the bridge, this time avoiding a dip in the cool, early morning water, Marcus tried to remember all of Merloy's instructions. The path was just where it should be. He pulled Tress to the left onto the stony path, just as Merloy had said, and guided her carefully across piles of small, then larger rocks. She snorted loudly, obviously not too happy about this route. *Even the horse would prefer an easier path!* thought Marcus with a slight chuckle.

Their progress was slow, and Rindel began whining about why Marcus had led them onto this awful path. "How far does it go, anyway? Is this even legal?"

Marcus ignored him, and Rindel kept on. "This looks like the path to nowhere, not some awesome kingdom! I wish I'd stayed in Erundel. I could have visited the grench port again, and I was just starting to make some friends down at that tavern. We can't even ride on Tress around here, it's so stony."

"If I hear you moan once more, Rindel, you won't get any of that fruit cake loaf," Marcus retorted.

Rindel sighed dramatically and kicked some stones off the path. Muttering more complaints under his breath, he refused to look Marcus in the eye and drooped his head grumpily.

Finally, they came to a clump of trees by a stream where they could rest for some food and shade from the midday sun. Lunch was a welcome distraction from the eventless day Marcus and Rindel had experienced so far. The path had been rocky and dusty, and the sun made them feel tired and thirsty.

"This is the best cake ever," said Rindel, licking his lips over the moist, fruity slice. "I can't wait to go back to Erundel to buy another. Hey—pass me the water, or I think I'm going to faint!"

Marcus handed him the water skin and warned him not to waste any by starting a water fight.

"We need that skin to last us till this evening. I mean it, Rindel."

Rindel's eyes widened as he made a mock movement as if to hurl the water skin over Marcus's head.

"Not even slightly funny, Rindel."

Rindel laughed. "I think I'm missing my brothers and sisters. There are more people to tease at home!"

Marcus munched on a piece of bread, the very mention of home making him think wistfully of his mother, at home by herself. At least she had wanted him to go. He hoped he was making her proud.

The boys ate till they were full and then rested a while before Rindel jumped up and stretched his arms out wide.

"Well, I think it's time!" he said jubilantly.

"Time for what?"

"Time for a little swordplay, seeing as there's nothing else to do around here. You up for it?"

"'Course I am," grinned Marcus. "Just take it easy; we don't want any injuries out here in the middle of nowhere."

Rindel grabbed his shiny silver ska-sword with the red glow-enabled feature on the handle. He'd convinced his wealthy uncle to get him one for his birthday a few months ago, and Rindel treasured it more than any other possession. He hardly ever took it out for fear that someone would snatch it from him. He pressed a button at the side, causing the blade to extend to its furthest point. The handle was decorated with symbols which he had chosen himself, and it was inscribed with a large, impressive "R." A thin band of solid silver was inlaid just beneath the blade. A sharp twist of this band would cause the glow color to change, while a slow twist caused the blade to retract to its original, compact size. The glow was particularly useful in sword training for groups of people, enabling night fighting and allowing easy recognition of who was on which side. Besides, it was a great way to impress friends.

Marcus threw off his tunic and drew his own sword from the scabbard by his side. Taking on a serious stance, both young men assumed their usual positions—rehearsed hundreds of times over the years, first using sticks as small boys, then makeshift swords, and finally rusty old swords discarded in the village. Many a time they had watched older cousins sparring and had meticulously studied their moves. Rindel's father had also taught them both skills whenever he got the chance.

Rindel lunged toward Marcus, left foot forward, swinging his sword toward his right shoulder. Marcus blocked him and then retreated slightly before sidestepping Rindel, who lurched forward again. Without skipping a beat, Marcus started his counterattack, thrusting his sword low near Rindel's ankles, then slashing it quickly up toward his chest. A clash of swords followed, each boy stepping back and forth in an attempt to wrong-foot the other. But Marcus's nighttime journey to the citadel had tired him out, and Rindel was moving considerably faster.

Finally, Marcus stumbled, falling on his back, steadied only by his left hand. Seizing his opportunity, Rindel pinned Marcus's right shoulder to the ground with the tip of his sword and shouted, "Do you surrender?"

Marcus pursed his lips, refusing to let out any response.

"I said, do you surrender?" Rindel pressed slightly harder with his sword.

"Ouch! Okay then—you win," Marcus replied with a groan. Rindel had won last time too, and a disappointed feeling of defeat nagged at him.

"I suppose your sword just isn't cut out for the big man's game, eh? D'you think you should get one like mine instead?"

Marcus grunted but didn't answer. His cheeks flushed with embarrassment and weariness from the fight. *Why did that man Brayman give me such a useless sword anyway?* If anything, his moves had been smarter than Rindel's, but his sword was heavier and his wrist movements less smooth as a result—besides, he was tired. He put the old sword away and began to consider trading it for a new ska-sword in the next town they reached. He'd seen a few in Prelanor's tent. Maybe they would run into the merchant again.

"Come on, let's get going," he urged Rindel, who by now was stretched out on his back, gazing at the clouds. "The path looks like it's getting a bit flatter now; we should be able to ride Tress again."

As they loaded up their bundles and climbed up onto Tress, Marcus remembered something he had read the other night. "Always be thankful for what you have on your journey. Others around you are less fortunate." Immediately, he realized that he was indeed thankful to have a horse at all, whether they could ride her or not; it wouldn't be much fun carting all their things around on a long journey. He smiled when he thought about how a kindly older man—a complete stranger—had given him a horse to accompany them.

He patted Tress and was relieved that Rindel didn't insist on sitting up front this time.

As they traveled along the dusty path, Marcus noted that there were no dwellings or inns in sight. It seemed a desolate place, with few plants and only a pitiful stream nearby that had all but dried up. Sometimes the path wound round sharply, making it difficult for Tress to maneuver.

Occasionally she stalled at big rocks or fallen logs and had to be coaxed forward. Whenever Marcus tried to speed up, she seemed to resist, as if reluctant to go fast in unsure territory. Growing impatient, Marcus began to handle Tress increasingly roughly.

"Oh, don't slow down here, Tress; it's just another fallen tree! You can easily jump over that. Come on!" He yanked on the reins and kicked her hard.

"Hey, take it easy!" Rindel called from behind him.

"Mind your own business!" Marcus snapped. He was sorry immediately but didn't take back the words. He didn't like being told what to do by his friend. The disagreement between them made each one reluctant to talk to the other, and the next hour of the journey was marked by silence.

Only when Rindel spotted something glistening on the ground did he break the tension. Stopping to reach down and take a closer look, he showed Marcus what he had found.

Holding up a metallic scrap, he asked, "Does this look familiar to you?"

Marcus at first thought it was part of a decorative scarf or waistcoat. But on closer inspection, it was plain to see—a broken remnant of a badge, the kind worn by Krinton's officials.

"It seems like we're not the only ones who've traveled this path. Might be patrollers—they could be up ahead or lying in wait for people like us."

"Cool!" grinned Rindel. "D'you think we'll get to use our swords against them? There's no way they're sending me back to the foundry!"

"I'm not sure I'm looking forward to any conflict. Let's be serious about this, Rindel."

Continuing their journey, Marcus rode nervously, with extra caution. He didn't like the thought of being confronted by patrolmen, and he started to think about how they might talk their way out of questioning or arrest.

Once they reached a wide cross section in the path, Rindel announced that this looked like a good place to hunt for their next meal.

"What do you fancy, then, rabbit or wildfowl?"

"Anything you can get your hands on," retorted Marcus with a smirk. He knew that Rindel was good at hunting, but he wasn't hopeful of finding much wildlife nearby.

His earlier grumpiness pricked at him as Rindel jumped down and started to examine their surroundings. "Here, would my knarl-knife be of any help?" Marcus asked.

"Thanks, I'll take it. Maybe I'll pin something up against those trees over there." Rindel pointed to a small clump of silver birch trees in the distance. "Are you coming?"

"Uh, no thanks. I think I'll try getting Tress to practice some jumps again. She needs to loosen up a bit. Don't be too long; we haven't got very far today. We've been moving so slowly. When you return, meet me up ahead at the path over there."

Rindel slung a cloth bag over his shoulder and waved at Marcus. He whistled as he made his way across the dry grassland.

As he watched him walk away, Marcus couldn't resist shouting after him, "Just make sure you don't disturb any gratsches today!"

"You think you're so funny!" Rindel yelled back.

Marcus turned his attention to Tress and tried to look stern. "Now, listen, you. You're going to have to try harder and start listening to me."

Tress snorted and flung her head to the side as if to say that she had no intention of listening to a harsh, incompetent master.

Completely ignoring Tress's displeasure, Marcus decided that he would trot her up ahead to the next curve and see if she could handle taking it faster this time.

It was a disaster. No sooner had they entered the curve than Marcus was jolted from Tress and thrown down awkwardly in a muddy patch close to the stream. Cursing under his breath, his legs sore from the impact, he sat up.

"What's wrong with that beast?" he pondered aloud. Standing up, he kicked the earth and started to brush himself down. As he slung his dirty bag back onto Tress, he glanced at her, seething, and saw that her eyes appeared somehow apologetic.

"Sometimes it's the rider, not the horse, at fault, my lad," came an amused voice out of nowhere.

Marcus stumbled and turned quickly on the spot, his eyes darting frantically around in search of the speaker.

"I'm up here!" the voice called.

Marcus looked over his shoulder into a chestnut tree about twenty steps from where he was standing. Indignant that someone had watched him clumsily falling off his horse, he huffed as he put his hands on his hips and said, "Oh, and what would you know about horses? You're not much older than me!"

The young man's eyes twinkled gray and green in the sunlight, his streaks of long blond hair glimmering in the midday glare. He took a last mouthful of a meat sandwich before licking his lips, wiping his mouth on his shirtsleeve, and clambering effortlessly down the branches to land facing Marcus. Approaching him with a huge grin, the man offered Marcus his hand.

"Delan Macantyre, pleased to meet you. And before you ask, I'm about ten years older than you, just small for my age. But as my grandfather would often say—that's no reflection on the size of my brain!"

Marcus regarded him with scorn and suspicion. Was this a trick? Was he about to be robbed by an ambush of this man's friends? Or could Delan possibly be a patrolman in disguise—though he didn't look even remotely like one of Treanthor's typical, fierce men? He quickly scanned the area for others hiding. He'd been fooled as a boy one time in the woods and wasn't about to let it happen again. Clutching his money and a few other treasured possessions tightly in the leather bag by his waist, he looked deep into Delan's eyes, examining his intentions. They were friendly and welcoming, making him feel at ease. Marcus relaxed and offered his hand.

"Marcus Macmillan. Tell me, just what did I do wrong back there?"

"Well, let's see. Suppose I pile up a whole load of these branches right in front of you on the path. You're walking along; how are you going to get past them?"

"That depends," said Marcus. "I might just walk onto the mud and grass to bypass the stack, or I might climb over them, or maybe I'll move them out the way for the next traveler."

"Exactly," said Delan. "You have a number of options. Just like your horse. When you picked up speed by that rock on the curve of the path, she assumed you intended her to jump over it. But you tried to rein her in to the side to curve around the rock. She was confused, so she stalled. You haven't trained her to respond to your voice and your movements."

Marcus snorted, skeptical. He wished it were that simple. He'd had difficulty with her quite soon after he had been given her. Oh, she looked so fine and silky and strong, and she had managed to get him and Rindel on their way. But she didn't know much about how to carry a man on a quest. No wonder the old man had been happy to part with her. She was meant to help make Marcus's journey easier, but so far, she'd caused him a few setbacks.

"Well, I'll bear that in mind next time, Delan, but I'm afraid I'm just not cut out for horse riding. She didn't come with any instructions, and I've been struggling since the day I got her. To be honest, I feel like just sticking to my own two feet—at least they're reliable."

He knew he sounded ridiculous, like a little boy trying to prove something instead of a man taking responsibility for himself. A lump rose in his throat, and he clenched his teeth, determined not to let any tears form in his eyes.

At thirteen years old, he'd already seen and experienced far more danger than most his age. He wished that he could be without responsibility and let someone else take all the slack. Oh yes, he had Rindel—but he seemed to see life as one big joke, and he certainly didn't take their journey seriously. Marcus had been trying to follow the book like his mother wanted him to, but it seemed like a heavy burden to carry. *Is this really the life I'm meant to lead, or should I just follow the way of the Wryxl people, most of whom seem to get along just fine? Why is everything so complicated? I'm meant to stay on this special, narrow path, but I've also got to live by a set of principles and do the "right thing" —whatever that might mean exactly!*

Marcus wished he'd never tricked his way into Treanthor's citadel and observed what he had—not knowing anything would have made everything so much easier. Then he could be happy-go-lucky like Rindel, blissfully ignorant.

"You'll be glad you found me then," Delan said, interrupting his train of thought. "I've been awaiting my next assignment, and it looks like you're it!"

Chapter 8

"Assignment? What do you mean?" queried Marcus with a confused frown.

Delan's expression was still cheerful. "Let's just say that I knew you'd be coming my way, and I'm here to help. I've been training horses ever since I was a wee lad. My uncle entrusted me with my own when I was nine, and I've come a long way since then."

"But you don't have a horse," Marcus stated, curious.

"Ah, that's where you're wrong, boy. Mine's just recovering from battle. Wounded from a spear in her thigh, she was, but she'll be fine soon."

"So you're not one of the Wryxl either?" inquired Marcus.

"Absolutely not! A people without a mission—I'd rather die than dwell happily beside those complacent sheep."

Marcus smiled to himself. Delan sounded like his great-grandfather. The Wryxl were a simple group. They loved food and merriment and would avoid battle at all costs. For generations they had supported an unwritten agreement to let Treanthor's guards roam freely among them as long as they were protected from outside predators and didn't have to fight. Treanthor had agreed to this on one condition: that the Wryxl would hand over anyone found training for battle or journeying on an unauthorized mission. The Wryxl were happy to go about their lives seeking pleasure as long as nobody tried to get them to consider the deeper questions of life. It had made Ree-Mya's grandfather incredibly angry. He used to say that the Wryxl weren't even like real men; they were little better than algae floating on a pond.

"Don't need to know, don't care either," was one of their favorite phrases, one that Marcus had seen his mother blow up over more than once. When one of their people started to question their purpose or point out the problems with their style of living, they were shouted down and derided. Worse still, some were threatened with being handed over to

Treanthor as his eternal slaves, though no one had ever really witnessed this for many years, and the threat was dismissed as scaremongering. Marcus now knew there was an element of truth to it—the scene of the weirdly transformed sick man being led down into an underground prison was etched clearly on his mind. To most, however, Treanthor projected himself as a benevolent ruler. It was considered a privilege to work for him, as there were many perks for being in his employ. Perks such as fine clothing and free housing, as well as a superior uniform and good pay.

Delan strode over to Tress, patting her gently and talking quietly to her. "She's a fine horse, my dear Marcus. Fit for any man or boy. We'll have her trained in no time. Come on, let me take you over to Farrow's Field."

Marcus flicked mud off his knuckles and wiped his nose. Some grass had lodged in his nostrils, making him sneeze three times very loudly. Tress startled and stepped backward.

Delan laughed and said, "Well that's not a good start, lad! Are you trying to make her run off?"

Marcus said, "It's all right; she's used to me sneezing. I'm allergic to dust and grass and all sorts of things. Come on, Tress, you're in for some real training now. But we'll have to wait for Rindel first. I said we'd meet him just up ahead there."

"Rindel?" Delan inquired. "Merloy didn't mention him."

"Merloy!" gasped Marcus. "He came to you too?"

"He's the reason I'm here. He sent me to find you and train you so that you can defend yourself on your journey—you may run into many dangers, my friend. Merloy told me that you are specially chosen. But I know nothing of Rindel."

Marcus didn't take in what Delan was telling him; instead, he focused his attention on his scrappy-looking friend, who was appearing on the path. "Look, I can see him coming now. Looks like he actually caught something!"

Rindel was walking toward them, carrying a bundle wrapped in cloth. He looked dirty and scratched but had a huge grin on his face. A pheasant was slung over one shoulder.

After being introduced to Delan and learning what the plans were for the rest of the day, Rindel was happy to go along with some horse training. And besides, he was happy to have more company—another person with whom he could share jokes and tell crazy stories. "The more the merrier!" he announced, beaming.

The three young men continued along the path until it narrowed further, leading them to a black iron gate, set under a stone archway—just as Merloy had said. The gate was well over six feet high, forged evenly into five bars. Weeds, vines, and cobwebs entangled the heavy bars, and the gate creaked noisily as Delan slowly pulled it open. Marcus's eyes lit up, but he said nothing, wondering what on earth Rindel would make of his encounter with the mysterious figure of Merloy. They dismounted to guide the horses through the gate, shutting it behind them, and followed Delan's lead as he headed toward a large overgrown field, just half a mile or so from where they had stopped for lunch. The field ran alongside the River Rothoy, which fed into the River Quinn at Erundel.

Out in the open again, Delan set to work with various obstacle courses and taught Marcus to use his voice consistently to command Tress and steer her correctly. At first Marcus wanted to respond obstinately, but he recalled another line in the book, which recommended that he should "Listen to advice and be ready to let others teach you."

So without complaint, he let Delan demonstrate the skills he'd thought he already had. Rindel was given the task of helping to set up obstacles and searching for hay for Tress—tasks which he was not too pleased about. But Delan promised that he would cook a fine roast meal for them all afterward, which appeased Rindel quite a bit.

Marcus welcomed the break from their journey and was glad to have met a like-minded character who seemed trustworthy. Delan was witty as well as skilled, and Tress responded unbelievably well to his training.

At one point while they rested from training, Marcus asked Delan about something that was confusing him. "You're a follower of PathOne, aren't you?" he asked.

"I am, of course," Delan answered.

"Then why are you here?" Marcus asked. "Shouldn't you be far ahead of us by now? And how do you have time to stop and train people like us when you should be trying to search for the kingdom?"

"Sometimes stopping is part of the search," Delan said, his eyes twinkling.

"Huh?"

"You've been reading the book, so you know that PathOne isn't just this physical path you're on—it's also a way of life."

Marcus nodded, though was surprised to learn that others knew about the book he carried. *There must be more of these books, after all,* he thought.

Delan began to roll up his sleeves. "Well, part of that way is serving others when Merloy calls us to. There are a lot of people like me—many of us are knights in a secret resistance, working against Treanthor and doing our best to make sure people can get hold of more copies of *The Book Beyond Time* and read it for themselves. Merloy has called me to be part of the resistance and train and defend other travelers. Doing so is part of my path."

"But how will you ever reach the kingdom that way?" Marcus asked, thinking Delan didn't really look like much of a knight – especially without any armor.

"I'll reach it when I'm meant to reach it," Delan said. "Merloy shows me new parts of the path when I need to take them. It may take years—

it may take my whole life. But someday I will reach the Kingdom of the North, and all of my dreams will be fulfilled."

Marcus was quiet for a moment as he pondered the idea of following this path for years. "You said I was chosen," he said. "What does that mean?"

"It means Merloy has a special role for you," Delan said. "But I don't know what it is. No two people on PathOne have exactly the same calling. But I know that yours is important."

As nightfall beckoned, Delan led them back onto the little stony path, away from open fields or farms in the distance. At times it was tricky to see which direction they were meant to go. Fallen branches and overgrown weeds often obscured the way, but Delan was familiar with the route and insisted that they keep going until they reached Tringham Forest.

Weary from the day's journey, the boys welcomed the sight of the forest and groaned with tired joy to find a pleasant clearing where they could build a campfire. Both friends relished the thought of someone else preparing a meal for them, and they looked forward to chatting about their quest. Rindel accepted the compliments upon the tasty meat with quiet pride. He had chased that pheasant for ages before outwitting it. Marcus was relieved that Delan had guided them well in the dark, and he began to feel safer about being in unknown territory.

After eating the fowl, which Delan had prepared on a makeshift spit over an open fire, the newcomer took out a dulcimer from his cloth bag and began to play and sing traditional folk songs. Marcus and Rindel relaxed under the beautiful night sky, at times joining in with songs they knew or watching the fireflies dart about in a pattern of lights.

Rindel was just about to fall asleep with his head resting on Marcus's shoulder when the sound of heavy thunder jolted him alert. A cluster of dark clouds approached rapidly from behind, and huge lightning flashes followed soon after. Then came the heavy downpour.

As the boys scrambled to unpack their thick cotton tent, it soon became apparent that it was too late. Within moments they were drenched. The thunder sounded again, as if to voice nature's supremacy, and Marcus began to imagine that he could hear Treanthor's voice behind the sounds of the storm.

As his heartbeat quickened, he began to feel exceedingly fearful. What if Treanthor had seen him leaving the citadel, or knew about his quest and was coming after him? What if patrollers had indeed seen them earlier and sent knights to plan an ambush ahead of them in the woods? Thoughts raced over and over in his mind as the three of them huddled under a clump of fir trees in an attempt to shelter from the pounding rain. By the time it stopped, Marcus was shivering not so much from the cold but from fear.

Merloy! Marcus remembered the unusual visitation and called his name quietly under his breath. "Merloy, I need you now. Where are you?" he whispered into his cupped hands.

Frustrated that Merloy did not immediately appear, Marcus allowed fearful thoughts to cloud his mind once more. He wanted to grab hold of Tress and Rindel and get away, just anywhere far from the forest.

Before he knew it, he was acting on his fears.

"What are you doing?" Rindel asked in exasperation as he was pulled roughly by the arm.

"I don't know. I, er, I just think we should get away from here. Now."

"And go *where* exactly? We may as well just stay here as planned. We're all tired, and the storm has passed. We can probably even get the tent up."

"But I think he's after us!"

"Who?"

"Treanthor, and his knights."

Rindel laughed heartily, shaking his head; Delan squinted his eyes in inquiring fashion.

Marcus released his hold on Rindel and looked all around, surveying the darkness for evidence of other men. In the stillness after the storm, he heard no other sounds apart from the occasional call of an owl.

Suddenly feeling rather foolish, Marcus cleared his throat. "You're probably right," he admitted. "It's probably best to stay overnight here after all."

Delan wisely chose not to bring up the subject of Treanthor again before they slept, and after finding dry clothing and getting their tent set up, they all settled down for an undisturbed night. Even Rindel was too worn out for silly tales or riddles.

* * *

Over the next few weeks, Marcus learned how to guide Tress swiftly in any direction he wanted and to jump over all sorts of obstructions. Not only a great horseman, Delan was also highly skilled in sword fighting. He seemed as able as a true knight, and Marcus found himself wondering where this young man had come from and where he had received his training. But Delan didn't tell them, and he dodged any questions that poked at the truth. He simply told them that his superior skills had been acquired from practicing every day.

With fascination and awe, the young men were inspired and challenged by Delan's swordsmanship. He made them practice over and over until they knew long sequences of thrusts, blocks, and feints by heart. He also trained them to respond to surprise attacks and how to react swiftly if disturbed from sleep.

Just when they thought that they had mastered all there was to know about fighting, Delan took them one step further—he taught them how to fight while riding a horse. A messenger arrived one morning with Delan's white steed, Opus, now fully recovered, and he set about charging at each boy in turn, daring them to attack with increasing ferocity.

Several weeks later, once he decided that Marcus and Rindel were well trained enough to respond to a variety of possible attacks and situations, Delan sent them on their way out of the quiet forest to continue their journey without him. Marcus looked wistfully at Delan as they rode away, unsure if Tress would manage without his guidance. Delan had been like an older brother to him, accepting him and always encouraging him to do better. Although they had only spent a few weeks together, Marcus had grown to really enjoy his company—not just his general good nature, but also his wit and sense of fun. He felt like family, a close friend. Marcus had even felt comfortable sharing the sad story of his errant father, and Delan had seemed to share his pain. He too had lost his father, who had been killed in a fight.

Marcus recognized that to have such a friend was worth more than anything he could possibly wish to buy, and thoughts of this reminded him of the "intangible treasures" spoken of in the book. Perhaps the treasures of the kingdom were worth more than gold and jewels after all.

Marcus had tried to persuade him to travel with them, but Delan was insistent that he needed to stay in the woods for a few more days. "I was instructed to stay here until my next budding warrior arrives for training," he said. "You'll have to continue without me." Tress was enthusiastic about going and keen to move into new territory and see new sights. Rindel had also become bored of the scenery and was eager to move on.

"Giddyup, here we come!" laughed Rindel as he sat in the front of Tress's saddle, imagining patrolmen or bandits around the corner and eager to show off his new skills.

"Steady on, Rindel, I nearly fell off there!" cautioned Marcus as Rindel galloped Tress along a stretch of path that widened for several yards before quickly narrowing once again between trees and huge boulders.

"Well, not much chance of going fast anymore. Here's a narrow stretch again—boring!"

They slowed to navigate carefully through a wooded area filled with bluebells and fallen branches. Nettles and thorns covered the ground, and Rindel had to concentrate to ensure he stayed on the path.

Marcus didn't bother arguing with Rindel; he had expected the journey would become boring again, and was in fact glad to have a trouble-free trip. All that fighting could wait till they had rested a while; they were both pretty exhausted from their intensive training, exacerbated by weeks of living on nothing but game and whatever else they could gather. He remembered Brayman's warnings about those out to get him and stop him from following PathOne, but he secretly hoped that no one would be bothered by a young countryman traveling with a friend cross-country—even if they were using unapproved paths. Thoughts of Treanthor's sinister citadel had frequently arisen in Marcus's mind, and he hoped he would never have to go back there again. He was still reluctant to tell Rindel about it, but soon his friend began to question him about his exploits that evening when they had been apart.

Marcus fobbed him off with vague explanations.

"Oh, nothing much, just had a look around at the merchants' goods."

"Well, you can't have done that all evening—I met loads of people. Surely you talked to some others?"

"Well, yes, I met an interesting clothes merchant."

"And?"

"And nothing!"

Rindel gave Marcus a skeptical glance and kept digging for information and details until Marcus relented and told him everything.

Rindel was not shocked in the slightest; rather, he was incredibly fascinated. "Treanthor's citadel sounds amazing!" he burst out, ignoring

Marcus's obviously negative feelings about the place. He asked Marcus dozens of questions, wanting to know all manner of facts and descriptions.

"Was there a throne?"

"I'm not sure, maybe. I don't remember exactly."

"Did you see Treanthor's bedroom?"

"No, I only saw a couple of main rooms and corridors."

"Oh, I bet he has loads of xanth-powered gadgetry. And the best ska-swords."

"Maybe. I'm not so sure about that."

"Not sure? He's the ruler of Krinton! He *must* have the latest inventions!"

"I suppose. I was just wanting to see what happened to the official who was dying."

"Well, never mind about him—did they have a huge feast there?"

"You only ever think about food!"

Rindel jerked suddenly, pulling on Tress's reins. "Hey, how can you accuse me of that?"

Tress stopped abruptly, and Rindel climbed down.

"What are you doing?" asked Marcus, perplexed.

Rindel winked cheekily. "I just spotted a plum tree—I thought we could enjoy some of those. After all, I was getting a bit peckish!"

Both boys laughed.

* * *

As they bit into their third or fourth plum, juice dripping down their chins, a short, wiry man with a limp hurried toward them from the road.

"What are you two doing?" he asked sternly.

"I think that's kind of obvious!" muttered Rindel quietly to Marcus.

"Shh," Marcus replied. "He doesn't look too happy."

The man stopped directly in front of them, looking down on them with a small nose and squinty eyes.

"Do you know who that plum tree belongs to?"

Rindel answered, "Uh, no, sir, we were just passing this way and thought—"

"No, you didn't think, did you? That's my tree, and I purposefully planted it out of the way here so that oiks like you wouldn't pinch them!"

"It's right off the road," Rindel said, defensive.

The old man snorted. "No one comes along this route anymore, what with it being all overgrown and difficult to pass."

"Sorry," mumbled Marcus. "We didn't know that the tree belonged to anyone. There are no houses here, and—"

"All right, all right," the man interrupted. "But maybe you can do something for me, now you've scoffed so many already?"

Rindel frowned and looked at Marcus.

"I wonder whether you could pick the rest of the ripe ones. You're both taller than I am, and I'm too old to climb up for the high ones."

Rindel groaned quietly; Marcus elbowed him in the side and said, "Yes, of course we can; that's no problem."

The little man handed the boys a few cloth bags and told them he'd be back later to check on them. And if they ran off with his plums, he'd get his friend, who was a friend of one of Treanthor's guards, to come after them.

Rindel sighed as the man walked away, and he turned on Marcus as soon as the man was too far to hear.

"What a soft touch! You're always too ready to help people, Marcus! We don't have time for this. What about us finding shelter tonight and some proper food?"

"Well, I thought maybe the old man could help us out," Marcus said. "There doesn't seem to be much in the way of shelter around here—

he might know where we can stay. Come on, let's fill these bags quickly and then rest in the shade for a while."

Rindel and Marcus were used to helping their parents with the harvest, and it didn't take long to fill the bags full of ripe fruit. The old man was nowhere to be seen.

"What if he doesn't come back?" asked Rindel. "And what if this *isn't* his tree after all, and we're helping him steal from someone else?"

"Well, we'll soon find out, won't we?" said Marcus, raising his eyebrows. "Look, I think I can see him coming now. Must be him — see how he's limping."

When the old man reached the base of the tree, huffing and puffing from the walk, he took in the sight of the bulging sacks with surprise. "So you've actually done it?"

"Yes, we've got five bags full," said Marcus with a smile. "We really didn't mean to steal from you, so we're happy to help."

"Well, you've done me a good turn, lads. What can I do for you in return?"

"Well," Marcus began, but Rindel rushed to answer. "We could use a place to stay the night."

The man quickly agreed, declaring he was always glad for company. He took hold of Tress and led her across the road and onto a path strewn with briars. After several minutes, it led to an overgrown back garden. After tying Tress to the gate, the little man led the boys through his kitchen door into a wooden house. The doors were quite low, and both Rindel and Marcus needed to duck their heads. Marcus managed to bump his forehead on the door frame into the living room.

Rindel laughed, and Marcus punched him in the arm.

"Sorry about that," said the little man. "My generation didn't have that problem. That's why all the older houses are so small. We never imagined our grandchildren would get so tall!"

After introducing himself as Stanrul, the man showed them the room where they would sleep. Two wooden beds, shorter than the boys were used to but still appealing, topped with feather mattresses and blankets that were worn but clean, stood at either end of the room.

"Beds!" gasped Rindel.

The old man looked curious. "Been a while since you've slept in one?"

"We've been camping for ages," Rindel explained. "We're on a journey, you see. A quest."

The old man smiled. "Tell me all about it in the kitchen, then, while I rustle you up some dinner."

After a hearty meal, Stanrul announced it was time for some fresh apple cider at the tavern. They'd be able to meet his son, Gledrik, who would usually join him there after work.

Rindel agreed enthusiastically, and Marcus nodded, though he felt they should have discussed it first. He'd only meant to spend the night here before getting back on the path — he wasn't so sure about going into the village. *Oh well,* he reasoned, *there's no urgent rush. Anyway, didn't Brayman and Delan say that we each have our own little side paths to follow?*

Chapter 9

The boys followed Stanrul along a long row of wooden houses. Most were single story, with a small front yard. They entered a square of shops, and their eyes quickly focused on the tavern on the opposite side. It was so full of people that many were standing outside. Others sat at wooden tables on a deck across the front of the building. Everyone seemed happy to be there, enjoying their cold drinks and laughing with friends. A group of young women were giggling and gossiping at one of the outside tables; several men were eyeing them up or trying to get their attention.

Stanrul led them through the crowded tavern and out the other side, where there was a small garden filled with three or four more tables. They sat down, and almost immediately a waiter appeared with a tray of drinks.

"Thanks, Mack," said Stanrul.

The cider was delicious, but it seemed more alcoholic than anything they had tried in Trynn Goth. Marcus noticed his taste buds almost sizzling from the concoction. Rindel raised his cup in appreciation. No sooner had they finished their cups when Mack appeared with another tray.

"Enjoy!" he said with a smile before rushing back inside the tavern.

As they finished their second round, a young boy about their own age, handsome and strong looking, sat uninvited at the table. He smacked the table top and hollered, "Mack! More drinks!"

"Thirsty, are you, Gledrik?" Stanrul asked.

"I'm a hardworking dairyman, Father," Gledrik replied with a grin. "And who are these young chaps?"

"Rindel and Marcus," Stanrul said. "Young travelers. They're staying with us for a bit. They helped me out this afternoon—picked me a pretty lot of plums."

"Welcome," Gledrik said, beaming. "I hope you'll stay a few days."

As they talked, several of Stanrul's friends gathered around and joined in the conversation.

"Have they got anything from the city?" asked one skinny man with a missing front tooth, poking his finger at the boys.

"Ask them yourself!" replied Stanrul.

Marcus and Rindel learned that Stanrul and his friends were full-blooded Wryxls whose forefathers had lived in the small town of Grentham since the Great Catastrophe. Most of them were involved in farming or woodwork. They were very friendly, and many offered them work or a place to stay, but Marcus declined.

Several young men sat opposite Rindel and showed him their ska-swords. One redheaded man with wild, curly hair let him handle his impressive new purple-handled sword. Rindel swiped at a chair leg, easily slicing off a thin sliver of oak.

Marcus began chatting with a man called Falk, who reminded him of his father. Falk wore a dark green cloak and a flat cap with a long feather in it. He rested his feet up on a nearby log, tapping his huge brown lace-up boots together.

Marcus shifted his chair to put one of his feet up on the log beside Falk when the book slipped out of his bag and fell to the ground. Marcus froze.

Falk spotted the book instantly. "Eh, what's that, then? Looks like a book, if I'm not mistaken! Not many your age have books nowadays."

Marcus mumbled something in reply, quickly put the book back in his bag, and tried to change the subject.

But Falk wouldn't let it drop. He reached for the bag and pushed away the edge of the cloth so the gold lettering on the front of the book could be clearly seen.

"I think I've seen that before. Isn't that that ancient book? Something about time?"

Marcus raised his eyebrows in surprise. Falk knew about the book?

"What do you know about it?"

"Oh, some old geezer used to go on about it a few years ago. Gathered people in his house every week to listen while he read it. Said it was the only hope for the future or something. Don't know where he found it, but we were all quite captivated by it."

"Did you believe it?" asked Marcus, cautious. He didn't want to get himself into trouble here, but all of these people seemed so truly friendly and welcoming.

"Yes, of course! We all did. Got to be something more to this life, hasn't there? It just got a bit boring, hearing the same things over and over, and we never did really understand half of what the book was saying. Some of it just seemed too difficult to believe. Anyway, the old man moved to another town and took the book with him, but we were certain there was some truth to it. Still are."

Marcus blinked, more surprised by the moment. "So you're saying that everyone here believes in *The Book Beyond Time?*"

"Oh yes, that's the one. Yes, most of us, I'm sure. All that stuff about new life and freedom sounded pretty good. In fact, I'd say we try to live it! Isn't that what we're building here? A new and better life, for we Wryxl and for everyone!"

Marcus couldn't believe what he was hearing. He wondered whether Falk had ever met Merloy, and why, if these people believed the book, they were settled so happily here. Why weren't they on the path to the north? But then, not everyone's journey was the same—perhaps for some, following PathOne meant staying put.

The thought made his head hurt. He wondered about Merloy again.

"Did you—I mean, did an unusual person ever, um, visit you?"

"What do you mean, unusual person? Well, there's the milk delivery boy—he always acts a bit strange!"

Their conversation was interrupted when another friend came over to Falk and took him away to play chess at another table.

He winked as he stood. "Nice meeting you, young Marcus. Hope to see you again soon."

As they evening went on, everyone became louder and livelier. Jokes were traded, and the laughter increased. Quieter Wryxl soon became minor entertainers, showing off tricks and sharing tales of farmyard humor, mostly related to manure.

After a third cup, Marcus became aware that the cider was affecting his ability to think properly. He felt relaxed, but not really in control. Still, the more he drank, the less it bothered him. He joined Rindel and Gledrik in mimicking some ladies dancing and enjoyed the laughter and whoops of approval from the Wryxl men.

As night fell and another round of drinks was offered by Mack, a couple of unusual winged creatures swooped down just above their table and hovered above their heads. They looked like birds, with brightly colored feathers and brilliant orange beaks, but then again, they weren't quite like birds at all—they had long, scaly tails like lizards, and as Marcus looked up at one of them, it flicked a forked tongue at him.

Marcus thought the birds must belong to a rare species in this part of Krinton, for he had never seen anything like them before. And yet their screeches sounded familiar—like the sounds he had heard on entering Treanthor's citadel that eerie night. Surely these could not be the same birds he had seen flying overhead there? But everyone just ignored them and carried on with their chatter.

With a swoosh of air, a bird with orange and green feathers flew quickly past Marcus's left ear. In a high-pitched voice, the bird squawked, "Make it funnier, add colorful words!" and then flew up to the roof of the tavern.

Marcus didn't know what to think. Since when did birds talk? And what did it care about their conversation? He was too fuzzy from the cider to figure the problem out, so he ignored it. But then it swooped down low again and began screeching rude words and phrases. Everyone heard it, and many began repeating the phrases, laughing.

Rindel joined in with the silly conversation, taking it one step further.

Marcus glared at him, but Rindel was incredibly funny, and he too soon found himself joining in the laughter. The laughs merged with sneering, mocking and putting others down.

Another strange bird, with equally striking wings—of yellow and red, with a smattering of green—swished above Rindel's head squawking ever ruder and meaner phrases. "Join in, lads, it's just a bit of fun! Say it, lads, haw haw hee hee!"

Everyone roared with laughter as Stanrul pulled a weird face, and his head jerked sideways as he repeated a string of obscene words, followed by taunts about those on another table.

"Hey, listen to this joke!" said the toothless man. "Yer mother won't like this one."

Through the haze of cider and laughter, Marcus thought of his mother at home. He envisaged her sitting there right now across the garden, listening to all this nonsense. A lump rose in his throat, and coughing wouldn't make it go away. He tried, but he couldn't dismiss the image of her watching him there, her concerned expression seeming to express sadness more than anger.

He took another look around him. Were these people really followers of PathOne? Was this really the life the book described?

Marcus put down his cup and decided to pour the rest of its contents on the grass beside him. Everyone else nearby thought he was trying to be funny and started pouring out their drinks too. One man poured his cider over Stanrul's head, and all the others roared with laughter.

Stanrul, however, was not amused. He jumped to his feet.

"Oy, what did yer do that for?" he demanded.

"Oh, it's just a laugh, mate, what you worried about?"

"Well, I guess I'll do the same to you then!"

The man jumped to his feet, his face an odd shade of purple. "Nah, get away, you old git!"

"Who you calling 'old'?"

Stanrul lurched toward the man, attempting to grab him by his shirt collar.

Marcus shook his head and intervened quickly.

"We were just leaving. Thank you!" he called out as he grabbed Stanrul by the sleeve and pulled him through the tavern doors. Rindel got up and followed them. Gledrik stayed behind, interested in a girl who had just arrived.

"Mack, here's your money," slurred Stanrul as he passed the bar on the way out.

"Cheers, mate! See you next time!" replied Mack with a grin.

Once they had returned to the house, Marcus helped Stanrul to bed. Rindel had already staggered off to find a quiet place, his face rather green, holding his stomach. He had drunk several cups of the strong drink quite quickly.

Marcus went to their room and lay on the bed. He pulled the book out of his leather bag and began to read a few lines, but started to drift off to sleep. As his eyelids slowly closed, he could hear Rindel throwing up in the garden.

* * *

"You've gotta watch out for those jeruni sometimes," said Stanrul over breakfast the next morning.

"Jeruni?" queried Marcus.

"Those twitchy, chattering birds. They always like to join in where there's a gathering, start stirring up a bit of nonsense."

Marcus leaned forward, deeply interested. There had been something strange about those birds. "Where do they come from?"

122

"Not sure, but in the last ten years or so they've been breeding like crazy. Always buzzing around in the towns and villages, especially at nighttime. People didn't like them at first, but now everyone thinks it's hilarious, all that bad language and jeering. I try to avoid it, but what can you do? Everyone talks like that these days." The old man sounded like a child trying to convince himself. "It's just a bit of harmless fun, isn't it?"

Marcus frowned. "Looks like they played a part in starting a brawl, if you ask me."

"Well, yeah, that kind of thing can happen now and again, but hey, nobody got hurt."

Gledrik, who had returned later in the night, smirked and gobbled down his last mouthful of bread.

"Yep, nobody got hurt—till after you left. Somebody started teasing Falk about his girlfriend, and then some punches were traded back and forth."

Once Gledrik had left for work, Marcus cleared his throat. "Stanrul, have you ever heard of *The Book Beyond Time?* Falk said many of the Wryxl have read it—at some old fellow's house?"

Stanrul wrinkled his nose as though he smelled something bad. "Oh yes, I remember that book. What a load of nonsense! You haven't been fooled too, have you? It's just a load of fairy stories, silly stuff. Can't believe there's still a few idiots who will believe it!"

Marcus blushed, while Rindel leaned forward, captivated by what he'd just heard.

"It's just a big distraction, that book," Stanrul continued. "Lots of people believed in it because they were scared of another catastrophe. It's for losers—people who don't know how to live their lives now. Claiming to have all the answers, all the 'truth,' and to be showing people a 'right way' through this world—what a joke! I mean, who would possibly believe such things in this day and age? And as for claiming to talk to some higher being – more like an airy-fairy imaginary friend ..."

123

Marcus didn't know what to say, and he got up to get a drink of water. He mumbled something about, "Maybe there's some truth to it," but Stanrul shot him down.

"No, there is no truth, and no right way. And that's that! No one tells me how I should live my life or where I should be going! And as for that nonsense of following a narrow path—who ever heard of such a ridiculous idea? Everyone wants to travel the easier path; I know I certainly do. Isn't that what progress is all about—making our lives easier?"

"But the Kingdom of the North," Marcus started to say, but Stanrul cut him off again.

"It's nonsense—ridiculous rumor. Everyone knows there's nothing to be found in the north—it's a virtual wasteland, and still part of Krinton besides. Anyone who's traveled in that region has returned with nothing." Stanrul fixed Marcus with a direct, accusing gaze. "This one thing I'll say: if you were to take it into your head to try to get to the Kingdom of the North, you'd be doing nothing but wasting your time!"

Rindel complained suddenly of a terrible headache and announced that he needed to go back to bed. Stanrul said he had to go into town, but Marcus didn't want to join him, saying he should make sure Rindel was fine.

Once Stanrul had left, Marcus went to find the book and took it outside to read on a bench in the garden near Tress. He was confused and uncertain about where to go next, and he needed to find some answers.

He read some words about not trying to hold on to "worldly possessions" which would not last, and some other things about being careful who to trust. But he flicked over the pages, looking for something to help him right now.

Marcus then stumbled upon the words, "Be patient, make the choice that seems right, and Merloy will direct you."

124

But Marcus hadn't seen Merloy for weeks. He had started to wonder if the visitation hadn't just been his imagination, as Stanrul claimed. Could his mind have been clouded that night by the smoky air wafting around at the citadel?

Then he remembered the words spoken to him that night on the roadside back to Erundel. *"I am always near."*

But Merloy didn't feel near. Marcus felt nothing at all. It was frustrating, just like that night in the woods during the storm. He had been scared silly, but Merloy hadn't shown up.

Weary and confused, Marcus let his emotions build. He was disappointed that they still seemed so far from finding the Kingdom of the North, and he questioned why they even had to rejoin the narrow path. He wanted to know where it would lead to next, or whether they would be traveling that overgrown path for a long time. Here among the Wryxl, with their happiness and simple ways, the kingdom didn't even seem real. Just a big joke, like Stanrul had said. *How long will this quest take, and why are there so many distractions along the way? Surely we can just head north and then find the narrow path right at the end?*

Sitting quietly for a while, Marcus was still contemplating these thoughts when he became aware of something speaking into his spirit, pricking at his conscience. He looked around, but no one appeared. Yet a voice seemed to speak quietly to him.

It said, *"When you speak out harshly in anger, or let yourself be influenced by others and join in with negative talk, you distance yourself from me. And if you drink too much, you close your mind to good choices or hearing from me. When you let fear take control, you lose sight of the way I am guiding you. I am not of this kingdom, and my ways are beyond your understanding right now. You need to trust that I will walk with you on the narrow path. Go back the way you came and find it once more."*

Marcus felt sudden remorse. He had indeed acted in a manner that he would be ashamed of back home in Trynn Goth. He was thankful that nobody knew where he was from, so they wouldn't gossip about all his faults.

But somebody knew what he had been doing and saying. Merloy!

Marcus hung his head low, feeling worthless inside. How could he ever measure up to the standards in the book? Even being fearful was considered a weakness! How could he trust in the book and do the right thing? He had read several excerpts about making the right choices, but it all seemed so difficult.

He burst out, "Why does it matter how I live and behave? Surely if I follow PathOne I'll get to the final destination—isn't that good enough?"

Merloy's voice became louder, as if speaking right into his ear. *"PathOne is not just a destination; it's a transformation."*

Marcus looked puzzled. "A transformation?"

The voice sounded as though Merloy was smiling. *"Once you begin to follow your destiny, and follow PathOne in all seriousness, it will change you—your thoughts, your behaviors, your hopes and dreams. Without that transformation, you cannot enter the kingdom. On this path you will discover more about me and the mystery of my kingdom, and you will become a part of that mystery. For when you travel on PathOne and live my ways, you bring a taste of the north to Krinton."*

"I'm not sure I get what you're saying," Marcus replied softly.

This time Merloy was definitely smiling. *"That's fine. You will understand more as you keep going and listen for my voice. But it's up to you — I will not force you into my kingdom. It's up to you to find it. And if you look for it, you will find it."*

Marcus looked ahead in surprise as the voice became louder still, and he heard the sound of footsteps. Merloy stood directly before him, his gleaming robe brushing Marcus's feet.

"I promise to help you if you want to continue on PathOne."

126

"But—but I thought you had distanced yourself from me and my ways?" said Marcus, not raising his eyes to look at Merloy's face.

"Not at all. *You* chose to distance yourself from *me*. Did I not say that I would always be with you? When you come to recognize that you need me and are willing to give up your former ways, then you will be aware of me guiding you continually."

Marcus looked up slowly. Merloy smiled kindly at him and rested his hand on Marcus's shoulder. As he did so, Marcus felt a surge of energy, like supernatural power, flow through his body to his feet. It jolted him backward, so great was its force, and then Merloy reached out his hand to pull him up again.

"What was that?" asked Marcus, breathless.

"That is my power. It is a taste of the Kingdom of the North, and it is readily available to you on your journey through Krinton."

"You mean I can actually have some of your power?"

"That's right. It will help you make wise choices and overcome evil along your way."

Marcus was quiet. "Last night at the tavern—none of that seemed evil. Foolish, maybe."

"Evil takes many forms," Merloy said. "One form it often takes is to distract people so much with seemingly harmless things that they never listen to the words of the book or take the Kingdom of the North seriously. Many of those men at the tavern have heard my truth, but they have chosen empty distraction instead."

Marcus bowed his head again. Rubbing his hand across his face, he mustered the courage to ask the one question he had been wondering about since his first encounter with Merloy.

"Who *are* you, Merloy? Are you really the ruler of the Kingdom of the North?"

Merloy waited until Marcus looked him in the eye, and said, "I am indeed the king of the northern kingdom."

The answer was both surprising and expected. Although Merloy was an impressive sight, he wasn't adorned with gold or silver, and he wasn't wearing a crown—he looked more like a warrior than like a pampered ruler. But Merloy's whole being emanated a definite supernatural power, which was alluring and mesmerizing.

"I just hope—"

He stopped. Merloy was gone again.

But this time, he was pretty sure he wasn't really alone.

Chapter 10

"Wake up, Marcus, we have a visitor."

Rindel shook Marcus, who had fallen asleep in the garden after doing some weeding for Stanrul. The mid-morning sunshine shone hazily through blossoms on the trees and cast interesting shadows on the grass as the wind softly blew. A cat sprang down from the fence, knocking down a couple of old tins stored near the back door, and Marcus noticed that the back window frames were badly in need of a lick of paint. Stumbling as he rose to his feet, nearly tripping into the row of clothes pegged on a line, he stopped and glared at Rindel.

"What are you talking about?"

"I think you'll like her. Says she's Gledrik's cousin."

Marcus followed Rindel back into the house, where a beautiful girl with long, wavy hair was sitting in a comfortable seat by the window. Her blonde locks glistened in the sunlight, and her smile revealed lovely white teeth.

She introduced herself as Shurama and said that she had come to visit Gledrik. Stanrul, who was scrubbing potatoes over the sink, explained that Shurama would stay for a few days.

Rindel and Marcus stumbled over their words as they introduced themselves, they were so taken aback by Shurama's beauty. Her voice was soft and sweet, and her eyes were startling blue.

Shurama said she would organize a party for Gledrik and his friends later, and she insisted that the young travelers join them.

"It's a full moon tonight, and you've just got to take any excuse for a party, haven't you?"

"I, er, I'm not sure if we can make it—"

"We're coming!" Rindel interrupted Marcus.

Marcus didn't argue. How often did he get the chance to go to a party? Especially on this journey. Somehow he doubted PathOne majored in parties. But as soon as the words "Yes, why not!" escaped from his lips, he knew that he should have said no. Merloy had told him to make haste and return the way they had come, not to fall prey to the distractions of villages like this one. He was convinced now that Merloy was very real and to be listened to. Yet he couldn't bear to look like an idiot, especially in front of a girl, and he bit his lip. Surely they could just stay a little while longer.

Still, Marcus persuaded Rindel that they should pack up everything that evening so they could be on their way immediately after the celebration.

* * *

The party that night was held in a field not far from Stanrul's plum trees. Shurama had organized a folk band of musicians to play, and it seemed that everyone under the age of twenty-five was there. There was dancing and singing, and barrels of beer and cider. Marcus chose to have only one cupful this time and reminded Rindel that he had been sick the night before.

Rindel wasn't bothered about the beer; he was distracted by all the pretty girls. Even Shurama showed interest in Rindel, putting her arm around him as she introduced him to Gledrik's friends.

Marcus was unable to relax. He felt that something was wrong but couldn't put his finger on it. There was no sign of any jeruni—it was still early in the evening—and he felt that all the Wryxl young people were incredibly fun and welcoming. Still, he was unsure that this was where he should be. When a couple of young men who sat nearby kept staring at him and whispering to one another, he grew more uncomfortable. *Could these be patrollers like the ones Prelanor talked about, ready to report anyone found traveling or not in employment?*

"Make wise choices, and I will guide you." The words resounded in his head.

Suddenly, Marcus was finished with this place. PathOne was calling, and he didn't want anything more than to be on his way. "Come on, Rindel, we need to leave. We have to get on with our journey!"

"But I haven't had a dance with Shurama yet!" protested Rindel.

"I'll go without you then," replied Marcus with a determined look.

"Oh, all right," groaned Rindel. "Just wait a moment, would you? Do you *always* have to spoil my fun?"

Marcus waited while Rindel finished his drink and said goodbye to everyone. He lingered by Shurama for quite some time before leaving her, his face beaming.

"Guess what? She's given me her contact details. Said we can drop by to see her when we pass her way. Can you believe it? I think she fancies me!"

Marcus eyed Rindel skeptically. "Who would fancy you? You haven't even got your shirt buttoned up properly!"

"Hey! You—you—I'll get you for that!"

Marcus darted away from Rindel, knowing this would be the best way to make a quick exit. But before they had crossed the field to the gatepost, where Marcus hoped to gather their things and saddle Tress, a couple of young men stopped them in their tracks.

"Where are you two going? The party's only just started!"

Rindel caught up with Marcus and patted him hard on the back.

"See, they don't want us to leave yet."

"Come on," said one of the lads, "maybe we could interest you in a barn dance?"

Marcus's shoulders sagged. The music was playing loudly, and laughter wafted through the air from the party. There was no way he was going to get Rindel to leave now. He felt strongly that they shouldn't go back, but he found himself giving in to Rindel's persuasion once more. "Well, I suppose just one dance wouldn't hurt."

They dropped their things and went back to the party.

As they began to form a group for the next dance, the sound of hooves distracted them, and a man on a black horse rushed toward them, his drawn sword gleaming in the early sunset hues.

Everyone scattered. The man looked fierce in his suit of armor, and he glared down at the crowd as though they were a bunch of criminals.

"Marcus Macmillan!" he announced.

"Yes, I, er, who are you?" stuttered Marcus.

The man's face was mostly hidden behind his helmet, but Marcus could see that he had startling green eyes and a broad mouth. Strands of light brown, spiky hair stuck out from one side of the helmet.

"I'm Jez Droy. You should pack up your things and be on your way at once."

"But why? We just—"

"There will always be another party, Marcus. Wryxl people do nothing but work, drink, and party. It's their way of life—but it is not for you. You will never get to your destination if you party every night! Follow me. We must get you back on PathOne!"

Rindel and Marcus looked at each other and promptly followed Jez, untying Tress on their way out of the field. Rindel thought Jez looked pretty cool, despite being another crazy follower of PathOne, and kept eyeing up his polished suit of armor. It was some consolation for being forced to leave the party.

No sooner had they gone than the music started up again, and they could hear the sounds of laughter and singing as they went.

* * *

Jez led them two or three miles out of Grentham toward a region of undulating hills. As they trotted along beside each other, maintaining a comfortable speed, Jez began to explain why he had come looking for them.

"I was at a tavern in the city to the east and overheard some patrollers on lookout for a young man of your description, Marcus, along

132

with a companion. Someone has reported that you have a copy of *The Book Beyond Time,* which makes you an automatic enemy of the empire. Did you not know that Treanthor has issued a permanent decree against PathOne and its followers? It was thought that all remaining copies of the book had been destroyed. Do you have any idea who saw you in possession of the ancient volume?"

Immediately Falk's name sprang to Marcus's mind—the friendly older man at the tavern the other evening in Grentham. He had seen the book in Marcus's possession and commented on it. But why would he have reported them? He had seemed favorable toward PathOne and its followers. It just didn't make sense. Who else could have been responsible?

"The reporters let slip something about a merchant in the city of Erundel," said Jez.

The blood drained from Marcus's face. Prelanor, the clothing vendor! He must have sneaked a peek through Marcus's belongings when he was following after the Emperor's entourage, and he would no doubt have spotted *The Book Beyond Time.* Marcus imagined that the merchant hadn't been happy about losing out on a sale after all the time he'd spent trying to help Marcus.

Rindel piped up, "See, you should have joined me at the saloon that night! Much safer to socialize with some happy drinkers!"

"You're not being helpful, Rindel!" retorted Marcus, scowling. "But Jez, I need to know: why did you come down here to rescue us from impending capture? Are you also defying Treanthor's decree?"

"Most certainly! There is a growing movement of us who are intent on following PathOne, and it is my mission to warn others of impending danger or to lead them to safety. Many of us have descended from the Treegle people. We're quite a stubborn bunch!"

That explains why my Mum wouldn't give up on the idea of PathOne—she also has Treegle blood in her! Marcus smiled inwardly before asking further questions.

"My mother didn't seem to know anything of any other PathOne followers still alive," Marcus said. "Her Treegle relatives who spoke of PathOne visited when she was young but never returned. Yet you speak of a growing movement?"

"We have to keep a low profile. It's hard to know who to trust and who will turn you in to the authorities. But there are small pockets of resistance springing up all over Krinton, all intent on pursuing PathOne. Treanthor is determined to stamp out any followers and destroy the book. He has managed to track down most copies and confiscate them. He doesn't want deserters from Krinton or people who will stir up others against his kingdom. You carry a rare treasure, my friend."

Rindel looked a little scared for the first time. "Maybe we should get rid of it," he said. "No sense carrying a thing like that around—it's just asking for trouble!"

Jez gave him a curious and disapproving look, but he didn't bother to reprimand him. Instead, he fixed his eyes on Marcus again. "It's not just the book that endangers you now—it's you yourself, Marcus. Treanthor will see you as especially important because you are the youngest follower of PathOne that we know of."

"But I've reached adulthood," Marcus stammered.

"Treanthor fears younger citizens starting to follow PathOne, since he knows that they will become more passionate about the cause, more likely to resist him. Wryxl people and other communities show contempt for the old and laugh at the things they value. People like you, Marcus, are very dangerous to Treanthor's empire. He knows that you could influence a whole generation of people away from him and into the Kingdom of the North."

Jez's face looked rugged and single-minded, and his eyes seemed to delve deep into Marcus's soul.

Marcus's mind was frantically sorting through everything he'd just been told. He was frightened, but underneath that, he felt a growing sense of importance and even strength—as though the power Merloy had touched him with was starting to make a difference inside him. "Now that we know we're being hunted down, what shall we do?"

"They won't be very far behind us," said Jez, picking up speed as they followed the hill path down into a wide valley. "I came across more patrollers in Grentham when I was looking for you. They are rarely seen in these rural parts of Krinton and are most definitely in pursuit of you."

Jez sounded concerned, but also confident. He looked as though he knew exactly where they were going. "They won't be familiar with the route I'm taking you, but you need to be sure of your pathway."

"What do you mean?" asked Marcus.

"I can only guide you some of the way," replied Jez. "Everyone on PathOne has his own distinct journey."

"But how can we protect ourselves when all we have is these swords?" whined Rindel.

"You will be equipped with armor when the time is necessary," came Jez's simple reply.

Once they passed through the valley, Jez pointed out the familiar narrow path at the foot of a dark hill. "That is the main route of PathOne, one you already know as well as I do. But there are other paths, lesser known—it is there I must take you now."

"Other paths? Doesn't that mean leaving Marcus's precious PathOne?" Rindel interrupted.

Jez humored him with a smile. "You need to remember that PathOne consists of several offshoots which twist and turn through all kinds of territory. Following it is not a simple journey—it will be the challenge of your life. And at times you'll lose your way and will need help getting back. Just don't give up, like many have done. Nothing great in life is attained by sitting back and taking it easy! You must focus on the final destination, that magnificent eternal kingdom. You don't just walk the way of PathOne; you live it and breathe it."

Rindel just looked more confused than before. Even Marcus found it hard to take in all that Jez had spoken. The words "challenge of your life" kept resounding over and over in Marcus's mind.

They rode in silence for another hour, at first paralleling the main route and then veering off in another direction. In the darkness, Marcus could make out little of their surroundings. He knew he'd be lost in a moment if he had to try to come back alone. Finally, Jez reined in his horse at a heap of boulders. He pointed out a narrow, barely visible path of stone gleaming in the moonlight.

"This is the route you'll take from here. I have to leave you now, but I'm sure you will journey well without me from here. Make sure you stick to the path. You'll find it leads westwards to the small town of Penryth, where the people weave wool and sell cloth. Rest there, but do not stay too long before continuing north. And don't stop reading the book. There is always more to discover about PathOne in its pages."

"Seems like a lot of strange stuff in that book, if you ask me," muttered Rindel under his breath.

"You are absolutely correct to question what it says," countered Jez. "Don't just take my word for it. Find out for yourself, and take time to dig deeply into the text. It's full of mysteries, but at the same time it is a simple message for all to understand—if only they will open their minds to the truth."

Rindel sighed heavily. There it was again—talk of "truth," that elusive word which described something he wasn't sure even existed. He couldn't believe he had missed an opportunity to dance with lots of beautiful girls—and all to get back to this stupid path!

Marcus thanked Jez for guiding them back to the route and on to their next destination, and he asked when they could meet again.

"That's not for me to say," said Jez. "Who knows if our destinies will collide once more? All I know is that you must stay true to the quest. I have come to you today to get you further along the path to the north, and to save you from the likes of Shurama—she is a force for evil and could cause your downfall. If I had not come for you this evening, she would have most likely persuaded you to settle in Grentham instead of following your destiny."

"The likes of Shurama? A force for evil? What could possibly be wrong with her? She doesn't look like she would kill a fly!" said Rindel.

Jez glared at Rindel before continuing his warnings. "Likewise, you should also watch out for the heavy force called *Santon*. Treanthor let it loose in this land long ago, and now that he knows of you, it will not be long before he sends it to attack you."

"Santon?" inquired Marcus.

"Yes . . . it is like a heavy spirit that will try to get you when you're feeling weak or down. Santon will try to rob you of your determination and make you weak. It's a persistent force that loves to discourage PathOne followers and make them feel useless and shameful. Whatever you do, don't give in. You have to fight it with what you know is true— you've been chosen for PathOne. But it's up to you to follow that calling. If you give up, you might never arrive at the Kingdom of the North."

"But how will I recognize Santon if it's unseen . . . a spirit?"

"You will know. It will try to flood your soul with guilt and despair. Now be on your way. Goodbye!"

Jez kicked his legs against his huge, dark horse and turned and rode away into the night shadows.

Rindel sighed heavily again, watching Jez as he left. "I'm really not sure about that Santon stuff—no one's ever spoken of that before. Sounds a bit weird to me."

He glanced at Marcus, who was dabbing his watery eyes with his shirtsleeve. Dust from Jez's departure had triggered his hay fever.

"Oh well, here we go again!" Rindel tried to sound chirpy, despite his disappointment at leaving the party. I hope we meet some girls!"

Marcus sniffed and then laughed. "You're probably in need of a good wash first!"

137

Chapter 11

A fierce wind blew around the two young men as Tress carried them out of dense woods and into a lush valley. They had been traveling for several days across difficult territory and hadn't seen a single soul. Their disappointment grew as they could not even catch sight of Penryth. Rindel had started to question its existence, saying, "Maybe Jez was just trying to make us feel better about taking this stupid path. Or perhaps we're actually on the wrong road." Marcus didn't like to think about Jez being wrong—he had seemed so certain—but secretly he wondered whether Rindel might be right. It felt as though they had been going in circles.

Marcus began to cough repeatedly as the cold wind blew against his open tunic, and he wished that he could drink his mother's hot ginger tea to soothe his sore throat. When he paused to tighten his neck scarf and button up his waistcoat, Rindel pointed out a familiar figure, waving at them in the distance. "It's Delan!" he exclaimed.

Marcus was instantly cheered, happy to see a welcoming face once more. "Hold on!" he instructed Rindel as he started to gallop as fast as he could across the valley toward Delan, who was leaning against a fence next to his horse.

"You're nearly there," announced Delan with confidence. "We just need to head across this valley and then we'll be in Penryth."

Rindel looked at Marcus, eyebrows raised to express his skepticism.

"We've been wandering around for four days, up and down hill, through virtual wasteland, forest and now valley, and now you're sure we're nearly there?" asked Rindel indignantly.

Delan looked back at Rindel and smiled. "Yes, I'm sure. My grandfather lives in Penryth, and he's just a short ride from this place. He sent a messenger to the village I was staying in, instructing me to come and find you here. The city is just hidden by those hills."

"Was the messenger someone named Jez?" asked Marcus, curious.

"No, but we know Jez well. He's one of our dearest family friends."

"So does this mean that you and he are part of the same resistance group against Treanthor's rule?"

"That's right. We're all part of the same network, supporting followers of PathOne and warning everyone of Krinton's destruction."

It was all starting to make some sense in Marcus's mind. He couldn't understand how Delan—or Jez for that matter—knew where to find them, but he had begun to accept that the journey of PathOne was a "mystery," just as Jez had explained a few days before. He was simply glad to know that they were not the only ones pursuing this strange path. It gave him a sense of security. Surely they could not *all* be terribly misguided?

The wind picked up some more, blowing Delan's hair in different directions. His horse stumbled slightly, uneasy about the impending storm as dark clouds moved faster toward them.

"Come on, lads, we need to hurry before we get caught in the storm."

Marcus was relieved that Delan was taking the lead. He was tired of Rindel's complaining and looked forward to staying in a proper home once again.

"Does your grandfather have a bathtub inside the house?" asked Rindel.

"He absolutely does," replied Delan. "But you'll have to haul some buckets of water in from the well at the end of his garden if you want to use it."

"Have you got a grandmother too?" inquired Marcus with a loud voice, trying to make sure he was heard over the sound of the wind.

"Yes!" shouted Delan back to him. "And she's a great cook! Makes the finest chicken and vegetable stew in Krinton!"

Marcus's mouth watered. They hadn't eaten much in the last few days, mainly fruit and nuts and some stale bread from Grentham.

Delan picked up speed across the valley, and Marcus was glad that Tress was happy to follow suit without showing any signs of nervousness. It felt good to ride at this pace after struggling along over rocky terrain and hills for days.

As they followed the path around a huge curve between the hills, they immediately saw the small city of Penryth, attractive and clean, with houses made of stone and thatched roofs with smoke ascending from red-clay chimney pots. The oak smell from wood-burning stoves was pleasant and reminded the boys of home. They couldn't see many people in the streets—most had likely returned home to avoid the storm. Only a man selling vegetables and flowers from a cart on the main street remained, though he too had started to pack up.

As they reached the vendor on the cobblestone street, Delan paused to buy a large bunch of purple flowers with leaves that smelled faintly of mint.

"My grandma will like these!" he said with a grin.

Rindel wondered aloud whether the man had any fresh bread.

"Sorry, only vegetables. The bakers have just gone."

Rindel groaned. "Oh, how could we miss the bakers? I'm dying for a fresh, crusty loaf."

"You'll be dying of other things if you hang about when the storm comes, lad," said Delan. "I remember one drunk man slumped in the street who came to ruin when a chimney pot fell on his head. What a sorry sight next morning! Come on, let's go."

Delan trotted his horse slowly through the village until they reached a huge well in the square. There he dismounted, motioning for the boys to do the same, and guided them through a dark, narrow lane. The end of the lane reached an archway, through which Delan led his friends, leading them into a neatly kept yard.

"Grandpa!" announced Delan in a cheery tone. "You have visitors!"

As they tied up their horses in the yard, a man in a huge cloak appeared, his face mostly shielded by a hood. The heavens suddenly opened, and heavy rain began to pour down.

"Ah, Delan, it's good to see you again! And I see you have found your friends," the man said, glancing at the other two. "Quickly, come inside."

Marcus cocked his head. Why did the man seem familiar?

They followed him into the warm kitchen, removing their boots by the door. Delan's grandfather removed his hood and said, "Welcome to my home!"

Marcus and Rindel stared at the man and then looked at each other.

"Brayman?" said Marcus.

"Yes, it is I."

Brayman reached out his arm to rigorously shake Marcus's hand. His eyes looked intensely into the shocked boy's face, just as on that afternoon at Horcum Hill when he had rescued Rindel from the claws of the gratsch.

As their hands clasped, Marcus felt a minor jolt of power rush up his arm and through his body. He recognized the feeling—it was the same power he had felt when Merloy visited him in Stanrul's garden. Though it was less forceful this time, Marcus knew immediately that Brayman must know Merloy too.

He watched closely as Rindel shook hands with Brayman, but Rindel showed no signs of having experienced anything strange. If anything, he treated the old man with suspicion.

Brayman's wife, a short woman with long, graying hair, entered the room and smiled warmly at Delan.

"Grandmother. I bought these flowers for you."

"Thank you. It's so good to see you, Delan; it's been a while. What have you been up to, dear young man?"

"I've been training these young gentlemen, Grandma, and others too. Meet Marcus and Rindel."

The boys smiled at her, not knowing whether to shake her hand. She stepped forward and patted them both warmly on the arm.

"Welcome. My name is Magreanne. Come, sit by the fire. I'm making a big stew, and it should be ready very soon."

They all followed her into the adjoining room, where a huge painting of a house on a rock hung on the wall. In the background of the faded painting was a cliff path down to the sea, the shore covered with pebbles. Magreanne placed the flowers into a vase on a large oak table as they found seats around the fire. Outside, rain was beginning to patter the windows.

Marcus stared at the painting, trying to imagine the sea. All around Krinton, high walls had been erected along the shores to prevent anyone leaving—or possibly anyone arriving. People had grown up to fear the sea, with tales told of the Great Catastrophe when the waters turned deadly and dark, killing thousands who drank from it once all the wells and rivers had run dry. Treanthor declared that all other lands had been wiped out, leaving only savages and monstrous creatures who would try to invade Krinton. But something about this painting drew Marcus's imagination and made him long to see the ocean for himself.

"Grandpa, how do you know my friends?" Delan asked.

Brayman winked at Rindel. "Do you want to tell the tale, Rindel?"

Rindel looked sheepish. "I've already told him the story about the gratsch. Delan, you remember the part where a stranger rescued me? Well, that was your grandfather."

"It was you, Grandpa?" asked Delan, astonished. "I thought you were no longer active in battle."

"Well, sometimes I still need to respond to a challenge. There are not enough people willing to step forward and take my place in our mission. If I had not been journeying that day, who knows what would have become of these two? I have to follow my calling, Delan."

"Your calling?" said Marcus, intrigued. "I've heard of that before . . . does everyone get called?" The more Brayman spoke, the more Marcus felt drawn to him. Somehow, he knew deeply that this man's home was nothing like the Wryxl village of Grentham.

Brayman held his hands together and looked Marcus in the eye.

"Everybody is called to follow PathOne and to find their destiny therein. But few will choose to take up the challenge and complete their life's quest. Everyone's ultimate purpose in life can be found by pursuing the ways of PathOne, and those who follow it have a common bond that unites them beyond family ties. We are all in this together, friends."

Marcus and Rindel fixed their gaze on Brayman, whose hands rested on his knees. His voice began to quiver as he blinked several times. He seemed very emotional.

"I am thankful that at last, Delan has befriended other young men who will walk away from Treanthor's Era of Pleasure and seek the better kingdom."

Rindel spoke up. "Why is the Kingdom of the North the better kingdom? What can it promise that is better than the future we have been promised here in Krinton?"

Brayman's wife brought food and a huge jug of water to the table. The smell was amazing, but for once, even Rindel was staying focused on the conversation.

Brayman laughed. "If only you knew. Treasures in Krinton are like worthless trinkets compared to the diamond gems to be found in the north."

"Diamonds?" said Rindel, his eyes wide.

"I speak in metaphors, dear boy. Even diamonds cannot compare to the riches you can gain on PathOne."

As they ate a hearty chicken and vegetable stew—remarkably good, as Delan had promised—Brayman began to explain some of the history of Krinton and how Treanthor had seized power. He talked about the brave Treegle knights of old, who had risked their all to defy him. Men like Vowter, Delan's great-uncle, who had lost his life in a gruesome battle at Erundel. Vowter had refused to join Treanthor's forces and fought for an equal government that promoted freedom of choice— something very foreign to Treanthor's principles of absolute authority.

"Treanthor has ruled for three generations. It is believed that he will never die, as he has sourced a unique formula of edible xanth crystals to sustain him. Only he knows the exact source of these special crystals, and rumor has it that if the formula is slightly altered, it will kill him rather than sustain him. This is why he closely monitors the production of xanth. If the ordinary people get hold of it, they too could invent all sorts of things or find a way to live forever. Of course, he does not tell them that.

"But *forever* in Krinton is not a positive future. Krinton may appear to be making progress. But its progress is based only on becoming more wealthy and getting more things. And these things will not last. Nor can Treanthor's Era of Pleasure—which promises endless happiness, yet leaves people feeling sad and empty after a while. They continually long for the next visit to a grench port, or for the latest shiny gadget, but shortly later their happiness has gone. That is why you find few men of my age there. They have learned that happiness here cannot be bought or experienced for long. But those who seek answers elsewhere are encouraged to sniff sekrin, to forget about their fears and not to bother with rumors of PathOne. But they need to know that Krinton will not continue forever. The time is short, and one day it will be utterly destroyed. Anyone who tries to hold on to what remains will try only in vain."

Marcus recalled his vision of Trynn Goth disintegrating all around him. He interrupted. "Tell us about PathOne. We've been following it, and yet there's still so much I don't understand about it. Has it always existed? What about before the Great Catastrophe?"

Brayman smiled. "As you have learned, PathOne is more than the physical road you've been following. It's also a way of life — the right way of life. The book describes it as a 'transformation' as well as a journey, but it also describes the road as a 'narrow way' which needs to be found and followed. It has existed since the beginning of time, when it was clear and uncluttered. But various cultures emerged over time and rejected the way of PathOne. They built cities on top of the road and made new paths, massive highways that could take you quickly anywhere you wanted. Kings and leaders didn't like PathOne, because there was talk of a greater leader in the Kingdom of the North who would overthrow all other kingdoms. They did not wish their people to go and seek him. They found that if they could distract people with other pursuits — like getting bigger houses and fine things to put in them — or if they simply spread the word that PathOne was nonsense, just a fairy tale, then people would ignore it and would give their all to serve the leader of the land.

"PathOne used to be the way of the majority, but now it is the way of only a few. Everyone wanted an easy life, an easy path to follow, and they gave up on PathOne. The obstacles along the way discouraged them from sticking to the path. And as many fell away, it became difficult being the odd one out in a family or community. It is always easier to follow everyone else than to stick to the original path, but doing as you please does not bring peace of mind. Such peace is one of the diamonds of the kingdom. It cannot be bought or traded, and so there is increasing uncertainty and fear in people's hearts. They just don't want to admit it to others, because they fear that people will laugh at them or reject them."

Brayman looked at each of the boys in turn, his eyes stern but kind. His glance rested on Rindel as he said, "It's not much fun to be around a serious person who is questioning the meaning of your existence! 'Tis

146

easier by far to simply join in with the current pursuits of the world, or to take sekrin to help you forget about all your concerns. People think that to be happy is the point of life. But they are entirely misguided. The point of one's life is to know one's purpose and to follow it wholeheartedly. But your destiny can only be found in one of two places: either you will follow PathOne, or you will follow the way of Krinton. Of course, Krinton appears to have several options or ways of life—but ultimately they are all the same and lead to emptiness of soul."

Rindel gobbled up his last piece of bread and spoke up, seemingly oblivious to the challenge in Brayman's tone. "I want to know more about these knights of old. Where did they come from? Did they win many battles?"

"Ah, the knights," Brayman said, leaning back as if he were settling in for a long story. "Originally, all knights adhered to the rules of PathOne—they looked after the community and protected the weak and the poor. Knights were honest and just. They fought against the jeruni, against gratsches, and against the Bevrugi and Tolsiqs—violent tribes of thieves and marauders. They helped the world begin to rebuild after the Great Catastrophe."

Brayman grimaced. "Then one knight arose who demanded special treatment. He wanted to be the leader. He claimed that he could protect the people better than any other, but he required them to give up their freedoms in exchange. Many did—the Wryxl were first. His name was Treanthor."

"I know that story," Rindel interrupted. "The people saw the wisdom in Treanthor's ways and hailed him as leader. Besides, he was so powerful—more powerful than anyone else in Krinton!"

Brayman shook his head. "But have you ever wondered about the source of that power?"

Rindel started to answer but shut his mouth. Marcus and Delan were listening with rapt interest.

"Few know the truth of it," Brayman said, "but I will tell it to you. In a vision, a strange spirit came to Treanthor and said that if he drank the blood of a vulture, he would become the most powerful man in Krinton. He did so, and the next day another vulture brought him a tiny xanth crystal from a crag in a high rock. The vulture spoke to him and told him to liquefy the crystal and drink it. When he did this, his mind became consumed by all sorts of evil, selfish plans—plans to see the people of the land become weak servants who would follow his every command while he lived in luxury. It's the reason why he chose the vulture to feature on the new kroen coins thirteen years ago. He's obsessed by the birds. Treanthor sold his soul for power over Krinton, and ever since, no one has been able to overthrow him or defy him completely.

"The other knights resisted at first. They held on to several counties for over fifty years. But Treanthor's forces grew—especially when he offered them the latest technology and highly paid apprenticeships. Eventually, most of the former knights died trying to resist him or decided to join forces with him. Those men lost sight of their high principles and commitment to help others; instead, they too wanted power and prestige."

Rindel shuffled on his wooden chair and looked inquisitively at Brayman. "But who should we follow if Treanthor is all that bad?"

Brayman looked seriously at Rindel before meeting eyes with Marcus. "Have you not met Merloy yet?"

Marcus coughed and nodded.

Rindel frowned. "Who? Merloy? Never heard of him."

Brayman leaned back on his chair and held his chin in his hand. "Ah, I see. Let me explain it to you . . . Merloy is our guide out of Krinton. He is, in fact, the ancient king of the north. He only befriends those who believe *The Book Beyond Time* and follow PathOne, and he is the one who will ultimately defeat Treanthor. He is looking for those who will stand up to the Wryxl way of life and the lies that Treanthor spreads, and he reveals truth to those who search for it. He has promised real life to those who are not afraid to follow the book. For this world here in Krinton is only temporary. It is not a permanent home for us."

Marcus interrupted as soon as Brayman paused. "But we met a man, Stanrul, a very kind and helpful man who let us stay in his house, and he insisted that PathOne was a fairy tale and that we were stupid to follow it or read the book."

"That is *precisely* what Treanthor wants people to think," said Brayman. "If he can make followers of PathOne appear to be foolish and outdated, then no one will bother to even find out about it, to see for themselves whether the book is true. Most people will just readily listen to others' opinions without properly finding things out for themselves. No one wants to appear stupid or crazy. But that is indeed what you will be called by the majority of Wryxl—indeed, by nearly everyone in Krinton."

"Nobody's going to call me stupid!" said Rindel indignantly.

Brayman ignored Rindel's comment, focusing his eyes on Marcus. "Are you willing to risk the ridicule of those around you for the sake of the truth found in the book?"

Marcus looked down at his hands, fidgeting with an old, silver napkin ring. "I don't know. I hope so."

Rindel spoke up. "Brayman, you said that PathOne is the only way to save us from the coming destruction. But how are people supposed to find things out for themselves when most people haven't heard of *The Book Beyond Time,* and most people can't even read well anymore? Surely it's unfair that so many people won't find out about the wonderful Kingdom of the North?"

Brayman looked thoughtfully at the boys across the table.

"Followers of PathOne, as you know, are not welcome in Krinton. Trenathor's officials have been instructed to report back on any rumors or sightings of individuals who carry or mention *The Book Beyond Time.* He sees it as a threat to his own kingdom, and his knights have already destroyed most other knights who opposed his rule. Treanthor also controls the jeruni—those nuisance birds that like to interrupt conversations. They have been trained to listen out for any talk of PathOne in public places and follow those people on their journeys. Many have been distracted from continuing their journey because of them, joining in with their endless, mindless chatter.

"Those who are in possession of a rare, ancient copy of the book are generally aware of the need to keep this secret from others. Only if you are completely sure that you can trust someone should you say anything about *The Book Beyond Time.*"

"How can we know who to trust?" said Marcus. He winced inwardly, his conversation with the Wryxl people in the tavern still fresh in his mind. He had almost certainly said too much. If he'd harbored any hopes that Treanthor didn't know about him, they were fast slipping away.

"You will soon learn to recognize who is trustworthy and who is not. And you will see that some people genuinely want to find answers and not just argue with you about everything. They will see that there is something different about you, and they will want to find out more."

"Yes, but how can we give them the book to see for themselves when we only have one copy? And Marcus says the pages are starting to fall apart already!" Rindel interjected with some exasperation.

"I was just getting to that," said Brayman calmly. "There are obviously more copies, although most were destroyed during the Great Catastrophe and are now buried under the rubble along with everything else. Most others were seized and discarded by Treanthor's knights. I and others in the resistance have begun to print more on handmade machines and tried to spread them throughout Krinton, but Treanthor is always quick to find and destroy them, and he has destroyed most of our secret print shops over time as well. However, most followers of PathOne now have a better way to learn about the north."

Marcus and Rindel stared at him and Delan before casting frowning glares at each other.

"Do you mean through communicating with Merloy?" asked Marcus.

Brayman smiled. "No, I mean through a special device that was invented just two years ago. Though you would do well to communicate with Merloy every day, at dusk—or whenever you pause to rest on your journey."

Brayman inserted his hand inside his cloak and pulled out a tiny silver item that looked like a stone or kernel. He inserted it into Marcus's ear and pressed it.

Marcus pulled away, a little alarmed. His minor fear soon turned to awe as he heard the voice of Brayman speaking words from *The Book Beyond Time* through the earpiece.

"I can hear your voice!" he said, amazed. "How did you do that? Delan, why didn't you tell me about this?"

"You didn't ask!" said Delan. "Besides, those old books are treasures—we should value them even if we don't necessarily need them."

"That's right," Magreanne put in. "I'll always prefer reading a book, myself."

"How did you make this?" asked Marcus, taking out the stone-like device and placing it into Rindel's ear. "Is it powered by xanth?"

"Of course, how else?"

"But how could you possibly have gotten it approved by Treanthor's panel of official inventors at the NewTech Department?"

"It's not approved at all. But a lady, a former cook at his citadel, snatched a large pile of xanth crystals from him before fleeing to live in the hills. There she met an ironmonger, a follower of PathOne who owned a copy of the book. As he told her more about the Kingdom of the North, she was convinced it was all true and begged him to teach her to read. When she revealed that she could pay him in xanth crystals, the ironmonger realized he had a golden opportunity to find a new way to spread the messages of the book. He spent six months testing out various devices before inventing the earpiece you now see. He visited Magreanne and me, requesting that I record my voice for the text. I happily obliged."

Delan interrupted. "Since he does have a voice that's timeless, you know!" He winked at Rindel, who frowned back at him, somewhat perplexed.

"Unique, timeless voice . . . *The Book Beyond Time!*" Delan emphasized the last word.

"Oh, I get it," answered Rindel.

"But couldn't you get into trouble for this?" asked Marcus seriously.

"Of course!" replied Brayman. "Anyone who decides to pursue the way of PathOne risks getting into trouble with officials. Our way is not for the fainthearted—as I'm sure Delan has shown you already. Why do you think he took the time to train you in horse riding and swordplay? PathOne is not for cowards. It is the way of the brave, those who are willing to stand out from the rest and follow their convictions with all their hearts."

Marcus took the earpiece from Rindel and held it between his thumb and forefinger, marveling that such a tiny thing could contain the whole of *The Book Beyond Time*.

"Can I keep this?"

Brayman smiled at him. "I've been waiting to give it to you. I had it specially made in silver for you."

The rain pounded down on the roof, splashing down onto the window panes and hitting the windowsill with force.

"And you'll be glad to know that it's waterproof."

"Awesome!" grinned Marcus. "That's just amazing. My mum would never believe it! What do you call this thing?"

"We've called it a podbook," replied Brayman. "I have one for you, Marcus, and also for Delan, who lost his in the River Quinn last year."

Rindel was impressed, but he thought to himself that the grench port in Erundel was more worthy of the word "awesome" than this little device with Brayman's voice rambling on—even if his voice, with its distinct regional accent, was timeless. *Maybe we can trade the earpiece later on in our journey?*

"Just be careful not to part with it," said Brayman as he stood to leave the room. He glanced over his shoulder at Marcus. "If Treanthor hears of it, he will track down our production facility and put an end to it."

Brayman swept his cloak aside as he went through the door. As he walked along the wooden corridor, the young men heard him yawning loudly.

"It's bedtime for old men like me!" he called back.

The boys laughed. It was only around nine. Delan had promised them a game of cards earlier, and they certainly wouldn't be going to bed until they had played a round or two.

No sooner had they dealt out the cards than they heard the sound of shuffling footsteps along the corridor. Marcus and Rindel were surprised to look up and see an attractive, dark-haired girl around their age pop her head through the door. Rubbing her eyes, she looked as if she had just woken up. Despite her messy, dark locks and frowning eyes, Marcus thought she looked incredibly beautiful.

"Delan? You're back? Who are these guys?"

"Ah, Keriss, good to see you again!" smiled Delan. "This is Marcus, and his friend Rindel. They're new followers of PathOne. Keriss is my younger cousin—she lives here with my grandfather."

Keriss glanced at the visitors, trying to raise a faint smile before yawning. "I'm sorry I can't join in your game, I need to go back to bed— I've been ill the last few days. Good to meet you both, though."

She held her gaze just slightly longer on Marcus before leaving the room again, and Marcus was certain he felt his heart quicken at the sight of her. He felt himself blushing slightly. He wanted to talk about her, to find out some things about her, but he was too embarrassed to say anything to Delan in front of Rindel.

They resumed their game, but Marcus kept thinking about Keriss, hoping that they might see her again.

After Rindel lost two games and stormed off to bed in a bad mood, Delan moved closer to Marcus and opened the book.

"Have you ever read this section?" he asked, opening the book just a few pages from the end.

"No, I don't think so," Marcus said curiously. "I mostly skimmed over some of the pages at the end. I'm trying to read through from the beginning, but it takes a long time."

Delan's eyes sparkled as he looked at Marcus. "This is my favorite part. It describes the final journey of PathOne, right before reaching the Kingdom of the North. See here; it describes a strange, desolate place of huge boulders you need to cross. 'Once you pass through this valley of rocks, you will know the destination is near, and all you have believed for so long will come into being. The city of lights awaits you. You need only to walk into the full, sun-cast shadows of my vast rock face, and I will lead you through. If you face resistance or trouble, keep on going, don't turn back.'"

Marcus followed Delan's finger across the page as he read the intriguing words.

"But do you know anyone who has ever come across this place of huge rocks? Does Brayman know of it?"

"He knows of it, but no, he has never found it yet. He says that his great-uncle spoke of reaching the desolate valley, but he was driven back by a fierce wind. Merloy once told me that if I am faithful to PathOne, I will not be disappointed—I will reach this valley and make great progress toward his Kingdom. I hold on to that hope every day, Marcus.

It's what keeps me going with this quest; it's what drives me along those rotten, unkempt paths every day."

Marcus marked the page by folding over its top corner and put it away again in his bag. "Merloy told me that he was the king of the north, but we know so little about him. Do you know anything more about him, or could he just be a messenger from that kingdom?"

Delan's eyes widened. "Merloy created the Kingdom of the North. It's been his plan all along for people like you and me to find it—but only if we truly want to be with him."

As he went to sleep that night, Marcus couldn't stop thinking about what Delan had said. *Merloy wants people to be with him in his Kingdom of the North.* When Marcus thought of Merloy, his power, and the way he had made Marcus feel like he had a father again, he knew that he wanted it too. *But why is it such a riddle to find the place?*

Chapter 12

A hissing sound, followed by a thud, alerted Marcus to activity beyond his window. Peering through the scratchy pane, he watched Keriss pull back another arrow, ready to take aim at a target hung on a tree trunk in the corner of Brayman's back yard. Impressed by her skill, he mouthed a silent 'not bad', when he saw how accurate her aim was. He was disappointed that after only two days getting to know her, Delan had announced that it was time for them to move on.

They had certainly refreshed themselves at Brayman's house, filling themselves with Magreanne's hearty meals and freshly pressed apple juice. Marcus had enjoyed the time getting to know Delan's relatives and had fun playing several challenging card games. Keriss had joined them some of the time, and Marcus found out that she too believed *The Book Beyond Time*—in fact, she was involved in helping Brayman print new books and distribute podbooks. Delan had praised his cousin for her archery skills, having been trained by Brayman himself, but Marcus didn't really believe it until he had seen her practice outside. Even Tress looked healthier after a well-deserved rest. She had made the most of an unlimited supply of fresh hay and been pleased to relax alongside Opus, Delan's horse.

After packing up and saying their goodbyes, the three friends chatted non-stop as they traveled through the city. Marcus and Delan discussed everything Brayman had told them and shared thoughts about what they had discovered in *The Book Beyond Time.* Delan seemed to know the book inside out and could even retell obscure or funny parts of the text. Marcus didn't know that such a serious book could contain so many funny stories, and he tried to get Rindel to listen too.

Rindel, however, was distracted by a swarm of green flies that kept getting stuck in his wild hair. He clutched a parcel of bread rolls and flapjacks as though his life depended on it and thought to himself that finding a bakery must become a priority wherever they journeyed. He had thought about asking Magreanne to travel with them so that she could prepare food, but he knew that Brayman would allow no such thing, especially if they should wander into gratsch territory again.

On the other side of the city, Delan led them away from the main street and through the courtyard of what appeared to be the remains of a castle. Marcus imagined how majestic it must have appeared before being destroyed in the Catastrophe. Now there remained mostly only the low rubble of the original walls.

"Hey, Delan, can you imagine the kinds of battles that would have been fought here centuries ago? Has Brayman ever—"

"Argh, watch out!" yelled Rindel as he ducked, narrowly avoiding being hit by a large stone.

Delan turned to see a group of men lurching toward them, some coming from the street they'd just left, a couple more hiding behind a pile of rubble just up ahead. Two carried yellow-handled ska-swords; the others brandished sticks and stones.

"Head back to the city!" yelled Delan. Marcus reined Tress around, but another rock hit him in the shoulder, making him wince in pain. Another rock hit Tress, who startled and jolted backward. Marcus was thrown from his saddle and landed on his leg, twisting his ankle. He gave a shout of pain.

Rindel was nearly thrown off too, but he managed to pull himself back up. Red-faced with anger, he hurled a bread roll at one of the attackers. It bounced off the man's head. The bandit laughed.

"Is that all you've got? Bread rolls? Ha ha ha!"

"No, it's not!" shouted Rindel defiantly, reaching for his ska-sword. Another man saw him, took careful aim, and threw a rock so expertly that it hit Rindel's hand, causing him to drop the sword.

"I think you're outnumbered, young man!" the bandit shouted. "Come now, we don't want trouble. Give us your money, and we'll let you go."

Delan had stopped several yards away, and he scanned the scene with concern. Marcus hadn't gotten back to his feet, and his leg was still twisted beneath him.

"We surrender!" announced Delan with his hands in the air.

"What are you thinking?" Rindel shouted. "We can easily beat these thugs! They don't even have horses!"

Delan ignored Rindel and approached the attackers, whose faces were partly covered by neck scarves. They were likewise ignoring the noisy young man on the horse.

"Who's in charge here?" shouted Delan.

"I am," said a man with a husky voice and tattooed arms. His sleeveless tunic revealed a menacing tattooed dragon which weaved its way from his wrist to nearly his shoulder, where the beast's mouth spewed out something like a chewed-up dog.

"Give us your money and I'll let you go," he demanded gruffly.

"Only if you promise not to harm our horses."

"Done," said the leader of the gang.

Marcus lay on the ground in intense pain, but he still wanted to get up and beat his attackers. Only his sense of Delan's control over the situation prevented him from interfering.

Delan reached into the back pocket of his long tunic, his left hand still in the air. He retrieved a small, brown leather purse and threw it to the man with the dragon. He then got down and pulled Marcus up onto his horse.

"Wait a minute," growled the chief thug, who proceeded to check the contents of the purse. "Is that all you've got?"

"I have one more coin under my saddle. Here," said Delan, retrieving a kroen from a hidden pouch. He threw it at the man before motioning to Rindel that they should make a hasty exit.

"That's all you're getting," said Delan as he turned and made speedily back toward the main city gate. Rindel followed in close

159

pursuit, hoping he wasn't about to get hit by a rock. But they escaped easily, the robbers happy with their purse full of coins.

Once back in the city, Rindel quizzed Delan over giving up so easily.

Delan winked at him. "Have you never heard of counterfeit coins? I always keep a supply in my back pocket when I'm traveling."

"Counterfeit coins? Where did you get hold of them?"

"My grandfather knows an ex-convict who can make them for him. He's turned away two sets of robbers already with them. Brain over brawn, you see, my friend."

"But what about the poor merchants who'll be fooled into giving their goods for worthless money?"

"Ah, Rindel, the merchants aren't so stupid as the robbers! They always check the money they're handed; you don't need to worry about them. We just need to hide away and keep a low profile for a few days in case the bandits come after us. They won't be happy once they find out my trick."

"Where will we go?"

"Back to my grandparents." Delan cast a worried glance over his shoulder. Marcus was pale and having trouble staying on the horse. "Marcus needs to recover."

* * *

Back in Penryth, Magreanne expressed surprise at seeing them again so soon. But Brayman was not home, and she said he had left in a hurry and had no idea when he'd return.

Delan suspected that he had gone off on another mission. Deciding that he didn't want to risk Magreanne's safety in case the robbers were to track them down, he decided to take Marcus and Rindel to his cousin's house in the city center instead.

Delan's cousin, Farlack, lived in a three-room dwelling above a butcher's shop and beside a jeweler's. The dwelling also included

Farlack's own store—a modern gadgetry shop selling all the latest inventions, both big and small.

Delan's cousin was delighted to have visitors and introduced himself with much enthusiasm.

"Welcome, my friends! I do hope you will stay long enough to help me sell to passersby! The frequent storms of late have kept many townsfolk and visitors away. Tell me, cousin, what brings you back to Penryth? I heard that you were here, but rumor had it you were leaving today."

Delan appeared a little embarrassed as he explained how they had been set upon by robbers and that Marcus had badly injured his ankle. But Farlack was very understanding and found Marcus a comfortable seat with a footstool by the window. He brought them a large clay jug of freshly made apple juice, insisting that they rest from their ordeal before apologizing that he couldn't chat any longer as it was time to open his shop. He invited Rindel to join him.

Rindel didn't hesitate for a moment, but jumped up immediately and followed Farlack into the shop. He gasped when he saw the shelves stacked with intriguing and glistening weapons, games, and gadgetry. He had not seen such an impressive display in Erundel, mainly for lack of time to visit every merchant. But here was every type of gadget he could ever wish for. The walls were cleverly painted to resemble the inside of a grench port.

Farlack busied himself behind his cash box and began to straighten up items on shelves. He was a lean man with blond, slicked-back hair which parted roughly in the middle. He wore a sapphire stud in each ear and three silver rings on his right hand. His clothes were all charcoal gray and tight fitting, with even his waistcoat tightly buttoned up. Rindel thought he looked distinctly cool.

"Is that a new knarl-knife?" he asked as he looked over Farlack's shoulder to the weapon he pulled out from under the counter.

"Yes, I was the first merchant to sell these in Krinton, as far as I know. I got my orders in first for all the latest NewTech inventions, you see. This version of the knife has the fastest flick mechanism ever."

"Wow," was all Rindel could think of replying.

He looked around at other shelves. "And you've got loads of torbs — they look fun."

"That's because they're my most popular item. I should hopefully sell at least five today."

A torb was an unevenly shaped disc that was rough on one side and smooth on the other. They were popular gifts for children who would spend hours throwing them sideways across rivers or lakes. The discs would bounce effortlessly across the surface of the water, producing amazing rings of water before hitting a tree or the other side of the river and then floating back slowly. Children would run along the river's edge or beside the lake to retrieve their brightly colored toys.

"Awesome." Rindel's eyes lit up as he spotted a wall of fishing rods. "Can I have a go with one of these kixans?"

"Yes, but handle it carefully. I'll make you pay for it if you break it."

Rindel handled the unique fishing rod as though it were a delicate crystal vase. His eyes widened in amazement at the clever design of the spin feature on the handle. He had heard that you could catch five fish in quick succession with the special mechanism, saving all the frustration of regular rods. Farlack watched him as he fiddled with the spin feature.

"Unfortunately I don't sell many of those, since people were starting to contract illnesses if they ate too much fish from the still-contaminated waters in most of this region. In some areas farther north, there are no fish to be caught at all."

"But fishing's still fun!" replied Rindel. "Even if you can't take the catch back for dinner. I'd love one of these."

The ringing of a bell alerted him to the arrival of a customer. Rindel quickly placed the kixan back on the shelf and smiled at the young man who had entered the shop.

"I'm looking for a new hammer," said the customer.

"Oh yes, we have some fine ones over here," said Rindel enthusiastically. He looked across at Farlack, who smiled and nodded at him to continue.

Rindel led the man to the back of the shop and pointed out a row of xanth-powered hammers that would double the strength of each blow.

"May I recommend this one?" said Rindel, passing the man a chrome-handled hammer. "It's a wonderful choice for any discerning young man, and see here—that extra light is only found on this latest design. It means you can continue working after dusk, without having to return home for a lantern. And if you press here," Rindel paused to show the man a tiny button in the end of the handle, "the hammer will retract into a smaller, handier size. See, now it can fit into your pocket easily."

The man looked impressed, handled it briefly, and said, "Yes, I'll take it, thank you."

Rindel led him to pay at the large mahogany counter. Farlack greeted him with a friendly smile and said, "You will like this invention, I'm sure. I have one myself, and it's very useful. Can I interest you in anything else?"

The man declined, but thanked him and left the shop.

Farlack grinned at Rindel. "I think you have the natural talent to be a salesman. You did a great job with that customer."

Rindel beamed with pride. He imagined owning his own shop one day, never to return to the foundry—or the road north—again.

"I just have to tell Marcus all about these gadgets. He'll never believe it!"

Rindel rushed back into the living room, where Marcus was slumped in his chair, nearly asleep.

Rindel shook him, and Marcus groaned in pain. He motioned for Rindel to leave him alone, so Rindel decided to search for a snack in the kitchen instead. He found some currant buns in a cupboard and called out to ask Farlack if he could have one.

"Only if you help me with some more customers later," called back Farlack.

"Okay, no problem," said Rindel, already tucking into the delicious bun, which was covered in sticky lemon icing.

While Delan tended to the horses in the street, Rindel ate two more buns and then returned to the shop, where he engaged with customers, persuading them to buy various gadgets. He was excellent at convincing people that various objects were just what they needed.

When Marcus awoke, he hobbled into the shop and found a stool to sit on. He watched and listened as Farlack and Rindel engaged customers in conversation and showed them how things worked. Marcus began to scan the shelves, deciding what he liked best and thinking that he would have to trade something with Farlack before he left.

He decided that he liked the fawb torch most of all, as it rolled down neatly into a pocket-sized shape and would be useful on their journey. A fawb not only contained a xanth-powered light which never ran out, it also doubled as a lighter—it could start a fire anywhere, without the need for kindling.

But the sunglasses which had a zoom feature, allowing you to see over a mile away, were a close second. He wanted to dash around the shop with Rindel and have a turn with each gadget, but his ankle was too painful to stand on. He would just have to rest.

Delan came in after a while and found Marcus, and he made him recline in the living room again with his leg raised. He fashioned a bandage out of an old shirt and tied it firmly around Marcus's ankle.

"Ow," complained Marcus with a frown. "Is that really necessary?"

"It is if you want your ankle to heal faster," said Delan. "And you'll have to keep off your feet for several days."

Marcus scowled. He hated sitting around.

"Well, can you at least get Rindel to show me some of those gadgets in the shop? I'll be bored stiff otherwise."

"You could always pop in your new podbook and listen a while. It's good preparation for the journey, you know."

"Mmm, yup, I'll do that later," said Marcus. "Rindel! Where are you?"

Rindel rushed into the room, holding a currant bun.

"You always find the best food first!" jested Marcus.

"This one's for you. I've had three already."

"You greedy piglet! I hope there are more for the others."

"Er, I'm not sure about that. But I can buy some more later."

Marcus asked Rindel to show him some things from the shop and from the high shelves in the living room, which were also packed with interesting games and devices. Farlack had countless little cupboards behind chairs and tables, each one filled with amazing inventions.

Rindel brought him a game in a shiny tin. Inside were four large flashing dice which alternated their colors, along with a black-and-white board. It was something like draughts, but much more fun. He and Rindel played for a while before Rindel said he should get back to help Farlack in the shop.

"I'll see if he doesn't mind you handling some things from the stock."

"Great, thanks," replied Marcus.

Marcus nodded off again, waiting for Rindel to return. It was nearly dinnertime when Rindel finally came back to the living room, his arms laden with gadgets.

"Farlack says you can take a look at these, as they're for customer demonstrations. You'll love these," said Rindel, holding up a pair of neon ropes. "They can recoil neatly in just a second or two with a sharp flick of the wrist—look! And how about this little beauty?" Rindel held up a bright orange, shiny ball. "It doesn't matter where you throw it, it will always bounce back to you—as long as no one intervenes and stops it. Look!"

Rindel threw the ball behind Marcus and into the corridor. Amazingly, it bounced up high and made its way back into Rindel's hands.

"How cool is that? I love all this NewTech stuff."

Rindel was beaming like a loon. He explained that the ball used xanth technology and contained a special homing code. He handed it to Marcus, who threw it out the open window.

Marcus heard the ball land on the street outside and then gasped when it whizzed back through the window toward his open hand.

"Incredible!"

* * *

Over the next few days, Marcus began to get used to this season of rest and relaxation. Rindel showed him every possible game and gadget, and he found countless ways to occupy his time. He knew that Delan was keeping an eye out for patrollers or other threats, and under his protection, Jez's warnings felt less ominous. Even when his ankle had started to heal and the pain was almost gone, Marcus didn't attempt to do much. He was growing accustomed to having a long afternoon nap, and he would stay up till after midnight playing one game or another with Rindel. Farlack's sales were up since Rindel had started helping him in the shop every day, so he was in no rush to see the boys leave.

Delan, however, was busy buying food at the market, taking care to avoid being recognized by the thugs who had tried to rob him, and cooking meals for everyone. He didn't want to take his cousin's hospitality for granted and thought that cooking and cleaning were the least he could do to thank him for letting them stay. He worked hard to keep everyone well fed and the place in good order, though Rindel definitely ate more than everyone else. When he wasn't working, Delan sat with his own podbook and listened to the book for lengthy stretches, a thoughtful expression on his face. At one point, Marcus saw him sketching maps—presumably of the journey ahead.

"Don't you think you could walk again now with a stick?" he asked Marcus one morning. "I'm sure Farlack has one with a glow feature!"

"Uh, I don't know about that yet," replied Marcus feebly. "I wouldn't want to damage my ankle again. I think I should rest some more."

Delan grunted something under his breath before saying, "Well, okay, if you really don't want to. But I was hoping we could leave tomorrow."

"Leave?" Marcus looked puzzled. "I, er, I was hoping we could stay longer. Maybe we could learn how to use some of these gadgets in battle. Like the accuracy arrow—it's called an *ambor*. You point it at your target, press a rectangular button, and it will hit your target every time, as long as no obstruction appears."

Delan huffed in annoyance.

"No, Marcus, we don't need all of this stuff. It will just slow us down and distract us along the way. You only need your sword and some basic armor—but Farlack doesn't have what we need anyway. He's just got thousands of toys and gimmicks. You could waste all your money here, but none of it will do you much good. I think we need to move on soon. You can't just sit around here forever. It seems like you've been taken in by sikarl. That's a common thing around here."

Marcus looked disappointed and began to chew on his fingernails. His mother had mentioned *sikarl* a long time ago, and warned him about it. It meant becoming so lazy and indifferent that you really didn't bother to achieve anything in life. You just wanted to play and sleep, never work or help anyone. Sikarl was an attitude that was common among country

167

folk, who enjoyed sitting in the sun and chatting all day but didn't bother to do much else. Their houses began to deteriorate and fall apart, but they were never bothered to fix them, and their clothes appeared tatty and smelly because they couldn't be bothered to wash them very often. People who let their lives be dominated by sikarl wondered why they were poor and why they didn't achieve much in life—but they never made an effort to go out and do something. Instead they blamed everyone else for their lack of success.

Delan claimed that sikarl was like an unseen cloud that settled above your head, and that Treanthor was surely involved in spreading its influence.

"But how can something you can't see have any influence over you?" inquired Marcus, genuinely puzzled. It reminded him of Jez's warning of Santon. *But I haven't seen any sign of that,* Marcus thought. *Maybe they're both wrong.*

"Treanthor possesses unseen powers of persuasion. If he can spread sikarl into the towns and cities, it will ensure that people do not bother to rise up against him. They'd sooner sit around and do nothing than learn to fight or find information about PathOne. He wants the people to be apathetic, to not care much about anything but themselves. Sikarl makes you want to keep your head down and take it easy."

"But how can you resist sikarl if you can't even see it over your head?"

Delan pulled out his podbook and tapped it with his forefinger. "Keep listening to this little thing. It will make you wise and keep your head clear."

Marcus raised his brow before glancing above his head and contemplating the possibility of sikarl trying to infiltrate his mind. He remembered the caverns in Treanthor's citadels where sekrin and hakrin were produced. Was it possible that Treanthor created and released other kinds of drugs into the air? He shook his head and sniffed into a hanky.

Once Delan left the room, Marcus took out the silver earpiece from Brayman and placed it in his ear. He pressed the button to turn it on but soon fell asleep in the sunlight streaming through the window. Two hours passed before he heard noises outside.

Life would be easier if we could just stay here and avoid any conflicts, thought Marcus after carts being unloaded outside stirred him awake. His ankle still ached, and thoughts of the road north weren't pleasant. It might be different if Merloy was still coming to him—but he hadn't seen or heard from Merloy for quite some time, and as he soaked up the sun, he began to question his intentions.

How can I even be sure that I can rely on Merloy, anyway? My father promised that we would travel together one day and build a new home for Mum elsewhere. But where is he now? He just left, without even saying goodbye. For all I know, Merloy will find some other young man to visit, and he won't appear to me anymore either. Even Brayman's not in Penryth at the moment.

And as for the book, well, it's all a bit complicated. I'm supposed to follow PathOne, but it seems like PathOne is more than one path—and for some people, like Brayman, it even means stopping and living in a place like this for a while. The book seems to say different things on different pages and contradict itself. How can I be sure what to follow?

As if reading his mind, Delan came alongside Marcus and put his arm on his unhurt shoulder.

"You need to take this journey step by step, Marcus. The book can guide us along different sections of the path at the same time. Where it directs you one day may not be where I or my grandfather are meant to go until next week or next year. You can't just figure it all out immediately. You need to trust Merloy. And have faith."

"Faith. What are you talking about?"

"The book talks about faith. It's the ability to believe despite all the seemingly good reasons not to believe. That means trusting in PathOne even when you don't understand everything. It means following your destiny and trusting Merloy even when you face setbacks and troubles, like that attack the other day. It means allowing the journey to transform you. Faith will help you keep your heart set on the final destination — the ultimate prize. But you should never stop asking questions. Faith can handle whatever you might throw at it."

Marcus looked unsure. The book seemed to have more and more crazy ideas. Who had ever heard of trusting in someone who could let you down? What if he didn't want to be transformed? And would the prize at the end really be worth it?

Delan continued, still seeming to read Marcus's thoughts. "Being a follower of PathOne doesn't mean you will never run into trouble again or that Merloy will step in and fix everything in two seconds."

"Well, what's the point then? We may as well just ignore it all and live like everyone else! Farlack seems to be doing well for himself, doesn't he?"

Delan snorted. "Farlack is a nice guy, but he doesn't have the reassurance that Merloy will always be near him and help him. He has to struggle through life on his own. He may look like he's got everything sussed out, and that everything's tickety-boo, but that's just how he acts in front of strangers. I know him better than that. He gets troubled and down like everyone else, and he even doubts himself at times. You also need to remember that Farlack has settled in a doomed city that lies under the firm grip of that tyrant, Treanthor. I've tried to warn him that Krinton will be destroyed, but he won't listen. I've even had dreams about it. He's convinced that the Emperor is good and will continue to improve life. But Treanthor is a liar, who tricks people into thinking he wants what's best for them when really he only cares about himself."

Delan swept his hands across his forehead and looked up at Marcus. "Merloy's not like that. Merloy is more real than anyone else you could meet, and he is closer than all others. Once you learn to trust him, you'll find that he captivates your very soul and permeates your whole being. Merloy becomes part of you! Those who don't understand like to mock his followers and try to undermine belief in his existence." Delan paused and held his gaze firmly on Marcus. "You didn't imagine your encounters with Merloy, Marcus. Don't let anyone convince you otherwise. He will always be your friend; he won't walk away like your father did."

That last comment set off a torrent of emotion inside Marcus. Tears formed in the corner of his eyes, and then he couldn't contain them any longer. He began sobbing uncontrollably. Delan knelt down and put his arms around him as Marcus sobbed on his shoulder. It was the first time he had felt a warm embrace since he had left his mother in Trynn Goth — and it was the first time he had ever cried over his father's departure.

It felt good.

Chapter 13

Early the next morning, Marcus plugged in his podbook and listened to readings from the book that sounded like gritty, honest poems. He found them oddly comforting: it sounded as if someone else understood his own feelings and insecurities. He pressed the button twice, and the text forwarded to another part of *The Book Beyond Time*. He began to hear the story of a woman who saved a group of people's lives by her cunning. Marcus was intrigued. *This really does speak to everyone,* he thought to himself. *There seems to be a message for every kind of person in this book.*

Rindel began to stir on the makeshift bed next to him on the floor. He started talking some random nonsense in his sleep, which made Marcus chuckle.

Marcus got up carefully and found the walking stick which Delan had placed at the foot of his bed the night before. He held on tightly and found that he could walk much better than his previous hobble. His ankle was mildly sore, but nowhere near as painful as the week before. He walked through the living room and kitchen and into the shop. The shutters were still down and it was dark, but Marcus noticed something glistening in the far corner, where a ray of light sneaked in through a broken slat. It was a purple ska-sword—the latest version. It had five diamond-shaped buttons set in the handle. Marcus went over and picked it up. He found that he could twist the inlaid silver ring on the handle and the blade would extend automatically. The top three buttons caused the handle to flash or glow or resound with a zoom when waved around. Engraved in the blade in small letters were the words *Designed by NewTech.*

"The other two buttons can cause the sword to seem like it's invisible or twice its actual size."

Marcus turned to face Farlack. He tried the fourth button. Immediately a shadow emanated from the sword, making it seem nearly invisible. Someone far off wouldn't be able to see the sword at all.

"Impressive, isn't it?" said Farlack with a smile that curved up in one corner of his mouth.

Marcus pressed the fifth button, and a beam of silver light shot up along the blade, giving the appearance of an incredible, enlarged sword. It looked threatening and sinister.

"Unbelievable. I've never seen that before." Marcus looked at Farlack. "Do *you* have one of these?"

"One in every color!" grinned Farlack.

"No way! That's awesome," said Marcus, his mouth open wide in disbelief.

"Rindel has nearly earned himself a blue one. Which one would you be interested in?"

"Well, I think, I think I, I'm not sure if I really . . . I dunno. I just don't know if I really need one."

Farlack laughed, one eyebrow raised. "You are a strange young fellow. Everyone wants one of these, and you don't think you need one? What has Delan been saying to you, I wonder? You really shouldn't listen too much to him, you know. He's a nice bloke, but he's got some old-fashioned ideas. Bit odd, if you know what I mean. I've known him all my life, and he's always been that way. If you ask me, he listens to our grandfather too much. Now *there's* an out-of-touch old man."

Marcus started to speak again, but he found himself stuttering and unable to reply properly. He felt embarrassed and stupid. He sniffed two or three times while Farlack opened the shutters and the room filled with light. Marcus looked around the shelf of ska-swords and pulled out a dark red one. He handled it carefully and realized that he really did want to have one. The sword Brayman had given him was so—old. And plain. This one made him feel powerful and confident, like he could take on every robber in the city.

Rindel burst into the shop, his hair sticking up in all directions as he had just awoken.

"I knew it! Didn't I say, Farlack, that he'd pick the dark red one?"

Marcus nearly dropped the sword and stumbled back into a row of magic card games, knocking them onto the floor. Bright red in the cheeks, he began to pick them up. "I'm really sorry, Farlack. I'll sort out this mess, I will."

Rindel laughed. "And I said he was clumsy too—right?"

Farlack came over to help tidy up. "Don't worry, Marcus. It's one of the effects of handling a shiny new ska-sword. It makes people so full of awe that they start doing silly things. We've all been like that sometimes. Even Rindel tripped over a rope yesterday by the window there, didn't you, Rindel?"

"Yeah, but I didn't cause a mess like this, did I?" replied Rindel. "Anyway, are you really going to give him a red ska-sword? He hasn't done anything to earn it."

"You're right there, Rindel. No, he'll have to pay for it or trade with me if he really wants one. They don't come cheap, you know."

Marcus placed the red sword on the shelf and cleared up the game pieces from the floor. He bit his lip as he picked up his walking stick.

"I'll make some tea," he said as he left the shop.

As he waited for the water to boil in a huge tin kettle, Marcus couldn't get the idea of his very own ska-sword out of his mind. Even his heart was beating harder at the prospect at owning the dark red one. Arguments tumbled and tangled in his head over the matter.

He didn't need one; Brayman had given him a sword already. The ska-sword would lose its appeal after a week or two and not seem so awesome after all. It would be a waste of money, and thieves would just try to take it off him anyway.

But just imagine being able to handle a sparkly new red ska-sword, with its amazing features and the ability to fool an attacker from afar! He'd be on an even par with Rindel in their sparring matches and show him his superior skills next time. Better still, he'd feel like a real man if he owned a genuine ska-sword. Not just an overgrown boy, a real man—like Farlack and Prelanor, and his older cousins back home.

That last thought decided it for Marcus. He put the teacups on the table in the kitchen and found Farlack getting dressed in the bedroom.

"I'd really like that red sword, Farlack. I'll trade you anything for it, but I don't have enough money."

"What *have* you got then?"

"I'll show you my stuff."

Marcus emptied his leather satchel, his bundle of belongings, and his purse onto the bed.

Farlack ran his hands through it all, glancing briefly at trinkets and silver napkin rings, little tokens Ree-Mya had given Marcus to help him pay his way. He looked disappointed.

"And what's this book? I didn't think anyone read these anymore."

"Oh, er, that's nothing. Just an old thing my mum gave me. I didn't think you'd want that."

"I don't. Haven't you got anything else?"

Marcus flushed with embarrassment. "Well, there are a couple more things; just a minute. They're hidden under the mattress."

Marcus brought out the heavy green and silver sword from Brayman, along with a gold necklace that his mum had given him to trade.

"That's interesting," said Farlack, picking up the sword. "I haven't seen one like this since my great-uncle showed me something like it when I was about five. Where did you get this?"

Marcus remembered Farlack's disparaging remark about his grandfather earlier and decided not to mention Brayman's name. "Oh, an old man gave it to me."

"Mmm, looks like an original . . . not bad. Just needs a good polish. I'll take it—and the necklace too. Go and get your red sword!"

Marcus hobbled back to the shop and picked out the red ska-sword. He couldn't believe that it was actually his now. As he placed it in the scabbard, he heard Delan coming up the stairs. He was carrying a basket of eggs and bread.

"I think we'll have a big breakfast today! Looks like you'll be able to travel this afternoon, Marcus."

"Did someone say breakfast?" Rindel ran into the room with a huge grin. "I could eat a horse!"

After cooking up a massive breakfast, Rindel went to help Farlack in the shop while Delan and Marcus sorted out their things, getting ready to move on. Delan insisted that Marcus would sit behind him and let Rindel handle Tress by himself, at least for the first few days. He reluctantly agreed and continued to help Delan fold up bedding and other stuff.

A repeated banging on the back door caused Delan to look up suddenly, every muscle tense. He motioned for the others to duck out of sight while Farlack went to answer it.

A scruffy boy in a faded jacket was standing at the door, out of breath.

"What do you want?" demanded Farlack.

"Does Delan live here? This is where he told me to come!"

"Yes, do you have a message for him?"

"That's right, sir, he promised me two coins if I told him straightaway when I saw Treanthor's patrollers in the market square. I've just seen four of them near the water fountain, and they're heading this way!"

"I'll pass the message on."

Farlack was about to close the door when the boy slipped his foot inside. "What about my coins?"

"Ah, yes—of course." Farlack rummaged about in his pockets to find two shiny kroens for the boy.

It was clear that they needed to make haste, though Farlack was sad to see them go. He had enjoyed their company and Rindel's help in the shop.

"If ever you want to return, I'll have a job for you here, Rindel. Here's your sword."

Farlack passed him a brand new, bright blue ska-sword.

"Thanks, that's just awesome. I'll definitely drop by again."

Delan and Marcus dashed about, gathering up their bags and belongings. Rindel gazed at his new sword, running his fingertips delicately along the handle before hurriedly placing it inside the scabbard.

Delan paused and sighed, smiling slightly. "I suppose I should have known better than to bring young friends anywhere near your store. No wonder they haven't wanted to leave! It's just too tempting." Delan slapped both boys on the shoulder. "Come on then, men! We need to get going quickly. It's a good thing Tress and Opus have fully rested—they should be ready for a gallop today! Thanks for your kindness, Farlack. Here's a bag of buns for you—just don't let Rindel anywhere near them before we've left!"

Farlack grinned. "It's been my pleasure. Have a great journey, all of you, and stay safe!"

* * *

Marcus twitched and turned but was unable to get back to sleep. The crickets in the nearby bushes repeated their rhythmic chant as a mosquito whizzed around the makeshift tent. Each time he heard a familiar buzz by his ear, Marcus attempted to swat the pesty fly, but every try was unsuccessful, and he tired of slapping himself across the face and flapping his arms around.

He scratched the bites on his leg and wondered why mosquitoes had ever survived the Great Catastrophe. As Rindel snored soundly nearby, he also wondered how his friend could be so oblivious to the bloodsucking creatures. He vowed to himself that if he ever got hold of a xanth crystal, he would invent some surging power box that would blast mosquitoes to death on slightest contact. *Yes, that would be satisfying,* he thought to himself in the darkness—just before slapping his cheek when he felt another mosquito.

The last few days had been difficult for Marcus. He still doubted his reasons for journeying across the country at all when he could have enjoyed the comforts of home or Farlack's house. If he left PathOne, surely Treanthor and his patrollers would lose interest in him. After leaving the city of Penryth in a dash to escape Treanthor's patrolmen, they had entered uninspiring territory once more, crossing fields and valleys and rocky paths by streams. Although he had Delan and Rindel to talk to, it was often lonely, and he found himself thinking of his friends and relatives at home. There was always something fun happening in Trynn Goth, always an interesting face to greet you in the square. But here in the countryside, nothing ever happened. He hadn't even had the chance to use his red ska-sword, apart from some practice fights with Rindel. But seeing as they both had the same model of sword, it wasn't really that exciting after a few days.

I mean, where's the surprise when your opponent presses the same button that you've just used to enlarge his sword? I must have pressed those buttons a thousand times already!

Marcus thought a great deal about why he was even on this journey. Delan had said he was "chosen"—but he was just an ordinary village boy with no special talents.

I may as well go home. Delan can go and find battles to fight against Treanthor without me. Why would Merloy choose me when he has people like Delan and Jez—confident and clever? I can't get anything right. I got injured so easily back in the city. I couldn't even see it coming, and I let the others down. I might as well let them continue without me.

Such thoughts recurred throughout the remainder of the night. He didn't think of putting his earpiece in. Besides, the thing was so small, sometimes it was hard to locate in the bottom of his satchel. No wonder Magreanne had said that she preferred a book—at least that was easy to find! Once Marcus thought about pulling it out to read, but it was dark, and he didn't want to bother with trying to get a light.

Marcus finally drifted off around sunrise, dreaming of the comfortable bed at Farlack's home and the currant buns from the baker's nearby. He dreamed of living like a king while others brought him food, drink, and inventions to play with, while he had nothing much to do apart from enjoy the view out the window down to the bustling street below.

When Rindel woke him with a gentle kick in his side, the last thing Marcus wanted to do was pack up the tent and find water for Tress. He just wanted to sleep longer and lie in the sunshine.

Why do we have to keep moving every day? This is getting so boring! It's just the same thing all the time—get up, pack up, move through uneven, stony territory, maybe cross a lush field if we're lucky, make a campfire and go to bed. And the Kingdom of the North never seems the slightest bit closer! I think I'd prefer to be told to stay somewhere like Penryth, like Keriss and Brayman do. At least they have the chance to have a life.

If he was honest with himself, Marcus had assumed they should reach their destination within three months at the longest. But they didn't appear to be anywhere close yet, and he had no idea how much longer the journey was supposed to take. Delan had been following PathOne for years, and even he had never reached the kingdom.

Marcus was too embarrassed to voice his true thoughts to Delan, and he didn't want to be rebuked for being lazy or giving up too easily. But later he whispered his thoughts to Rindel, who nodded furiously in agreement.

"There's not a bakery in sight on this route!" he whispered back. "I don't think this could be PathOne at all. More like PathGlum!"

Rindel pulled a funny face, with his tongue stuck out to one side and his eyes crossed. Marcus laughed for the first time in days, and Delan asked him what was so funny.

"Oh, nothing special, just one of Rindel's silly jokes," replied Marcus.

Just at that moment, a small swarm of jeruni flew high overhead. As they passed near the young men, two of them began to swoop down alongside them.

Delan moved like a bolt of lightning, flashing his sword at the strange birds before firing a succession of darts at them from his saddlebag. One of the birds, wounded badly on the side of its head, flapped vigorously before falling to the ground. Delan stomped over it on his horse, yelling at the others, "Get out of here—go!"

The remaining birds squawked in dismay and retreated. "Not a place for us then, not a welcome place for us. We'll be off then, we'll be off. Not a welcome, nasty man."

Delan yelled once more, and the creatures flew out of sight.

"I think we must be nearing a town. The jeruni like to find a good crowd to influence. If I'm correct, I believe we're near Shakel."

Rindel whooped loudly and winked at Marcus.

"And where there's a town, there's a baker!" he exclaimed. "I'm so desperately in need of a fresh loaf of bread; I never want to eat an apple again."

"Well, you *do* know what the book says about that, don't you?" chortled Marcus.

"No, what?"

"It says you can't just live on bread alone!"

"You mean we're supposed to eat lots of vegetables too?"

"Oh, something like that! Tell us, Delan, what does it mean?"

Delan paused and drew Opus alongside Tress despite the narrow path. His eyes squinted in the sunlight as he smiled.

"It means that you can't survive only on food during this quest. You need to absorb the words of *The Book Beyond Time* to sustain you and keep you strong against enemy attack. Treanthor's not just out to control people's bodies—where they go and what they do. He wants to control their minds and souls as well."

Marcus and Rindel looked at Delan as though he were crazy. Marcus was sorry he had asked—Delan was becoming so serious lately. And he still didn't like to be reminded of what he had seen at the citadel.

After a moment's silence, Rindel couldn't resist saying, "Yup, well, I'm still going to want that fresh loaf—enemy or not!"

Delan replied in all seriousness, "Just don't forget to feed your soul, Rindel."

* * *

Shakel was a small town with a meandering path that wound through the outskirts of streets lined with bright-terraced houses, ultimately leading to a bustling market square that was open three days a week.

Rindel commented cheerily on the misshapen houses that were painted in an array of colors.

"Look at that light green one," he pointed out. "The roof is lopsided, and the windows aren't quite square."

"Houses in Shakel were constructed in a hurry," explained Delan. "The poorer townsfolk were moved on from another overgrown city which couldn't provide enough well water for everyone."

"They must have been in a real hurry—look, that yellow house doesn't even have any windows at the front!"

Just as they turned a corner into a busy street at the edge of the market, they could see some sort of scuffle up ahead. It appeared that a group of men were angry at another man. They began poking and shaking him, pushing him into a corner.

One very tall man, wearing tough laced boots and a dark hooded cape, grabbed the victim's face and spat in it. The others lashed out at him, taunting and kicking him repeatedly.

As Marcus and his companions drew closer, they could see that the victim had a crippled leg. Delan looked across at Marcus, who simply frowned in response. This wasn't right, but what could he possibly do? There were too many men—and besides, Marcus was still injured. Sort of.

Marcus nudged Tress's sides with his heels. "Move on," he told her quietly.

But Delan didn't seem to have heard him. "Hey, what's going on here?" shouted Delan, his face furious. Before waiting for a reply, he surged toward the group as Opus let out an angry neigh. The men withdrew in fear, their backs up against the sides of a wall, worried that Opus would trample them. The man with the broken leg slumped to the ground, blood pouring out of one side of his mouth, groaning as he clutched his stomach.

Delan drew his sword, glaring at the gangsters. "Who wants to pick a fight with me?"

The men cowered up against the wall, while the tall one suddenly turned and ran off toward the main road out of Shakel. The others said nothing, refusing to even look at Delan.

He drew Opus right up beside them, daring them to stand up to him. "Well, who's brave enough to attack an able-bodied man of his own strength and size?"

No one moved. The only sound to be heard came from vendors selling their wares at the market and Opus swishing away flies with his tail.

"Be on your way!" shouted Delan. The other thugs scampered, one of them dropping his bag as he went. Delan went to the injured man and lifted him up onto his horse. He poured water over his wounds and tied a scarf around his head.

"Thank you," whispered the disheveled man. Delan picked up the discarded bag and place it around the victim's shoulder.

"I think you should keep this for yourself now—that thug won't be returning for it. Where's your home? I'll drop you off there."

"You should have beaten up that gang of thugs before they got away," said Rindel to Delan. "They were just a bunch of cowards, mistreating a weaker man."

Delan glared at him. "I don't seek out fights for the fun of it," he replied. "But I think we should look out for those in trouble—step in and do something when help is needed. This man didn't have a chance on his own." Delan looked across at Marcus, fixing his eyes on him for several seconds. "You were well able to have done something back there. What have you become, Marcus? I thought you wanted to make a difference in this world!"

Marcus looked down, feeling his face heat up. He had only thought of himself. He hadn't wanted to intervene or go to the trouble of saving this stranger. Suddenly he was ashamed of his inaction and knew that his mum would have scolded him for ignoring someone in a desperate situation. She always helped others, in whatever way she could. And he was supposed to be a traveler on PathOne, someone trying to live differently!

He stared down at the ground ahead before mumbling some excuse about not knowing how to handle the situation. Rindel said that he'd thought some of the poor man's own friends would come to his rescue.

As he watched Delan tenderly care for the injured stranger, Marcus felt a deep calling in his inmost being that he too had a purpose in life and a reason for being—just as Brayman had tried to explain to him on that night they arrived in Penryth. Marcus had experienced the effects of sikarl these last few weeks, like a heavy robe on his back, slowing him down. Yet he realized now that he had welcomed sikarl, letting its spirit wrap around him and influence his attitudes and actions. And yet—he hadn't been happy. Not really. Living life that way was easy and safe, but a prolonged time of laziness was also unsatisfying. He had never felt that more than now.

How could I have missed an opportunity to fight off bullies in the street? Marcus asked himself. *I passed it by because it was easier to do nothing — when I could have achieved something amazing by defending this poor man!*

His thoughts weren't pleasant, but he allowed them to continue. Somehow he knew he needed to face up to his own failures. *But here I am today, not even bothering to scare off a bunch of mean attackers. Even though it was safe to do so, in the light of day, I just wanted someone else to sort it out.*

Entertainment and new things had seemed so important at Farlack's house. But all of a sudden, all of those things seemed empty. Inside, Marcus recognized that he would rather live like Delan, who was not trapped by the need for every worldly possession and yet seemed satisfied with his life and his journey on PathOne.

What kind of person will I become if I gain every single costly possession, but have no concern for my fellow travelers? He made a silent promise to himself that in future, he wouldn't selfishly ignore anyone in need but would stand up for justice.

The man directed them to his narrow orange house with brown shutters at the end of a wide stone street. The house next to it was identical, except that the other had black shutters.

"Who can take care of you now?" asked Delan.

"It's just me and my older brother—but he's a fieldworker, gone for the season. He won't return till the end of harvest. But I'll be fine," said the man weakly.

"I can't leave you here like this," insisted Delan. "I will stay until you recover. My friends here will have to continue without me."

Delan addressed Rindel and Marcus with clear instructions. "You must not stay here in Shakel. The jeruni from the road may well have alerted patrollers to your presence; you'll need to move on before anyone has a chance to track you down. Purchase enough supplies from the market and continue toward the mountainous region west of here."

"But will you meet up with us again soon?" asked Marcus, his face marked slightly with worry.

"That is not for me to decide now. All I know is that I cannot leave this fellow alone in this state. It is good that we came by him when we did. Minutes later, and he might not have survived the attack."

Delan's tone softened as he saw the genuine concern on Marcus's face. Somehow, he seemed to know that his friend had experienced a change of heart. "I must do what I know is right," Delan continued. "That is one thing I have learned from Merloy. I'm sure he will reunite us if it is beneficial for all of us. Until then, do not worry about your next steps. The book will direct you, if you take time to let it speak to you. And Merloy will protect you as you journey."

Delan smiled at Marcus, trying to encourage him to see their separation as something positive.

"Now is the time for you to take the lead, Marcus. This is your chance to find your own way on PathOne and make all the decisions. Maybe you will finally use your training to ward off any pursuers!"

Inside, Marcus knew with all his heart that Delan was right, and that he needed to focus his life on following PathOne and becoming transformed in any way necessary. Their departure from Shakel would force him to find his own way rather than following his friend's. It would mean following PathOne at his own pace and standing up for what he believed in.

Standing there in the street, outside the injured man's house, Marcus heard Merloy's voice. It was clear, as though he was standing behind him. But when Marcus turned, he saw no one.

"Pointlessness does not a pretty picture paint," said the voice. *"Rather, its random scrawls depict only confusion and standstill. You thought idleness would make you happy, but it only destroyed your passion and made a coward of you. Don't forget that."*

Marcus looked up in the air, still expecting to see Merloy, but heard only the voice. It was obvious that Delan and Rindel couldn't hear it.

The voice continued. *"Purpose is like a river, flowing from the mountain out to the sea. It is forever in motion, continually a delight to behold through the changing of the seasons. Follow your purpose in life, Marcus. Follow the river now."*

He felt a breeze swish past his ear, as though Merloy was brushing past him, and a vivid image sprang to Marcus's mind: one of the maps he had studied in the book. The map showed a winding river into the wilderness. Their path. Along with the image came the ability to understand it more clearly than he had ever understood a map before.

One last message from Merloy reached his mind: *"Whatever happens, stay close to the river, Marcus."*

Delan was speaking with Rindel now, continuing with his instructions: "And make sure you practice your swordsmanship with Marcus every day. You must not forget the training. Treanthor is already aware of Marcus, and he will only grow more determined in his pursuit once he hears of the podbook production unit. You must be ready for action at any given moment. Don't get complacent and think that he's not interested in your quest. You are more important than you know."

Looking back again at Marcus as he dismounted Opus and untied his belongings, Delan said, "Marcus, your new ska-sword is shiny and fancy, but I think you should continue to practice with the old sword my grandfather gave you. Make sure you sharpen it and keep it to hand at all times."

Marcus could not bear to admit that he had traded Brayman's sword with Farlack for the red ska-sword. He simply nodded and turned to leave.

Delan patted him on the back and insisted that Marcus take a handful of coins. He had been a great companion, more like a brother, and Marcus felt sad to part. Yet, as they waved goodbye, for the first time Marcus really felt like he was now a man, ready to take on responsibility and face any challenge. A lump rose in his throat as he could almost hear the words of his dad to him when he was younger—"Keep going, Little Fighter, you can do it!" It was time to move on and take responsibility for himself.

At the market in Shakel, Rindel chose a wonderful assortment of baked goods, despite Marcus's protests that they wouldn't taste fresh in a few days' time. They also bought some potatoes and chicken for their evening meals. The town appeared to lack any interesting features, and trees and flowers were scarce. Marcus thought this must be the reason for painting all the houses so colorfully—they were attempting to brighten up the town somehow to compensate for its dull outlook.

As they rode out of the unusual town, Marcus inserted his silver earpiece, listening to battle stories of men and women who made mistakes and of those who won great victories. Rindel chanted folk songs from Trynn Goth while munching on a large loaf of bread. As he dropped crumbs, several birds followed along, scooping up the leftovers. One of them was a young pink and purple jeruni, which, after gobbling a chunk of dropped bread, flew close by and dropped something round and small onto Rindel's lap. Rindel saw nothing—his eyes were nearly shut as he tried to keep out the glaring sun.

The small item unraveled itself and rose as a column of vapor. Rindel breathed deeply, inhaling it, and grimaced—but neither boy saw it.

Chapter 14

Once they were at a safe distance from Shakel, Marcus felt he could relax a little, and he slowed down to enjoy watching the clouds move across the landscape ahead.

"Isn't it time for me to ride up front again?" asked Rindel.

"Not this time. Maybe tomorrow," said Marcus with determination. "Besides, I'm still getting used to handling Tress again—it's been a while since I rode any distance. Hey, you look after the food this time. No slinging it at robbers!"

"Yup—and you could try actually staying on your horse when people come to attack us!" retorted Rindel with glee. Marcus took the teasing in stride, grinning back at him.

"I'll do my best!" was his good-natured reply.

As they rode through a stretch of long grass, past a farmhouse and a cluster of tall houses, Marcus began humming a traditional tune from Trynn Goth. The sun glistened through hazy clouds, edging its way out over the tops of tall houses. It was an unusually warm day, and his desire to sing could not be contained for long. As they made their way beside a farmer's field toward the hilly region, humming soon turned to raucous singing, with Rindel banging a spoon on a tin cup to add rhythm.

It is the season for singing, when the sun comes up,
The season for singing through the night.
When the good times roll
And the harvest's on its way,
Come on and join our celebration on the hay.

The song brought back memories of late summer barn dances with friends and family back home. Not for the first time, Marcus felt a twinge of homesickness—and yet, he was happy to be on the road again. This was where he was supposed to be.

"Hey, at least we don't have to gather corn this year," piped up Rindel. "That's one good thing about being on this journey. And you won't have to help your mum put jam in all those pots."

"I'm glad you can think of something positive about traveling with me!"

"Well, I only really liked the parties that came along with harvesttime—not any of the work!"

Marcus chuckled. "That doesn't surprise me, Rindel. But you do realize that we'll still have some work to do out here? I don't think our journey will be over too quickly. Might have to take on a bit of farmwork to raise funds for next month's meals."

"Oh." Rindel sighed. Then he perked up, suddenly enthusiastic again. "Well, instead of harvesting, maybe we can find work with another shopkeeper—someone like Farlack."

"Maybe," replied Marcus unconvincingly. He knew that where they were heading would not lead to many shops. He had seen the route that Merloy had whispered to him: it was on the largest, main map of the book, tucked inside the center pages. Having studied it earlier that day, he was sure that it could be as long as two weeks before they reached another town. But he had decided not to share this with Rindel.

Marcus cleared his throat and started up the singing again.

"It is the season for dancing when the sun goes down, the season for dancing round the hay . . ."

They trotted along an overgrown path by the river known as Oswill as Tress stepped over briars and twigs.

" . . . when the good times roll and—aaargh, come on, Tress," Marcus urged as they slowed with a jerk.

Rindel leaned to one side, peering down. "It's no use; we've hit mud. Looks like Tress will be crawling for a while."

Tress heaved each hoof out of the sludgy dark mud, snorting at the frustration of having to work so hard. Every few steps, she stumbled on a sharp rock which protruded through the mire.

"Hold on to the bags, Rindel, we don't want to drop them in this dirt." Marcus wrinkled his nose as a putrid stench from the mud rose around them. Clouds of flies buzzed around their heads, disturbed by Tress's hooves.

"I was just thinking that! When are we going to get through this? I don't fancy pitching our tent near any of this—look at all those flies!"

The path was narrow and winding, hemmed in between a steep hillside and the slow-moving river. Marcus could only see about a stone's throw ahead.

"I have no idea, but we must stay alongside the river no matter what."

"I hope we don't fall into it. Shouldn't we try going up and round this hillside instead?"

"No!" snapped Marcus, irritated. "Besides, even the hill is muddy—look at it. It's steep *and* slippery; we won't go any faster that way."

Tress halted again. Marcus kicked her. "Come on, girl, you can do it! Lift up out of the mud!"

But Tress was well and truly stuck this time. Her front left hoof would not shift out of the dense sludge.

Marcus climbed down and found a small branch to dig the mud around Tress's hooves. Then he coaxed her legs out and forward, talking gently as he worked to calm and reassure the horse. His own feet sank halfway into the mud, and he fought to keep from slipping.

"There we go; just hang on while I cover this part of the boggy path with twigs and stuff."

Marcus hastily gathered some small branches and leaves and threw them over the worst of the mud just ahead.

"That should do the trick!" Marcus said with a smile, trying to stay positive.

Rindel, who was still on Tress's back, frowned. "Well, yes, there's one problem sorted for the next few yards, but what about when we turn the next corner? Maybe we should head back and try a different route. It could take us all night just to get through here."

Marcus shook his head. "We'll just have to take it as it comes. I know we have to stay by the river. That's the last thing Merloy told me to do, so that's what we'll do. I can't worry about what's coming up ahead. One step at a time, that's the only way."

Marcus brushed off the worst of the mud from his tunic—his breeches and boots were impossibly covered—and mounted Tress once more. As they navigated the awkward path, Marcus asked Rindel something he'd meant to ask him for a long while.

"Do you really believe everything Brayman explained to us at his house, or are you just with me for the adventure? What I mean is, I think, um . . . I just want to know whether you want to follow this book and everything."

Rindel was quiet for a few moments and then replied. "Yes, of course I believe it. I mean, I wasn't sure to start with. But Brayman explained a lot of things, and I do think he's right. I don't want to be part of Krinton's downfall, if that's going to happen, and so, yes, I am sure about following the right way. It's just hard to believe that we're going the right direction sometimes. I mean, why doesn't that Merloy fellow come and help us now and again?"

Marcus sniffed and scratched his nose. "Look, I don't understand everything either, but I know he wants to help us. Delan says we need to listen more, and he'll guide us."

Before Marcus had finished speaking, Tress stumbled on a rock and slumped down, her front legs obviously causing her pain.

Marcus and Rindel dismounted immediately and tried to comfort her by rubbing her legs.

As they did, rain began to fall, slowly at first and then becoming increasingly heavy. Droplets splashed in the mud, making the smell even worse.

"At least it's warm rain. We could all do with a wash!" said Marcus with a smile.

Rindel looked worried. They were stuck in the middle of nowhere with no hope of seeing a friendly passerby with a horse and cart. No one else would be foolish enough to try to bring a horse through here.

Tress pulled herself up and tried to take a few steps but without success, her right leg buckling.

Marcus looked around for shelter and spotted a large oak tree just up the hillside, on what appeared to be firmer ground. "We'll just have to rest here a couple of hours until Tress regains her strength. Let's sit under that tree, at least until the rain dies down."

Rindel nodded and followed Marcus a few yards up to the tree, which provided a little shelter from the downpour. Both boys felt weary, and they soon fell asleep leaning against the broad tree trunk.

* * *

The sound of rain in the tree branches woke Rindel slowly. He rolled over, saw that Marcus was awake, and said, "Well, this is miserable."

Marcus was leaning against the tree trunk, wet and uncomfortable, but he sat up straighter and shifted at Rindel's words. "It will be worth it, Rindel."

Rindel grumbled. "I don't know why you're so convinced of that. What are we going to do now?" He pointed across at Tress, who lay slumped in the mud. Her flanks were covered with sludge, and she looked woefully over at them. At least the rain had driven the flies away.

"Well, we could always eat something," replied Marcus. "I hope you covered the bread well."

Rindel pushed himself up on his elbows. "Of course I did. It's right here under my tunic—warm and dry!"

The bread wasn't fresh anymore, but it still satisfied their hunger as light rain continued to fall, dripping off leaves around them.

As they ate, Marcus took a deep breath and decided to tell Rindel about the times he'd encountered Merloy and all that he had said to him. He had hesitated to mention his encounters with the awe-inspiring figure before now, but his friend deserved to know.

Rindel listened wide-eyed, inwardly feeling a little jealous that such a being had spoken with Marcus so much.

After a while, they stepped down across the path to the river's edge, taking turns to throw sticks into the rushing water.

Tress snorted loudly behind them, and when they turned to look, they saw that she was standing firmly on all four feet again. The rain was ceasing, and although it had made the mud worse than ever, they were eager to be on their way. A little further up the path, the ground was stonier, giving Tress a better foothold.

As the sun began to set, it reflected a bright pink haze on the river to their right. Marcus insisted that they keep going until they were too tired.

"Now the rain's gone, we may as well keep going as long as we can."

But they had barely turned the next corner before a deafening noise came from the hillside on their left, as without warning a rush of mud and rocks came tumbling down. Tress reared, and Marcus fought to keep her under control. He could feel Rindel clinging to him desperately, trying to keep from being thrown off. Mud and small stones stung their faces and bodies, and Tress tossed her head and rolled her eyes. But there was no way out. The surge blocked them on all sides and pushed them up against the riverbank.

"It's a landslide!" shouted Marcus.

"You don't say!" huffed Rindel in annoyance.

Mud was still flowing down the hill, though more slowly now, and Marcus patted Tress's neck to calm her. "We'll have to sit tight till it's completely stopped. Hold on, Tress."

Tress had no intention of moving. She had wanted to turn and bolt but was blocked on all sides by mud. She threw her head back and neighed violently to express her dismay.

"Easy, girl," whispered Marcus in her ear. "We'll be okay; just hold on now."

Thankfully only grit and small pieces of rock came tumbling down with the mud. Nothing weighty or sharp hit them as they braced themselves against the deluge.

After two or three minutes, there was an unusual silence. No movement, no birdsong, no rain or falling of leaves. Silence. Marcus turned to Rindel.

"Do you think that's it now?"

"Yup. That's what my dad would say. Once the silence sets in, there won't be any more movement of anything—at least not till after the next rainstorm."

Marcus looked down. The mud came midway up Tress's legs.

"You always said you wanted a mud bath!"

"This is not what I had in mind!" retorted Rindel. "But—" he started to dismount, "seeing as we're in this mess, we may as well make the most of it!"

"Rindel, don't you dare! We haven't got time for this. We need to dig our way . . . ugh, you rascal!"

A lump of mud and earth hit squarely on Marcus's face. The muck dripped off his forehead and down his nose. Rindel cackled with laughter.

"It's not fair! I haven't even—"

Thud. Another clod of mud landed on the back of Marcus's head, sliding through his hair and onto his neck.

"Rindel—you!"

Marcus clambered down, grabbing two clumps of mud and grass. He pretended to throw with his right hand, then aimed cleverly with his left at Rindel's tummy. Both clods hit exactly on target.

Rindel lurched forward, wrestling Marcus down into the huge mound of mud. Marcus overpowered him, turning him over and forcing his full weight on him.

"Well, and how does it feel to be truly stuck in the mud, eh?"

Marcus submerged Rindel's head in the mire, laughing at the sight of his friend's screwed-up eyes getting covered in the dirt.

Rindel pulled his arms out, grabbing Marcus by the scruff of the neck and yanking him over his head behind him. He threw some fistfuls of mud over his shoulder, somehow targeting Marcus's face again.

"Enough!" shouted Marcus. He fought his way to his feet, laughing. "We need to free Tress and set up camp before it's too late."

Rindel looked disappointed to let the fight end so soon. "Just one more?" he pleaded.

Without waiting for Marcus's response, Rindel pulled himself up out of the mud and threw a big armful over him.

Marcus didn't bother to even shield himself, letting Rindel cover him in the slimy mud.

"I said you win. Okay? Is that it now . . . can we sort this out now?"

Rindel suddenly appeared serious. "Shh! What's that? Did you hear it?"

"What?"

"There—it's happening again."

Marcus stood still. His eyes widened as he heard it. Rindel was right: a growing roaring sound indicated another landslide.

They had no choice but to kneel in the mud and cover their heads with their hands.

Marcus whispered Merloy's name as more mud and earth tumbled down the hillside. He was scared, but somehow peaceful at the same time. Merloy didn't appear or stop the landslide, but Marcus was confident that they were not alone. He could sense Merloy nearby. And that was reassuring.

It was only a minor landslide this time, covering them in just a few inches more of the dirt. But the mud had piled up between narrow rocks ahead, blocking their passage. It would take three whole days to clear their way out and move on.

* * *

After three days of struggle and path clearing, Marcus and Rindel were tired and disappointed. They hadn't seen a single soul, and they had only progressed about two hundred yards an hour.

"I didn't realize this journey could possibly get any more boring or frustrating!" moaned Rindel. "What I wouldn't give for a warm stew and a comfy bed at home!"

"Yeah—Brayman said it wouldn't be easy, but I can't say I was expecting all this. At least no patrollers are likely to follow us out here — and the mudslide has probably covered our tracks." Marcus grimaced. It wasn't much of a comfort, but it was something.

"And I'm just desperate for a fresh loaf again. All we've got left is this hard crust and a bag of walnuts."

The mud got easier to navigate the farther they went, and the brilliant blue sky and warm autumn sun overhead cheered their spirits a little. They had managed to wash their clothes and belongings in the river and hang them to dry overnight. The early morning sun had worked its magic, leaving their things dry—albeit crumpled.

There was one benefit to the terrible road: their awful surroundings made them both more interested in the book. Marcus and Rindel spent the evenings taking it in turns to listen to the book through the pod inserted in their ears. Marcus was encouraged to hear that it was normal to expect setbacks and difficulties along their way and to be reminded to be persistent in following the path. Rindel secretly thought the book seemed a bit duller than he expected it to be, but at least he kept trying.

The path grew more wooded, and they used their swords to cut away low-lying branches and bushes. Rindel talked at length about how excited he was to eventually get the chance to use their swords again. Delan had practiced with him often in the evenings at Farlack's house, and he was sure that he could overcome any opponent—especially men who were older, yet often much shorter than he.

They finally reached the end of the mud-covered path. At the same time, the steep hillside fell away, widening the path. The way ahead was stony but dry.

"Do you see that?" Marcus blurted, pointing ahead. He could swear he saw a man in a gray cloak, though he was hard to make out among the stones.

Rindel peered ahead. "There's someone coming!"

Both boys grinned and laughed.

"Hey, maybe he's got fresh bread!"

"Or maybe he'd like to play a game with us!"

"No use him continuing this way," Marcus said. "We'll warn him about the landslide."

Their spirits were lifted as they approached the tall, pale man in a gray cloak. Gray hair and a beard poked out from under his hood. He walked with a stick and waved at them. Marcus and Rindel waved back.

Tress stumbled awkwardly over large stones several times, but this time Marcus didn't lose his patience. He was just delighted to see another face. Maybe this man knew how far they were from the next village.

Moments later, they were face-to-face.

Vrayken was his name. He seemed friendly but hesitant. Rindel didn't think he'd be much fun to play cards with, but he was overjoyed when the stranger offered them two fresh bread rolls.

Marcus inquired about the path ahead, but Vrayken shook his head for several seconds before saying that it was no use continuing that way.

"It leads to a bridge where you cross the river. But the bridge has collapsed, and the current is too strong to try wading across on foot. I'm heading off here eastward, just a little way beyond those trees. There, you'll find a proper path that's much easier to travel. None of these awful rocks."

Marcus was unsure, but the man seemed trustworthy.

What's the point in continuing this way if we won't be able to cross the river anyway? he thought. *We can come back to the river later.*

"Will you travel with us, sir? We have some other supplies if you need anything."

Vrayken declined the offer, saying that he needed to rest a while.

"Just head in that direction; you'll soon find the path you need. Have a safe journey."

Marcus and Rindel thanked the man, relieved at the thought of making better progress after their slow pace of the previous few days.

As they munched on the bread, Marcus felt happy about their change of direction. Tress was equally happy to head toward woodland, away from sharp rocks and jutting branches, and she showed her appreciation through gentle snorts.

But once they reached the wide path Vrayken had spoken about, Marcus felt suddenly unsure.

Chapter 15

Tress trotted effortlessly along the broad, clear path, following a small number of other travelers. Most were making their way west, away from the dangerous road that Marcus and Rindel were leaving. This broader road had likely been constructed in the last year or two, with huge beautiful stone slabs laid out for miles ahead. All trees and bushes had been cut back to prevent obstruction, and as they passed through the valley, it was clear that the path had been leveled to enable swift travel. Marcus was surprised at the numbers of people they encountered—judging from the map Merloy had shown him, he had thought this whole area was uninhabited. Apparently the map had been wrong about that.

"Can you believe this?" Rindel's eyes widened. "Not one bump, rock, or obstruction! I can't wait till we get roads like this in Trynn Goth. Dad could get to the foundry in half the time."

Marcus nodded in agreement. The road had been constructed with skill and was a marvel to behold, shining in the sunlight like a pathway of gold. Yet, he still felt uneasiness in his spirit—a growing dissatisfaction he couldn't quite put his finger on.

He quietly thought through everything they had endured the last few weeks, wondering why Merloy had instructed them to go through that landslide when he surely knew what lay ahead. *What was the point?* he thought. *We couldn't have even continued that route if we'd wanted to—the bridge was broken!*

Rounding a bend in the road, Rindel interrupted his thoughts.

"Hey, check out those buildings back there!" he said, pointing at some amazing, new houses, set far back from the path. Stony driveways led through perfectly manicured gardens to the shiny, modern homes. Marcus stopped and stared. They were so impressive, even compared to the best homes they had seen on their way out of Erundel.

"My cousin, Finn, told me about the plan for those!" gushed Rindel. "They must be the brand new homes designed by NewTech. There's even talk of creating xanth-powered vehicles soon – imagine that – no more horses and carts!"

"Wow. But who lives in these houses?" replied Marcus, admiring the huge windows and angular, quirky styles. They reminded him of the grench port.

"They're rewards for the Emperor's top government workers", I think. "These could be the first ones made. Finn heard that Treanthor wants to attract the best, highly skilled people, especially those who can advance xanth in homes."

As they mused, a bigger crowd developed around them. Rindel dismounted, opting to strike up a conversation with some young men nearby. They were transporting goods from their ironworks, and Rindel took an interest in their trading opportunities and how much money they could make. They let him climb aboard their wagon so he could continue chatting with a young boy wearing a flat cap.

Marcus looked around at the other travelers. They were young and old, some well dressed or official looking; others were laborers dressed in dirt-smeared work wear. Everyone seemed to be happily on his way, many chatting animatedly to one another. Some hurried along while others went along at an easy pace, but no one appeared concerned about anything. Children played tag and raced each other alongside their parents' wagons; several people had stopped on resting benches to the side of the road, drinking ale from brass cups. Others were singing local songs.

The scene aroused memories of home and of the Wryxl village where they had stayed. *Everything seems as it always was—except better,* he thought. *No sign of any coming destruction or danger. Everyone's just getting on with their lives. Simple!*

* * *

At their next stop in the early evening, Rindel watched a group at the rest stop across the road. It appeared to be a family with four children. The oldest was an attractive young lady with green eyes and long, dark hair. Rindel couldn't take his eyes off her. She wore a dark red dress with a black shawl. Once they had set off again, Rindel encouraged Marcus to ride closer to their wagon so he could strike up a conversation with her. He had washed his face at the fountain and now started to press his hair back into shape.

The noise of the wagon wheels made it difficult to share more than a few words with her, and Rindel was embarrassed that everyone could hear what he was saying in a raised voice.

"It's, er, a lovely day. Looks like we're traveling the same direction."

The girl smiled back at him but said nothing.

"My friend and I have been on the road for quite some time. We're from Trynn Goth, a village."

"You're Trim Froth?"

"No, I'm *from* Trynn Goth . . . uh, never mind. What's your name?"

"I'm Leisha. Pleased to meet you."

"And you. Has, er, has anyone ever told you that your eyes are so pretty?"

The wheels on her wagon creaked some more. Leisha looked puzzled.

"Sorry, I didn't quite hear you. Did you say that 'lies can be witty'?"

"No, no, not lies. Eyes! Your eyes, they're so pretty!"

Leisha smiled coyly and looked away. Rindel's face began glowing red. He jumped down and hurried alongside the family's wagon. Very soon, the father, a man wearing a wide-brimmed hat, invited him to ride with them. As they slowed to let him in, Marcus continued on ahead, glad that Rindel was no longer whining about the journey as he had all last week and that he could make friends easily along the way.

It was effortless trotting along the road, even in the low light of evening, and Marcus began daydreaming. He thought again of their journey so far and of his mum left at home. He began to feel overwhelmed at all that had happened and started to worry about whether he was doing the right thing. He suspected this would all be easier if they still had Delan alongside them. He began humming an old favorite tune from home, sneezing and coughing as Tress kicked up dust.

After two or three more miles, Marcus stopped to get water for Tress. As he sat down at the bench, he looked around to see very few travelers. A few individuals rode by on horses, but there was no sign of Rindel or the wagon he was traveling on.

Where have they gone? Did they turn off at a crossroad I missed? Surely Rindel would've called out to let me know! Probably too busy gazing into that girl's eyes to notice. Now I really am all alone!

Marcus sighed in annoyance. But he also felt fear. It was getting dark and cold, and although the road was lit with occasional oil lamps, he was positive that once they went out later that night, they would not be relit until the next evening.

* * *

Rindel sat close beside Leisha as her father drove the wagon and her mother busied herself with feeding a baby and keeping another young boy occupied with a game of draughts. They talked about harvest dances, summer fountains you could splash in, grench ports, ginger ale, dice games, and festival time. There was no talk of PathOne or *The Book Beyond Time,* and that suited Rindel just fine.

Mesmerized by Leisha's wide green eyes, Rindel didn't notice when her father turned at a crossroad onto another, less traveled path heading west. It wasn't until they stopped to get water that Rindel realized the road was no longer so wide and impressive and that Marcus was not just up ahead of them anymore.

When Leisha's father stepped down to offer everyone a drink and some dried meat, he offered his hand to Rindel.

"Well, young man, I see you're getting on well with my niece here. Let me introduce myself!"

The man removed his wide hat, revealing distinctive black hair and piercing eyes. His voice deepened, and his whole manner seemed to change—it was almost as though he grew and became dark like a cloud. "I am Treanthor, your Emperor."

Rindel stumbled out of the wagon.

"Uh . . . she's your niece? I, er, thought you were Leisha's father. Treanthor, is that really you? I, er, I thought you had a special, uh, special carriage and officials and, uh, um, oh, your majesty."

Rindel went red with embarrassment and fell into a bow to show his respect. The man certainly appeared to be Treanthor, but he wasn't wearing his usual robe, and there was no sign of his dogs. "I, uh, I am—"

"Rindel!" Treanthor interrupted him.

Rindel was alarmed. "How do you—?"

Treanthor laughed in a mocking fashion. "Of course I know who you are, Rindel. I know all about you. I make it my business to know about all of Krinton's citizens—especially those who seem so especially gifted and talented as you!"

Rindel was still bowed, quivering slightly at the shock of seeing Treanthor before him. But his ears began to prick as Treanthor complimented him. Was he truly specially gifted?

"Be at ease, young man. At times I wish to travel without hordes of people or the blast of trumpets following me. And besides, my sister here required a safe journey with her children back to her village. It is off the beaten track, and alas, it is hard for Leisha to make friends with others of her age. I'm so glad she met you today—I know that you are a responsible, highly regarded man."

Rindel felt a sense of pride swelling inside him and smiled. *The Emperor thinks I'm talented and responsible. And a man—no longer just "young." I must well be fully grown now.*

Treanthor urged Rindel to take the reins and ride the wagon for the next section of their journey. Treanthor would ride beside him up front where they could get to know one another better. Rindel was keen, but a slight concern niggled at him. Marcus.

"But what about my friend—"

"Marcus?" interjected Treanthor. "Yes, I know all about him too. Don't worry yourself about him; we will join up with him again soon. Besides, I have a proposition for you. Only you can serve the Emperor's wishes for this very special task."

Rindel was in awe. His incredible Emperor knew all about him and had selected him for a special job.

"Will I get paid to serve you, my lord?" Rindel asked with hesitation.

"Of course. The Emperor is always very generous to those who fulfill special tasks."

"Tell me all about it as we journey!"

Rindel smiled across at Leisha and winked at her before moving up front to sit next to Treanthor.

As they rode along in the low light of a half-moon above, Treanthor excited Rindel with promises of an important mission that would earn him a permanent, well-paid job at the citadel. In the meantime, a superior ska-sword and a year's worth of wages in the form of gold coins would suffice to pay for this first task. The Emperor also spoke of something extra special that he had in mind for Rindel.

When they approached another stop, Treanthor once more took charge of the reins and offered Rindel a cup of his special ginger beer, handmade at the citadel. Rindel drank it all, noticing only afterward that it had a very strange flavor, unlike anything he had ever tasted back in Trynn Goth.

The Emperor continued to describe all the benefits that Rindel would get if he chose to show his allegiance to him—fashionable clothing, a good horse, and an assistant. He also hinted at the possibility of a future marriage to his niece, Leisha, which would of course entitle them to a luxury house of their own, as well as personal servants.

Treanthor then reached inside his cape and pulled out a small, black velvet sachet. Rindel wondered whether his chance had now come to taste sekrin, and he looked over his shoulder, a little nervous of the prospect of someone else watching him.

But the sachet did not contain the familiar silvery strands of sekrin or hakrin. Inside were three perfectly formed, sparkling crystals—almost as bright as diamonds and about the size of small coins.

"Are they real xanth crystals?" asked Rindel, eyes wide as he examined the precious gems.

"That's right, Rindel, and these are not the common variety found at the base of Mount Zorbin. No, these are the most treasured, rare kind of xanth stones ever to be mined. Each of these has the power to fuel all manner of gadgetry and devices."

Treanthor held one of the crystals up high between his thumb and forefinger, allowing the moonlight to bounce around its hexagonal edges. Rindel fixed his eyes on it.

"This one is for you now, the other two will be yours once your mission is complete. You will have my permission to work with one of my NewTech inventors to create whatever you wish with them."

Rindel pocketed the sparkling crystal silently. He could not believe his luck.

By this time, Treanthor could have requested that Rindel should clear all the streets of manure for the next year, and he would have said yes—so powerful were Treanthor's persuasive words and promises of fortune and praise.

"So what exactly is this special mission, sir?" he asked, enthralled by Treanthor's voice and still captivated by the precious gems in his hand.

"Well, as I told you earlier, I know all about your friend, Marcus." Treanthor frowned as though what he was about to say troubled him deeply. "You need to know that he is not all that he says he is."

Rindel sat back a little. "What do you—"

"Now, don't be alarmed—I have only his best interests at heart. But you need to know that Marcus is a traitor. I am certain that he has problems in his mind and is starting to have some mental disturbances— seeing visions and the like."

"Oh, but that's ridiculous. Marcus isn't crazy, and he's certainly no traitor. He—"

Treanthor interrupted once more. "Now listen, Rindel—do you want the job and all the rewards or don't you?"

"Yes, I, er, just—"

"Then listen carefully and trust what I tell you! Marcus may mean well, but as I say, he has a few problems. Ever since his father died, well, he just hasn't been the same."

Rindel nodded and poured himself some more of the strange-tasting ale. He hated to say it, but it was true.

Treanthor continued, "Marcus does not know it himself, but by following the path he is on—PathOne, isn't that what they call it?—he is trying to undermine me and my kingdom. He has thrown his lot in with schemers and plotters who plan to destroy Krinton—and our whole way of life. Especially dangerous is the one they call 'Merloy.' I have reason to believe Marcus has spoken with him and is coming under his sway. He wants to seize power and take over from me so that he can control everybody and make their lives a misery! Have I not improved

208

everyone's way of life? Do I not care about the people and provide them with jobs and food and homes? And fun and merriment as well? It is I who discovered xanth crystals and created grench ports so that our towns and cities could be wonderful places to live in. And the followers of PathOne want to do away with it all, and make people work more!"

Rindel looked across at Treanthor, who locked eyes with him. His heart falling, Rindel simply nodded once more. It was true. Brayman, Delan, Jez—they had all been against Treanthor, against the peace and prosperity of Krinton. Come to think of it, Marcus's own mother and grandfather had been the same way. And now Marcus had been sucked in too. For that matter, even Rindel had almost been sucked in!

Treanthor shook Rindel's arm. "What you must do, only you can do, Rindel! I need you to get hold of that dusty old *Book Beyond Time*, where Marcus gets his ideas, and bring it back to me immediately. Then you must return to him and convince him that he has been fooled by PathOne and that Merloy is a fantasy for desperate, weak people. He'll listen to you—after all, you are his childhood friend. Without the book, he'll be far more open to hearing what you have to say. I want you both to come and work for me in future—I want you to tell other young people that PathOne is a dangerous, miserable delusion and that happiness is found in my service. I'll make celebrities of you. You'll be famous, heroes. But first bring me that book."

"Why don't you just capture Marcus yourself—seeing as you know so much about him and his whereabouts?" asked Rindel.

Treanthor scowled, beginning to show exasperation. "Of course I can find him and bring him in; I have all the power in Krinton! But I want to avoid raising suspicion from those other PathOne followers or stir up any kind of rebellion. If we can get through to Marcus calmly, we'll be able to convince his other new friends to also abandon their pursuit of that pretend kingdom. If we don't, their silly fables will destroy the peace and progress of Krinton—just as they did before the Great Catastrophe.

PathOne has caused nothing but trouble, and frankly, everyone in Krinton would be far better off if it were totally forgotten."

As they drew up outside Leisha's family cottage, Treanthor stepped down to bid his relatives good night and instructed Rindel to stay seated. They would not be staying. As the Emperor hugged Leisha goodbye, he whispered something in her ear. She skipped across to Rindel and flung her arms around his neck before kissing him on the cheek.

Rindel's heart leapt a little, and he hugged her back, feeling good about the fact that such a pretty girl could like him so much.

As they rode away, Treanthor told Rindel to hold on tight. Then the Emperor took a big breath, tapped his feet several times, and took off at incredible speed. The wind on Rindel's face was unlike anything he had felt before, the force of it pulling the skin from his cheeks as his hair flew behind. He wondered whether the horse had been specially trained for speed or whether Treanthor had special powers, because in a moment they were back on the wide, stone path.

The Emperor then slowed, put on his broad-rimmed hat, and told Rindel to jump down from the wagon.

"You'll find Marcus just ahead up. Make sure you get that book and find me at the citadel. Tell any of my officials who you are, and they will take you there immediately. Do it, Rindel—the happiness of Krinton depends on you. Don't change your mind!"

Treanthor turned the wagon around before speeding up incredibly once more and disappearing into the distance.

The night air was now much cooler than before, and Rindel found that it stirred him from his drowsy state after the wagon ride. He rubbed his hands on his arms to warm them and walked hastily along the smooth path.

Now, where is Marcus? Just up here? Can't see anybody on the road! What if I can't find him? Why didn't Treanthor drop me . . . oh, wait, yup, I see him!

Rindel spotted Tress about a hundred yards away, tied to an ash tree set back from the road. Under the tree he spotted Marcus's tent and a glowing light from one of their swords shining through the canvas.

When Marcus finally saw him, he was pleased to find he wouldn't be alone all night after all.

"Rindel! Where did you get to? What happened to you?"

"Oh, it's a long story," Rindel said, not meeting Marcus's eyes. "Just, uh, got a bit lost. That's all."

Marcus was desperate to know all about it. He had been studying the faded map, but he was feeling a little lonely and insecure. It was obvious from the map that they were heading in the wrong direction and that this road would never rejoin their original path. That was why the area was so much more populated than he had expected. The map hadn't been wrong—they were on the wrong road entirely.

"Well, tell me about it then!"

"Yeah, tomorrow—I'm kind of tired, you know."

Rindel yawned hugely and plonked himself down on a mat.

"Switch off that torch will you? I, er . . ."

He stopped midspeech, apparently having fallen asleep with exhaustion, and began snoring gruffly. Marcus groaned. "Typical! He's gorged himself on food and drink, and now he can't even get dressed for bed!"

He switched off the light on his sword, pulled up his covers, and turned onto his side, listening to the sound of the crickets and a lone owl. *Tomorrow we'll head east before finding the path that runs north along the river,* he thought.

As he slept, he dreamed that he was being sucked into a disintegrating world, just as he had on his bed that evening in Trynn Goth.

Chapter 16

Rindel breathed nervously as he rummaged around in Marcus's rucksack, feeling for items in the darkness. A towel, a knarl-knife, three apples, a leather belt, a handkerchief, some loose coins, a waistcoat, a felt cap, a box of dice. Everything, it seemed, except the book. He continued searching near Marcus's pillow when his friend twitched and rolled over, pulling the book close to his chest.

Gently, Rindel tried to pry the book away from Marcus's hands. But Marcus spoke in his sleep and began coughing, and Rindel sat on his heels in alarm.

"Get over your side of the tent, Rindel!" muttered Marcus sleepily.

Rindel sighed in annoyance and retreated back to his bed. He would have to wait till morning.

He slumped his head. The excitement of the day had tired him after all, and he was asleep within a moment.

As sunlight streamed through the canvas, Rindel awoke to find Marcus emptying his bag.

"What are you looking for?" quizzed Rindel.

"Oh, I can't find that earpiece from Brayman. I thought I'd listen while brushing Tress down. Maybe it got lost during our mudslinging fight! Oh well, guess I'll have to read the original book again."

Marcus sat upright with the book balanced on his knee, opening the pages, trying to find the one with the corner turned back.

"You wouldn't believe what I discover in this book, Rindel. Just when I think I know all about it, I find out something new. And there's this map—it seems to feature this wide road we're on, though the original wasn't quite so wide as this."

"Mmm," muttered Rindel. "So, er, where does it lead to then?"

"Looks like some city called Warsap further west. But we don't want to go there, or we'll never get back on track. I'm looking for a little path that will get us back to the river."

"It's a bit boring by the river," Rindel said, trying to keep his voice calm so Marcus wouldn't suspect that anything was wrong. Can't we just go visit Warsap first and then head north later?"

"It doesn't work like that, Rindel. Besides, if we miss out a whole stretch of our journey, then we're not fulfilling the quest. Remember when Brayman said that we each have a destiny to follow and that it can be found through the book? But we must work it out for ourselves, and listen for direction from Merloy, to discover which path we must take. Merloy clearly instructed me to stay by the river."

"I think I'd like to choose my own."

Marcus looked up, frowning. "Your own what?"

"Quest. I mean, why should we just do what that book says all the time anyway? It's an ancient text for people from previous times, since before the Great Catastrophe. It's just not, what's that word—uh, relevant—anymore."

Marcus looked surprised. "You've changed your tune, Rindel. Just the other day you were saying you believed in it all and you wanted to pursue the quest. And what do you mean by relevant?"

Rindel fidgeted. "Yeah, well, I guess I've changed—grown up a bit since being on this journey. I don't think we should just follow everything some old book says. I mean, isn't it kind of old-fashioned to do everything that old people like Brayman say we should? We're young. We should be finding new ways."

Marcus scratched behind his left ear, still balancing the book on his knee. "Well, Delan and Jez are hardly old, and they seem to think that PathOne is worth following."

"Mm, well, they're exceptions."

"I really don't know what's got into you today, Rindel. Did you have a bad sleep or something? Let's just get going as planned. After all, we read the other day that we should expect our journey to be full of difficulties and opposition. The book states that several times, remember? It won't be easy, but it will be worthwhile."

Rindel rolled his eyes and turned to leave the tent. "I suppose we'll follow that map then, won't we? Sheesh! What are we looking for next anyway? Another hill?"

"Actually, there's an interesting sundial we need to watch out for. See, here on this section of the map—looks like it could be close to the river. Hopefully it's not covered in soot or submerged under water."

Rindel wasn't in the least bit impressed. As Marcus went to clean his boots, Rindel continued to mutter to himself, "Man, can't he ever just think for himself once in a while? The book says this, the book says that. Blah blah blah. Treanthor was right—that book is really messing with his head."

Marcus remained in the tent a while longer, examining different maps carefully and trying to memorize several key landmarks. He decided to pull out the main map from the center pages and tuck it into his front tunic pocket. That way he could glance at it easily as they traveled. He wasn't discouraged by Rindel's change of heart—after all, Rindel was often moody first thing in the morning. He'd be fine later. Nevertheless, Marcus was aware that Merloy had not shown himself in a while. He'd promised that he'd always be near, but it bothered Marcus how often he seemed far away.

"Help us, Merloy," he spoke aloud. "Lead us safely back to the river."

There was no answer. Marcus sighed and told himself to trust. For all he knew, Merloy was hovering invisibly around the tent.

Marcus found Rindel sitting on a rock, building a fire.

"Why are you making a fire now?"

Rindel looked up smugly. "I'd like to eat fish."

"Fish? Who's selling fish? I thought the rivers didn't produce fish round here. Too much toxic waste still lingering after all these years — everyone knows that."

"That may be so, but I just met a man from up north who said that a fishmonger would be passing through here in the next hour. Apparently, where he comes from there are loads of fish in the river. Salmon and trout."

"Really? I hope that wasn't a joke."

"No, seriously. The man said the fishmonger was a bit slow on his cart, but he'd be along soon."

Marcus laughed and lifted his head up to face the sky. "You've got to laugh. I mean, we never know what will happen from day to day on this journey, or whether we'll be eating walnuts for a week or fresh salmon! I'm glad you're good at making fires, anyhow!"

Rindel smiled. "My mouth is beginning to water already. I can't wait for some grilled fish."

Marcus joined him in throwing sticks on the fire and then went to dismantle the tent and pack up their belongings. He had been right; Rindel had already started to cheer up. And as he rolled up their blankets, Marcus was relieved to find the little podbook amidst the mess. He twiddled it between his thumb and forefinger before tucking it securely into his waistcoat, grinning to himself at the marvel of such an invention. *Now if only it also had a "return to owner" function if you whistled or something, then it wouldn't be so easy to lose!*

Unfortunately the fishmonger never showed up, and toasted bread wasn't so tasty without any cheese or fish to go on it. Rindel kicked at the dust, scowling.

"I'm really sorry, Rindel. You know I was looking forward to grilled salmon too."

Rindel grunted and threw a couple of stones onto the path.

Irritated by his friend's bad attitude, Marcus continued, "I don't know why you were concerned about following PathOne this morning but were so quick to believe some random stranger. You really need to evaluate everything people say and see if they're trustworthy or not. I mean, what would you do if—"

"Oh, shut up, Marcus! Yeah, you were right again, but I happen to know some things you don't. So there!"

Marcus bit his lip, stopping himself before he started a massive argument. If he wanted to get going on their journey, he would have to swallow his pride and say nothing. He decided to change the subject.

"Well, we can find some cakes from one of those bakers before we leave this main route. How about that?"

Rindel grunted again. "And I want to ride up front this time."

Marcus shook his head, barely hiding his exasperation. "Okay, come on."

* * *

After purchasing a small sack full of cakes, the young men soon came to the first landmark Marcus had memorized: an ancient sundial, set back from the path at a crossroad. From there, they headed eastward before turning south, finding themselves on a less traveled, though pleasant, road. Rindel grumbled about going south when they were supposed to be searching for the Kingdom of the North, but Marcus insisted it was a necessary detour, marked on the map, and Rindel eventually stopped his sarcastic remarks. They passed several friendly people on the way, occasionally stopping to chat and talk about their travels. One plump lady convinced them to buy a large bag of cherries.

The road began to twist and turn and then turned steeply down a sharp incline, which meant that Tress struggled to balance her footing. Rindel tried to handle her carefully and ensure he didn't hurry her—he didn't want to be thrown off. Now and again, Marcus spit out a stone from a cherry, aiming like a peashooter directly at Rindel's head.

"I'll get you back later!" snapped Rindel. He was concentrating too much on keeping Tress steady to think of retaliating.

Marcus grinned. He had one up on Rindel for a change.

He was certain they would soon find the second landmark on the map: a pile of rocks that was some kind of memorial to an historic queen—Queen Sholpa or something like that. But he had miscalculated distances and grew frustrated at their lack of progress. He hated to admit it, but Rindel's attitude was starting to rub off on him.

Once they came to an open clearing and the path leveled out once more, Marcus suggested that they rest a while and let Tress graze on the grass.

When Marcus struck up conversation with another young man passing by on a horse, Rindel seized the opportunity to find the book. Delving hurriedly into two bags, he felt around for the distinctive hard cover, all the while glancing over his shoulder, worried that Marcus might suspect something.

As he reached into the third bag, pushing aside some items from Farlack's shop, Marcus called to him.

"Hey, Rindel, come over here! This man wants to know if we noticed some weird vegetables on our way here from the wide path. Do you remember seeing anything?"

Rindel stopped his search, gritted his teeth, and walked over to the others. He listened briefly to the young stranger's description before answering, "Sounds like you're talking about mushrooms. Dad said he used to have them when growing up in the country over in the west. I don't think I saw any—but you should be careful. Some types of mushroom can be deadly poisonous."

The three of them began talking about what types of plants could be eaten raw or cooked and the best places to search for berries. They then compared their knives, Marcus proudly showing off the knarl-knife he had found a long time ago in the woods. In the end, they chatted so long it was late afternoon before they got moving again. Before they parted, Marcus inquired about both the memorial stones and the next landmark, a high granite rock. But the traveler was not familiar with either of these.

Marcus regretted being distracted by the traveler, who was obviously in no hurry to get anywhere. He remembered Merloy's urgent voice saying, "Whatever happens, stay close to the river, Marcus." The words began to echo repeatedly through his mind, and he started to panic. Why hadn't he listened?

What if we get lost, or the map is out-of-date? What if we find the wrong river? How will I know if it's the right one?

He kept his thoughts to himself while Rindel began to loudly bemoan the fact that this path was not half as nice as the other one and that they hadn't seen a pretty girl all day. This last comment finally distracted Marcus from his worries.

"Have you ever thought about whether girls might actually think *you're* nice to look at, Rindel?"

"Well, I must be," Rindel shot back. "That girl I met the other day — Leisha was her name—really liked me. Even kissed me on the cheek!"

Marcus felt a small pang of jealousy. No girl had ever kissed him — other than his little cousins, who definitely didn't count.

"Maybe her eyesight's bad!" he quipped.

"Oy—I'll get you for that! Well, she wasn't interested in you, so I must be better looking. Ha!"

Marcus let Rindel have the last line; he needed to focus on the road again. There was meant to be a narrow path lined with cedar trees leading up to the memorial, but he could see nothing of that description up ahead.

* * *

Two days of meandering and wandering passed before Marcus and Rindel made any real progress. Rindel gave up another attempt to snatch the book, deciding it would have to wait until Marcus was injured again and unable to move. He was just considering how he might cause Marcus to sprain his weak ankle when he heard a loud cheer.

"Wahey!" Marcus punched the air and pointed out the distinct landmark.

"Look at that! That's it!"

Rindel gazed ahead but saw nothing noteworthy.

"Off there to the left! I can see a hill with a jagged, granite rock at the top."

Rindel cast his eyes across to a dark, imposing mountain in the distance that towered into the sky with a jagged rock face at the summit. He groaned.

"And? I really hope you're not going to suggest we climb that mountain—it looks far too steep and dangerous."

"No, but it's the next landmark I've been trying to find. See that huge stone facing partly this way with the chipped edges? That must be the ancient marking we're looking for. It's dislodged from its original position, but there's no mistaking the markings on it. The book showed a rock just like it on one of the maps. We missed the memorial en route, but it doesn't matter anymore—come to think of it, I wonder if Treanthor had it dismantled. It's the sort of thing he would do, not wanting anyone to remember any past greatness that isn't his. Now I know we're close to the river again. I'm pretty certain we'll find a stream on the other side of that mountain which will take us back to the river. We've been on the right track all along—it was just longer than I thought."

Rindel sighed. "Aren't we ever going to find another city? I'm getting bored of the countryside."

Marcus was so happy to find the granite rock that he didn't even sound annoyed when he replied, "Yes, Rindel, it's just going to take us time. But let's set our sights on our goal. Wherever else we might stop on the way, we're heading for a wonderful, unspoilt kingdom—a city of wonders that won't be under Treanthor's rule and won't fall, even when

Krinton is no more. It might take us years to get there—or maybe we'll find it quickly. Maybe it's just around the mountain for us!"

Rindel grimaced inwardly. *Marcus really is talking nonsense now. There's no place that's not ruled by Treanthor. He sends out spies and officials across the land to make sure that everyone follows his decrees. I can't believe he actually believes the stuff spouted by Brayman.*

Rindel cleared his throat. "Uh, so show me where it says that in the book. I want to read it for myself."

Marcus pulled out the book from the leather bag across his shoulder and slowed Tress to a halt. Turning around to half-face Rindel, he opened the book to the page with the corner turned back.

Rindel's heart began thumping furiously in his chest. He knew this was another chance to grab the book. But he also knew that Marcus and Tress would easily catch him if he ran. He bit the corner of his lip and pretended to listen.

"You see, right here, it mentions this city of lights. It sounds so awesome!"

Marcus quickly read two or three lines to Rindel before shutting the book abruptly and putting it back in his bag.

"We can read more later. Right now we need to focus on getting to the other side of that mountain."

Marcus turned back and urged Tress to move on quickly. They splashed through shallow puddles and across an overgrown plain before coming into clearer view of the mountain. There were no main roads approaching the gigantic hill and no sign of any nearby villages, but Marcus showed no signs of fear; he knew he was heading in the direction that Merloy had instructed him to go.

Light rain began to fall as they approached the foot of the mountain. And that was when they noticed that there was going to be a problem. The left side of the mountain was wholly unapproachable: a dense covering of tall pine trees and thorny briars stretched out and up all across that side. The right side would have been easy to navigate—if there were not such a huge lake surrounding it. Marcus knew instantly from the sight of the red, claylike earth along the lake shore that it had likely been the site of an old quarry—the water would be exceedingly deep and dangerous. Any possibility of wading through it was out of the question.

At the foot of the mountain there was not even a narrow path. The lake's water lapped right up against the steep, rocky hill.

"So that's it then," said Rindel matter-of-factly. "We'll have to access that little path cut into the mountain there. It's probably used by herdsmen to reach this water at the lake."

Marcus rubbed his hands across his forehead and eyes. The tone of his voice grew low and serious. "Rindel, do you see how narrow and steep that path is, and how high it goes before it curves round to the other side? And did you notice that there's no safety fence or handrail? I just don't see how *we* can handle that, let alone Tress."

"But it looks kind of exciting, though, doesn't it?" Rindel punched Marcus in the arm. "We'll just have to walk and lead Tress along—she'll trust you."

Marcus wasn't so sure. Now it was his turn to express regret.

"I just wish we'd never left that path last week. We probably could have waded through the river to continue on our way. Now we have to navigate this nightmare of a road, and we don't even know if there are any obstructions ahead of us. If we meet another traveler, we'll have to go back and start again—there's no way two horses could pass each other on that path!"

"Oh, come on, let's look at it as a challenge! We could even try it with our eyes closed! What's the matter with you . . . scared of heights or something?"

Rindel watched Marcus intently. If Marcus would just take the dare, he would probably get hurt and have to stay put for a while. Then he could seize the book without fear of Marcus pursuing him.

Marcus continued to rub his forehead, screwing up his eyes and looking anguished.

"You're right, Rindel! We just have to try. Come on!"

They dismounted Tress, and Marcus walked on ahead, leading the faithful horse. Rindel followed, already feeling slightly less brave at the prospect of slipping off the path to plunge into the lake.

The path wasn't as narrow as it appeared at the base of the hill, so the first part of the journey didn't seem too difficult. When a small rock looked like a footing hazard for Tress, Marcus would remove it and throw it into the lake. Rindel would normally have protested at the unfairness of this, wanting to be up front and hurling the rocks down himself, but he was too focused on thinking about how he could cause Marcus to slip and hurt his ankle without making him fall into the lake. After all, he didn't want his friend to be *badly* hurt.

As they curved around the side of the mountain, they discovered that the path narrowed sharply, and they had to slow down immediately. Tress snorted and kicked up a fuss, wanting to retreat, but Marcus coaxed her along, rewarding her with bites from a crunchy apple.

When the rain began to fall heavily, they found a crevice in the rock side where they could shelter and rest for a while. Looking down into the lake, they could see the reflection of the full moon and cascading patterns as the raindrops landed on the water's surface. It seemed a long time before the rain slowed to a gentle patter and Marcus urged them onward again.

Wet, cold, and aching from the steady uphill climb, Rindel walked behind Tress and grumbled to himself, keeping a close eye on Marcus and wishing with all his heart they were somewhere warm and dry and close to a hot meal. His lack of success was making his mood even worse. This wasn't what he'd wanted when he came with Marcus on this journey. If only they didn't have to follow that stupid book, they could have been having a grand adventure in a place of their own choosing instead of struggling up a dangerous path in the middle of the night.

Just ahead of him, some of the path crumbled away from the force of Tress's hooves. "Watch your footing, Rindel!" Marcus called back. Rindel glared up ahead. *Like I don't know how to take care of myself,* he thought. *Watch your own footing, you . . .*

Without warning, he hit a loose patch of earth that slid away beneath his feet before he could think. With his stomach in his throat, he fell and clutched at the ground, trying to stop the slide. Rain and mud were in his eyes, blinding him, and he was aware that his legs were over the edge, and his body, and the deep, terrible lake was below . . .

A strong hand caught his, and he heard Tress whinnying. "Hold on!" Marcus bellowed. His clutch was tight, almost desperate. Rindel held on to Marcus's arm and wrist with both hands and felt his body swinging out over the open air.

"Help me!" he screamed.

"Hold still!" Marcus called back. "I'm trying to pull you back up, but you've got to cooperate with me!"

His heart pounding wildly, Rindel forced himself to hold still. He could feel Marcus pulling him up. Mud and gravel continued to slide away from Marcus's feet, but he seemed to be holding on to something with his other hand—something that kept them both from pitching over the side.

As Marcus strained to pull Rindel's weight, something inside his tunic shifted. In the low light of dusk, Marcus didn't notice the book coming free and falling—but Rindel did, and he let go with one hand just long enough to snatch it and tuck it into his own shirt.

"Watch it!" Marcus yelled. "Hang on!"

Rindel grabbed Marcus's wrist with his other hand again, hardly able to believe he had reacted so fast. Treanthor would be proud.

As quickly as he had fallen, Rindel's feet were on the path again. "Don't let go," Marcus told him. In the moonlight, Rindel could see that

Marcus was clutching a rope with his other hand—one that was lashed to Tress's saddle. The horse was leading the way.

Moments later, they were on surer footing. Marcus released Rindel and went to work untangling his hand and comforting Tress. Shaking hard, Rindel sat with his back against the rock wall. *Go on,* he thought, *comfort the horse.*

He closed his eyes. This was as far as he was going. The path ahead only looked more treacherous. He wouldn't say anything to Marcus—he would just slip away quietly while Marcus was concentrating on Tress—but he didn't intend to take another step. His friend's delusions weren't worth risking his own life.

Chapter 17

Marcus stood up and dusted down his trousers. The particles of fluff and earth stirred upward, causing him to sneeze and cough. Only silence answered. He quirked a smile and called over his shoulder, "Hey, that's unlike you, not to poke fun at me. I mean, usually you —"

Marcus paused and turned around. "Rindel?"

He scanned the empty road and mountain slopes around him — nothing. Rindel must have retreated a little to find a spot to pee. Right? Minutes passed, and when Rindel didn't return, Marcus drew in a huge breath of air and yelled, "Rin-del!"

His voice echoed ominously across the mountainside, but no answer came back to him. Again he shouted out, "Rindel!"

He stamped his feet in frustration, startling Tress. It was clear enough that Rindel had abandoned him — probably unwilling to take one more step on this difficult road. And after everything Marcus had done for him!

"Why do you do this to me, Rindel? Now I suppose I'm going to have to go it alone while you wander off in search of another pretty girl and some fresh bread. And you were the one who was so sure of going this route! An adventure, you said! How about a challenge! Well, thanks a lot for leaving me now!"

Marcus scowled at Tress, who gazed at him with apologetic eyes. Somehow the horse understood that this was indeed a tricky situation in which to find themselves.

Determined not to give up, Marcus tightened his bootlaces and continued round the curved edge of the mountain, at times gripping the rocky side of the path, which narrowed perilously. Looking out the other way caused his stomach to churn — the sheer drop was unlike any other he'd encountered. He paused regularly to take in breaths and steady himself.

Each and every step required careful maneuvering and consideration. The slate path was extremely uneven, and Marcus was aware that he could easily slip as Rindel had earlier. To make an error or misjudge a step would not be an option. Still, he ensured that the rope attached to Tress's harness was attached securely several times around his wrist.

Once they turned a corner, Marcus was relieved to arrive at a wide ledge which jutted out from the hillside, giving way to a breathtaking view down to the valley and the lake. A tiny stream provided fresh water for them, and Marcus was cheered by the sight of orchids and lilies growing in a wild spray beside the water. They reminded him of his mother, who so loved fresh flowers, and that in turn reminded him why he was journeying this way. In the distance he could just make out the lights of a town or city. For the first time since Rindel had disappeared, he felt himself feeling hopeful.

After resting a while, Marcus cut down an overhanging branch and used his knarl-knife to fashion it into a walking stick. It would help to balance him on treacherous parts of the path ahead.

Darkness descended quickly over the mountain, and it became eerily quiet. Marcus realized it would be foolish to move on further, and he settled down for the night, thankful that he had found a safe spot to put up the tent. He used rocks and sticks to hold its shape and was glad that the earlier downpour had dripped off down the side of the ledge. His loneliness grew as he settled in for the night, missing Rindel's teasing and even his complaining. Still, he couldn't shake from his mind the words he had read weeks earlier in the book about the "difficult path" being the right one. Marcus reflected on this now and hoped that it was true.

It was too dark to even consider reading, and Marcus didn't notice that the book was no longer in his possession. He rummaged around in his waistcoat to find the tiny podbook and gently inserted it into his left ear. As he began to drift off to sleep, perched alone high up on a ledge on a menacing mountain while listening to the sounds of Brayman's familiar voice, Marcus felt flooded with a sense of calm, and his fears were forgotten. He realized that this secure feeling in his heart was worth more than anything he could possibly buy or trade. *This must be one of the "intangible treasures" of the Kingdom of the North,* he thought. *I shouldn't feel calm right now, but I do. I feel safe. I know I'm doing the right thing by continuing this journey.*

He awoke startled by the sound of an eagle's call overhead. Opening the tent, Marcus was disconcerted to find the whole mountainside shrouded in misty cloud. He could barely see to the other side of the ledge, and panic began to claw up his body like menacing scorpions. Fear returned.

What if it stays like this for days and I starve to death? What if a huge eagle plucks me from this ledge and decides to have me for dinner?

Just then Marcus felt some words speak to his spirit, though he was sure that these were not his own thoughts.

"Take one step at a time; don't look back."

It was crystal clear what he should do. Marcus sighed with relief, realizing that he didn't have to depend on himself only. Merloy had promised to go with him and guide him. And despite the lack of physical signs of Merloy's presence, he knew for sure that he was going to be all right. His breathing slowed down, and the feelings of panic were replaced by feelings of safety. He didn't need to worry.

After packing his things, Marcus soon began to enjoy the thick mist, feeling as though he was right in the clouds. The air was crisp and smelled of fresh flowers and grass. He began to think again of Rindel and where he might be now.

Maybe he's heading back to Trynn Goth and will report back to Mum everything that's happened so far, he thought.

* * *

Rindel rearranged the cushions in the luxury wagon and put his feet up on the seat opposite.

He had found his way down to the foot of the mountain and retraced his steps to find a familiar path, where he soon encountered travelers who agreed to take him back to the wide main road. From there he had walked several miles before finding an official wearing a special felt hat with the distinctive "T" sewn in gold lettering on the front.

After Rindel explained his mission and showed the official the rare xanth crystal which Treanthor had given him, the man had agreed to transport him to Treanthor's citadel, on condition that Rindel promise to put in a good word about him to the Emperor. Like most officials, he was hoping for a higher position or higher wages.

Rindel smirked as he considered the reward he would get for turning the book in. And it wouldn't be hard to find Marcus later and convince him to give up the journey: although two days had now passed, he was sure that Marcus was still navigating slowly around that treacherous mountain. By the time he was finished, he'd be miserable and ready to give up.

Rindel confirmed what he thought to be true by asking the dark-eyed official: citizens of Krinton were permitted to travel only on the main paths and routes. This law had come into effect about sixty years ago when a few individuals had spread rumors of another kingdom and way of life. The official explained that Treanthor was concerned about talk of another king, supposedly mightier than he, and that he wanted to dispel all reasons for believing in such a fantasy.

"Besides, Treanthor is also known for his shrewdness with money," the official continued. "I think he feared an invasion from a ruler who could get hold of the people's taxes for himself. That's why he sent out information declaring the Kingdom of the North to be a fantasy—just a silly story for idiots. In fact, no one's really talked about it for quite some time. But Treanthor is right, regardless. There can't be any such place.

After all, no other king has ever shown up after all this time. We all know it's just a myth."

Rindel interrupted. "Yes, but don't some of the Wryxl still believe it could be true? Don't some of them talk about some ancient text that will lead them to the Kingdom of the North?"

The man gave a scornful laugh. "Not these days. A while back there was some man named Bremin or Brayman who was spreading the lies, but he was killed or banished—I can't remember. Anyway, even if it were true, as Treanthor likes to remind the Wryxl now and then, who would want to rule over them or choose them as a people to govern? They are such an unworthy, stupid people—and they should be thankful to have such a wonderful Emperor. Who else would want to govern simple blacksmiths or farm laborers?"

"Nobody!" piped up Rindel, laughing. "Nor drunk barmen!"

"You're right there, young man. Yet Treanthor provides them with everything they need, and since he's been in power there have been no wars or invasions."

The official shouted ahead at the driver, "Next left!", and looked across again to Rindel.

"Anyway, you know what the Wryxl say—"

"Stay with what you know!" Rindel chimed. "Never question the status quo. Never question at all." *Not like Marcus,* he thought. *Marcus has always been a questioner, and look how much trouble it led to.*

The official grinned. "That's right, that's what they say. It's worked for them all this time—they're generally a happy bunch. And there's always loads of sekrin available to cheer them up. Given away freely at some taverns now."

The wagon turned off the smooth, wide road and veered over a bumpier path toward woodland. Rindel smirked again at the thought of being a guest at the Emperor's palace and looked forward to trying some sekrin for himself, now that Marcus was not around to deter him. *A little bit can't hurt,* he thought.

Rindel drifted off to sleep as the wagon rocked over sticks and stones, his hair falling across his forehead and a little spittle dripping out of the corner of his mouth.

* * *

After an hour or more of treading slowly and carefully along the mountain path, away from the ledge where he'd spent the night, Marcus noticed the thick mist beginning to disappear as strong sunlight banished the clouds. It was a glorious day, and he could relax, finally able to see clearly. The narrow path continued to wind round to the far side of the mountain until it stopped abruptly. The only way to keep going would be to climb some wide, steep steps which had been carved into the side of the mountain.

Marcus gazed up at the steps, concerned that Tress might not manage the incline. They appeared to be dry and free from slippery mud, but he was unable to see where they reached. "There could be hundreds," Marcus thought aloud.

He pursed his lips, deciding to tie Tress to a tree root and investigate for himself. He scrambled up about thirty steps before arriving at what seemed like the entrance to a large cave. Raising his hands above his head, he reckoned that Tress would be able to pass through easily, but first he flicked on the torch from his ska-sword and shined the red beam inside to check that it was safe.

The cavern was broad and largely empty apart from rocks set in a circle and some stalagmites jutting into the air around head height. On the ground were several large puddles of water. On the far side Marcus could see that the cave narrowed greatly, leading to a tunnel entrance. Again, he thought that he and Tress should easily be able to pass through. He should have felt fearful; the cave was exceedingly dark and unwelcoming. But Marcus felt confident that he should continue.

232

Retracing his steps back to Tress, he coaxed her gently to follow his leading as she reluctantly, and with great difficulty, climbed up the steep steps. Several times, Marcus had to pull her along, encouraging her with persuasive words and promises of treats.

"Way to go, Tress!" Marcus cheered once they reached the cave entrance. "I knew you could do it!" He patted her and rewarded her with their last green apple.

Shining his torch ahead, Marcus led the way into the tunnel. Apart from their steps and the dripping of water from above to the stony ground, it was silent. Marcus could no longer hear the wind or the sounds of birds or other creatures. He picked up speed, deciding that the sooner they could emerge from the tunnel, the better. Tress followed close behind, keeping pace. His heart beat faster than normal, but somehow Marcus was not afraid. In his spirit he thought, *I have to do this, I can't give up.* He felt a kind of supernatural confidence that he had not really known before.

His eyes soon adjusted to the dim light of the tunnel, and Marcus made good progress. But he was discouraged when his hungry stomach alerted him to the fact that it was nearly lunchtime and the end of the tunnel was still not in view. Rustling around in one of the sacks Tress was carrying, he became angry.

"Rindel, you beast! You took the last loaf!" Stamping his feet, he found a handful of squishy berries and stuffed them into his mouth.

"I've got a bag full of useless gadgets here, Tress, and no more food!"

Tress snorted in agreement and scraped her hoof along the ground, as if to mirror Marcus's stamping.

Still angry but unable to keep raging at no one, Marcus sighed and straightened his shoulders. "Well, we'd better get going and see where this leads."

Marcus rearranged the bags and set forward with determination. *We have to get out of this tunnel while there's still daylight outside,* he thought.

Increasing his pace now, he made great strides ahead, following the tunnel as it twisted to the left and then the right, then up a bit and down quite steeply again. He was glad Rindel wasn't there to distract him with mindless chatter or complaints. For the time being at least, it was easier to do this alone.

* * *

Rindel jerked awake as the wagon ground to a halt. He pulled off his scarf to wipe the sleep from his eyes and sat up to find himself in a far more spectacular cave than he had ever imagined. Awed by the stalactites and xanth-powered colored lights, he followed as the official led him through corridors toward Treanthor's chambers.

A huge, imposing door was opened before him, and Rindel was instructed to sit and wait on a small bench near the fireplace.

Curiosity tempted Rindel to get up and look around. He couldn't resist taking a closer look at Treanthor's possessions. A huge black sword hung on a wall alongside a suit of armor that appeared to be made from solid silver. Rindel ran his fingers along the breastplate slowly, watching as lights stirred in its surface at his touch, and jumped as he heard the door open. A breeze followed Treanthor in as his cape swished with each step.

"Sit down, young man!"

"Yes, sir," quivered Rindel, bowing low as he moved back to his bench.

"The book."

"Yes, sir, it's right . . . right here, sir." Rindel stumbled over his words. His confidence had evaporated as the Emperor entered. Here, in his own citadel, Treanthor was a far more terrifying figure than he had been in disguise on the road.

Rindel handed over the book and watched as Treanthor handled it like it was a snake.

"And Marcus?" Treanthor said. "Is he nearly ready to join my side?"

Rindel found his voice. "He will be," he said. "I've been trying—trying to convince him that we should quit this PathOne business. He's been stubborn, but you should see where he is now! He's rounding some horrid mountain. If you show me a map, I'll point out his position to you. It's a terrible mountain, where I almost died. It's just south from here. I can take you there if—"

"Enough!" Treanthor blurted out, drops of spit emerging from his mouth onto the large table. "I have no need to go there." He narrowed his eyes. "Why are you so sure this mountain will make Marcus want to give up?"

Rindel cleared his throat. "Let me show you. You do have a map, don't you? Surely the Emperor has managed to preserve an old document or two. Or made a new one?"

Treanthor laughed, a deep, mocking cackle.

"Come here and sit by the table."

Rindel got up and sat on a high-backed chair opposite Treanthor, trying hard not to fidget.

Treanthor reached his hand under the mahogany table to slide a lever which pulled open a large hole in the table. A wooden slot gave way to reveal a large screen.

Rindel gasped as Treanthor blew on the glass-like screen, which lit up to show a colored map.

"Wow! Where did you get that?"

"I have my ways," laughed Treanthor. "You do realize that I have the largest quantity of xanth ever, and that all the best inventors work solely for my benefit?"

"No, I, er, I never knew."

"It took ten of those crystals I showed you the other night to create this. People are working around the clock at my NewTech Department to create such things as this! Now place your finger on it and show me where that troublemaker is!"

Rindel placed his finger on what appeared to be Treanthor's citadel. Sliding it across the screen, he was amazed that the map moved in every direction to display rivers, towns, forests, and major landmarks. Following the wide path he and Marcus had earlier traveled on, he was soon able to retrace their position to the foot of the distinctive mountain.

"You see?" he babbled. "It's such a dangerous route, and he has a horse with him, making it even more treacherous. By the time he comes down, he'll be ruing the day he ever left Trynn Goth. Just—well, I don't think there's any need for me to rejoin him until after he gets off that mountain, do you? Plenty of time once he's on safe ground to talk him into—"

Treanthor wasn't listening anymore. He tapped on the mountain two times, causing a black "x" to appear at the position Rindel had showed him, and leaned back in his chair.

"Well done," he said with a cold smile. He reached into the top drawer of the desk and retrieved a dark red pouch containing shiny, golden coins.

"This is for you. You'll find thirty inside – a month's wages as promised. You'll get the other two xanth crystals I promised once you've helped steer Marcus away from PathOne."

Treanthor handed the little drawstring velvet bag to Rindel, who eagerly received it, wide-eyed.

The Emperor leaned back, rubbing his hands and looking to be in deep thought. "The mountain," he mused. "Not many people ever get that far anymore. I am not convinced that the mountain alone would defeat him. But now that he no longer has access to the book, he should easily fall prey to discouragement."

Rindel cleared his throat. A terrible thought had suddenly come to him—but maybe he could find a way to profit from it anyhow.

"Well," he said, "he doesn't *exactly* not have access to the book."

Treanthor turned a strange shade of red and stared at Rindel as though he were a rat. "What?" he asked with a voice like a lava flow.

"Er, that is, he has a podbook," Rindel stammered.

Treanthor roared, "A *what?*"

"A—a podbook. It's the book, but they make it with xanth crystals and—"

"*Who?*"

"B-Brayman, sir. Personally, I don't think he can do you much harm, sir. He's quite an old man, you know."

"Personally, I'd stick to carrying out my commands and leaving your opinions out of this," snarled Treanthor, his scowl taking over his whole face as his eyes pierced right through Rindel. "I wanted the book taken away from Marcus, and now you tell me you've left him with full access to it!"

For a moment, Rindel was terrified that Treanthor would throw him in the dungeon or worse. But the Emperor appeared to calm down after his initial outrage.

"I've changed my mind," he said. "You are not going to rejoin Marcus. I'll put you to work convincing other young fools not to follow PathOne—you were on it long enough to make them think you were truly committed to it once. When the time is right, you'll help me convince Marcus to quit his pursuit of that fantasy kingdom. But first, you are going to tell me everything you know about Brayman and his podbooks. And you are not going to leave *anything* out this time. Do I make myself clear?"

Chapter 18

Marcus shielded his eyes from the dazzling sunlight, which blurred his vision as he emerged finally from the winding tunnel. Unable to see properly for almost a minute, he stood still, trying to scan ahead.

He had come nearly to the foot of the mountain, facing north. There was little water on this side, just a gentle stream trickling into a narrow river that flowed down toward woodland. Marcus mounted Tress, relieved that he could finally ride again and rest his weary legs and blistered feet.

Sitting astride the horse, he looked around for any sign of people. No one. He reached into his tunic pocket, pulling out the folded map.

"Stay by the river."

Merloy's words echoed once more in his head. He tapped Tress with his feet, and she led them forward alongside a dusty path with a ravine to the right and thick trees on the left.

"This is the way, Tress. Keep going, and we should soon get to a city. That's what the map shows."

Marcus urged the horse forward, feeling tired and hungry and wondering what this next city would be like and whether he would find any welcome there. He didn't have Rindel's way with people. He jangled the few remaining coins in his pocket, hoping he would find some food before storekeepers packed up for the evening.

The river widened once they neared the forest's edge, its rushing waters drowning out all other sounds.

By the time Marcus heard the hoofbeats of someone approaching from behind, he panicked, reaching clumsily for his sword. His grip slipped, and he dropped it on the path along with one of the bundled sacks.

"Marcus!" a firm but calm voice called out.

Marcus recognized it instantly and turned to face Delan.

With relief rushing through his body, Marcus fell forward, hugging Tress, and began to laugh. His laughs turned quickly to quiet sobs. His emotions were overwhelming, and he found that he couldn't get them under control.

"I thought someone was coming to attack me," he cried.

Delan patted him on the back.

"It's good to see you, brother, but where have you been all this time? I was instructed to meet you in Kalpos two days ago. I've been waiting and then came in search of you. Merloy said I would find you in the city."

"Kalpos?" sniffed Marcus. "Is that the city up ahead?"

"That's right. It's less than half a mile from here. It's a bustling city full of distractions and all manner of strange but interesting people. I have somewhere for you to stay the night, but I'm afraid I'll be moving on, as I have somewhere else to be now. If you'd come earlier, we could have enjoyed some time together."

Marcus hung his head low, unable to hide his disappointment. He was lonelier than he wanted to admit without Rindel.

Delan saw Marcus's dejection and forced his voice to be cheerful. "Anyway, I should have time to show you around a little before I leave. What kept you so long, Marcus? If you'd gotten here sooner, I could have stayed and helped you a while."

Marcus sighed and began to recount all the events of the previous few days as they rode side by side on the river path. He explained how the landslide and the chance encounter with an unusual traveler had made them decide to move away from the riverside path and journey instead on the wide, smooth road.

As obvious disappointment grew on Delan's face, Marcus felt increasingly stupid and small. His friend looked almost angry.

"Did you not suppose that your 'helpful' stranger could have been one of Treanthor's messengers? The Emperor knows of you, Marcus, and he does not want you to continue following PathOne."

Marcus's jaw dropped. The thought had never occurred to him, but in that instant he knew that Delan was right.

"How could you know? Why didn't I see? I, er, I—"

Delan stopped his horse and looked directly at him.

"Marcus, you should expect traps and deceptions along the way. You need to be ready and on the lookout for such pitfalls. Did you not learn anything from your time with me and Brayman?"

Marcus cleared his throat and twitched his nose.

When he described how Rindel had nearly slipped off the side of the mountain and then deserted him, Delan looked even more incredulous and shook his head in dismay.

"Were you instructed to journey together and stay together at all times?"

Marcus admitted that neither the book nor his mother nor Merloy had encouraged him to travel with Rindel.

"I thought it would be less lonely to bring Rindel along, and he can be such fun. I've never traveled such a distance alone, and besides, Rindel said he believed in PathOne too and wanted to follow it."

Delan looked at Marcus with disapproval. "It is better to journey alone than to travel with someone who will lead you along wrong paths."

"It wasn't his fault!" protested Marcus. "I agreed to follow that stranger's advice too."

"That may well be so," said Delan with a deep frown, "but you would think more carefully if you didn't have some fool-headed half-wit along with you to influence your every decision. If you had stuck to the original path, you would have had plenty of time to navigate the mountain and still reach Kalpos in good time." Delan shook his head. "I had my doubts about him when I first met him, but you insisted on him staying and learning to train alongside you."

Marcus was at a loss for words. Delan had never spoken so harshly to him before, and he stared straight ahead, refusing to look him directly in the eye.

Delan's voice softened a little. "I am sorry for being so strong, Marcus. It can't be easy for you to have lost a friend."

"But I don't understand," Marcus blurted, hardly noting Delan's apology. "If Merloy cares about people, why didn't he appear to Rindel like he did to me?"

"Merloy has been reaching out to Rindel," Delan said. "He allowed Rindel to travel with you all this way. He directed my grandfather to save Rindel's life from the gratsch, and you to rescue him on the mountain. Rindel has heard the words of the book and the mysteries of PathOne from you, from me, from Brayman, and from Jez—but he has chosen to reject all of that. If Rindel would only respond to Merloy, Merloy would help him believe like you do. But instead, Rindel has chosen to reject all of that for the sake of worthless pleasures."

Delan grimaced. "And _you_ should never have trusted him so implicitly. He gave you plenty of reason to realize that his heart wasn't in this journey."

As they approached the bright lights of Kalpos, Marcus said very little. Resentment at Delan's sharp rebuke set root in his spirit, and he grew disappointed that the friend he had so looked forward to seeing again was in fact chiding him for all his mistakes. Besides, for the most part, Rindel had been willing to follow his leading and to continue their journey as planned. Yes, he could be foolish—but he wasn't that bad!

When Delan began to offer words of advice and wisdom about staying in the city, Marcus chose to let his mind wander and tuned out Delan's voice. It was a childish response and Marcus knew it, but at the moment he wasn't quite up for leaving childish ways and attitudes behind. Likewise, he didn't pay much attention when Delan started telling him about a wild beast he had tackled on his way to Kalpos and how he had managed to escape.

242

It was dusk as they entered the city. A huge iron sign hanging on a post by the city walls stated, "Welcome to Kalpos — City of a Thousand Delights, 50,000 inhabitants."

Marcus sat up a little straighter in his saddle, wondering how a city could have so many delights and looking forward to the sights and smells of such a thriving metropolis. It felt like he had been far from civilization for years, and he yearned for companions once more.

Delan led him through narrow winding streets, past shops and taverns to a little house on a corner. He pointed out a good place to find hay for Tress and showed him how most streets ran parallel to one another, all leading to the main square. After tying up their horses, Delan opened the blue wooden door with a large key and led Marcus up creaky stairs to a room with a small square window which looked out across the street. A flashing light beamed intermittently through the pane.

Marcus approached the window to pull the curtains shut when he saw the source of light. A grench port was situated yards from the house, its lights beaming out onto all the other buildings around.

Delan handed Marcus the large key, along with a smaller iron key for the room.

"I'm afraid you'll have to share the washroom with the other travelers down the hall. Remember everything I told you, and let's hope we can spend more time together next time."

Marcus didn't know what to say. He nodded and dragged his belongings across the room. He lit a lamp on a small table by the bed, and Delan threw a cloth bag at him before saying goodbye.

Inside the bag he found a fresh loaf, some meat and a ginger cake. There was also a bunch of grapes in there, his favorite fruit.

Marcus called out his thanks as Delan left the room, and he slumped down on the bed. He meant to start eating but drifted off to sleep instead, the events of the day circling around in his mind. He kept reliving Delan's harsh rebuke and the steps around the treacherous mountain.

He imagined Rindel falling off the perilous path, screaming as he descended to the dark lake, when he suddenly bolted straight upright.

Sweat drenched Marcus's forehead and back, his breathing heavy and distressed.

He shook his shoulders nervously and stretched out his legs before getting up to pour a cup of water from a glass decanter on a dresser across the room. His eyes blinked again at the flickers of light still flashing through a gap in the curtains. Pulling the ragged curtain aside, he looked out, amazed at the number of people still up and about in the middle of the night, gathering on benches, chatting to one another or queuing to get inside the impressive building. Some young men and women sat around a nearby fountain, sharing little sachets of sekrin, which they gathered up in cupped hands before closing their eyes and inhaling the fragrant substance.

One attractive girl threw her head back and began laughing. Marcus recognized her but couldn't remember where from. As he continued to observe her, she flicked the blonde hair from the side of her face, and he remembered. *Shurama. That's her, the girl from the barn dance.* Rindel had been besotted by her.

But Rindel's not here anymore. And he's found another girl anyway.

Marcus moved away from the window to sit back on the bed and start eating the food which Delan had brought. He tried to think of other things or consider what he might do the next day. But he couldn't shake the image of Shurama from his mind.

He scoffed the small loaf and cleared the crumbs from his lap. He fidgeted and sniffed and rearranged the covers on the bed.

Then he looked out the window once more. She was still there.

He began to sort through his bags haphazardly and fill them up again. But he could not focus on the task.

Breathing in deeply, Marcus went to wash his hands and face over a cracked clay bowl before grabbing his overtunic and dashing out of the room. He jumped down three steps at a time, forgetting the last time he had done so—he had crash-landed in a heap at home. This time he managed to land on his feet.

As he strode across the street, he heard the town clock sound midnight. His eyes met hers in an instant, and in that moment he was hooked—like a fish on a reel. It didn't take much persuasion before Marcus found himself following Shurama into the grench port.

Just as Rindel had described, the grench port was a feast of sensory amazement—a constant, overwhelming mix of rides and music and excitement, like an entire carnival captured in one place. Despite all this, Marcus realized that he was more enamored by Shurama than by all of the fun activities of grench. Not that he wasn't fascinated by the buttons, the lights, the sliding floors and levels, or the impressive design of the place. No—they were amazing, every last one. It was just that he was even more impressed by Shurama.

There was a certain way about her that he had not really noticed in a girl before. The way she flicked her hair from her face, the way she fluttered her eyelashes, her tight-fitting clothing and the soft skin of her neck. And her voice. Her voice was somehow captivating; everything she said seemed to lead him on, like she was trying to take him somewhere, though he wasn't yet sure where. When she spoke to him, her eyes sent additional messages.

When she said, "Shall we try this game capsule?" Marcus knew instinctively that her eyes were saying, "I really like you, and I want you to follow me."

When she suggested, "Let's stand by this platform and watch what's happening on the level below," he interpreted this (correctly) to mean, "I want to stand near you and touch you."

With every word, every brush of her against him, intense feelings stirred inside Marcus which he had never experienced before. Although he realized that he did not know Shurama well yet and that he should take care to learn more about her, he ignored his reservations. It felt good to be noticed by such an attractive girl. And she seemed so carefree and happy. He'd had nothing but worry and hardship for so long—surely it wouldn't hurt to let go for once.

As they leaned against a railing, watching crowds of people below, Shurama pointed out a funny-looking fellow wearing red boots.

"Isn't that the strangest-looking man you've ever seen?" she giggled.

Marcus couldn't make out where she was pointing, and she leaned across him to point more accurately. He gasped softly as she pressed against him.

When she turned to face him, her eyes locked with his. Clasping his hand in hers, she whispered in his ear, "I know of a quiet spot—come with me!"

"I, er, where . . . what do you mean?" mumbled Marcus nervously.

"Oh, come on, I'll show you."

Shurama winked and pulled his hand, leading him across the platform, round a corner, and down some narrow steps. From there she led him to a quiet corner where two or three couples were embracing and kissing.

Marcus's heart began to race as he anticipated what might happen next. His whole body demanded that he follow his desires and do whatever Shurama wanted, but in a small part of his mind he was aware of something warning him to get out of the port and away from her.

Shurama did not allow much time for thinking. She pulled him close and pressed her lips to his. Marcus resisted lightly, taking a half-step backward, but Shurama closed in toward him, and he couldn't take it anymore—he just had to kiss her. One of her hands ran behind his head and then around his neck while her other hand clutched his lower back.

It felt so good, but it also felt wrong. Marcus didn't even know her last name, but he couldn't stop himself.

As they stood in the low light, their bodies entwined, Marcus chose to ignore his doubts and follow his urges. He felt weak at the knees as she pressed her body against his.

Only the clunking sound of something falling onto the floor by their feet and rolling around distracted them.

Shurama bent down to pick up the pod-like gadget.

"What's this?" she asked curiously.

Marcus coughed and blinked. His eyes widened as he recognized the little item.

Snatching it from her hand, he replied, "That's mine. I've been looking for it—it must have fallen out of my tunic."

"What's it for?" inquired Shurama. "Let me see."

"No," snapped Marcus, standing back from her. "That little thing is why I'm on this journey. I need to go."

Somehow, the appearance of the podbook had changed everything. The words of Delan reverberated round his mind—"You should expect traps and deceptions along the way"—and he knew he needed to get away from Shurama.

She would not help him focus on completing his journey or finding the Kingdom of the North. She would only slow him down or distract him altogether from his quest.

Shurama looked disappointed and upset.

"Don't go now—we were having so much fun. Come on, let's sit over there a while. We can try out a game on that spark wall before you leave. It's amazing."

Marcus twiddled the podbook between his finger and thumb before placing it carefully inside his inner waistcoat pocket. The urgency he'd felt a moment before was fading . . . it would be more polite to stay a little while longer, wouldn't it?

Shurama pulled his arm and led him to a bench by a glowing wall with changing, lit-up shapes which increased and decreased in size depending on where they touched them. Shurama showed him that the object of the game was to touch different parts of the wall so quickly that the shapes matched in size and color.

She laughed sweetly as Marcus was unable to complete the task—it was far more difficult than it appeared. "Have another go," she told him, stepping up beside him again. "Watch—this is how it's done."

Marcus wasn't really interested in playing any longer. He wasn't sure he should have stayed this long instead of running when his instincts first told him to, and now that he was still here, he began to see the pointlessness of it all. The grench port wouldn't earn him any money, it wouldn't help him on his journey, and it wouldn't help him reach Merloy. It was just a waste of time. Oh, it was fine for a few minutes of fun. But did he really want to spend the rest of the night there, punching glowing shapes on a wall?

"No," he said aloud.

"No what?" asked Shurama. "Shall we go through that tunnel and find a better game?"

"No, I don't want to stay here now. I need to leave."

Shurama's eyes turned sharp, and she cast an angry look at Marcus. Her previously soft voice turned almost menacing. "Nobody turns me down!"

He shook his head. "I'm sorry, I should never have come here with you. I—"

Before he could finish, Shurama leaned forward and grabbed his head, trying to force another kiss. When Marcus pulled away, she started to run her hands down the front of his tunic. She was forceful and skilled in her maneuvers. Marcus recognized that she must have done this at least a dozen times before.

This time, he refused to be swayed by the feelings that still raged in his body. He peeled her arms off him, pushed her aside, and walked away. After three or four steps, he could hear her behind him.

"Wait!" she called out. This time her voice was whining, pleading. "You didn't even try some sekrin with me. I have another pouchful — you've got to try it before you go; it's awesome stuff."

She caught up with him and waved the fragrant bag of powder under his nose. But the very mention of sekrin reminded Marcus of his father, and something twisted inside of him.

He snatched the pouch and threw it down the steps to his left.

"I won't ruin my destiny for the sake of some cheap thrill!" he thundered.

His steps turned to running, and he refused to look back as Shurama continued to pursue him and call his name. Marcus lost her in the crowds and slipped through a small door on the floor below. Tears were stinging at his eyes as he thought of his father, and he angrily swiped them away.

Once he emerged out of the grench port, away from the pounding music, he found that dawn was already starting to break through the misty early morning air. He had spent half the night with Shurama, something he had never intended to do.

As he ran across the street and turned the corner to the little house where Delan had left him, he stopped suddenly in his tracks when he heard the sound of heavy footsteps and caught sight of the distinctive hats of knights.

Treanthor's men!

He darted inside a shop entrance and hid himself in the shadows as four officials marched by.

Once he was sure they had passed and gone a fair distance, Marcus fumbled in his pockets to find the keys and return to his room. He needn't have bothered to search for the keys.

Both doors were slightly ajar.

Chapter 19

Entering the room with his heart pounding, Marcus groaned aloud as he found all of his belongings upturned and strewn across the room. Had it been Treanthor's men or just thieves? And what had they taken?

He was surprised to find his coin purse remaining, including the gold necklace it held, as well as the gadgets from Farlack's store. Most of his clothes appeared to still be there too. Only after half packing up his things did it occur to Marcus what they had come for—the book. *They must have taken the book!*

He searched everywhere but couldn't find it. He cursed himself as he searched. This was the *one* time he had left the book behind since he had started reading it in his bedroom back in Trynn Goth. One time—and now it was gone. The precious gift his mother had entrusted to him, the book he needed to show him where to go, was now in the hands of some stranger—probably one who worked for Treanthor.

Marcus slumped down on the floor and started punching the bed repeatedly.

"You stupid boy—you couldn't even take care of the one important thing in your life!" he berated himself. "Now you don't have all the maps, just the listening device. But Mum will want to have the original book back. She said I must not part with it! And the only map I have doesn't show all the details I need. How will I ever find my way now? And Delan . . . and Merloy . . . what would they say?"

Unable to think clearly, Marcus didn't realize that Treanthor's men, having not found him in the room, would still be in pursuit of him. He did not even consider that Rindel might have taken the book or betrayed him; that would have been unthinkable.

Marcus felt a cloak of shame surrounding him as he nearly drifted off to sleep on the wooden floor. Memories of Shurama only made it worse, filling him with guilt as he thought about how willingly he had given in to her. As he slid down to the floorboards, he felt worthless and disappointed in himself. If he hadn't gone to the grench port, he would have heard the men coming and could have escaped out the window *with* the book. At least he still had the podbook—and as far as he knew, Treanthor's men didn't know about those. *No thanks to me,* he thought; after all, he had let Shurama see the podbook like a fool. How long until rumors started to circulate and put Brayman's whole operation in danger?

He closed his eyes, but sleep refused to come. Instead, he saw a dark cloud before him that circled around, instilling him with fear. He shook his head awake and blinked, but saw nothing. As he closed his eyes again, the dark cloud pressed in toward him menacingly.

And then he heard a voice. *"Don't try to resist me. Lie there and wallow in me. Just accept it—you are a failure, and I have come to draw you into my comfort. When you can't stand it any longer, run and take yourself to the tavern three doors down the street. We can enjoy a drink together and just accept the situation—there's no use fighting it."*

Marcus froze. He had little strength to counter this strange force; his body was desperate for rest. He opened his eyes once more and saw nothing in the room. Still, the words pierced his mind and refused to leave it. Something Jez had said—a warning about something called Santon—niggled at his mind, but he couldn't focus on it. The voice was too compelling.

"Go to the tavern." It was all he could think about. He climbed back on the bed and tried to sleep, but sleep continued to elude him. The dark cloud encircled him every time he closed his eyelids, and whispers echoed in his ears. *"It's no use—accept it—you are a failure. You let that girl get to you; she's weakened you now. It's no use. Run to the tavern. Go. Go."*

For more than an hour, Marcus wrestled with these words and with images, the scenes from the grench port replaying in his mind. His responses swung from guilt to regret. Maybe he should have given in to her all the way instead of resisting. Otherwise, why was he in this difficult situation now? Maybe he deserved it for being so foolish.

He retrieved the little podbook from his waistcoat pocket and rolled it around in his hand. But he couldn't bring himself to insert it in his ear and switch it on.

"You're a failure, Marcus—face it, a failure. You'll never get to your destination. You may as well give up now."

Santon swirled around him, and he felt utterly useless, his powers of resistance already spent in the grench port.

He clasped a small tankard on a wobbly bedside table and threw it against the wall, yelling out in frustration.

Getting up from the bed, he pulled on a cap and coat and left the room. Hurrying along a few houses to the left, he found the tavern still open at dawn. Only a few heavy drinkers remained, slumped at tables. Marcus approached the bar and sat on a stool.

"I'll have a large beer, please. Make it strong ale."

The weary-looking barman wiped a towel across the bar before pouring a large mug of ale and placing it before him.

"So what brings you here at this early hour?"

Marcus turned away from the man. "I just wanted a beer—not a conversation!" he snapped.

He gulped down the beer within a couple of minutes and requested another. The barman obliged, this time saying nothing. As Marcus drank alone, he considered once more how much easier life would be if he just followed the Wryxl lifestyle, enjoying himself and leisurely pursuits instead of worrying about following some strange path. What would it even matter if he did take things further with Shurama?

"Why do you always have to get so hung up about everything?" Rindel used to say. "Lighten up a bit—live for the moment!" Bitterly, Marcus began to think that maybe Rindel had been right. *I mean, look at me and the state I'm in! I can't possibly belong in the city of lights I once glimpsed. Why would Merloy even let me in? I think he made a mistake, saying I was chosen—he must have meant someone else. I'm just not good enough!*

After drinking two more beers, Marcus stumbled out of the tavern and back to his room. He was nearly sick at the foot of the stairwell, but he managed to contain it, steadying himself there for a while before climbing the stairs.

Maybe now the clouds of Santon will leave me alone, he thought. But as he collapsed on his bed, the clouds—now darker and thicker—enclosed him as though they would strangle him as he closed his eyes. He heard eerie laughter as he tried to turn his head.

"You can't get away from me," mocked the voice. *"The beer might make you sleep, but I'll still be here tomorrow!"*

Marcus's head swirled in a drunken stupor, and his stomach churned. If he lay perfectly still, his stomach would just about settle. As his body finally submitted to sleep, Marcus entertained the thought that maybe it would be better if he never woke up.

* * *

The sounds of hoofbeats and barking dogs emerging from the direction of the grench port stirred Marcus abruptly awake. It was now mid-morning. He dashed across the room to peer out the window, his raging heart beating wildly, his head pounding from the earlier drinking fest.

Just across from the fountain, market stall holders were selling their fruits and vegetables. Beyond them, through the misty morning air, he saw a figure who appeared to be Treanthor's captain of the guard on a dark horse, leading seven or eight other horsemen. The growing crowds had forced them to slow their approach, but Marcus was certain of one thing.

They were coming for him.

Hurriedly packing up his things, Marcus fled the room and darted across the hall, down the stairs, and out to the front, where he found Tress still tied to a lamppost. He mounted her nervously, nearly dropping one of the bags, and whispered "Go" into her ear, steering her in the opposite direction from the approaching guards.

The flight meant that Marcus had to weave through winding streets and past pedestrians and market carts before he could make a swift departure. He didn't dare look back, pulling his cloth cap low over his forehead to keep a low profile. Once he approached the city's boundaries, away from the bustle of the center, he could clearly see three possible exit points. The first pointed in the direction he had entered the city with Delan—that was out of the question. He was reluctant to backtrack when he had made it this far. The second seemed to point to hill country; the third pointed toward open fields, where a low fence to one side continued into the distance. The other side was flanked by hedges and fruit trees. Marcus quickly chose the latter route. There was cover in the trees, and he reckoned that at least he'd find something to eat en route.

Picking up speed, Marcus soon heard the sound of Treanthor's greyhounds in hot pursuit. Horsemen followed not far behind. Reluctantly he pulled out the remaining strips of meat from the food bag Delan had given him. Pausing momentarily, he broke the strips into several smaller chunks and threw them behind him, to the right. He then pulled out one of his grubby shirts, rolled it into a ball, and threw that in the same direction.

Kicking his heels, Marcus galloped off across the field as fast as he could. At one point he threw off a bag of goods from Farlack's shop, deciding it was too cumbersome and awkward to bother carrying any further. The *lighter my load, the better,* he thought. Leaning forward, he flicked Tress's reins and galloped away.

* * *

The discarded items served their purpose of distracting the bloodthirsty dogs and Treanthor's men. Among them was Rindel, who confirmed that the bag and the shirt did indeed belong to Marcus.

"He'll be heading north," said Rindel confidently. "And if there's a river up ahead, he's sure to be traveling alongside it."

The captain yelled out orders concerning the horses and hounds, dividing them in two groups to head in slightly different directions. "Don't kill the target," he said sternly. "But use whatever force necessary to bring him in. Is that understood?"

Now that Marcus's scent was fresh in their nostrils, the eager parties focused their energy on the chase. This was, after all, their sole purpose in life: to pursue and detain enemies of the Emperor. And they relished the thought of terrorizing a frightened victim.

* * *

Marcus slowed Tress up, looking wildly around for someplace to take cover. He could hear the sounds of pursuit behind him and knew he could soon be caught. Then another sound—cows lowing—came to his ears. A farmer was leading a large herd of cows across the field just ahead of him. He breathed a huge sigh of relief, knowing that this would delay his pursuers further and confuse the dogs away from his scent. Careful not to be noticed, he rode Tress into the herd for a little while, hoping the scents would be confused, and then ambled away on his own again.

Continuing another half-mile, the field dipped to one side, enabling Marcus to move out of view from his attackers. The grassy verge leaned steeply down toward a dark copse, forcing him to move slowly through low-lying branches. At one point Marcus saw a narrow, overgrown path leading to a stream. Tress skillfully trotted over thick bramble and dense trees to reach an open area, which appeared to have been used in the past as a place to camp and build fires.

Marcus stopped and listened. He heard nothing. He jumped down from Tress and listened again—still nothing. A damp mist circled around the trees, the haziness seeming to play tricks with his vision. He squinted and turned all around.

Maybe they've kept going north on the path, he thought to himself.

Unsure if he even wanted to continue his journey, Marcus was still certain of one thing: he did not want to accept Treanthor's lies or have any part in his kingdom. He could never trust that man with the piercing eyes and haunting laugh. His mum, Ree-Mya, had only ever shown mistrust and scorn at the mere mention of his name. Even if he couldn't stand to follow the book any more, he would just become a typical Wryxl man—enjoying life and work, and relaxing with friends. Anything to keep a low profile and stay out of trouble. Someone else would have to follow his destiny; someone else would have to find the Kingdom of the North.

Marcus sat on a tree stump and tightened his bootlaces. He considered the previous night and his time spent with Shurama. She had been almost as intoxicating as the beer—he couldn't deny that. Yet he hadn't liked her forceful, controlling manner. She would try to make him be whatever she wanted him to be—and that really wasn't attractive.

Yet no matter how hard Marcus tried to convince himself that he was not the right person for this quest, the more he remembered words from Merloy and Brayman—words which cut deep into his mind and soul.

How can I walk away from the truth? I have been chosen for a purpose—that's what they said. It's up to me now. I can either press on to reach that city of lights and place of ultimate fulfillment, or I can ignore everything I've seen and risk going down with everyone else when Krinton is destroyed. That is, if it really is going to be destroyed. But why else would Mum and I have such similar dreams—the world fading beneath us?

The conflict raged in his heart as he recognized that there were no easy options for him now. He could choose to join the Wryxl, but he would forever remember the words in the book and his experiences with Merloy, along with the beautiful vision of the amazing city. Or he could return home to Trynn Goth and face the crushing disappointment of his mother, as well as having to deal with the pointlessness of getting this far and turning back. Joining Treanthor was simply not an option. Not now, not ever. But in some ways, Marcus wished he had never picked up the book in the first place or experienced his shocking vision. He wished he had never seen the distant Kingdom of the North or trespassed in Treanthor's citadel. *To be ignorant of the truth must be an easy way to live,* he thought.

The sound of rustling leaves disturbed Marcus's train of thought. He leapt to attention, searching over his shoulder and all around. Clutching his ska-sword, he expected to be confronted by one of Treanthor's knights at any moment. But the sight that appeared before him was fearful beyond his imagination.

A creature of considerable size lurked in the shadow of the trees, grunting and kicking its heels in the dirt. An unusual moaning sound emerged from its mouth, rattling Marcus to the bone.

His heart began to race as he vaguely recalled some of Delan's words the other day, on their way into the city.

"Watch out that you don't run into the den of a mak . . ." Oh what was it, *a mak-something, something about a menace to overcome. Makhtamn! That must be it; I'm sure he said something about moaning and droning.* Unfortunately, Marcus could remember nothing Delan had said about how best to trap or avoid the weird creature.

Holding his ska-sword ready in his right hand, Marcus pulled out his knarl-knife with his left hand and flicked it open. Walking backward slowly in Tress's direction, he hurriedly mounted her, all the while scanning the area for evidence of more than one of the creatures. He saw no more and decided to focus on the approaching, scaly beast.

As it emerged from the trees into the light, its massive head swung around and focused on Marcus with lizard-like, unintelligent eyes. The creature stood on four powerful legs, and its scaled skin was crowned by plates along the length of its spine and long tail. Tufts of hair grew from its joints and from between the plates, spiking up like needles. Though it paused to regard Marcus, when it did move, it was quick — surprisingly quick for something so big.

As the creature came forward at a remarkable pace, swinging branches aside with its head, Marcus laughed softly for a moment. He knew that he would not be able to outrun the makhtamn through dense trees. Here he was, sword in hand, ready to launch an attack on a creature he had never even heard of until the day before—and he had only been trained to battle other men!

"Why did I agree to even following PathOne at all?" Marcus muttered to himself. "I've had nothing but trouble since I walked out the door! So much for the difficult path leading to life! Now it looks like I'm going to die here in the middle of nowhere, beaten by some scaly beast! Well, at least I'll put up a fight."

His voice was rising, making sure the creature could hear him. "I won't go down easily!"

Marcus steadied Tress, warning her to be ready for action. She kicked the dirt beneath her, aware of the approaching creature, and retreated slightly. Despite his doubts, Marcus found himself mumbling, "If you want me to continue this journey, you'll have to get me out of here, Merloy! I can't do this on my own."

Once the makhtamn's head was in full view, Marcus could see properly what he was up against. The creature's eyes were clearly intent on its target—him and Tress. They appeared as dull silver balls. Its scales were dingy green and brown, its frame more than twice the size of Tress. A horrible odor wafted through the air as it grunted and snorted.

Marcus's heart began pounding furiously in his chest. He braced himself, ready to launch his attack. Aiming carefully toward the animal's eyes, he hurled the knarl-knife. It rotated several times through the air and lodged in the makhtamn's head, just above the brow.

The creature let out a deafening moan and stomped its front legs in fury. Shaking its head against a tree, the animal managed to dislodge the knife. Blood poured from the makhtamn's head, dripping onto its misshapen mouth and down onto the leaves below.

Marcus could tell in an instant that the wound had only angered the creature and that its strength had in no way been hindered. If anything, the knife attack had stirred up the animal's rage against its attacker. The creature grunted loudly and darted toward Marcus, its heavy breath audible from across the open woodland.

Marcus geared up to lunge at the animal, lying low across Tress to shield his head from the anticipated impact. He thought he could come against the creature from one side and plunge his sword into its belly.

The makhtamn had other ideas. It rushed against Tress, the impact flinging Marcus from the horse onto a pile of sticks and twigs. One of them pierced through his clothing into his side, and he cried out in agony.

Marcus's shrieks alarmed the makhtamn for a moment—the unusual sound of a young man yelping unsettled it. As the creature remained still, just a few steps away, Marcus mustered up the strength to seize another opportunity for attack. Sword in hand, he leapt up and ran full strength into the monster, plunging his sword into its underbelly.

To his dismay, the sword barely pierced the animal. It maybe went in two or three inches before shattering and falling to the ground.

"Useless sword!" he called out.

Unarmed, Marcus pushed himself away in a panic. He remembered how he had traded the trusty sword from Brayman for a flashy-looking ska-sword, a fine-looking weapon—one that had proven to be useless. Regret came over him.

The creature moaned loudly, enraged that Marcus had wounded it a second time. It stomped the ground and hovered down over Marcus, ready to grab him. Marcus rolled away to the left before huddling over his knees, cowering from the impending danger. There was no possibility of escape.

The makhtamn came after him quickly before awkwardly losing its footing and plunging dramatically through the thick pile of sticks. The massive creature let out a haunting moan as it landed in a pit right beside where Marcus lay.

Marcus blinked once or twice, letting what had just happened sink in. Sweat poured down his forehead as his heart beat wildly in his chest. When he had recovered from the initial shock, he peered down into the hole before lying down on his back and panting in relief. He was safe. Someone else had laid a trap for this creature, and now it had saved him. He lay quietly for several minutes before realizing that he was still lying on sticks which could also give way into the pit. Rolling carefully away from the hole, Marcus thought that if his movements had been slightly different, or if the twigs had shifted differently, he could have fallen through the trap first.

When he was sufficiently far from the pit, Marcus pulled himself up, only to collapse to the ground again in agony. The ankle he had previously injured had given way once more, and he was unable to walk on it. Pulling himself up again, Marcus steadied himself against a tree before hobbling on one leg back to Tress, who had retreated in the direction they had come from.

Eerie moans continued to erupt from the pit, but Marcus was convinced there was no way of escape for the creature. Calling out to Tress, he tried to soothe her.

"It's okay now, he can't get out. He's trapped, Tress. Come on, come here, girl."

Marcus winced as the pain from his side started to get to him. Looking down under his tunic, he found his shirt soaked in blood. Pressing his hand onto the wound to stem the flow, he began to feel incredibly weak and tired. He had just about summoned the strength to mount Tress and steer her in the direction back to the field when he lost all focus and drifted out of consciousness.

* * *

Delan had just turned on his bed to avoid the early morning sunlight streaming through the broken wooden shutters of his window when he was roused by a heavy banging at the door. Jerking awake, he leapt up, sword at the ready.

"Who is it?"

"Messenger boy. Sent by the one called Brayman from the town of Penryth," replied the voice behind the door of the little inn bedroom.

Delan relaxed and moved slowly to unlock the door before slumping back down on the bed.

A scrawny young man with a dirty face, wearing scruffy clothes, came in. He sounded breathless from his hurried journey.

"Are you Delan Macantyre?"

"That I am."

"Sir, an urgent message for you from Brayman. He's had a dream warning him that some people are in perilous danger. You must go to save them immediately!"

Delan sighed. "But who are these people and where shall I find them?" *Could Rindel have returned to Marcus and led him into some foolish trap?*

"Brayman said he saw two men, maybe three, cowering in a dark room, scared for their lives. He didn't say who they were—I'm just the messenger, sir. Then he saw you en route to find them, following the range of mountains that leads to the place of the volcano in the west, Mount Zorbin. He says you must leave immediately. I've been looking in every hostel and inn for you. This is the fifth one I've been to."

Delan started to pack up his things haphazardly and asked if there were any further instructions.

"None, sir. That's all he told me."

"Thank you. Here's a tip for your troubles."

Delan tossed two kroens at the boy, who caught them awkwardly and went on his way.

Delan began to wonder how this new mission might unfold. He shook his head, not too happy about the prospect of tackling the paths around Mount Zorbin. Delan knew that many of the rumors about the mountain's extreme dangers were just rumors—but that didn't mean it wasn't dangerous all the same. Just as he was about to leave the room, having hurriedly downed some breakfast, he paused to close his eyes and call on Merloy. He would need clear direction if he was to find his way.

Chapter 20

Marcus's eyes gently flickered. His side ached, and his ankle throbbed in pain. Opening one eye, he gazed up at the dark ceiling above him. Too weak to focus on his surroundings, his body still locked in slumber, he blinked at a scene where everything appeared to be blurred. Closing his eyes once more, Marcus moved his hands around, trying to gauge where he was. It felt as though he were lying on wood. No wonder he felt so sore.

When he breathed in through his nose, he became instantly alarmed. Sekrin! He could smell sekrin. Both eyes shot open, but he remained lying down.

His eyes functioning alertly now, Marcus scanned the room to discover that he was not in the woods, nor in a guesthouse, but in a fearsome cavern. Long, sharp stalactites jutted out on every side, the light from two sconces casting eerie shadows which danced around the jagged, icicle-shaped formations.

Treanthor! Immediately, the wafting aroma of sekrin made Marcus realize where he was—the citadel below Mount Zorbin. But he was alone in the cavern, his only company the huge spider which had spun its web from one huge stalactite down to the floor. His head started to pound as the frowns on his forehead burrowed deep, and he wondered why he was lying on a table, elevated high above the floor.

Just as he raised his head to look for an exit, a heavy hand came from behind and pushed him harshly down.

Marcus winced. "Ow, who did—"

"I did," a voice rasped.

Treanthor had been watching him. He stepped around to tower high above his prisoner, his cape blocking the candlelight and forming a menacing shadow beside Marcus.

Marcus was overcome with despair. He had managed to escape the clutches of a makhtamn only to land straight into the lair of the evil Emperor. He didn't want to be there.

"Look at me, Marcus."

Marcus scrunched his eyes shut and turned his head away.

Treanthor grasped his chin and pulled it to face him. "Open your eyes, peasant!"

He slapped Marcus across the face.

Once he had his attention, he pulled out a ragged cloth from inside his cape.

"Do you recognize this?"

Treanthor dangled the stained, gray cotton item just inches from his nose.

Marcus knew instantly that it was the shirtsleeve he had torn on the spiked gatepost during his flight from the citadel that first eerie night. But he refused to acknowledge it, and he remained silent.

Treanthor started to laugh. His mocking, cruel laugh.

"You are brave, you know. No one else has ever dared creep in here to see the truth for himself. But you have never been out of my sight. I have always been close behind you, watching your every move. And I know about the resistance movement and the production of those wretched podbooks. Rindel has been quite helpful. Even now, my men are tracking down the secret production unit."

"Rindel doesn't know where they're being produced!" protested Marcus.

"Yes, but following you led us straight to Brayman, and he is being watched at all times. We'll soon put a stop to his illegal activities."

Marcus gritted his teeth and restrained himself from spitting in Treanthor's face.

"Why don't you just kill me now? You've got what you want," he snarled.

"You're no use to me dead, Marcus. If you were, I would have killed you long ago—before you even ventured onto my wide path. Don't you see that I have plans for you? I want you to become one of us."

"One of us? There's only one Emperor."

"You are quite correct. But my people, my loyal people, are of one heart and purpose with me. We work together to ensure the future of my kingdom."

"There is no future for Krinton!" argued Marcus.

Slap. Treanthor struck Marcus across the face again, this time scratching his cheek with the gold and sapphire ring on his middle finger.

Blood trickled down Marcus's face and ran into the corner of his mouth.

Marcus trembled but tried to hide his fear. "What do you want from me, Treanthor?"

Treanthor smiled coldly. "You know that PathOne is virtually impossible to follow—that is why so few even attempt to travel it. I want you to tell others how miserable you have been, how PathOne nearly ruined your life. I want you to wipe out all remaining traces of that route, along with every offshoot and side route, and to spread the word about the easy way of life along the wide path. The good way. *My* good way."

Treanthor unraveled a sachet of sekrin from his pocket and rubbed some of the powder between his thumb and forefinger just above Marcus's nose. Marcus flinched as he tried to avoid inhaling the substance, but he couldn't help breathing in a small amount, which caused him to cough and sniff.

"I'm allergic to that stuff. Get it away!" he protested.

Treanthor laughed as he drew his hands to his own face and sniffed in the distinct drug. He then breathed out over Marcus, spreading the fragrance across the cavern.

Marcus held his breath for several seconds, not wanting to consume even a little of the mind-numbing powder. He needed to stay alert. He contemplated his options and decided to humor Treanthor by feigning interest in his schemes.

"So tell me, why I should possibly want to join forces with you?"

Treanthor smiled a sly half-smile. "You already want to join forces with me, Marcus. You have proved that over and over again. You prove it every time you allow yourself to be sidetracked and stay in one of my cities, enjoying its entertainments and distractions, forgetting about your destination. You proved it with Shurama too. And if you give in, if you admit that your real allegiance is with me, you will see great success. You will rise up the ranks steadily to gain high position, and nobody will deter you or mess up your chances of a good life. Everything and every gadget will be provided, and I will never send you on ridiculous, impossible missions!"

Marcus grew quiet. "Do you mean that I won't have to do anything really difficult?"

"That's right. All I want you to do is be a hero by proving once and for all, to every young person in Krinton, that PathOne is a lie and a waste of a life. Of course, you also get to enjoy unlimited pleasure on your days off: grench, sekrin, beer, girls—I know some incredibly pretty ones—and all that comes free with the job."

"And you promise that I won't end up alone in a dark wood or on a treacherous path round a mountain?"

"I do! You will always have a group of friends to accompany you, and they won't make ridiculous demands of you. And if ever you should run into any trouble, I guarantee that I will send a squad of my finest men to come to your rescue."

For a moment, Marcus was slightly tempted. He could not deny that an easy life with lots of benefits was appealing, even that he had sometimes given in to the temptations. But deep down, he knew he could not trust Treanthor. He quickly recalled the warnings of Brayman—how Treanthor was described as "the deceiver"—and remembered the cruel way in which he had tricked his own loyal adviser, turning him into a mindless slave. Not only that, but he remembered how truly good to him Delan had been, and Brayman, and Merloy. Like fathers and brothers.

Marcus's mind returned to the scenes he had absorbed beyond the door in his vision of the city of lights back home on his bed. Oh, how he longed to return to that place, to experience that total freedom and elation. Nothing else in life had compared to that awesome feeling—not Shurama's embrace, nor the finest clothes, nor the thrills of grench. Treanthor's trinkets and attempts at a grandiose lifestyle couldn't even come close to what the Kingdom of the North had to offer.

And no matter what Treanthor said, Marcus knew deep in his heart that he wanted to follow PathOne, and he had proved that over and over—because no matter how many times he had given way to temptation and distraction, he had always gotten back up and kept going.

Still, Marcus decided to string Treanthor along further, pretending to be interested in his schemes. He covered his face with his hands, pretending to struggle with the choice available to him.

"So you would be willing to give me a special room to live here, and provide me with all the latest xanth gadgets, as well as giving me plenty of free time for every pleasure I could want?"

"Absolutely. Isn't it an incredible offer?"

Marcus removed his hands and turned to look Treanthor squarely in the eye.

"Never!" His demeanor instantly changed from agreeable to angry. His pursed lips and stern eyes reflected that he meant it.

The sudden change in response enraged Treanthor, who did not like to be taken for a fool—much less by a young man. He yanked Marcus by the scruff of his neck, pulling him off the table and across to the other side of the cavern where a fire burned in a massive hearth.

As Marcus's heart sank, Treanthor snatched something off the mantle and held it up, gloating.

It was the book.

Marcus closed his eyes. He'd been through so much because of that book—had hoped for so much. And now it was in Treanthor's hands, and so was he, and it was all over. He had to fight tears as Treanthor held the book over the fire.

"It's not nice to watch your whole life burn, is it?" Treanthor asked. "But this is the end for every fool who refuses to believe in me and live in *my* world!"

Without another word, he threw the book on the fire. Flames leapt up as though they were eager to devour it.

A cruel smile formed on the Emperor's face, and he grabbed the scruff of Marcus's neck once more. "As for you," he said, "something a little . . . colder is in order."

A wave of devastation swept over Marcus as he glanced at the flames starting to devour the precious book. He felt sick to his stomach as the Emperor dragged him away.

As Treanthor pulled him swiftly through a door in the side of the cavern, a guard stood watching the fire in disbelief.

The book wasn't burning.

Instead, it seemed to regenerate even as the flames did their best to tear it apart. He peered closer, stepping forward. He could see words forming, circling in the fire, landing back on the impenetrable pages. Wonderingly, he took up an iron poker and carefully pulled the book from the fire.

* * *

Treanthor led Marcus along a cold, windowless corridor, down a stone flight of steps, and through another cavern with an uneven, rocky floor. "Let's see if this is what it takes to convince you of my ways. If you can't listen to reason, you can learn to endure some real hardship for a while!"

Marcus yelped as his ankle twisted on the steps, the Emperor dragging him harshly along.

"Where are you taking me?" demanded Marcus. "You can't make me work in your drug factory. I won't do it!"

"No. Worse than that, I'm taking you to the dungeon!" was Treanthor's cold reply. "We'll see how long it takes before you come to your senses and start doing what I say. I'll never let you free otherwise!"

At the far end of the cavern they approached an iron grate, in front of which stood a guard in full armor.

"Open it!" ordered Treanthor.

"Yes, sir."

The guard fumbled nervously with a bunch of keys before opening the grate.

"Throw him in!"

"Yes, sir."

The guard moved to grab hold of Marcus, who shrank away.

"Get off me! I'll climb in myself."

Marcus hoisted himself up the half-wall and through the hole into a damp, dark dungeon. The cavern they had come from seemed like a pleasant field of poppies in comparison to where he now found himself standing. He shuddered—the chill in the air was startling.

The guard slammed down the grate and locked it. Treanthor turned to leave.

"Call me when you've changed your mind!" he growled. "If you don't, I will turn you into one of my slaves at the hakrin production unit! You'll never be the same again!"

Leaning against a wall, Marcus slumped slowly down to the ground and hugged his knees. Then he started sniffing and sneezing, the change in temperature triggering another allergic reaction.

All of a sudden, a voice came out of the darkness.

"So how did you land your—"

"Augh!" shrieked Marcus, sitting up. "I thought I was alone in here!"

The voice was strangely familiar. "No, I'm here too. I wondered how you ended up here."

"It's a long story," said Marcus.

"I've got the time," came the reply.

"I can't see you. And I don't know if I want to talk about it."

The other prisoner lowered his voice. "Join me over on this side."

Marcus sighed. "I'm quite happy here, thank you."

"Shh . . . no, seriously, it's a bit warmer over here. There's a nook here, away from the draught."

Marcus reluctantly shifted from his position, hoisting his bad leg up and hobbling to the other side of the dungeon.

An arm grabbed him and pulled him into a dark corner.

The man kept his voice low—barely more than a whisper, as though he feared being overheard. "We're hidden from view here. It's Marcus, isn't it?"

"What, how do you know me?" whispered Marcus. "Tell me who you are!"

"Wait." The other man pulled him further into the corner before pulling out a match and lighting it. He held it up to his face.

The flickering light revealed a man with scraggly hair and an unkempt beard whose face and body had been badly beaten. Both his eyes were blackened, his lips cut and sore.

Marcus pulled away, shocked. "I, er, I don't know who you are. What do you want from me?"

"Marcus!" The man slumped his head low. "I've been alone here for weeks. I realize—"

Just as the flame died out, Marcus recognized the voice and the distinct green eyes. "Jez! Is that you?"

"Yes . . . you remember now."

"Yes. I, er, I'm sorry . . . you looked so different, I didn't recognize you at first. And you have no armor. How did you end up here?" Marcus's emotions were reeling. What was his friend doing here?

"Probably much the same way you did. I had camped for the night, traveling alone, when I was surrounded by Treanthor's men. They hit me over the head with an iron bar just as I was stirring awake, and I woke up here in the citadel. I refused to comply with Treanthor or listen to anything he said. I argued with him that he was doomed and that he would never succeed. It made him so mad he sent me to be beaten and thrown in here."

"How long ago was that?"

"Oh, about four weeks. I've barely eaten, and I'm constantly cold. Come here . . . sit close by me. Please. I need some warmth."

Marcus moved closer to Jez and threw an arm around him, hugging him tightly.

"We must think of a plan, Jez. We have to get out of here," he whispered.

"I've been thinking for the last few weeks. I see no way out, and I only have two remaining matches. Guards are now positioned all over the citadel, not just outside. You are my only hope at the moment. Do you have the book, Marcus?"

Marcus shook his head. "No, I . . . it got . . . no, I don't anymore." Marcus saw no point in explaining how he had lost it.

"And what about that listening gadget, the podbook? Brayman told me he gave you one of the few remaining ones created."

Marcus realized that he had no idea if the pod was still lodged inside his inner waistcoat pocket. Treanthor's men had stripped him of any items of worth on his body, including the gold ring from his right hand which had belonged to his father. But they might not have looked there.

"I'm not sure, I'll see if . . ."

Marcus searched the inner pocket in vain and then began to delve into every little pocket and crevice in his clothing. The inner pockets of his tunic were also empty, as was his shirt pocket, and he sighed with disappointment. The folded map was gone. Still he fumbled through his clothing, realizing how easy it would be for the little podbook to dislodge and end up somewhere unexpected. He felt along his sleeves and up the back of his shirt before searching the partly unstitched hem of his tunic and then the crevices of his upturned trousers.

Still nothing. He had just about given up when he decided to untie his boots and look there. Taking off the left boot first, he felt around the laces and the leather tongue at the front.

And there it was—nestled between two laces, held in place by the leather.

"It's here!" Marcus announced as quietly as he could, trying not to attract the guard's attention.

"Well done!" whispered Jez.

For the first time in a while, Marcus felt pleased with himself. Somehow the tiny gadget had escaped the guards' body search. A moment later he realized it wasn't himself he should be pleased with— more than likely this was a sign that Merloy had been watching out for him.

He handed the podbook to Jez, who inserted it into his ear and started listening. He repeated the words he heard, whispering encouraging words about being "bold and fearless," "willing to tear down walls" and "enter new territory." Everything they heard from the book seemed to speak directly into their situation. Though weak in body, both Marcus and Jez felt wholly strengthened in spirit.

* * *

Delan scanned the foot of the volcanic mountain where Brayman's dream had sent him. It lay far west of the mountain where days before Marcus had struggled along the risky northern pass, part of the same range but very different in appearance. It had taken Delan several days

274

to travel across high peaks and low hills to get to this point, avoiding towns and cities. Mount Zorbin stood like a dangerous, smoking guardian over Treanthor's citadel. Delan shuddered. He only hoped he would reach the men in time.

He searched for a hidden entrance by a low-lying crag just under a twisty path. Merloy had directed his attention to a passage of the book that spoke of a "hidden way" under the mountain, telling him to "stay low" and "search for hidden treasure." But now he was wondering whether this was the correct place. Or should he climb higher up to find it — risking the treacherous path?

No, he definitely remembered the part about "staying low." And the "hidden treasure" — did it mean actual treasure, or did it mean that he would find those in danger? Delan was confused. He wanted some easy answers, but he knew from experience that the book did not always offer them. Most of the time he had to work the answers out for himself.

He continued to cut away branches, searching for an alternative way into the mountain. He knew from old maps that there was another way into the mountain at the top of some rocky steps, but he had been clearly instructed to stay low.

Delan scrambled under the thickets and over tree roots, using his sword to secure his steps as it steadied him around the awkward mountain. He wished Brayman was with him, but the old man was busy trying to move the secret production facility for the podbooks — Merloy had warned him that Treanthor was coming after it. Delan soon came to an area right above a deep, dark lake and grimaced. He knew he had to stay at the foot of the mountain, but he wondered how he could stay there, so close to the water, when the angle of the mountain was virtually straight down. It was very similar to Marcus's description of the lake by the treacherous mountain in the east. The brambles and plant life started to fade out as this part of the hill turned rocky, the redness of the clay coming off on his hands. He knew that this too was a former quarry that had been made into a lake. The water was surely perilously deep.

Delan was brave, but he always assessed a situation before taking any risks. When he heard a voice that seemed to be Merloy's telling him to *"Go lower still!"* he grew frustrated.

"I can't go any lower than this—I'll end up in the water!" he complained aloud.

As soon as he said it, he knew in his spirit that he had to go into the lake, which lapped gently just feet from where he stood.

With great difficulty, he secured his bag tightly around his shoulders and returned his sword to its scabbard. He clung to the mountainside several seconds before taking a deep breath and jumping backward into the cold lake. Keeping his eyes open underwater, he looked around before deciding to keep going away from the shore and close along the mountain's edge. Pushing aside debris and plants, he caught sight of a small, dark shadow—a way into the mountain!

Delan grew desperate for oxygen and decided to come up for air. Just as he surfaced, he heard voices.

"There he is. Shoot!"

An arrow flew just above his head and lodged in a gap in the rocks. Delan inhaled deeply again and disappeared into the water. Treanthor's men. He had no more time.

This time he made it quickly through the hole and swam into a water-filled cavern. He wondered if he had made an awful mistake and whether he might have to risk facing the knights again when he looked up and saw a rope ladder leading to another entrance.

He kicked his legs hard and climbed the ladder, gaining access to another cave which was only half-filled with water.

He gasped as he finally surfaced and managed to breathe air once again, and he remained still for a few minutes to regain strength. Pulling out a little xanth torch which Brayman had given him, he could see that the cave led to a tunnel. He swam across until he reached higher ground. It was dry. The tunnel appeared to be an ancient feature of the mountain.

His suspicions were confirmed when he saw lots of writing on the walls, etched in by slate markers.

He paused to read some of the writing, and his heart nearly descended into his stomach. The words he read shocked him to the core.

"Been here 27 days now. Still no sign of life out there. No lake, just fumes and dust. No sign of the sun. The stench is unbearable. Never thought I'd survive it, but now I think I will die in here. Jonil Rethy, 2025."

Other, similar stories unfolded on the walls of the tunnel, but Delan saw no evidence of skeletons. Maybe they had washed out to the lake or been cleared away. It was obvious that these people had been survivors of the Great Catastrophe—but had they even survived? One thing was clear—an explosion of some sort had kept them trapped in the tunnels for nearly a month. Delan shuddered when he imagined the fear they must have encountered all that time ago.

He continued to read more stories, hoping to find more reliable clues about what had happened. So many voices in Krinton said so many different things that no one really knew the truth. And Treanthor didn't like people to talk about history. He often declared, "Why bother with the past, when we can focus on our glorious future?" But Delan knew that they should look at the past to learn how best to navigate the future.

Treanthor claimed that "his world" was indestructible, no matter what the book said. But if the old world could be so completely wiped out by a single catastrophe, then Krinton was no less indestructible. Delan stepped forward with renewed focus. It was crucial that he and the other followers of PathOne defeat Treanthor and expose him for a liar.

And right now, that meant pursuing the mission from Brayman.

Chapter 21

The busy sound of chisels, saws and hammers could be heard above the dank dungeon. Treanthor had ordered the extension of his citadel for reasons no one quite knew—perhaps he was expanding his drug production or raising more jeruni. Jez had overheard tidbits of information when the guards changed over at midafternoon and had explained the developments to Marcus.

With every bang, Marcus and Jez moved around the walls of the dungeon, tapping at the walls with their tin cups and pressing their ears against the cold rock, desperately trying to listen for any differences behind the stone walls—trying their best to find a thin, weak place.

This was no easy task, since the racket overhead masked both the sounds they made and the ones they were listening for. In the end, they agreed that the guard was so clearly distracted by his dinner that he wouldn't notice if they tapped occasionally when there was a brief break from the builders upstairs.

But the investigation was painstakingly slow, and Marcus was quick to give in, certain that the walls of their prison were impenetrable on every side. He imagined being left to rot there in the dungeon, a fate that was too hard to bear.

The clunking above stopped momentarily, and Jez tapped twice on a wall near the iron gate before dashing across the dungeon in the darkness to tap on an opposite wall. He clutched Marcus's arm.

"Did you hear that?"

"To be honest, it sounded much the same to me, Jez."

"Not to me! This wall is definitely not part of the original thick stone wall. I think there's wood behind there, or perhaps just a thin stone wall. We can get through!"

Marcus was reluctant to start cheering quite yet. "And once we get through the wall, what then? How can we possibly hope to escape the citadel with Treanthor's knights and workers everywhere?"

"I know it seems crazy, but we have to trust what we heard yesterday. And you know that it was meant for us—that message in your earpiece which said, 'Now is the time to tear down the walls and break free. It is for freedom that you shall be set free. No longer consider yourselves prisoners, but free men.' You heard that too!"

Jez paused for a moment before adding, with his voice still hushed and serious, "Our only alternative is to give up hope and maybe stay here till we die. I am not prepared to do that."

Marcus wiped his nose with his sleeve. He was encouraged by their discovery but was still scared and confused. "Why does Merloy make it so complicated? Why should we have to continually try to figure things out?"

"I'm not sure I know all the answers myself, friend, but I do know one thing." Jez faced Marcus. "Merloy does not wish to control us or make us do anything without questioning it first. He wants us to *want* to follow him and PathOne. Not because we're fearful, but because we enjoy experiencing his unique presence. And because we can be confident that he only wants what is best for us."

"So would you say that Merloy has only good plans for us?" The question almost sounded absurd here in the dungeon, but Marcus had to ask it.

"Well, sort of. He works everything out for good in the end, but sometimes we have difficult or dark paths to tread. But he promises to always be with us—and that's something I cannot live without. I know with all my heart that Merloy is good, yet evil is still present in Krinton, and so we must struggle against it for now."

Marcus nodded. He understood what Jez had just explained, and yet he didn't fully understand.

"We will never fully understand until we reach the Kingdom of the North—only then will it all make sense."

Marcus smiled inwardly. Jez often seemed to be in tune with his thoughts; it was uncanny.

"There's something else I need to know," he went on. "Why did Merloy choose me to walk this path? I'm not strong or anybody special. I don't have any particularly wonderful qualities." He glanced at Jez. "Apart from my fine looks, of course!"

Jez grinned, but his eyes were still serious. Marcus marveled at the contrast between this companion and Rindel. He had never realized how much his companions could affect his journey.

"That's probably something we'll never quite know. But I do know that Merloy chooses to reveal himself to those whose hearts are open and willing to believe. He invites everyone on this journey—young and old, rich and poor, clever and simple. But only a few respond to the calling, and many give up easily when the going gets tough. Mostly, though, people are happy to simply continue in their same old ways, doing things the way they want or ignoring any thought of another kingdom."

Jez released Marcus's arm and set about crawling on the floor in search of stones and small rocks. Once he had gathered a handful, he began chipping away at the weak wall, his clunking actions in sync with the hammering above the dungeon. Marcus joined him almost immediately. He had nothing else to occupy him anyway.

They were thankful for the darkness at the far end of the dungeon which shielded them from the observations of the guard, who was all too happy to eat his massive meal and fiddle with a new xanth gadget he had been awarded.

* * *

Delan groped about in the darkness. He had dropped his torch in a puddle, and the xanth crystals began to crackle under the strain of water that seeped through the damaged casing. The light flickered several times before going out. His progress would be slow now, and he scolded himself for not bringing a small oil lamp.

"Typical gadget—can't always rely on them!" he said to the enclosing walls, his voice echoing back at him.

He came to a crossroad in the tunnel, forcing him to choose between three different directions: straight ahead, left, or right. It seemed obvious that to go right would be foolish, as the tunnel turned sharply back, heading out again toward the direction of the lake, but he didn't know which of the other two to take. He started to feel the cold and drew his tunic closely around him, pulling up a hood to cover his head. He decided to turn left and keep going. After wandering for what seemed like several hours, he grew frustrated that his journey had left him still lost in the heart of the mountain. He was nowhere near finding those he was supposed to rescue. He kicked himself for thinking that he could work out the rest of the way without consulting Merloy.

"What now?" he inquired aloud. "Show me the right way, Merloy. I need you. I'm sorry for not thinking of asking you earlier." He knelt down, exhausted, holding his head in his hands.

Instantly, a bright figure shone in front of him. Delan gasped and shielded his eyes until they grew accustomed to the light. Before him stood a glorious creature, taller than a man but resembling a lion. The creature was shining with light, and brilliant wings unfolded from its back. Delan didn't know whether to welcome it or raise his sword for an attack.

"I am not sent by Treanthor," the creature said. "I am a cronjl, brought here to take you to your destination. Take hold of my wing and climb on my back."

Delan's mouth gaped open. "A *cronjl?*" He had read of the powerful creatures in the book but had never expected to see one. He stretched out his arms to clamber up and held on tightly.

As soon as he lay securely on the soft, glowing animal, the creature bounded off incredibly fast, tearing off down the tunnel to the left, traveling at immeasurable speed. Delan could hardly contemplate what distance they were covering—the walls flashed by so fast as they went through tunnel after tunnel. He clutched his sword close with his right hand and clung to the cronjl's wing with the other. His hood fell back, causing his hair to be swept back.

As Delan was whisked through miles of gloomy tunnels, he eagerly anticipated where his arrival point would be.

Will I arrive outside the rear of Emperor's citadel, or will I be taken straight to the darkened room? Will this creature stay with us and escort us away, or will we have to make our own escape?

Before Delan had even finished these thoughts, the cronjl ground to a halt, the momentum causing Delan to slide off. As soon as his feet hit the ground, the creature disappeared. In its place lay something barely discernible in the consuming darkness.

He approached it slowly, reaching out his hands to see what it was. He felt pieces of armor, several of them. It only took him a moment to realize that the cronjl had disappeared, leaving behind entire suits of armor—four of them.

Delan stood in the darkness, unsure of what to do next. And that was when he heard the *chink clunk bang* on the other side of the wall before him. He listened carefully, but the relatively quiet sounds were buried by the clamor of building works which had resumed above him.

When he reached to pull on a helmet, a hand emerged from the wall, and he heard Jez's quiet voice say, "We're through!"

Delan grabbed the hand, his mind quickly processing what he'd discovered—Jez, the strong friend he never expected to land in trouble—was trapped behind the wall. "Jez, I'm here. It's Delan!"

The shock of someone grasping his hand sent Jez tripping over himself backward.

"What is it, Jez?" whispered Marcus in an anxious tone.

Jez could hardly speak. He motioned toward the hole and simply said, "Delan."

"Marcus!" A harsh voice bellowing from across the dungeon interrupted their reunion.

Jez hurriedly stuffed a neck scarf into the hole and pulled Marcus to join him, slumped on the floor as though they had done nothing but wallow in misery since being thrown into the dungeon.

A guard Marcus didn't recognize jangled keys noisily as he unlocked the iron gate and shone a burning oil torch across the prison. The previous guard had left behind his plate of chicken bones and gone away. Marcus and Jez blinked and turned their heads as the light glared into their eyes. The guard came closer until he stood near their feet.

"What do you want?" asked Marcus as timidly as he could, not wanting to stir any suspicions. "Have you got some food for us?"

The burly guard leaned toward the two huddled figures and lowered his voice.

"No, but I believe this belongs to you." He reached into his cloak and pulled something out.

On the other side of the wall, Delan pressed his ear against the stone, desperate to hear what was going on. The voices were muffled. He decided to insert a finger into the gap in the wall, pushing the scarf slightly aside to enable him to see with one eye.

He nearly fell over with shock when the guard passed Marcus *The Book Beyond Time.*

"Where did you get this?" inquired Marcus eagerly. He recognized the book but was amazed to see that the guard had gotten hold of a brand new one. It looked as though it had never been read before.

"I fished it out of the fire!"

"What!"

The guard explained what had happened after Treanthor threw the book into the blazing fire.

"I watched the pages begin to burn, and then a weird thing happened. As soon as you left the room, I saw the pages uncrumple and reform. And then I saw words flitting around in circles in the flames and start to land back on the pages. The fire couldn't destroy the book—it was as if the book was, was—I don't know."

"Indestructible," finished Jez. "It regenerated because it cannot be destroyed! That's why it is 'beyond time'; it can never be destroyed or fade away. Treanthor has managed to find and discard many copies, true, but its message is eternal. Before tossing me in this dungeon, he took me to an old salt pit where he had thrown a large pile of the books. He took great pleasure in gloating over what he had achieved and said that by next year no one would ever be found reading such 'rubbish' again. It seems that Merloy has supernaturally protected this copy of the book to prove that no one can ever properly destroy it."

The guard looked seriously at Jez and Marcus, glancing over his shoulder briefly to check that no one was there.

"That's not all," he said quietly. "After I retrieved the book from the fire, I opened it in the middle—just to take a look—because I hadn't read a book since I was little, when my grandpa would make me read over and over about a fisherman lost at sea who finds treasure behind a rock. Anyway, I opened this book and the first thing I read was, 'To find the Kingdom of the North is like finding hidden treasure.'"

The guard lowered down to face his prisoners directly. "Can you tell me about this Kingdom of the North?"

Jez leaned forward and grasped the guard by the shoulders. "That is where we are going. Will you help us to escape from here?"

The guard's eyes lit up just as Delan began knocking through the wall. With the hole now big enough to push his head through, he called out, "That makes four of us!"

Marcus jumped up, excited to see his friend again, and they all set about pulling out rocks from the wall to be reunited with their ally. Once Delan came fully into view, they all observed a slight glow around his arms and legs. Just on the edges of his clothing, tiny sparks seemed to cling to his frame as if he had rolled in shavings of silver.

"What happened to you?" exclaimed Jez with amazement.

"You wouldn't believe it!" replied Delan, grinning. "And don't you look a sorry sight, friend!"

Marcus stepped forward to put his arm around Delan's shoulder, and as soon as he touched him, a warm flood of power shot through his body. Immediately, he felt his ankle strengthen and his leg being restored.

"My leg, my ankle! It's recovered. As soon as I touched you, the pain disappeared!"

Everyone smiled in amazement as the glowing shadow faded away from Delan's garments.

"That must have been the cronjl's power," exclaimed Delan. "Let me tell you about it as we get going."

* * *

Four scruffy laborers hunched over an old stained table, formerly used for slaughtering animals. A flickering lamp above them gave out just enough light for them to concentrate on their intricate task of putting together podbooks, inserting three miniature specimens of xanth crystals into each special item. They had been working every night from after dinner till midnight in the disused barn on the edge of a remote farm belonging to Brayman's oldest friend. The barn was situated about twenty miles from the town of Warsap. The four men used tiny tools fashioned from iron and lead to create their masterpieces, which would then be passed on to a stonemason who would work to house the devices in their tiny stone cases.

Brayman's young granddaughter, leaned across the table, carefully watching their handiwork, eager to learn and start helping with production. Outside the barn, two men practiced their sword movements, darting from one end of the barn to the other. Nearly every day, a new volunteer or two would arrive at the "Barn Factory," as it had become known, each one keen to spread the dispersal of podbooks across Krinton. The moon shone low against the backdrop of the barn that night as Merloy glided past gracefully, pleased by what he saw.

Treanthor was coming, and the factory would soon have to be moved. But the work—Merloy's work—would go on.

* * *

Treanthor retreated to his quarters and slammed the heavy door. Shortly afterward, he heard a couple of knocks.

"Go away!" he ordered.

He sat behind his desk but turned his chair to face out of the vast window behind him. From here he could see down across the valley to nearby towns, villages, and forests. He felt proud of what he had achieved and the kingdom he presided over. He thought about the grand reception he had received in the city of Shenoa the day before. When he had thrown coins out into the crowd, the people had practically worshiped him.

Bitterness consumed him as he considered how a few pesky rebels were trying to undermine him and turn the people against him. The audacity of it!

"I will not let them get away with this!" he shouted, causing his two greyhounds to retreat from him. "This is *my* empire, and they all belong to me!"

"Rindel!" Treanthor yelled. There was no response. He flew out of his chair and kicked open the wooden door.

"Rindel! I said *come here!*"

Rindel came running along the corridor.

"You told me to go away!" he stammered.

"Oh, do shut up, boy, and listen to what I tell you."

Rindel nodded and approached Treanthor meekly.

287

Treanthor thought for a moment. "Go down to that dungeon and tell the guard to report how my prisoners are doing. See if they're ready to give in or if they're committed to suffering more."

Rindel's face didn't betray how he might feel about checking on his old friend. "Yes, sir, I'll go straight away!"

Rindel turned and ran off down the corridor. He didn't consider for even a moment that he should defy Treanthor or try to save his former friends. Since staying at the citadel he had been totally consumed by desires for selfish gain and worldly recognition. At night he would imagine himself being appointed governor of a whole city such as Erundel, and he dreamed of the prestige and glory of one day standing beside Treanthor on a stage. He had no patience for waiting for future rewards in a mystical kingdom. No, he was now driven by a darker power which had taken root in his soul since the day he breathed in the vapor on that dusty, narrow path—a vapor created in Treanthor's chemical factories that enhanced doubt, dissatisfaction, and greed. He felt sorry for Marcus, being so foolish as to believe such an ancient, old-fashioned book. *Look where following that has brought him!*

And anyway, Marcus would be fine. Treanthor was just teaching him a lesson, and once that was done, Marcus would come around and join them too. Treanthor had special plans for him, after all. Rindel was almost jealous at the thought.

Minutes later he returned to Treanthor, looking pale and overcome with fear as he knocked on Emperor's door.

As soon as Rindel entered, Treanthor knew something was not quite right.

"What is it? What have they done?" he demanded.

Rindel stuttered as he tried to respond. "The g-g-guard, he, er, h-h-he's not . . . not . . ."

"Not *what?*" Treanthor shook Rindel violently.

"He's not there. And Marcus and Jez have gone too."

"*Gone!*" hollered Treanthor, pushing Rindel aside. "What do you mean 'gone'?"

"They, er, they made . . ."

Before waiting to hear any more, Treanthor stormed away down to the dungeon, his dogs following after him.

The Emperor grabbed a torch, still glowing outside the iron gate, from its holder and shone it inside the murky prison. At the far side, he saw rubble on the floor beneath the small hole they had escaped through. There was no sign of the guard.

Treanthor cursed loudly and threw the torch on the ground, smashing the xanth-powered light. Little bits of glass, painted panels, and xanth crystals scattered around his feet as he turned to leave. One of his greyhounds licked some of the crystals and swallowed them. They settled uneasily in the dog's stomach as it followed Treanthor back up the stairs.

* * *

Once back in his room, Treanthor pulled a lever on the wall near the door. Immediately, a deafening alarm resounded throughout the citadel. Within seconds, officials, workers, builders, and cleaners came running to line up outside the room. There were more than a hundred by the time a minute had passed. Heavily armed guards, who usually paraded outside the citadel, also joined them. Treanthor switched the alarm off and addressed his submissive followers.

"We have escaped prisoners—two scrappy-looking men in rags, as well as that guard Benton, who has betrayed me. Find them—dead or alive, just find them. You, you, and you, go down via the dungeon and follow after them. The rest of you, search the whole citadel on all levels as well as the grounds outside!"

"Yes, sir!" resounded a chorus of voices. They scattered in all directions, leaving Rindel still standing there, too shaken to move.

"What are you still doing here? Go!" snapped Treanthor. "And take my dogs with you. I need to get my horses prepared." Treanthor threw two leads to Rindel.

Rindel wanted to say something but decided it wasn't a good idea. He attached the leads and pulled the dogs away.

* * *

Benton led the way with his torch as Delan, Marcus, and Jez followed closely behind. All were now clothed in new armor, though Marcus and Jez were without their swords. Benton knew nothing of these underground tunnels and was certain that Treanthor had not constructed them.

"I think we have a good chance of escaping before they find us. Surely someone will come through that wall behind us when they find we have escaped, but there are no sounds of that yet, and my replacement guard is not due for hours."

As they hurried along, Jez soon began to tire. He had eaten little for several weeks, and his muscles ached from being inactive for so long. Delan insisted that they stop to allow Jez to rest and eat some bread he had brought, while he himself set to laying a trap for any possible pursuers. He had grabbed the first guard's dinner plate on their way out, and now he smashed it into several pieces on the floor and tied a thin rope low across the pathway just inches from the smashed pieces. Benton used nails he had been carrying for the citadel construction to pin the ends into the sides of the tunnel. Delan then carefully positioned the sharp parts pointing upward and pulled on the rope to check its strength.

"That should make them uncomfortable," he said with a grin. "Now come on—on we go!"

* * *

Rindel had decided to go back down to the dungeon, pulling the dogs up over the grate and through the makeshift hole in the wall on the other side. The greyhounds were eager to tear away, but Rindel held them firmly on the leads. He would let them loose once his targets were in sight. The thought of his huge reward made him smile inwardly. *If I can be the one to trap them, Treanthor will be especially pleased.*

The xanth crystals broke down into smaller pieces inside the smaller greyhound's stomach before dispersing through its bloodstream and entering the dog's nervous system. Its eyes started to glow red, and its muscles enlarged rapidly as they pursued the scents in the tunnels. Rindel was too focused on making progress to notice that the greyhound had nearly doubled in size and strength, or that its body had contorted into a disturbing shape. When the other greyhound barked and shifted nervously, Rindel ordered it to settle down and be quiet.

He soon came across the three officials Treanthor had sent down the tunnel earlier. One was swearing and bandaging his wrist. Bloodied fragments littered the ground.

"I don't know where they got the glass from," complained one of the men.

Rindel flashed a torch on the ground. "It's not glass, it's a cracked plate—I can still smell the meal off it!"

The dogs tried to lick the men's wounds, but Rindel pulled them away. "I have to be on my way now. Go back to send for more help."

The man bandaging his wrist snorted. "Like we're going to let you get all the glory, you little squirt!" The guard advanced on Rindel menacingly when, to all of their surprise, the greyhound stepped between them and bared its teeth with a growl.

"That's right," Rindel said, not sure what was going on but happy to take advantage of it. "I said go back and get more help."

Eyeing the dog warily, the guards nodded.

Only when he came to a lighter area, with daylight streaming through gaps in a tree at the tunnel's exit point, did Rindel see what had become of the dog.

Startled greatly by its transformation, his eyes widened. "Sit!" he squeaked.

The animal obeyed and sat down. Relieved, Rindel ordered it to do other things he had heard Treanthor say.

"Heel!"

The animal came to his feet.

"Down!"

The animal lay down as best it could. Rindel smiled.

"Bark!"

The animal growled so ferociously that Rindel jumped.

"Stop!" he commanded.

Moments later, he and the dogs emerged from the tunnel, pushing aside branches and twigs to find themselves in the woods. Mount Zorbin rose, dark and threatening, behind them. In the distance he could hear the voices of the missing guard, Benton, and his former friends — apparently just chatting!

Rindel grinned as he realized how easy this was going to be. He hushed the dogs and crept slowly along, keeping hidden behind trees. Treanthor would reward him well for this. A path widened into the center of the woods, where the men, all dressed in armor, sat on a log.

Unbeknownst to Rindel, they were sharpening the two swords — Delan's and Benton's — while discussing their next steps and what had happened earlier.

"Have you seen that happen before?" asked Benton. "That regeneration thing? How did you know?"

"I didn't," replied Jez. "I just know what the final words in the book are — *'These words will never fade away. Be careful to take note of them.'*"

"Do you have your own book?"

"Not anymore. Delan and I used to share a partly torn book, but once when we were lodging at a small village, someone stole it from my bag when we went bathing in the river."

"What else does it say?"

Rindel came closer to the four and hovered behind a large bush. Before he could give the command, the transformed greyhound growled and pulled loose from him to attack the escapees.

"Watch out!" yelled Jez. Delan ducked down low to dodge the raging, wolflike beast as it leapt at them. Thrusting his sword in the air, Delan poised himself to counterattack. The creature growled once more to reveal fierce-looking fangs. Its eyes were fixed on Marcus as it stopped momentarily before lunging at him. Marcus bounded to one side, jumping over the log, just as Delan came from behind, thrusting his sword into the wild animal and killing it instantly. The creature landed on Marcus's back, which would have been badly clawed were it not for the armor he wore.

The other greyhound, now also loose, set about to attack the group, but Benton commanded it to be still. The dog recognized the guard's voice and submitted, growling at his master's enemies. Everyone stopped still in their tracks, looking at one another.

Jez stood straight and pinned their hunter with his green eyes. "Have you come here to turn us in, Rindel?"

Rindel looked at Jez with proud eyes.

"You are defying the ruler of Krinton!"

"Yes, but should he rule over us? Is not freedom to believe worth fighting for?" replied Delan. "You were with us once, friend. Come back to our side."

Rindel tightened his hand around the sword at his side, ready to strike. He glared at Benton and the others.

"You will die for turning against the Emperor!"

The guard spat on the ground. "I'd rather die for something of worth than give my life for another's evil plans!"

"Then let's see who should die!" challenged Rindel, ready to draw his sword against the guard. He stood resolute and determined, certain

293

of his victory against the older man —and determined to shut out Delan's invitation any way it took.

Beneath their feet, the ground began to tremble. As one, they turned to see who was approaching.

Chapter 22

As Delan and Benton drew their swords and positioned themselves in front of Marcus and Jez, the sky seemed to darken. Behind them, Mount Zorbin smoked and shuddered. Jez slowly bent down and picked up a long stick, wielding it like a staff. Marcus felt frozen by dread.

No one was paying any attention to Rindel anymore.

Through the trees, something heavy was approaching. A rush of air whirred overhead, and a flock of jeruni burst through the trees, swooping down over their heads, jeering and cackling as they flapped their bright wings and pecked at Marcus and the others. "Give up, give up, give up!" they shrieked. "You are dead, you are finished!"

Delan and Benton tried to chase them off, but it was hard to hit jeruni with swords. After a minute, the birds pulled back but kept circling overhead. The air had darkened even more, and now creatures were appearing on the ground: heavy, lizard-tailed makhtamn, at least six of them, stared at the friends with sinister eyes. Smaller than the one Marcus had encountered already, they appeared to be its offspring—but they were still just as menacing. Greyhounds trotted through the trees behind them, baring their teeth and growling.

Most frightening of all, behind them walked Treanthor himself, with a contingent of knights wearing black and carrying red flags to signify battle. And all around him floated dark clouds, clouds that had voices and were whispering things as they approached.

Treanthor raised his hands, and every eye fixed on him. The jeruni overhead chattered incessantly, calling, "Hail, Treanthor! Hail, Master! Hail your doom, ha ha ha!"

"Going to fight me with sticks and swords?" Treanthor called, his voice mocking as he stared the escapees down. "You know that you are doomed! This fight is pointless—*feel* the pointlessness of it!"

As Treanthor spoke, one of the clouds—gray and almost sparkling—drifted from beneath his cloak and wafted all around the companions. Delan and Benton seemed to sag where they stood, their arms suddenly losing strength to hold their swords high. Jez's mouth twisted, and Marcus felt suddenly very strange—as though nothing at all mattered, as though all he wanted was to leave this place and take a nap. Who cared about fighting Treanthor, anyway? Better just to give in and live like the Wryxl did. Surely the Emperor would give them another chance.

Sikarl. Apathy. Marcus closed his eyes and tried hard to fight it off.

"Join me!" Treanthor called. "All three of you. You know you want to. Only the self-deceived follow PathOne. Admit the truth—that you just want to join me and live an easy life like everyone else in my kingdom!"

"You're a liar!" Jez called out. "You lie and deceive! We cannot trust our feelings at this moment, for you are influencing them with your accursed clouds. But we will stand on what we know!"

Marcus and the others rallied to Jez's voice, forcing themselves to fight past their feelings and stay focused on the truth. They could not join Treanthor. They *would* not.

Forming a line on either side of Treanthor, the makhtamn stamped and the greyhounds snarled.

"Fight me, then," Treanthor said with a smile. "Fight me and die where you stand."

Without another word, the greyhounds charged forward, snapping and growling. Delan and Benton sprang forward to meet them, and Jez batted one away with his staff, dealing it a strong blow to the head. Marcus felt like a stupid child, trapped behind his friends, unable to help them without a weapon. He looked around for a rock or something, but saw nothing except a stick. Still, it was better than nothing. He picked it up, snapped the end to form a sharp point, and drew a deep breath.

The makhtamn were still coming, their heavy footsteps shaking the ground. They had almost reached Delan, who was now fighting two greyhounds and a trio of diving jeruni. More of the birds careened down toward Marcus, who dealt the first one a good blow with his stick. For one second, he felt triumphant.

And then darkness hit him like a blow. A voice laughed through his mind and said, "*Give up . . . die now. Kill yourself before Treanthor's men torture you. You are worthless, a failure, not worthy to be here. You are all, all going to die—your friends and everyone you care about. And it is all your fault.*"

Marcus knew this voice—Santon. And yet, even knowing it was a trick of Treanthor's, it was almost impossible to resist. The stick fell from his hand, and his eyes filled with tears as he saw Benton struck down by a knight in black. Delan was going to die. Jez, facing a makhtamn now with only a staff, was going to die. And it truly was all his fault. They were here because of him.

"Join me, Marcus." This time the voice was Treanthor's. Even though the Emperor still stood away from the battle, positioned by the treeline, his voice sounded as though he were right in front of Marcus. "That's all you need to do. Become a voice for my cause, like your friend Rindel has done. And I will call my forces away and let your friends go free. Just join me. Give up your path to the north and become mine."

Marcus didn't know what to do. He couldn't join Treanthor—but Santon was still filling his lungs, filling him with despair, and his friends were going to die. Shouldn't he at least try to save them, even if it meant giving in?

He took one more desperate look around. He could not even see Delan anymore. Jez had broken his staff on the makhtamn's scaly back and was scrambling to keep his footing. Benton was outnumbered by knights and dogs who seemed to just be toying with him.

He had no other choice.

But then a fleeting thought came to him.

Merloy.

Hadn't Merloy promised to be with him? And hadn't he once said that Marcus could carry some of his power?

Marcus reached down and groped for the stick he had dropped, and then he closed his eyes and called out, "Merloy!"

Nothing happened at first. The jeruni darted around his head, taunting him, and the grip of Santon grew stronger. But he called out again.

"Merloy, please help me! Merloy! I want to be strong and follow you! Merloy!"

In his hand, the stick hardened into metal and grew heavy. He opened his eyes: it was his sword—his old iron sword, the one with the green jewel that Brayman had given him and he had so foolishly traded away. And it was glowing with light. But this was not some cheap trick, some xanth-powered light triggered by the press of a button. It was a much greater power.

Marcus raised the sword and yelled, "For the Kingdom of the North!"

Hardly even knowing what he was doing, he pointed the sword straight at Treanthor. A beam of light shot from the sword, cut through the clouds of sikarl and Santon, and sliced through the flocks of jeruni. It struck Treanthor and pierced his right eye.

The Emperor shrieked and recoiled.

The jeruni jerked away as though they were puppets being yanked away by a string. The makhtamn let out frightening howls, and the dogs whined and dropped to the ground, rolling over and trembling in fear. Even the knights dropped to their knees. Amazed, Jez helped a bleeding Delan get to his feet, and they positioned themselves on the defensive again. This time Marcus joined them, brandishing his still-glowing sword. His hands were shaking—but with awe, not with fear.

Pillars of light suddenly blazed around them, and thirteen enormous cronjls appeared, forming a defensive line in front of them. The strange and beautiful creatures charged against the makhtamn and the knights and drove them back.

Standing all alone on the other side of the clearing, Rindel sobbed with fear and regret.

In the midst of the battle, a robed figure materialized and held out his hand to the three young followers of PathOne who had traveled so far.

"Come," Merloy said.

* * *

Delan, Jez, and Marcus found themselves standing in a place they had never seen before. It was broad daylight, and Treanthor and his hordes were nowhere to be seen. They could not see Mount Zorbin or the citadel, either—somehow Merloy had transported them far away. Merloy himself had disappeared.

Marcus handled his old, worn sword with awe, holding it up to the light to inspect it more closely; he knew for sure that it must have been used by others before him in battle. He wondered how many victories it had helped to win. The signs of clashes with other weapons were marked all along the blade as well as the handle. He wondered how he could have been so foolish as to trade it away. He knew he would never forget how it had been used against Treanthor.

Delan, bloody and streaked with grime, raised his hand in a salute.

"You refused to give in, Marcus. You're a right little fighter, my friend. Your mother would be proud."

Marcus beamed at his friends, simultaneously ashamed and prouder of himself than he had ever been. The words "little fighter" again brought to mind memories of his father, who used to call him by that name as a child and tousle his hair. A lump began to form in his throat, but he smiled and nodded. He thought of his mother and knew that Delan was right: she would be proud.

My dad may have messed up and let her down, but I refuse to disappoint her further, he thought.

Jez was looking around. "Where are we?" he asked.

Instantly, all of their thoughts left the battle behind and focused on where they were now. A pile of huge gray rocks stretched out for miles from east to west, forming something of a path.

"I know no more than you do, brother," said Delan, "but I sense something important will arise. Do you not recognize this place?"

Jez and Marcus looked around again. They were in a virtual wasteland of rocks and low hills, and a slight river had practically dried up—it was just a small trickling stream that flowed between the boulders.

"I don't see anything remarkable," said Marcus.

"But don't you recall this description in the book?" Delan's comment was met with blank stares. Delan continued, his voice full of enthusiasm. "Don't you remember that night around Brayman's table, after we had played cards—when I was reading from the book, and it described this very scene we're standing in?"

Marcus's eyes lit up; he did remember that night.

"And did it not say that when you find yourself in a dry land surrounded by rocks on every side, look out, for you are not far from the final destination?"

"That means we're about to find the Kingdom of the North!" Jez said, the excitement in his voice building as he spoke. "That's why Merloy brought us here!"

Delan was still smiling. "We're in this together. We just don't know how close we are. I think the final landmark we need to see is the formidable, high rock face."

"That's right" said Jez. "When we see the high rock we must walk into its shadow and wait. I heard that on Marcus's podbook in the dungeon!"

"I can't believe we're finally going to see it!" Marcus whispered. He had thought it might take him his whole life to find the kingdom —and now they were almost there.

Standing there, together, the three friends felt like they had found their ultimate purpose. The anticipation of what was to come was tangible, and they all sensed it.

As one, they navigated the maze of rocks. Merloy clearly expected them to work—it was a journey of hours. By late evening they turned around a large boulder and stopped in awe of what lay before them: a gigantic, towering rock, just as the book had described. It stretched high into the sky, about ten miles from where they stood. Only a vast expanse of dry land separated them from their destination. Their desire to see the kingdom drove them like a fire, but after the battle and the day's journey, they were in desperate need of rest and water. Besides, it was getting too dark to see the way.

After setting up camp for the night, Delan brought out his dulcimer, and they sang heartily together. Songs from their boyhood, as well as new funny songs Delan taught them. And they laughed over and over. After all their traveling, they had just about reached the place they had hoped for so long. All three slept soundly despite the sound of crickets and Jez's loud snoring.

* * *

Treanthor lay back uneasily on a raised bed in the center of a whitewashed room. A physician wearing small round spectacles and a long white tunic peered over him. As the Emperor stared straight up to the ceiling, the man carefully removed Treanthor's eye patch and forcefully inserted a glowing red-and-black eye into the vacant socket. It made a clicking sound as it fell into place and flickered at random intervals.

Two previous prototypes had been rejected already, met with violent rages from Treanthor. Just the day before, he had yanked the eye out himself and thrown it across the room, yelling obscenities. His physician, a short man with a pointy nose, stood a few feet away, watching nervously for a reaction.

Treanthor blinked three times and looked in every direction around the room before voicing his satisfaction.

"Perfect," he said. "This one is just perfect. This xanth eye has restored me to full, no, even greater power." He smiled. The eye allowed him to see through people and objects if he chose.

He let out a roaring cackle of laughter which resounded off the walls and sat up. His guardsman beside him stepped back in alarm. Treanthor was truly terrifying!

* * *

At first light, Marcus and his companions set off again. The land was flat and relatively easy to pass, a straightforward journey compared to the previous day, though still eerily desolate. Few had crossed this way before. Conversation was scarce as each one's mind was filled with thoughts of what it might be like in this mysterious kingdom they had learned about.

Marcus was glad that the others did not ask him what he was thinking. In all truth, he felt something like fear. Although this was what he had been searching for all along since leaving Trynn Goth, a small part of him still felt strongly attached to Krinton. Krinton had been his home for so long; it felt familiar. It was a part of him. Even though he had experienced countless disappointments and trials, he was slightly reluctant to fully embrace this new kingdom.

Will the Kingdom of the North really be all that the book describes? he thought. *What if it's disappointing in some way?*

But then he remembered how utterly safe and secure he had felt whenever he met with Merloy. The Kingdom of the North was Merloy's realm, so he knew that it could only be good.

It was mid-morning when they approached the south face of the imposing rock. The sun was mostly hidden behind a cluster of dark clouds, and Marcus felt a twinge of anger as he knew that they needed to cross into full, sun-cast shadows to enter the Kingdom of the North. That was what the book described.

"Let's be patient," Delan spoke up. "We know it can't be long now."

The others said nothing, continuing to advance closer to the rock. As they came nearer, a breeze brushed past them, and all three sensed something supernatural about the rocky mountain face. The breeze grew in intensity until a strong gale prevented them from taking any further steps. Marcus and his companions linked arms and stood still, in awe of the remarkable wind which blew in their faces until their eyes watered.

Staying virtually unmoved from their position, it was nearly an hour before the sun pushed out above the clouds, covering one side of the rock face in brilliant sunshine and the other in dark shadows. Sunlight filled the spot where they had remained, bathing them in warmth.

The wind began to die down, and the three looked at one another.

"It's time," said Marcus. "Our journey is just about over. I can't believe it!"

"Let's go!" exclaimed Jez as he loosened his arms from the others and began running into the rock's shadow.

Marcus and Delan raced after him, full of excitement and wonder. Marcus overtook Jez easily and was the first to step into the shadow.

In an instant, everything changed. Gravity was no more as he felt the earth's pull dissipate beneath him, and he was suspended upward as though in flight. Set before him was the kingdom he had tried so long to envisage. A fast-flowing, sparkling river ran through the center of the kingdom, and new sights, colors, and smells enveloped him. A lush green mountain, drenched in unrelenting light and covered in amazing flowers he did not recognize, was the furthest thing Marcus could see.

Looking down, he witnessed his body fading away, his clothes seeming to melt from him as he was flooded with an incredible sense of happiness. This was unlike anything he had felt before in Krinton: mesmerizing, ecstatic, and freeing at the same time. This was it! He was totally free—free from worry, free from pain, and free from fear. He heard himself shout for joy, surprised to note that his voice remained fully functional while his body was no more. Looking down, it was clear that only three things remained from Krinton: his sword, his spirit, and the book. His mind was fully aware of what was true and what was merely an illusion. And he knew without a doubt that all he had known before could not compare even the tiniest bit with what he now knew.

When he turned back to examine the view, Krinton could not be seen at all. Marcus was surrounded only by the brilliant sights of the Kingdom of the North. His whole being seemed to absorb freshness and light. *This is my home, where I belong,* he thought. And it was as if he had always lived there.

Suddenly, Merloy stood before him. Marcus ran to him and embraced him with his new kingdom spirit. Even as he did, he felt a new body forming, becoming real and strong.

Merloy held him close and then spoke to him.

"Well done, Marcus! You accepted the challenge to find my kingdom, and you did not give up." His eyes glowed with something like strength and power, but Marcus could not describe it.

Recognizing his friends among a group of others nearby, Marcus turned away from them, fixating his gaze only on Merloy and the light emanating from him. As Merloy drew closer, Marcus felt an elevation in his spirit, confirming that he had transcended into a whole new atmosphere or dimension. Although his earthly body was no more, his spirit and his senses assumed a level of euphoria that was unexplainable. The new, physical body which had formed around him was incredible. It took him only moments to adjust, and he felt himself smiling broadly.

Merloy spoke once more. "Your mother is here."

Marcus spun round to see Ree-Mya beaming and dressed in unusual clothes. Her eyes shone crystal blue and he knew she could see perfectly.

"Mum, I... it's you! You're here, how did...?" Marcus's words trailed off as he caught her up in a long embrace.

"I've been waiting for you, Marcus; we're here now, where we were destined to be!" Ree-Mya seemed to have adapted to the new kingdom already. She appeared energetic and somehow much younger since Marcus had said goodbye.

"But how...?" Marcus shook his head, trying to comprehend it all.

"I fell one afternoon in the village. I think I must have tripped on a discarded barrel or some bricks left on a village street. My head crashed against a wall very hard and I collapsed in a heap. Even as a lady came to help me, I started to slip out of consciousness and was surrounded by these amazing creatures."

"Cronjls? Delan saw them, too!"

"That's right. Even as the lady spoke, they swept me up in the air and I watched Trynn Goth fade into a small speck in the distance. I knew I was on my way to the Kingdom of the North, and that everything in Krinton really didn't matter anymore – the house, my possessions, the village. They all became... uh..."

Marcus interrupted "... insignificant?"

Ree-Mya looked Marcus in the eye. "Yes. Everything that seemed so important there suddenly became a blur, as though it had all happened in just one day."

"And you can see properly now?"

"Perfectly – clearer than I ever did."

Delan, Jez and the others were speaking excitedly with Merloy, and Marcus couldn't wait to introduce his mum to his friends. Leading her across to them, he began to tell Ree-Mya how they had got to know one another.

Treanthor stirred uneasily on his silk covered bed, letting out mild groans which escalated into an agonised scream. "Aarggghhh, somebody help me!"

An assistant came running in, but covered his mouth and ran straight out again. Treanthor rolled off the bed and started to crawl toward the door. "Doctor!" he yelled. "Aarrgghhh!"

He started to scratch at his face and skin, overwhelmed by weird sensations of burning all over, even though he was not on fire. Inside, Treanthor felt as hot as volcanic lava. His skin started to dry up and crack open from head to toe, as a foamy substance began to ooze from the crevices that had formed.

"Aaarggghhhh!"

Treanthor threw his head back and writhed about on the elaborate, tasselled rug.

The assistant rushed back into the oak paneled room with Treanthor's personal doctor. A look of horror came over both of them.

"Stand back!" ordered the doctor. "We mustn't touch him."

Treanthor's skin was quickly turning purple and red as his face contorted into a disturbing shape.

"I didn't know the chemical would take effect so soon", said the doctor, covering his mouth with his sleeve. The assistant glared at him.

"What have you done? What's wrong with him?", whined the assistant, almost too scared to watch Treanthor any longer, who was now cursing and shouting in between writhing around.

"It's the eye we inserted."

"The xanth-powered eye? I thought it would help him!"

"It would have done, um, that is, if we hadn't changed the design. The Emperor insisted that I use more xanth with this eye, to ensure it worked and to make sure it gave him superior powers of vision. I decided – *we* decided, we *all* did in the pharmacy – to put a stop to his tyranny. I wasn't going to at first, but then I had a dream about it."

The small physician explained what he had done in a matter of fact tone. "We mixed a potent chemical with the xanth, using the same liquid Treanthor used to subdue his former assistants, turning them into mindless slaves. The eye I inserted has started to leak. Treanthor's suffering from the radioactive content that's absorbed into his system. He'll soon be fully toxic and die."

Both men watched aghast as Treanthor succumbed to the lethal effects of the chemicals and his body shook violently.

"He built up Krinton with the promise of xanth, but now it will be his downfall". The doctor stepped further away toward the door.

Treanthor began to hiss and splutter, his hands and fingers twitching uncontrollably, before breathing his last. His body then started to disintegrate, the chemical literally consuming him.

As Treanthor's once strong and superior body dissolved before their eyes, the citadel, Mount Zorbin, the cities to the north and south, and the whole of Krinton started to also dissolve. Lava spewed furiously out of Zorbin, as though making one last plea against its demise. But the mountain was powerless to prevent its own ruin. Over at Erundel, the metal beams supporting the grench port melted like wax and slithered into the crumbling earth. Great towers and buildings across the land toppled like matchsticks, unable to withstand their downfall.

* * *

Standing beside Merloy, Ree-Mya, Marcus and his friends stared incredulously as Merloy pulled aside something like an invisible scroll or curtain, enabling them to watch the scene as Krinton turned and twisted and faded, sucked down as though through a funnel. It was exactly how Marcus had envisaged that night on his bed back home.

It was as if Krinton had never existed, merely an illusion or a trick of the eye. It was an alarming thing to experience and no one said anything. Merloy closed the unseen scroll and turned to face them.

Just as he opened his mouth, a figure emerged among them, as if flung into their presence from afar. It was Keriss, her windswept hair fallen across her face as she knelt, her hands over her eyes. Her breathing was heavy and she appeared to be exhausted.

"Keriss, you're here!" Delan called out.

She fell over, letting out a small scream.

"What's happened? Where am I?" Keriss looked up at everyone staring down at her. "Marcus, is that you? How did I get here? I...I should be dead, I, er, I've been attacked... Treanthor's men, they, they killed me!"

Merloy reached down to lift Keriss up. Her face and body transformed before them, all trace of her former self in Krinton disappeared.

She laughed; Merloy laughed.

"You are now fully alive! Treanthor's power is no more; welcome into my eternal Kingdom."

As Merloy led them away toward a vast table set with amazing food they had never eaten before, Marcus saw crowds of people approaching the table from the other side. Hundreds, no thousands, of people swarmed around Merloy. Marcus searched frantically for Rindel among their faces but couldn't locate him. He desperately hoped that Rindel might have found his way to the northern Kingdom, too.

He then caught sight of the book. A pristine copy set on the center of the table, its gold lettering on the front glimmering brightly. It looked as though it had never been opened.

Merloy gestured toward the book. "All of your destinies were intertwined in *The Book Beyond Time*, even if you didn't realize it."

Marcus was sure that Merloy was going to show them the maps where their paths had crossed. But when Merloy opened the book and held it up for them to see, he turned to the final page, before licking his finger and turning that one over, too. There were no maps or familiar lines of text. The content appeared completely changed; though Marcus was sure he'd seen the last page so many times – he knew exactly what it looked like.

Stepping forward to see what was now written on the pages, he observed something he had never expected – column after column, and page after page of people's names, handwritten in perfectly symmetrical writing. The book seemed to go on and on, even though its thickness had not changed. Merloy moved a finger lower down one page, which Marcus followed with his eyes. And there it was – Marcus Quinton Macmillan.

Marcus noticed a twinkle in Merloy's expression, a mesmerizing, but welcoming, look, before realizing that they were all floating, hovering around the table.

Merloy stretched out his arms, raising the book high above his head. "You also are eternal, which is why the book now also contains your names. You are beyond time, too."

He closed the book with a thud. The lettering seemed to come to life, sparks of gold streaming out as if to highlight its invincibility. Marcus felt a further lift in his spirit and smiled. Everything he had gone through in Krinton had been worth it.

Reaching out his arms, Merloy beckoned the throngs of people. With a loud voice, his words resounded above them all. "And now it's time for the greatest party you could ever imagine. Come and join in!" Marcus's eyes locked with Merloy's and a massive bolt of power surged through his body. He had never felt more fully alive.

I'm saying yes to You
And no to my desires
I'll leave myself behind
And follow You

I'll walk the narrow road
'cause it leads me to You
I'll fall but grace
Will pick me up again

I've counted up the cost
Oh I've counted up the cost
Yes I've counted up the cost
And You are worth it

Lyrics: Rend Collective Experiment
Song: The Cost
From the album: Campfire[1]
